Strokes at Midnight

LAYLA PINE

This is an adult romance, containing multiple, explicit intimacy scenes. It is written for 18+ audience.

This book contains scenes / references to the following, which may be distressing for some readers:

- Unplanned pregnancy
- Emotional and mental abuse
- Physical abuse and violence
- Homophobia
- Fat shaming
- Breast cancer
- Infant death
- Parental death
- Abuse of prescription drugs
- PTSD and emotional trauma

For all the girls who have ever compared themselves to someone else, and felt like they were less.

Contents

CHAPTER ONE

What Did You Do

AMANDA

"I can't believe you think that going out, getting drunk and *losing my virginity* to some random guy is going to help me get over feeling the way I do when I drink!" I hissed to Alison, my best friend since we met back when we were just little nursing students navigating the stressful environs of Sydney University.

"Look, I know I got a bit enthusiastic earlier about the whole 'find a guy, bang the psycho out of your system' thing. And yeah, I was probably a bit out of line," Alison admitted. "I'm not advocating for you to lose your virginity to some rando in a bar!" Her voice was loud enough that a mother who was browsing racks with her teenage daughter nearby gave us the stink-eye. "I'm just saying, you need to make some new, happier memories around drinking, so you don't always default to *that* night and *that* arsehole!" More stink-eye from the mother.

"Keep your voice down," I mumbled. "I've already agreed to your ridiculous plan, despite my misgivings. I just don't see why I can't wear something I already own out tonight, that's all."

Alison thrust a pair of denim shorts into my hands. "Just try them on already!" she demanded. "I swear to God, they will look divine on you!"

I sighed. Alison was a total pain to take shopping. She always tried to push me outside of my comfort zone when it came to fashion—my comfort zone being stretchy tights with oversized t-shirts for every day, and maxi dresses for going out. Both styles ticked the Three C's for me: cute, comfortable, coverage. And they hid the three B's: boobs, belly, bum. Not to mention the two T's: my good old Thunder Thighs.

"I still don't think—"

"Amanda McGregor, you are absolutely not going out for your first official night of Immersing Amanda in just any old thing! Get that peachy butt of yours into the changeroom, or I'll come in there and change you myself!"

"Alright," I grumbled, stepping reluctantly into the change room. I pulled the curtain closed, avoiding the mirror as I stripped out of today's maxi dress, too late realising I had nothing but my bra and underpants on. I had nothing to try on the bloody high-waisted shorts with anyway.

"You can thank me later," Alison snarked from the other side of the curtain as she shoved a black silk tank top through the gap to me. I took it with a roll of my eyes, slipping the tank on over my head, trying my best not to catch a glimpse of myself in the mirror until I dragged the denim shorts up my legs and buttoned them at my waist.

The first thing that shocked me was that I didn't feel completely horrific. The shorts, while … well … short, had a wide, flirty leg, so they didn't squish my bum until it looked like a raw whole chicken in a bag. They also, incredibly, fit comfortably at my waist.

I hazarded a glance up into the mirror.

"Oh!" I exclaimed, just as Alison, in typical Alison fashion, zinged open the curtain, making me jump.

"Total effing babe!" she crowed, stepping closer. "Only, you just need to fix this one little thing." Before I knew what was happening, she had her hands at my waist, inside my shorts, as she tucked the tank into them. I squirmed under her ministrations. No one touched me like that. Not even Thomas—my longest relationship by a good three months—had touched my stomach.

I shivered. Not just because of her touching me, but because I'd thought about … him. I hated thinking about him. I hated that, eighteen months after everything had happened, he still had the power to ruin my mood. Which was exactly why Alison had come up with this crazy plan of hers. Immersing Amanda was her strategy to help me get over the tipsy night that had started the whole traumatic experience with Thomas. I was just along for the ride. Alison's will was as fiery as her naturally bright red, curly hair.

"Much better!" Alison sighed in satisfaction, while I tried to shake off the memories, tentatively taking in my reflection.

"OMFG, look at that tiny little waist!" the sales lady cried out, shouldering Alison out of the way and coming in to turn me to face her. I flushed beetroot, staring down at my feet. I hated when people made my body the centre of attention.

"I keep telling her to stop hiding that gorgeous hourglass figure under baggy clothes!" Alison agreed, as both she and the saleswoman eyed me up and down.

"I don't have an hourglass figure!" I protested, but Alison slapped me on my arm, a scandalised expression on her face.

"Big, bouncy tits, little waist, gorgeous round hips and arse! It's the literal definition of hourglass! You're like Marilyn bloody Monroe, you twit!"

"Maybe if you stuck a bunch of Marilyn's together …"

Alison sighed dramatically. "I think you have no flipping clue, my beautiful, sexy friend. But whatevs. You're buying that whole thing, and you're wearing it out tonight."

"Denim shorts on a night out? Isn't that a little … casual?" I asked, feeling suddenly shy, as I peeked in the mirror once more. They were so short! My thighs were totally on display. I wore longer shorts than this to go swimming!

"Oh, don't be silly!" the salesgirl said, flapping a dismissive hand in my direction. "You team that ensemble with some heels, really pop those shapely calves of yours, and holy shit, you won't be able to fend the boys off! Now, take them off and I'll start ringing them up for you."

"It's your job to flatter people to get a sale," I muttered darkly as

I closed the curtain, handing the items out to the salesgirl. I changed back into my maxi dress, which suddenly seemed like a big, dark blue sack on my body. I felt fatter wearing the dress than I had showing all that skin, which was just weird.

———

Mel texted as I walked out of a shoe shop with a new pair of black stiletto pumps that Alison had insisted would look "so freaking sexy" with my new outfit.

> Mel: You free to catch up? I fly out for Dubai on Monday, miss you.

> Amanda: I'm at Eastmeadow, doing some clothes shopping (vomiting emoji). Can you meet me here for lunch?

> Mel: Sure, I'll get Joel to drop me off for a girl's only lunch - Sushi in 20?

> Amanda: Perfect!

"Mel's going to meet me for lunch. Do you want to hang around, grab some food with us?" I asked Alison. She watched me calculatingly. I really mistrusted that gleam in her eyes.

"I've actually got a special secret mission that I need to complete without you being around to make it difficult. So how about you text me when lunch is over, and I'll come find you."

I narrowed my eyes. "What special secret mission?"

Alison grinned, winking cheekily at me and flipping her long red hair over her shoulder. "It wouldn't be a secret if I told you, now, would it?"

I frowned, but let it drop, telling Alison I'd take my purchases to the car and then head to the food court to meet Mel.

"Have fun, MM!" she crooned as she walked off. MM? What on earth did she mean by that? My high school nickname had been Mandy-Moo, but Alison had never heard anyone call me that.

I was heading back from the carpark, up the escalator to the restaurant level when I realised what Alison had meant. I laughed in disbelief. Marilyn Monroe. For crying out loud.

Mel and I had been friends since high school, and even though our lives had gone in very different directions—hers into professional tennis and a jet-setting lifestyle, mine into university and a nursing career—we still made time to hang out whenever her busy life, and my work roster allowed. As I approached the table, she bounced to her feet and hugged me tightly, looking tanned and grinning. She'd never used to be such a hugger. Not until Joel came along.

"Before I sit down," I began, looking around dramatically, "am I going to get inadvertently papped sitting here with you, you big star?"

Mel rolled her eyes. "I fucking hope not. I can't guarantee we won't be harassed by randos wanting to get a selfie though. The downside to winning the Australian Open—sometimes I wonder if it's really worth it." She sighed dramatically, winking to let me know she was totally joking.

"You'd be well and truly used to it by now, wouldn't you?" I asked, hopping up onto the bar stool and eyeing the sushi as it travelled past on the little conveyor belt. "I mean, how many Grand Slams is it now? Three?"

Mel sighed. "Melbourne makes it four. I swear Joel's head gets bigger every time. You'd think he was the one playing the tennis, honestly!"

She sounded annoyed, but the quirk in her lips and the sparkle in her eyes told me otherwise. She and Joel loved teasing one another. I was sure that it was a form of protracted foreplay for them.

"What's that blush for?" Mel asked, reaching out and pinching my cheek gently. I reddened some more. It wasn't like I could say to her, 'oh, just thinking about you and your boyfriend using teasing as foreplay'.

"Alison just made me buy a risqué new outfit, and I am under strict instructions to wear it out tonight for drinks."

Mel grinned. "Ooh, I wish I didn't have dinner plans tonight, otherwise I'd one hundred percent be tagging along to see this outfit! It's high time you wore something that didn't hang off you like a sack!"

I gaped. Mel, who was the most clueless woman I knew when it came to fashion, had noticed that I dressed in baggy clothes all the time? I'd always thought I looked fine in what I wore—always thought that feeling comfortable would help me look less over-weight. But it seemed I'd let myself fall into a fashion rut.

I knew exactly how, and I was so cross with myself for letting him take up so much space in my brain today. He wasn't someone I felt comfortable talking to Mel, of all people, about. Not after what he'd done to her. But I needed to get something off my chest.

"So …" I began, opening a container of sushi and splitting the disposable chopsticks, busying my nervous hands. "Alison thinks that I need to make some new drinking memories, so that I don't think about that time in Melbourne, when I met … you know … every time I get drunk."

Mel stilled, a piece of sushi poised mid-air between the table and her mouth. I flicked my eyes to hers for a second, before letting them fall back to the table, focusing on drizzling soy sauce over my food.

"Are you trying to say that you still feel bad about drinking because of that fuckwit Thomas?" she asked, putting the sushi down, staring hard at me.

I shrugged. "Um … maybe?" I swallowed once, but the words were forcing themselves up my throat and out into the world. "I just think that if I hadn't been drinking that night, he might never have been able to—"

"No!" Mel snapped, slapping her hand down on the table. "That is such bullshit, Mandy, and you know it! He would've found some other way. He was a complete psychopath."

She flopped against the backrest of her stool, huffing out a frus-trated breath. "Have you been feeling this way since he confessed?"

I paused, shoving sushi into my mouth so I couldn't talk. And then I nodded.

"Amanda, you have nothing to feel guilty about! And you know what?" she added, leaning forwards, stabbing up a piece of sushi and shoving it into her mouth, "I think Alison is totally right! You need to go out, get tipsy, or write yourself off completely, I don't know—have a fantastic night, flirt with some random hottie in your sexy new outfit, maybe pool-shark him, that would be hilarious! And then go home with no regrets!"

She picked up another piece of sushi, poking it in my direction for emphasis. "I am one hundred percent behind this, and I want an update when I get back from Dubai."

"Alison has dubbed this experiment 'Immersing Amanda'," I said, dropping a piece of sushi directly into the wasabi and cursing.

"Yes! I always knew I liked Alison!" She stuffed the next piece of sushi between her teeth and chewed furiously. I thought I heard her mutter, "Fucking Thomas," under her breath.

"Melanie Black?!" an excited voice squealed. I bit back a smile as Mel tried not to sigh, turning and plastering a grin on her face as two teenage girls stood wide-eyed, holding out their mobile phones in shaking hands. "Can we get a selfie with you?

"Sure!" Mel said, flipping me some side-eye as she turned in her seat, picking a piece of seaweed out of her teeth and putting her arms around the two girls. Within seconds other people started realising who was eating lunch in the same restaurant as them, and there was a short line of people awaiting Mel's attention. She took it all calmly in her stride, as if this was her everyday life now.

I realised it probably was. I didn't envy her. I would never want that sort of exposure for myself. I was a low-key kind of girl. Being friends with a celebrity was enough for me.

"What did you do?" I asked, my eyes narrowing as I took in the smirk on Alison's face when we met at the car an hour later.

"I accomplished my secret mission."

I slid into the driver's seat and massaged my temples. Sometimes Alison's antics were just a little too much for me.

"Don't even think you're going to try and chuck a sickie on your first night of immersion, my buxom beauty!" Alison warned as I put the car into gear and reversed out of the parking spot. "I can see you gearing up to claim you're getting a migraine."

I shook my head as a flutter of nerves bubbled up from my belly into my chest. "I wouldn't dream of it. You know how much I love to make you happy, Alison."

She sighed. "This is about your happiness, not mine. The thought of you trying to process a misguided guilty conscience every time we go out … it's just not on, Amanda! Eighteen months of therapy hasn't seemed to make much headway, so it's time you took some practical steps towards realising that nothing bad is going to happen to you when you drink."

I snorted, trying to cover up my nerves with bravado. "I thought tonight was about getting a nice buzz, flirting with the first guy who so much as looks at me, and then I'll magically forget that the last time I got drunk and flirted with a guy it ended with two men dead, one in a critical condition, and one of my oldest friends in hospital with a gunshot wound."

"None of those things are your fault though! You need to realise that going out and having a few drinks with friends isn't something you should feel guilt over. What happened, it wasn't because *you* were drinking. It was because *he* was a perverted lunatic!"

"Look, I know, rationally, that I don't have a drinking problem," I agreed. "But I hate that every time I do it, every time I wake up a bit hungover, or sore from dancing, it reminds me of him …"

"Which is exactly why we're going to help you make new night-out-on-the-town memories," Alison reassured me. "Tonight is about you having a fun, *safe* night, and tomorrow we'll talk about how you feel. Tonight's your first baby step, my gorgeous girl!"

CHAPTER TWO

Freedom Tattoo

LEVI

"Any plans to unpack these boxes at some point? It's been a month since you moved your shit over here, and it seems like boxes keep appearing, but none are disappearing."

I was gingerly removing the plastic wrap from the fresh tattoo on my forearm. I looked up as my brother Xander walked into the living room, tossing his keys into the bowl on the hall table and glancing at the pile of boxes beside it.

"Yeah, yeah," I replied shortly, looking at the tattoo. I'd gone knowing exactly how I wanted to commemorate the end of three years of misery. Now I'd never fucking forget just how bad three years with Zilla, also known as my ex-girlfriend, had been—it was there, a constant reminder on my arm. A Freedom Tattoo.

We'd ended things a month ago, and when I went back the day after the breakup to move my shit out, I was shocked that she hadn't thrown it all into a pile on the communal lawn of the apartment block and had some sort of satanic burning ritual as revenge.

Xander headed to the kitchen, grabbing a beer from the fridge. "Want one?" he asked me, not even waiting for my response before pulling another out and popping the lids off both. He knew I'd never turn down an arvo beer.

"I mean, it might be a waste of time, to unpack that shit. I'm hoping Zilla sorts out her rental situation soon, and I can get out of your hair."

Xander collapsed back onto the lounge beside me. "I still can't believe you agreed to continue paying half the rent until she finds a roommate. You know she's going to milk that for as long as possible, right?"

"I just needed to get out. You have no fucking idea how good it feels to not have to go home to her. It was painful enough doing it before we split. If getting away from her means having no money spare to pay rent somewhere else, then that's a small price." I hooked a finger around the neck of my beer and took a long swig. "Have I mentioned how fucking grateful I am that you're willing to have me here, rent free?"

"How about you show your gratitude by moving those boxes so they're not blocking the hallway?" He swallowed his beer, running a hand through his dark blond hair. "You haven't forgotten lunch with Dad tomorrow, have you?"

I glanced over at him, in his navy scrubs, and barked out a laugh. Dad loved that Xander wore scrubs, because he could pretend he had a doctor for a son, and not just a veterinarian.

What you'd never see him acknowledge was that he also had a son who was an Olympic silver medallist rower. Rowing was supposed to have been a hobby, a way to keep me out of trouble while I was at school. To Dad, it wasn't a 'real' career.

"Been trying not to think about it," I replied, grabbing the tube of ointment and gently swiping some over the tender skin on my inner arm.

Xander leaned over to take a look. "Jesus, Levi! That's a statement!"

I scowled. "Once it's settled it won't stand out as much. I just needed the reminder."

"Well, one good thing will come out of that," Xander said, tilting his beer at my fresh tattoo, before tipping it back to drain the last of it. "If Zilla sees it, she's never going to want to fuck you again."

I barked out a hard laugh. "I don't need a deterrent, Xan. Just the thought of ever going there again makes me sick."

"And yet you stayed with her for three years."

I sighed, the bravado I'd been holding onto leeching out of me. "Yep. I'm a fucking idiot. I never even really liked her, now I think about it. I mean, the sex was wild—to begin with at least. But the rest …"

I took a giant gulp of my beer, trying to wash the lump from my throat. The last thing I needed right now was to cry in front of my big brother like a fucking wuss.

Clearing my throat, I muttered, "The rest was just shit."

Xander clinked his empty bottle to my half-full one. "Amen to that. See, this is why I steer clear of anything serious with women."

"Yeah, you keep telling yourself that, Xan," I chortled. "You steer clear of the serious shit because—"

"Shut the fuck up right now, arsehole."

My jaw snapped shut at the warning in Xander's tone. Even after all these years, he was still messed up over her.

"Here's to bros before hoes," I said instead, and downed the rest of my beer in a single gulp.

I tugged at the collar of my dress shirt, sweat pooling under my arms and dripping down my sides, leaving dark patches in my armpits. It was mostly from the scorching heat, but some of that sweat was stress from having to eat lunch in Dad's presence.

"Why the fuck has he chosen to sit outside on a day that's topping forty-five?" I demanded. Xander, who walked beside me, was apparently completely comfortable in dress pants and a shirt in the middle of the hottest day of summer so far.

"There'll be a breeze on the water side," Xander muttered. He always got quiet when we were seeing Dad. Like he had to get into the zone of being the respectable, responsible son, the one with a 'proper' career.

I sometimes wondered whether Xander hammed that shit up just to make me look like even more of a deadshit in Dad's eyes.

I let out a sigh of relief as we walked through the doors and into the frigid air-conditioning of the club. I took my time signing in, partly to enjoy the cold, but also because I really didn't want to deal with Dad's bullshit today.

"Beer?" Xander asked as he strolled off in the direction of the bar.

"Can we drink it inside?" I asked, knowing the answer would be no. I'd already caught sight of Dad's perfectly combed grey hair, sitting in his usual spot out on the balcony, overlooking Sydney Harbour. The Silver Fox, all the blokes he played golf with called him. Like they were so fucking clever. Maybe I should demand that title, being a silver medallist and all.

"Do you think if I wore the medal every time I see him, he might actually acknowledge it?" I asked as we weaved our way through the comfortable, climate-controlled dining room, and through a set of automatic glass doors that opened and transported us into the hellfire outside.

"Jesus," Xander cursed at the blast of hot air. "Honestly, Lev, I think it'd just piss him off more."

I chuckled with zero humour. "Even more reason to do it then."

Dad heard my dark laugh, and he turned his head, taking in the pair of us—Xander balancing a tray with two schooners of beer and a glass of Dad's favourite wine on it, and me slouching along beside him, hands in the pockets of my grey pants. His eyes swept over my tattooed arms, and he scowled.

"Why the fuck are you making me do this?" I mumbled out of the corner of my mouth to Xander before we got too close for any frank conversation.

"Because I shouldn't have to put up with his shit on my own," Xander replied under his breath. I snorted—Xander was the bloody golden child. The only thing he'd ever mis-stepped on was choosing vet science over medicine.

"Boys," Dad grunted as we scraped out our chairs and sat. I took the seat across from Dad, just for that tiny bit of extra distance. Not that it helped—I was now directly in his line of vision.

"A fucking perfect afternoon to be sitting in the blazing heat, sweating our balls off," I commented, leaning back and stretching my arms behind my head. Dad's eyes caught on the fresh tattoo. The scowl deepened further.

"How's the handover going?" Xander asked, distracting Dad. Always the peacekeeper. I tilted my chair onto its two back legs.

Dad's gaze swept from me to Xander, and the furrow in his forehead eased a fraction.

"As smoothly as can be expected. Robert's a complete twit, if he was left to his own devices, he'd drag the whole place down within six months, but at the very least Haley is capable of holding him off that long."

Dad was a renowned lawyer, and he ran a very successful practice. He'd been making noises about retiring for years now, but it never seemed to happen. I raised my eyebrows.

"You're actually going to do it this time?" I blurted before I could stop myself. Dad's eyes flicked to me. I hated that I'd inherited my unique eyes from him. It meant that every time I looked in the mirror, I saw him staring back at me.

And he never stared at me with anything but disapproval, verging on disgust.

"Yes, Levi. These things take time, if one wants to do them right." His voice was full of revulsion. "I couldn't just up and leave Robert in the lurch. He wasn't ready to take on the practice, he needed more experience."

And then he turned back to Xander and continued to talk about the handover logistics as if I didn't even exist. Which suited me just fine.

I was definitely going to need a drink or five tonight with the rowing boys, just to dull the itching sensation that crawled under my skin every time I had to deal with Dad.

Our food arrived, silence settling over the table. Both Dad and Xan had ordered the salmon salad—because that was what they always ordered when they came here. I tucked into my monstrous veal schnitzel with a double serve of chips and extra veg, drowned in Diane sauce.

Dad's disapproval scorched me as I took a massive bite of the schnitzel.

"What?" I asked through my mouthful, because I knew that would piss him off. "Did I spill sauce on my shirt?" I made a show of putting down my cutlery to check my polo, which I knew was spotless. I loved food, but I wasn't a fucking slob.

"One day your diet is going to catch up with you," Dad grunted, eyes narrowed, mouth pinched like a cat's arse. I returned his glare as I mashed some chips and a piece of overcooked broccoli onto my fork and stuffed it into my mouth. I chewed for a moment, just to get my anger under control.

"With the calories I burn at training, I'm pretty sure I'll be okay," I muttered through the last of the mouthful, cutting another massive chunk.

"Yes, well …" Dad murmured. I let my knife and fork fall to the plate.

"Well, what?" I demanded. Xander gave me a look that I knew meant *'don't poke the bear you fucking imbecile,'* but Dad always got my back up. It was his special talent.

"What about once this … hobby of yours peters out? What then?" Dad asked, taking his napkin and dabbing at the corners of his mouth.

So, we were going there again.

"Hobby?" I repeated, very deliberately shoving the largest piece of meat I could manage into my mouth, chewing with my mouth open, because I knew it horrified him. "I make a living off my 'hobby'. I have an Olympic medal thanks to my 'hobby'."

Dad huffed. "You make a piss-poor living only because sponsors see you as some kind of charity case!"

Fuck that noise!

I stood up, my chair tilting, falling to the decking with a clatter. My hands bunched into fists, and I leaned over the table, pressing my knuckles onto the hard surface as I got up close to Dad.

"Sit down, Levi, for crying out loud, you're making a scene!"

Dad hissed, glancing around, despite the fact we were the only ones sitting outside, because other people weren't idiots.

"I'm fucking full," I snarled, pushing up from the table and turning for the door. "Xander, I'll Uber home, I'll catch you there later."

"Lev," he called after me, but I wasn't turning. I just couldn't deal with the same bloody lecture all over again.

CHAPTER THREE

A Night to Remember

AMANDA

"What did you *do*?" I screeched.

I stood in my bedroom doorway, wrapped in my towel after a shower, and psyching myself up to put on the 'risqué' new outfit Alison had chosen for me. But lying on my bed was the evidence that Alison had chosen something else for me to wear as well. Two somethings, actually.

Dani, our other roommate and another fellow nursing alumni, came running first. "What's wrong?" she puffed, her long black hair half pinned up—she was clearly in the middle of straightening it. I pointed a shaking finger at the bed. Her eyes followed my finger, her shoulders instantly relaxing when she saw what I was pointing at.

"Manda, honestly?" she sighed, picking up one of the offending items and inspecting it. "This is hot, where did you get it from?"

"I *didn't* get it!" I exclaimed, picking up the other item between my thumb and forefinger. The lace was softer than I'd expected. But still, I wasn't going to …

"Oh, you found them!" Alison said slyly, sauntering into the room. I threw her a withering look.

"Of course I found them, you laid them out on my bed for me!"

Alison giggled, and Dani joined in. I scowled at the both of them.

"Oh, come on, Manda," Alison cajoled. "You can't wear that hot new outfit with your regular granny panties and a saggy old bra, can you?"

"I absolutely can!" I argued, but my fingers continued to stroke the satin and lace. It was so pretty. I never bought myself pretty lingerie. I skimped on Kmart undies and splurged on heavy duty underwire bras with the widest straps possible to hold up my giant boobs. "This won't hold up half of what I've got out front!"

Alison grabbed the bra from me. "It one hundred percent will. I took photos of you into the lingerie shop, and it's exactly your size. The salesperson said this brand is super supportive for the bustier ladies."

I turned to her, a horrified expression frozen on my face. "You … you took photos of me to show the lingerie salesperson?"

Alison held out the bra to me, completely unapologetic. "Yes, that's exactly what I did. You don't treat yourself enough. So, consider this me treating you. Imagine if you picked up tonight, you got back to his place, and he found your old, saggy-in-the-bum undies when he undressed you?"

I choked on a hysterical giggle. "There is no way I'm picking up tonight!" I protested. Dani and Alison shared a meaningful look.

"What?" I demanded.

"Babe," Dani began, but Alison interrupted.

"Going out wearing this outfit tonight, you'll have to take a stick."

I wrinkled my nose. "Why?"

"To fight the men off with, you dork! Now, put them on, get made up, and I'll curl your hair while you have a wine."

There was no arguing with Alison when she got an idea in her head. My stomach swirled with nerves … and maybe just a teeny, little flutter of excitement. I closed my bedroom door on their retreating backs, picked up the sexy black panties, and stepped into them.

LEVI

Two beers and a glass of Scotch. That's where I was at when I heard the knock on Xander's front door. I set down my tumbler, heading to let my best friend and teammate Theo in.

"You're early," I grumbled as I opened it. But it wasn't Theo and the rowing boys.

"Afternoon, Levi," Dominic, Xander's best mate, said mildly as he sauntered into the hallway. "That looks good." He pointed to the glass of amber liquid I was nursing. "You can get me one, too."

I turned and headed for the kitchen with a sigh. "Xander sent you to babysit?" I guessed, pulling a crystal tumbler out of the cupboard and pouring him a Scotch. He took a seat at the island, and I slid it across to him, leaning on the counter and staring into my glass, as if it could solve all my problems.

"Can't a bloke just drop in on his mate's little brother and share a drink?" Dom said with a smirk that didn't reach his dark eyes. He was a cold one, Dominic Timothy Fournier. Xander used to give him shit all through high school that his initials spelled out DTF. Because he never chased girls in high school. Ever.

And then he hit university, and it was all he did. Down To Fuck Dom. He really grew into that nickname.

"Cut the bullshit, Dom."

Dom sighed, scratching at his neatly trimmed black beard. "Yeah, he texted me, said your dad was a prick and to make sure you'd come home. He didn't want you taking off again like that other time."

My sinuses stung as I snorted Scotch out my nose. "What the fuck? That was ten years ago! I'm not a shitty teenager anymore, I'm twenty-eight! I have bloody responsibilities. I can't just disappear."

Dom's eyes slid towards the window as he sipped at his Scotch. I knew what he was thinking. What they all thought: *Levi's responsibili-*

ties aren't real responsibilities. He just mucks around at his hobby all day, and somehow scrapes enough money together to pay the bills.

"I have a team that I can't let down. I have a national race meet coming up, and it's an Olympic Qualifier year at Worlds. This *is* fucking important to me! This is my career!"

Dom lifted his hands, somehow managing not to slosh Scotch everywhere. "Alright, you've made your point! You're a big, important sports star, doing big important sports star things."

He was trying to lighten the mood. It wasn't going to work. I drained my glass but didn't reach for the bottle. I suddenly didn't want to get wasted tonight, because that was what they all expected of me.

"Well, I'm glad you're here to lecture me, Dom. I love being told my sporting career isn't valid by a fucking singing teacher."

Dom chuckled, grabbing the bottle of whiskey and tilting it over his glass. "Do you want to spend the evening arguing the merits of sport versus the arts? Because I'm free *all night.*"

I had to laugh then, and it did make me feel a bit lighter. Bloody Dom—he was always so goddamned calm. That was why Xander had sent him over. If anyone was going to talk me down from the ledge, it would be him.

"You do you, Levi," Dom said, clinking his full glass to my empty one. "Fuck the haters the same way I do. Now, is tonight's plan to find a hot, willing girl and screw the titty-monster out of your system?"

"Nope, no need. Zilla was out of my system months ago," I sighed, slouching around the island and collapsing onto the couch. "Fucking years, if I really think about it."

Dom watched me, those black eyes of his hiding his thoughts too well. I rubbed at my temples. I wasn't sure I was in the mood to go out with the boys tonight.

"All the more reason then," Dom argued, taking a seat in the armchair across from me. "If fucking has been a chore for you for years, then you need to find the fun again."

I couldn't really argue with that. But it had never been my style —to go out and chase tail. I'd been a serial monogamist since my early twenties. Boobzilla had lasted the longest, but most of them had been between six and ten months before her. And they'd all pursued me. Even Zilla, self-absorbed harpy that she was, had chased me. I knew now that it had been less to do with our non-existent chemistry and more to do with me being the cocky bastard that I sometimes could be, strutting around the bars of Newtown with my Olympic medal around my neck. She noticed *that* about me.

Apparently being on the arm of an Olympic medallist was great for her online persona. It had only taken this short-sighted imbecile three years to work out that was the only reason she was with me.

"Tonight," I announced, slapping my thighs for emphasis before standing up. "I'm going to hang out with Theo and the rowing boys, drink enough for a mild buzz, maybe play some pool, come home—alone—by midnight, stroke off in the shower, and fall into bed to sleep like a goddamned baby."

Dom laughed under his breath. "Sounds like a night to remember."

CHAPTER FOUR

Abandoned Intentions

LEVI

"Tell me again—why is he here?" I hissed to Theo. He'd been my best mate since kindergarten, and my teammate since we took up double sculls rowing together at fifteen. He knew exactly who the fuck I was talking about. We stood at the bar, ordering a round of beers for the boys—Grant, Harvey, Ryan and Patrick, one of the quad sculls teams from Sydney Rowing ... and Macintosh Fucking Graham.

Theo grimaced as he slapped a fifty down on the bar. "He overheard me telling the others. It was like he bloody appeared out of thin air, grinning like a dickhead and saying how it would be a great 'bonding experience' for us all."

Macintosh—what sort of parents named their kids something so stupid—or Mac for short, was a reserve at Sydney Rowing. Something about him had always rubbed me totally the wrong way. I was almost sure it was his people-pleaser attitude. I'd rebelled against that sort of bullshit my whole life, and he'd leaned into it. Hard.

Every time he walked into a room I was in, acting like a Golden Retriever whose red rocket popped out every time he got a pat on the head and a 'good boy', I felt like I was about to puke.

I sighed. "Well, it's not like we can get rid of him now. Unless we ply him with drinks until he's completely wasted and put him in an Uber home early."

Theo shrugged. "I mean, if you really want to go to that much effort, mate, I'll support you one hundred percent. But honestly, just fucking ignore him. He's annoying, but he's essentially harmless."

I didn't respond, grabbing the tray and heading back over to the bar tables we'd commandeered. It wasn't all that late yet, so the place wasn't crowded. The lighting was low, but still enough that I could make out a few groups sitting in the booths on the other side of the bar, near the pool tables.

"Did you clock that tiny redhead at the other end of the bar?" Harvey said, looking expectantly at Theo and me. I shook my head, but Theo nodded with a grin.

"Hot as fuck, man!" Theo said. "When I'm out with you bunch of dickheads and I see a girl like that, I thank God that you're all shacked up."

"Ah, but you've got competition again, Theo!" Harvey said, tilting his beer in my direction. "And my bet would be on Levi tapping that tonight."

I grunted. "I'm not putting my hat in the ring."

"Bullshit!" Ryan argued. "It's rebound time for you, man! The best no-strings sex of your life awaits you!"

"*Not* with the redhead!" Theo warned me.

I shook my head. "I'm not in the market for rebound sex. Not my style. Besides, tiny redheads aren't my thing."

After three years of Zilla, I wasn't even sure I knew what my 'thing' was anymore. And tonight wasn't the night I planned to find out. But I was curious about this redhead that had Theo all tied in knots. I took a sip of my beer as I turned to see if I could spot her.

I caught sight of the back of her fiery head as she slid into the booth closest to the pool tables. There were two other women with her. A tall, serious looking black-haired one. And a pretty, smiling blonde.

My stomach flipped.

Fuck. Me.

I was pretty sure I'd just figured out what my 'thing' was. Pretty smiling blondes.

"Looking at the blonde? She's cute," Mac commented in my ear, and I jumped, turning to see him watching the other end of the bar over the rim of his beer. "I might have to go and introduce myself. Please excuse me." And off he trotted, beer in hand, towards the booths at the other end.

"Jesus fucking Christ," I muttered, slamming my beer down on the table.

"Challenge accepted?" Theo asked with a chuckle. "You about to go cockblock old Macca?"

"Fuck off," I grunted. Because that was exactly what I was about to do. But not for the reason that Theo assumed.

I was about to break my rule. I needed that pretty, smiling blonde in my bed tonight, if it was the last thing I did.

AMANDA

"Holy shit, did you see that table of hotties at the other side of the bar?" Alison exclaimed as she tucked her wallet back into her purse. "Either they're a bunch of gym junkies, or they play professional sport." She was practically drooling as she eyed them, completely unashamed.

I sipped at the surprise cocktail that Alison plonked in front of me, glancing in the direction of the supposed hotties and almost swallowing my tongue. There were seven of them, all tall, muscled, and tanned. All gorgeous to a fault.

"I call dibs on the dark-haired one staring at me," Alison murmured from the corner of her mouth, ogling him right back.

Dani tittered, tilting her head to take a sip of her drink, but not before she whispered, "I think one of them might be a bit taken with you, too, Manda."

My cheeks heated as I tried to glance at them from under my

lashes, my attempt at subtlety no doubt failing miserably as I caught the eye of one of them.

"The blond one?" I hissed out of the corner of my mouth. "He looks nice."

"He's coming over!" Alison warned me, completely unnecessarily. I could see perfectly well for myself that he was weaving his way towards us.

He was exactly the kind of man I would normally melt over—cute, with wavy blond hair and a smattering of light freckles over his nose. Tall, muscled, but not in a super bulky way—some of the other ones he was with were much bigger than him. An open, friendly smile. He was the least threatening one in the group, by quite a margin.

I wondered what he would want with someone like me—he could pull any girl he wanted, with those boyish good looks. Maybe he'd been looking at Dani.

"Hello, lovely ladies, how are you tonight?" he said as he stopped in front of our booth, smiling at Alison and Dani before turning his attention to me, his grin widening.

Okay, so he had been looking at me. Even I couldn't mistake it. The temperature of my face went up another notch.

"We're doing great!" Alison replied, nudging me not so subtly in the ribs. I winced, hoping that I disguised it by flashing him an overly warm smile.

"I'd love to buy you all a drink, but it seems you're sorted for the time being." He glanced at our almost full glasses, a woebegone expression stealing across his face. It was so over the top that I giggled, averting my eyes, because the earnest look on his face made me uncomfortable.

LEVI

I approached the table where Mac was chatting animatedly with the three women. He said something and they laughed, and I felt like sprinting the rest of the way and spear tackling him to the ground. Mac was annoying as shit, but he was what women called a 'nice guy'. Easy on the eye, friendly, polite, inoffensively funny.

Probably exactly what the pretty blonde was after. Closer up, she looked even better than from a distance. Her skin was peachy, and not covered with a metric buttload of makeup. Her eyes sparkled as she looked up at Mac, flashing white teeth as she giggled.

My dick twitched at the sound of her laughter, stopping me in my tracks. I coughed, giving my crotch a quick adjustment, and surged forwards again. Reaching Mac's side, I barely glanced at the redhead and the black-haired woman before my eyes landed on the blonde.

Holy shit. I was in trouble. Grey eyes, pink cheeks, a little button nose. Glossy, pouty lips—but not because of fucking fillers, those babies were all natural. And then my eyes fell past her chin … to the most luscious boobs I had ever laid eyes on. Also natural, I would have bet my Olympic medal on it.

"Evening, ladies," I managed, dragging my eyes away from her rack with an insane amount of effort, meeting her wide eyes.

"I feel like playing some pool," I said to Mac, grabbing him by the arm. "If any of you ladies would like to join, you'd be … very welcome."

I couldn't help myself—my eyes dropped to her tits again before I hauled Mac away, pulling my phone out of my pocket and tapping it to the credit card scanner on the pool table nearest them.

"I really hope they join in," Mac said, making puppy-dog eyes at the blonde as I racked up the balls and grabbed a cue from the wall.

"Don't be so damned obvious," I hissed. "Just play. The ball's in their court now."

I fucking hoped my balls would be in the vicinity of her court before the night was through. I was officially abandoning my intention to go home alone tonight.

CHAPTER FIVE

Danger Boy

AMANDA

"I told you!" Alison crowed. "All we had to do was replace your sack dresses with some sexy clothes, and you've got two guys panting after you in the space of minutes."

I couldn't answer, still stunned as I slurped my drink, wishing the alcohol would put out the fire that was suddenly kindling low in my belly. But all it seemed to be doing was stoking it. I couldn't drag my gaze off that man. The one with the unbelievable eyes.

My head swam trying to work out what colour they were. I would probably have called them hazel, but they were … more than that. Like they were lit from within. And set in a face that was tanned, they seemed even lighter, like precious stones adorning his face. His manly face, framed by bronze hair that was short at the back and sides, but slightly too long on top, flopping down over those incredible eyes. His face, complete with high cheekbones, a strong jaw and a knowing smile.

But then there was the rest. A scar over one eyebrow—it looked like it might have been from a piercing that had grown out. His tight, grey t-shirt, with a black linework logo of two crossed oars on it, barely contained his bulging biceps and pecs. And then there were the intricate tattoos winding down both arms, to his wrists, the reds and pinks and blues and greens undulating as his muscles bunched under the skin, as he lined up and dropped shot after shot.

He practically exuded danger.

His game impressed me, and not many people could impress me with their pool skills. His blond, smiling friend barely even got a look in, but he didn't seem to mind. He stood to the side, leaning against his cue, grinning and occasionally making a comment to the dangerous one, who acted like he didn't exist.

"Manda, get over there!" Alison muttered, nudging me in the ribs again. I was going to have a bruise at this rate. "Those two are vying for your attention!"

I rolled my eyes, even as my heart attempted to break free of my ribcage. "You can't be serious! The one with the tattoos has barely even glanced at me."

Alison eyed me. "Why would that matter—you'd be aiming for the blond one anyway, wouldn't you? I mean, you'd swipe right on him in a heartbeat."

I swallowed a large mouthful of the cocktail, dragging my eyes back to the smiley one. "He looks …" What did he look like?

He looked like he wouldn't hurt me, that was what immediately came to mind.

As if she could read my thoughts, Alison leaned closer. "He looks like he's safe, doesn't he? Like he's not going to break you? I'm sorry in advance for what I'm about to say, but you need to hear it. Thomas looked safe, too."

I gasped, then coughed, almost choking on the piece of ice I'd been sucking on. Alison and Dani both reached out and patted my back as I got myself under control. It was honestly more for emotional support than because I was actually choking. They knew his name always made me feel a bit out of control.

"All I'm saying," Alison continued quietly, as the tattooed man sank the eight ball and glanced up at me. He arched his scarred eyebrow and his lip tilted up on that same side, but then his gaze slid away, and he tapped his phone to the side of the table to start another game, muttering something to his blond friend.

"Earth to Amanda!" Alison snapped, and I shook myself,

turning my attention back to her. "Oh my God, you don't even need me to tell you this—you're clearly making eyes at Danger Boy over there."

"I'm—"

"Don't. Don't try to lie to me. I just want you to hear this. You learned the hard way that 'nice' and 'unassuming' don't always mean 'good'. So maybe you should throw all those ideas out the window, and just go for what gets you hot."

She nodded very obviously at Danger Boy. "Go, play pool with him. See where it goes. This is a perfect chance for you to put the past behind you—he couldn't be more different."

I sucked hard on my straw, swallowing the last dregs of my cocktail. Alison was renowned for picking the strong drinks, so I was feeling pleasantly floaty, almost as if approaching a dangerous looking tattooed man and challenging him to a game of pool would be totally normal and easy for me.

Before I could think too hard about it, I stood, squeezing past Dani and out onto the floor. I turned back to give them both a cheeky salute. Alison winked at me, and Dani raised her glass.

Yep, I was going to go and flirt with Danger Boy. That's what tonight was all about, wasn't it? Getting out of my comfort zone, and realising that things weren't going to end badly.

Well, he was about as far outside my comfort zone as it was possible to be. And yet something oddly close to excitement fluttered in my belly as I approached the pool table.

CHAPTER SIX

Manifested Fucking Destiny

LEVI

I broke on my second game with Mac, managing to sink a ball on the break. I was on a roll tonight. I had no fucking idea how I was playing so well, when every nerve ending in my body was tuned in to the blonde with the pouty lips, and the beautiful tits straining to be free of that low cut black top she was wearing.

"You're on fire, mate!" Mac's impressed voice rang out. I bit down on my tongue to stop myself from telling him to piss off, focusing on lining up my second shot.

"I may as well just hang this cue up and go sit with the ladies over there," he added.

My cue slipped, catching the white ball at the wrong angle, and it spun off course, missing my easy shot at the top pocket. I glared at Mac, who grinned right back. The bastard had done that deliberately. I didn't know whether to be pissed off or impressed that he actually had the balls to do it.

"Well, you can't sit down now, can you?" I replied darkly, backing away and leaning on my cue to watch him line up, then miss a shot. He was fucking terrible at pool.

"I'll play the winner."

My eyes snapped up at the honey sound of her voice. And Holy fucking Jesus! I could see her properly now that she wasn't sitting in the booth. If that face and those tits had been enough to get my dick twitching, now I could add in her round arse in a tiny, flirty little pair of denim shorts, and smooth, creamy thighs, shapely calves, and a pair of black heels that I wanted digging into my back as I buried my face between her legs.

I let my eyes slowly trail back up her body, as I moved closer to the table to conceal the sudden raging boner I was sporting.

"Something worth fighting for, wouldn't you say, Levi?" Mac said, moving away from the table and towards the lush blonde. I wanted to strangle him.

"Levi," the blonde repeated to herself. The sound of my name on her lips … I needed her moaning it in my ear.

"I'm Mac," the prick jumped in before I could introduce myself properly. "It's lovely to meet you …"

"Amanda," she said, smiling at him, but her eyes strayed back to me. I flashed her a toothy grin, leaned down, and with a little bit of skill and a shitload of luck, I sank a ball.

"I can't wait to play with you, Amanda," I murmured, raising one eyebrow just enough that she understood I wasn't talking about pool. Those peachy cheeks of hers flushed so prettily I had to adjust myself before I took another shot. And sank another ball. There was no fucking way I was letting Mac be the one to play a game with her. I sank another, and then missed, scowling at Mac where he'd been chatting away to her.

"You're up," I grunted, and took my chance to go and stand by her, watching Mac assess the table and choose his shot.

"Do you play pool much?" I asked, grabbing the chalk and attending to my cue, while not-so-subtly checking out her cleavage. Her chest rose and fell with faster, shallower breaths as she noticed where my attention was going. Which just made her boobs even more fucking perfect. I wanted my hands on them, my palms cupping the weight of them. I wondered whether her nipples would be as pink as her lips. I wondered how much sucking and biting it would take to make them as rosy as her blushing cheeks.

"My dad used to play a bit. He taught me," she replied, her

voice slightly shaky. Was I making her nervous? I dragged my eyes from her rack, instead watching her lips move as she added, "But it's been years since I really played properly. I'll be rusty."

Her lips twitched, and she glanced up to meet my eyes, then away again. I got the impression she wasn't telling the full truth. Which somehow only turned me on more.

"I'm going to beat Mac; you know that don't you?"

She looked over at Mac, who had sunk his ball, but was struggling to work out what shot to take next. She turned back to me, giving me a little nod, and an even tinier smile. I wanted to see that wide grin, the one she'd shown to Mac earlier. I wondered what it would take to get her to smile at me like that.

"So, when I win, and it's our turn," I paused, letting those words hang for a moment, "Let's make a wager, yeah?"

"A wager?" she asked, her mouth popping open. I didn't have time to enjoy it, though, because fucking Mac bounced over and informed me that it was my turn again. As if I didn't know.

"A wager—you come up with your terms while I win this game." I said, ignoring Mac completely. I sounded like such a cocky prick, but the way she flushed and shifted her legs told me that act was working. I flashed a grin in her direction and turned to give all my focus to the game.

I had to freeze Mac out now. I had to be the one to play her.

I sank ball after ball, managing some tricky shots in the process. I glanced up every now and then, watching her watch my game. She was sizing me up, deciding if my offer of a wager was worth it for her. Fuck I hoped she decided it was.

I had one more coloured ball and the eight-ball still to sink. The table was littered with Mac's balls—I had frozen him out, but he seemed to be taking it just fine. He'd just returned from the bar with a beer for himself and a small glass of wine for Amanda.

They clinked their glasses together, and she turned to me, lifting it in my direction and watching me through lowered lashes as she took a sip. Fuck. Hard as steel again.

Focus, Levi. Two more balls, and then you get to play with her.

I sank the coloured ball, lined up the eight ball, and took my shot. It rebounded off the bottom pocket, and I cursed under my breath. But then it spun across the table and dropped with a satisfying *thunk* into the centre pocket.

"I totally fucking planned that," I said with a chuckle as I looked up. She watched me, eyes sparkling. She looked as excited as I felt. I imagined her bending over to take a difficult shot, me behind her, stroking my fingertips up the backs of those curvaceous thighs. And then she'd press that beautiful butt back against my groin, grinding against my dick.

I needed to stop. This was getting out of control. I'd never—not even as a horny teenager—had such vivid fantasies. I closed my eyes, willing myself to get my act together.

"I'll take your wager," her silky voice murmured, so close. I turned my head, looked down. She was there beside me, holding a cue in one hand, and her almost empty wine in the other.

"If I win," she continued, tipping the glass and letting the last of her wine slide past her moist lips. She was so sexy, and I wasn't even sure she realised it. "I want you to tell me what that tattoo means. It … intrigues me." She pointed at the fresh one. The freedom tattoo.

Fucking hell, I had to win this game. If I had to tell her the story behind that tattoo, I'd never get her in bed with me. I forced a smirk onto my face.

"And if I win, you have to come home with me."

Her expression crumpled slightly. *Too much too soon, Levi. Stop thinking with your dick and engage your fucking brain.*

She giggled nervously, sending more of my blood rushing south. "You might be a serial killer, for all I know," she confessed with a laugh. There was an edge to the sound and my stomach dropped.

"Okay," I amended, reaching out and taking the empty wine glass from her hand, putting it down on the bar, leaning closer and lowering my voice. "If I win, I get to kiss you."

The nervous look faded, and her cheeks pinked again. I wanted to reach up and drag a thumb across that heat, tilt her chin, and take my kiss right now, wager be damned.

"Um, okay, I can agree to that," she said with a shaky voice. "But I get to break."

I nodded in agreement, tapping my phone and getting the balls up onto the table, standing back to let her rack up. Which was a mistake. Watching her bend over the table to line the balls up, those shorts riding up and showing just a hint of the lower curve of her arse …

Fucking torture.

AMANDA

He was watching me.

And not in an innocent way, either. I could practically feel the heat of his eyes roving over my legs and bottom, like an actual caress. I was sure my legs were flushing, the same way my face, and chest, scalp and stomach and every other part of my body was burning.

Why did he make me feel this way? Okay, yes it was mildly awkward, to know I was being scrutinised by him so intently. But more than that, it was … titillating. Which was a word I had never, ever thought I would use when describing how a man looked at me.

Maybe he has a fetish for chubby girls, the nasty little voice in the back of my head suggested. I tried not to let that thought deflate me. I was feeling pretty for the first time in God knew how long.

So what if he does? I argued with the voice in my head, like a crazy person. *He seems to like what he sees, that's all that matters.* I wasn't fully convinced, but at least it stopped that intrusive little voice in its tracks. I took a deep breath, removed the frame from the table, and lined up the white ball to break.

Two stripes hurtled towards the bottom pockets, dropping in and making that satisfying rumbling sound as they made their way into the bowels of the table. I straightened, tilting my head in Levi's direction. The shocked gape of his mouth made me giggle. I tried to hide it behind my hand, but it burst past my fingers. I gave up trying to hold it in, clutching my stomach and shaking with tipsy laughter.

Levi's eyes darkened, his gaze fixating intently on my jiggling breasts. I sobered, realising that the way my arms wound under them pushed them up almost obscenely. I quickly dropped my arms to my sides as he stalked towards me.

"You're a pool shark," he murmured, continuing to advance on me until I felt my butt bump up against the table. I shook my head. Gosh I was such a liar.

"I just know some trick shots, that's all," I protested breathily. His chest was warm, and his Adam's Apple was directly in my line of sight. I watched it bob in his throat, as his hands rested on the edge of the table either side of me, his head dropping until his lips were at my ear. He smelled like the ocean, and of skin warmed by the sun. I sucked in a little squeaking breath, heart racing, warmth flooding my belly, and lower.

"I didn't realise that playing with you was going to be this much fun," he muttered against my ear lobe. Then just as abruptly as he'd caged me in, he stepped back.

"Well, take your next shot," he commanded, arms folded across his wide chest. Somewhat unsteadily, I turned, assessed the table, chose my shot. Bending down, I lined it up, pulling the cue back.

Feather-light touch on the back of my thigh. I jerked, the cue slipped, barely grazing the edge of the white ball, which meandered off to the side, nowhere near touching any of the stripes. My pulse beat wildly between my legs. His fingers were still doing a barely-there dance on my skin, just below the overly short hem of my shorts.

I didn't want to turn, to let him see how flustered he had me. I'd never been touched like that, and for it to be happening here, in a very public space, was shocking and exhilarating, all at once.

He leaned down, his breath tickling the back of my neck, heating my skin.

"Two can play that game, Honey," he breathed into the shell of my ear, making me shiver. "I really want my kiss." He straightened, my thighs shaking as he removed his fingers, took his pool cue and coolly assessed the table. How was he so calm, when I could feel my blood rushing through every part of my body? I was in over my head with Danger Boy, that was for certain.

His solid ball clunked as it sunk into the pocket. Levi stared heatedly at me, moving around the table to line up his next shot. As he passed me, he murmured, "I should have warned you … if I want something bad enough, I'll play dirty to get it."

Goosebumps erupted all over my skin, and for a brief moment, I wondered if throwing the game entirely and letting him kiss me wouldn't be the best outcome here. The thought of his lips, touching mine, his hot breath in my mouth, his tongue … I suddenly wanted it so badly. And I hadn't wanted anything close to that since Thomas. But letting him win seemed a little too desperate.

I could play dirty too, couldn't I? If he could touch me like that, why couldn't I touch him, too? It was the most forward thing I could imagine doing, but maybe I could win and still get my kiss at the end of it all.

My kiss? God, this was getting out of control.

He leaned over the table, lining up his cue. Before I could chicken out, I crept up beside him, reaching my hand out and slipping it into the back pocket of his jeans. I even gave a little squeeze. Oh my God, his backside was so muscled, clenching against my hand.

He grunted as his shot went wide, then cursed as the white ball collided with one of my stripes, sending it into the centre pocket.

He straightened fast, too fast for me to extricate my hand. Panicking, I tugged, and it came free suddenly. I teetered on the heels I wasn't really used to wearing. His hand flashed out, grabbing me by the wrist and steadying me before I could go head over heels.

"Truce time, I think," he said, his palm warm against my skin, a calloused thumb running across the sensitive veins on my inner wrist, those light-filled eyes sucking me in. "Fuck, I desperately want to win this, but not if you break a leg trying to stop me. Let's play clean, yeah?"

I nodded, not trusting my voice. He released my wrist, and it was all I could do not to melt into a puddle on the floor. So much for wanting a kiss—now all I could think about was going home with him, like he'd wanted to begin with. And the fact that maybe it was finally time for me to get rid of my pesky V-card.

LEVI

I was pretty sure she wanted to come home with me tonight, despite her earlier protests. And fuck, if she didn't, it was going to take me all of three strokes in the shower when I got home for me to blow. I'd never been so worked up over a woman before.

Our truce was going well for me. She'd missed her next shot, which I considered karma, since she'd almost made me pass out when all my blood rushed to my dick from her grabbing my arse. And then I'd sunk four in a row, before missing the fifth.

Amanda was up, chewing on her full, pink bottom lip as she weighed her options. I groaned quietly under my breath. Everything she did had me on the razor's edge of throwing her on the pool table and burying my face in those lush tits of hers. And then burying it lower.

Would she squirm? Would she scream? Would she rock her hips to ride my mouth? Christ I hoped so. Imagining how she might be in my bed was absolutely fucking torturous.

She took a shot, sank it. Flicked me a cheeky look from under those long, dark lashes of hers. Just like the rest of her, those lashes were natural—I knew how to spot a set of fake eyelashes a mile away, having seen them strewn all over the bathroom counter for the last two years.

"This is some truly epic foreplay we've all got a front row seat to," Theo remarked, sidling over as Amanda lined up her next shot. She was on the other side of the table, facing us. Just before she took her shot, she glanced up at me. Her eyes met mine as her boobs fought her top to try and get free.

"I fucking hope it's foreplay," I muttered, silently thanking God when her striped ball ricocheted off the pocket rather than dropping into it.

"She looks at you like she wants to be eaten alive," he continued. "Her friend tells me she never loses at pool, yet here you are, wiping the floor with her."

"Really?" I muttered, smirking over at her.

"And you successfully cock blocked Mac—he left as soon as you started the game with her." Theo added. I grunted at him, a warning, as Amanda approached. I had too much riding on this for him to ruin it with shit talk about Mac. I hadn't even given the guy a second thought since I started this game with Amanda.

"You're up, Levi," she purred, giving me a shy smile. This girl was a walking contradiction. Her honey voice was pure sex. Her body language was all innocence. Except when she squeezed my butt. And when she wriggled her sexy arse as I stroked her thigh.

And … I was painfully hard.

Head in the game, Levi! Win this and you might be in with a shot.

I took one last, lingering look at her, all soft curves and blonde curls. And then I manifested my fucking destiny.

And when that eight-ball dropped into the pocket, time stopped.

CHAPTER SEVEN

The Big 'It'

AMANDA

The clunk of that final ball descending into the pool table reverberated through my blood. My mouth went suddenly dry, my eyes flashing up to meet his.

The intent in his gaze as he tossed the cue onto the pool table and strode towards me turned my knees to jelly. I gripped the corner of the table to hold myself up, glancing around in sudden awareness that this big, muscled, tattooed Danger Boy stalking towards me planned to kiss me in front of everyone in this bar.

Not that anyone else seemed even remotely concerned with what he was about to do to me. Or if they were, they were making a very good show of feigning disinterest. Even Alison was too busy giggling and whispering into the ear of Levi's friend—Theo I thought his name was.

"Eyes on me, Honey," he murmured, the heat from his body seeping into every one of my pores. Long fingers grasped my chin, tilting my head up until I was taking in that strong, tanned jaw with its shadowy stubble, white teeth and parted lips, straight nose, and those eyes that practically glowed golden, framed by dark, dangerous, scarred brows.

Danger Boy.

Everything south of my navel turned to liquid heat at the fire in his eyes. Who would have thought that the bad boy vibe would do so much for me?

His mouth moved closer, his breath warm against my cheek, as he angled my head to get better access to my lips.

"Wait!" I whispered. He froze, his fingers suddenly tense on my jaw.

"Do you want to back out of our wager?" he asked, nostrils flaring. Oh my God, he was barely in control. Did he actually want this kiss that much?

I shook my head emphatically. There was no way I was missing out on his kiss, not when I'd been dying for it since he offered it.

"Just … not here, okay? I want to go home with you." The words came out in a strangled rush, before I could lose my nerve.

What was I doing?

Whatever it was, I was not going to think about it too deeply right now.

His eyes flashed, his palm sliding down my throat, across my collarbone, and then down my arm until his fingers wound through mine.

"Thank fucking God," he muttered fervently, his eyes slipping shut for a brief moment. A tiny, nervous giggle broke free of my throat as he turned and tugged on my hand, leading me towards the door.

I scanned the bar for Alison, needing her to know that I was leaving. She was still all over Theo, but Dani was sitting on a stool nearby, a couple of the other guys chatting to her. She caught my eye, lifted one hand in a thumbs up, and mouthed, *"Go get 'em, tiger!"* to me.

And then we were out the door, and into the sticky night air of Bondi in February. Even in the still, oppressive heat, my skin prickled under his scrutiny. Light pooled from the nearby streetlight, but we were just out of its reach, in the shadows.

Would he kiss me now?

No. He tugged on my hand again, heading off along the street at an easy pace that I could match even in my heels. Waves rumbled to shore on nearby Bondi beach, the burble of laughter and music from a number of bars combining into a buzz of sound that hummed through every one of my nerve endings.

"Do you live far?" I asked, stumbling slightly in heels I was so unused to wearing. "It's just that these aren't the best footwear for a long walk."

Levi paused, his eyes traveling up and down the length of me, heat coursing through my veins as if it was his hand, and not his eyes trailing me.

"It's only a couple of blocks. I just moved in with my brother, so I'm still getting my bearings around here," he explained, pulling me forward gently by our joined hands, stopping by a side street, peering down it.

"I've lived in Bondi for years now, what's the address?" I asked. Levi turned to me, eyes ridiculously bright as he rattled off a street number and name. I nodded, turning down the street he'd been peering into.

"You knew where you were going," I reassured him. "It's always more difficult in the dark." We continued up the street for a block, then took a right.

"So, you live close by?" Levi asked. I nodded, as we approached a cute white weatherboard place, with a picket fence and some cottage planting in the small front yard.

"Only a few streets from here, actually," I replied, pausing at the gate as Levi leaned down to unlatch it with his free hand. He hadn't let go of mine since he took hold of it back at the bar.

The click and creak of the gate, and the sudden, overwhelming scent of jasmine in the garden had my nerves spiking. I was going home with a man I knew barely anything about. This was not me.

But maybe that was the reason it felt right. Getting out of my rut, trying something new. Losing my virginity to a virtual stranger, because I couldn't deny the chemistry I felt with him.

Oh my God. What was I doing?

Levi tugged on my hand again and I followed him along the stone path, my thoughts in turmoil but my body still more than willing for whatever was about to happen. The porch light was on, and as he stepped under it, I saw him in full light for the first time.

He was devastating. How did someone that physically blessed choose to take someone like me home with them?

I realised at that moment, that this was the first time he would have seen me in proper light, too. I sucked on my bottom lip, that all too familiar swoop in the pit of my stomach heralding the nasty thoughts.

He can see how wide your bottom is now, how your arms have no tone. That lighting is doing nothing to mask your fat face.

"Hey," Levi said softly, his deep voice breaking through the static of intrusive thoughts. His thumb caressed my palm as he stepped closer. I sucked in a breath. Would he send me home?

"If you don't want any of this, you just have to tell me, okay?" His voice was quiet, reassuring, but that nasty voice piped up.

He's trying to let you down easy.

My hammering heart refused to be calmed. I did want this, but I was suddenly sure he wanted me to say no, to turn and walk away. The warmth that had been flooding my body rapidly cooled, as I loosened my grip on his fingers.

He tightened his. "You don't have to do anything you don't want to do, Honey," he murmured, and his use of that nickname melted me once more. "But for the record," he added, stepping closer, his free hand sliding up my neck, under my hair, cupping my nape as he drew me closer to him, "I want this so fucking badly."

His lips touched mine. A fleeting brush of contact. Lightning seared me.

"I'm a virgin," I blurted.

LEVI

I reared back in shock. In the bright light of Xander's front porch, I watched those grey eyes of hers slide away from mine, her cheeks going that shade of pink that had captivated me earlier.

Holy shit. She wasn't lying.

"How …?" I began but stopped myself. There were so many potential reasons why she wouldn't have had sex yet. And none of them were any of my fucking business, when it came down to it.

But seriously. Fucking how? Her gaze dropped to the ground, bottom lip trapped firmly between her teeth. I took in her gorgeous curves; big, perky breasts, those cock teasing shorts showing off her beautiful arse and hips, and then those creamy thighs.

She was a wet dream. How had no one tapped that?

"How old are you?" I asked suddenly, blood draining from my face. If she was barely legal, I was going to lose my shit. She had a face that could easily pass for just turned eighteen. And at twenty-eight, I'd be the worst kind of dirty perve, if I even thought about popping a teenager's cherry.

If cherry popping was still on the table. And fuck me, if it was … and she wasn't, in fact, a teenager …

"I'm twenty-four," she mumbled, that pink in her cheeks spreading, reddening.

"Oh, Honey," I sighed, relief that I hadn't been about to defile a teenager making my voice rough. "I think you just made my night."

Her eyes flashed to mine, curiosity overtaking her embarrassment. "How?"

I chuckled, but instead of explaining my dirty thoughts to her, I slid my hand from under her hair, down to the small of her back, pressing her against the bulge in my pants.

My dick jerked at her sharp little suck of breath. I pulled back, reaching into my pocket and dragging out the key. As I turned it in the lock, my stupid, overthinking brain started bombarding me with a bunch of bullshit worries.

What if she thinks she can't say no? What if she regrets it in the morning? What if she's so nervous that no matter what you do, she can't get off?

What if she turns and runs the second you show her your unusual dick …?

"Come in," I said, giving all those concerns a big mental *fuck off.* A couple of my partners before Zilla had been inexperienced, and I'd worked out pretty fast that consent, communication and control

—as in giving *them* the control—had helped them to let go and enjoy themselves.

But none of them had been virgins …

Piss off brain!

I led the way into the kitchen, grabbing two glasses down from a cupboard and filling them with cold water from the dispenser on the fridge. It wasn't quite midnight, but the house was silent. Xander must have hooked up—his usual Saturday night routine.

"This is a lovely house," Amanda remarked, her eyes roving the open plan living and kitchen. I had a feeling she was feigning interest in the place because it meant she could look anywhere but at me. I had to get her over these nerves, if anything was going to happen with us.

Had I decided that I'd let this happen if she wanted it? Was I making my peace with being her first?

Who was I fucking kidding? The thought of being the first man inside her was half the reason for my rock-hard dick.

"Yeah, my brother's been renovating it himself," I replied, playing her game. "The bathroom's his next project. It's just down the hall, second door on the left, if you need it."

She nodded, but made no move to use it, instead coming up to the island bench and reaching for the glass of water I'd placed there for her. She sipped slowly, her eyes finally meeting mine.

"So," she said timidly as she set the glass back on the counter. Her eyes flicked to mine, blinked once, and flitted away as she swept her ring finger over the corner of her mouth, wiping away a drop of water there.

My dick ached. I wanted to replace her finger with my tongue. I stalked around the island towards her, gritting my teeth because what I really wanted to do—spread her out on the island and feast on her—was impossible.

For now, anyway.

"So …" I repeated, stopping just shy of touching her. She spun on the stool until she faced me, her expression flustered and unsure and so fucking adorable my breath caught in my throat.

I had to make tonight good for her. No, fuck good—I had to

make it unforgettable, in the best possible way. Because I wasn't sure that one night with this girl would be enough for me. Not with the laundry list of filthy things I wanted to do with her growing by the minute.

"I'm going to ask you something, and I want your honest answer, okay?" I took one small step back, giving her space to answer without my body crowding her. She nodded, nibbling on her bottom lip.

Fucking hell.

"Do you want to be with me tonight?"

Her pale hand snaked out, reaching for mine, grasping it. "I want to be with you tonight," she breathed. "I wouldn't have come home with you otherwise."

Her eyes met mine, cheeks rosy, lips curved into a little, shy smile. That smile was going to bring me to my knees. Breathing deep, trying to calm my raging dick, I stepped closer, my hips nudging her knees, but no further.

"Okay. We're going to play a little game, Honey." Fuck I loved the way her breath hitched, her tits heaving, when I called her that. "Because we've already established that you and I like playing with each other. We're going to play a game called 'I want'."

Her tongue darted out, tasting her bottom lip. A low groan burst out of me.

"How do we play?" she asked, her hand slipping from mine, sliding up my arm, gentle fingers tracing the pattern of vines and flowers. My eyes almost rolled back in my head, and she was only touching my arm.

"It's simple. Every time you start a sentence with 'I want', I have to do whatever you say. Nothing more, nothing less than exactly what you say. If you don't like something, or you're not into it anymore, you can say 'I want you to stop'. Does that sound okay?"

Her eyes fixated on where her hand had moved to the bottom of my t-shirt sleeve, fingers tucking under the fabric. The moment dragged.

"Of course, if you were to say, 'I want you to bend me over the kitchen bench and eat me out until I'm screaming, then I'd be more than happy to oblige," I added, giving her a wink to let her think I was joking as her lips parted and her cheeks flamed so bright.

The silence continued to stretch. I waited, not breathing, for her answer.

"I … I want you to kiss me, Levi."

Perfect fucking start. My hands shook as I cupped her face, caressing the soft skin of her jaw. Leaning closer, until my nose brushed against hers, and her fingertips clawed into my bicep, I murmured against those sweet, plump lips, "Just so you know, you have free rein with my body. Anything you want to do to me is on the table."

She shut me up when she closed that last millimetre of distance and kissed me.

Her lips were soft, and pliant, and tasted like sunshine. And Christ, she might be a virgin, but she knew how to kiss. That pretty mouth opened, nipped at my bottom lip until my dick was uncomfortably hard, trapped in my jeans. Her tongue darted out, tasting my mouth, and that was the end of my fucking restraint. I tilted her jaw, slanting our mouths to deepen the kiss, tangling my tongue with hers, slipping my hand under her hair to trap her mouth to mine.

Hands grasping at my shoulders, she parted her knees, making space for me in the cradle of her fucking lush body. Groaning into her mouth, I stepped closer, her thighs hugging my hips, the warmth of her searing me through my jeans until my dick throbbed, threatening to rip through the fabric holding it in. I rocked my hips forwards, all my thoughts racing south to my cock, desperately seeking friction.

With a squeak, she broke the kiss, turning her head to the side as she panted.

Shit. I'd gone too far. I started to step away, to give her some space. She gripped harder to my shoulders, her thighs squeezing me, trapping me.

"I want you to take me to your bed, Levi."

CHAPTER EIGHT

Does Sex Feel Better With That?

AMANDA

My heart was trying to batter its way out of my chest. Yes, I'd made out with guys before, but no matter how hot and heavy it had been in the past (and it *had* been with He Who Must Not Be Named), it was nothing compared to how I felt when Levi's tongue licked mine.

And the way his light-filled eyes darkened; those pupils blown wide when I asked him to take me to his bed had me throbbing between my thighs—which were currently wrapped around his hips.

"I want that too—so fucking much," he murmured, nuzzling his nose against my earlobe and making me shiver.

"Eeep!" I squeaked as my bottom suddenly left the stool. I frantically clutched his shoulders as he adjusted his big palms to cup my butt cheeks. Heat flooded my face, and down there too, at the feel of his fingers kneading my flesh, our noses touching. The bulge in his pants rubbing on me turned me lightheaded. But not enough to stave off the rush of mortification.

"I'm too heavy!" I protested as he turned and walked down the hallway with me pressed against his front.

"That's utter bullshit," he replied, raising that scarred eyebrow, planting a tiny, soft, sweet kiss on the tip of my nose. "I bench press double you without breaking a sweat, Honey." He emphasised his words with another squeeze of my backside, and I squeaked for a totally different reason.

This man was going to melt me into a puddle on his bed … and despite a flutter of nerves that seemed to have taken permanent residence under my ribcage, I wanted it.

What 'it' was, exactly, I wasn't entirely sure. I mean, I knew I wanted the big 'it'—sex—but I wasn't certain about some of the other, less momentous 'it's. Some of them—particularly the one where his face was anywhere near the vicinity of my belly and thighs—sent cold chills up and down my spine.

You don't have to do anything you don't want to do, I reminded myself as Levi reached a closed door at the end of the hallway and somehow managed to turn the knob without dropping me. *He's made that promise to you.*

I couldn't comprehend the man carrying me, as he walked through the door and into his room, lowering me down to the edge of the bed. He seemed so … bad … with the tattoos and the curse words. But the considerate, sweet way he'd taken my inexperience and nerves into account, without me having to explain myself … that wasn't what I'd expected of Danger Boy.

And I liked it.

Levi closed the door and darkness swept over us. I heard his footsteps around the side of the bed, and the click of a lamp switch. Warm, soft light bathed one corner of the room, and my nerves kicked up a notch.

No one had ever seen adult me naked. Even I tried not to see adult me naked.

Oh God.

"What do you want now, Honey?" Levi asked, moving back to the end of his bed and leaning over me. I had to recline on the navy-blue comforter, propped on my elbows as his arms caged me in on either side, hands planted on the bedspread. He wasn't touching me, but the look in his eyes made me wonder what he would want to do, if he had control.

I wasn't sure I was ready for that. I wasn't sure I'd ever be ready for that.

I cleared my throat, letting my gaze sweep over his tight t-shirt, his bulging biceps, those intense tattoos—including the fresh one that had intrigued me earlier—and then, without my permission, my eyes dropped to his crotch. Where the fly of his jeans was straining. I ran my bottom lip through my teeth.

"I want you to take your clothes off," I blurted before I could lose my nerve. "All of them," I added for good measure, scrubbing my suddenly sweaty palms on my shorts.

His teeth flashed white as he grinned down at me, before straightening to his full height—which was much taller than any guy I'd ever dated.

"I'm used to taking control in the bedroom," he said, his voice deep and rumbly as he reached behind his head and tugged on his shirt, lifting it up and off his body, tossing it in the corner. "But I'm liking *you* being in charge."

I barely even heard his words, because those pecs and abs— before I knew what I was doing, I reached out to drag my fingers over them. I was sure muscles that defined couldn't be real!

"How did you get these?" I whispered. His chuckle rippled the muscles of his eight-pack.

"I have a very physical job," he replied. I wanted to ask for more details—was he in construction, perhaps? Or was he a porn star?

But then he undid the button on his jeans, dragging the zip fly down slowly and carefully over his bulge, and then he tugged them down his legs, stepping out of them and kicking them over with the t-shirt.

I sucked in a breath, saliva flooding my mouth at the sight of his erection, straining against the fabric of his black boxer-briefs. It was … well, it was in proportion with the rest of him.

"You want to touch this, too?" he rasped, dragging the heel of his hand along the length. Oh, I wanted to. I wanted a lot more than to touch. The familiar throb down low at the thought of taking him into my mouth, working my way down his length … tangled with the sick swirling sensation in my stomach that memories of blow-jobs past always elicited in me.

As much as thinking about wrapping my lips around Levi had me achy and hot and damp, I knew I wouldn't be going there tonight. There was too much emotion tangled up with the act for me.

"I want to see it," I said instead, leaning back on my hands, putting some distance between my lips and his penis.

Another deep chuckle, but perhaps tinged with a hint of nerves? I wondered why, as his thumbs tucked into the waistband of his underwear, lifting them over his length and sliding them down his legs. I lost my breath completely, my pulse throbbing through my veins and centring between my legs.

"Oh my God," I gasped. "You're pierced!"

LEVI

Well, that went very differently to how I'd imagined it.

Amanda was practically salivating as she stared at my dick. The light glinted off the jewellery, and I might have stood straighter, letting it thrust closer to her gaping mouth. Fuck, the thought of those pink lips taking me in … my cock jerked fucking obscenely, and she made a little sound, not quite a moan, but close.

As she stared on, wide eyed, I gripped myself, stroking from base to tip, playing with the silver barbell that protruded from the head of my dick.

She squirmed, pressing her thighs together. I stroked myself again.

"I bet if I touched you now, you'd be so wet for me, Honey," I said. She hadn't stopped staring at my hand, moving along my shaft, squeezing the head, and back down again.

"I want you to touch me," she breathed, wriggling again. She was clearly horny as hell right now. Thank fuck.

"I want you to … to get me off. With your fingers."

The tip of my dick leaked precum onto my hand. Fuck, I needed to stop stroking it. Watching her watch me was so fucking hot. I'd never had a woman get me this close to blowing without even touching me.

Her eyes flicked to the lamp in the corner, her fingers tensing, clawing the comforter. I let go of my dick, lowered to my knees on the floor, so my face was closer to her eye level.

"We can turn it off if you want," I suggested, reaching out and taking her hands, relaxing her fingers in mine. "Touch feels so much more intense in the dark."

She sighed a little relieved breath, confirming my assumption. She didn't like the thought of me seeing her body.

As much as that disappointed me—fuck, I wanted to spread her out on my bed in broad daylight, not a stitch of clothing on her, and lick every single inch of her skin—tonight was about her.

If I played this smart, like I was trying to, this might not be the last time I saw her in my bed.

I stood, walked buck naked to click off the lamp. The room plunged into darkness, but before I even made it to the bed, my eyes had adjusted enough that I could make her out, hair and skin silvery in the night light filtering in through the partially closed shutters.

Fuck, she was beautiful.

I climbed onto the bed, leaning back against my pillows. She twisted to face me, still seated at the end of the bed. I bent my knees and spread them wide, patting the mattress between them.

"Come and sit here," I suggested. She lingered for a second, then crawled up the bed, kneeling awkwardly just out of my reach. Her tits … fuck they were works of art. I needed them out of that top, out of her bra. In my hands.

"Where do you want me to touch you?" I asked. *Fuck, say I can touch your tits, please!*

That tiny little smile tugged at her lips. My cock swelled, bobbing between my legs. She reached out, her soft, gentle fingers feather-light on my balls, stroking up the underside of my dick.

My eyes fell closed as she reached the barbell, tugging on it gently. "Does sex feel better with that?" she asked me, suddenly brazen now that the light was out.

I barked out a strangled laugh. "Yeah, it does." I sucked in a sharp breath. "You need to stop touching me, or this will be over way too fucking soon, and I've got a job to do before then."

"I want you to touch me … here," she murmured, her hands reaching up to cup her beautiful tits. I groaned, but didn't move, waiting to see what else was allowed.

"And … I want you to touch me here." She reached between her legs and rubbed herself through her shorts, biting her lip.

Fuck me sideways. How was I the fucking amateur in this situation? I was about to blow, while she tormented me by touching her pussy like that.

"Turn around," I commanded, forgetting for a second that I wasn't in charge tonight. But fuck, if I really was in charge, my face would be buried so deep in that pussy right now, my fingers thrusting, getting soaked with her fucking hot wetness.

I cleared my throat. "Turn around and lean back against me."

She complied faster than I'd expected. Holy fuck she must have been as close to the edge as I felt.

When her warm, soft arse nestled back against my dick, I grunted. Shit, I was already regretting this position. My dick, rubbing up against that arse. I was going to come all over her back at this rate.

Nope. I was going to last. Through sheer fucking willpower, if nothing else.

I gripped the fabric of her top on each side of her waist, slipping it out from her shorts and dragging it up her body.

"Arms up, Honey," I whispered, and she complied. I nuzzled my lips against her neck, breathing in the warm, flowery scent of her skin and hair, before I lifted it off her entirely. Her hair flipped back down, swaying against her soft back as I tossed the top away.

Black satin and lace. I shifted my arse backwards, trying to get a bit of space between my dick and her body. Fuck, I wanted her to be facing me, so I could put my mouth all over those insane boobs.

But I'd chosen this position because it meant I couldn't see much, and that seemed to be what she wanted.

So instead, I stroked my fingers down her arms, her skin like silk. My callouses probably felt like fucking razorblades on such softness, but she didn't seem to mind. She pushed out a breath, melting just a little more against my body.

I trailed my palms back up her arms, and then over her shoulders, collarbone, and finally down further, to knead her tits through the lacy cups of her bra.

Fuuuuuck.

Her nipples were two rock hard points, pebbled and pressing through the lace. I brushed my thumbs back and forth across them, until she was squirming, pressing those amazing tits into my hands. I gave the flesh a squeeze, then pinched her nipples between my thumb and forefinger, rolling them as she gasped and shivered.

"Have you been touched here before?" I asked her, giving them another pinch. Her head fell back against my shoulder.

"Not like this," she muttered breathlessly. I tweaked them again, watching her hips undulate off the bed. Could she be any more fucking perfect? She was so primed for me, and I hadn't even gotten my fingers wet yet.

"Can I take this off?" I asked, sliding a finger under each bra strap. She nodded against my shoulder. Within seconds it was across the room with her top, and my hands were finally skin to skin with warm, giving flesh.

I'd forgotten what real tits felt like. They were so much fucking better than the rock-hard baubles I'd had the misfortune of fondling for the last three years. The way they moulded to my palms, her nipples all tight and firm as I strummed them until she was writhing. I probably could have gotten her off just with nipple play, she was so fucking responsive.

But I wanted more.

"Can we take these off?" I asked her, fingering the button at the waistband of her shorts.

"Please," she moaned, tilting her hips so her butt lifted off the bed as I pushed them down her legs. Her panties were lace and satin, too, just like her bra, and just like her bra, I wanted them off. Hooking my thumbs into the sides, I drew them down and she nestled her warm, soft, naked arse back against my dick. My about to go off like a fucking firework dick.

Clenching my teeth, I let my fingers trail up from where they rested at her knees. She shook under my touch, like it felt so fucking good she couldn't handle it. But then her hands clamped down over mine, stopping my progress halfway up her thighs.

"Not there," she whispered, an edge to her voice. "Just," she took my right hand and placed it directly over her pussy, "here."

I wanted to know why, but then I crooked my fingers just slightly, feeling silky curls, and she let her legs fall wide, and my fingers slid along her hot, slippery pussy lips.

"Please," she begged again, and just like I'd fantasised about earlier, she rocked her hips to my hand.

"Jesus fuck," I hissed, pinching the head of my dick with my free hand, willing myself back from the fucking ledge, even as I gathered wetness from her entrance, dragging it up to circle her swollen clit.

"Don't stop doing that!" she groaned, turning her head to press her lips to my neck.

AMANDA

My breaths were short, sharp gasps against the warm, damp skin of Levi's neck. His fingers, slightly rough with callouses, felt nothing like my own when I touched myself.

No, they felt about fifty thousand times better, and he'd barely even started touching me there. His fingers dipped, just breaching me, then sliding up, teasing me, circling me, tickling with barely-there pressure, and then pressing down, before easing off to tease me some more. My thighs dropped wider as I rocked my hips, seeking more pressure.

"Tell me what you want, Honey," he murmured, hot breath tickling my ear, making everything between my legs throb. "Tell me what you want, and I'll do it."

His penis was like a hot rod nestled at the very top of my butt cleft. And, oh, I wanted it. I wanted it in my mouth. As his finger dipped again, I changed my mind. I wanted it in there. His body over mine, thrusting, those hard abs pressed against my softness, his hips pounding, grinding. But not yet. Not until I'd climaxed. Because I wasn't sure if I could with sex alone. Especially not the first try.

"I want you to … I need you to fuck me with your fingers," I panted, shock at my language clenching my muscles.

"Fuck yes," he whispered. But he didn't stop circling, pressing, circling … oh my God, did he just pinch my clitoris? I virtually levitated off the bed, a choking moan slipping between my lips at the wicked sensation. His other hand snaked around my body, and without touching my belly or my thighs, he circled my entrance and slipped one finger inside me.

All the while the other hand kept tickling, pinching, pressing, circling. Desperate, wanton throaty sounds burst from my lips, and I was rocking to meet that finger, as a tingle started in my toes, in my hands. I clawed at the comforter.

"So wet for me, Honey, and your clit, so fucking swollen." He added a second finger, filling, stretching. I looked down. In the dim light filtering in through the blinds, I stared, mesmerised, at his muscular, tattooed arms draped over me, that bad-boy skin against my pale flesh, his hands, his fingers, working me over, as his penis jerked against my back, the dampness of his own arousal and the metal of his piercing leaving little cool spots on my heated skin.

"The sounds you're making, fuck, it's driving me crazy," he muttered, his fingers moving faster inside me, the wet, slick sound of him fingering me, the tension in his arms increasing with the tempo of his thrusts, the tickling of my clitoris, the almost animal sounds I was making.

"You're about to come on my fingers, aren't you?" he asked. I nodded, incapable of actual words. My hips were meeting his fingers thrust for thrust, my pelvis rocking to seek more friction from that circling finger. The tingles spread, shooting up my legs, through my body. My nipples ached, and everything pooled in my abdomen, and deep within me.

"How hard are you gonna come, Honey?"

"So hard … so close!" I gasped, and with a groan, he thrust his fingers deeper, curling them inside me.

I saw stars as my body convulsed, a keening sound erupting from my throat.

"Fuck, that feels …" his words trailed off as my head fell back against him, the aftershocks of my orgasm still pulsing around his fingers, and I reached up and pulled his face down to mine, showing my appreciation in a searing kiss.

LEVI

I was leaking all over her back, so fucking close to just spurting my load onto her. Fuck, the way her hips moved to my fingers, the noises she made—and she wasn't quiet either. She'd gotten so lost in that orgasm that every inhibition she was worrying about had just flown out the window.

And I couldn't be fucking gladder. If only I wasn't about to lose my masculinity by coming on her rather than in her.

And then she gripped the back of my neck, dragging my mouth down to hers, nipping and licking and sucking at my tongue like I'd hung the fucking moon or something. I groaned into her mouth, breaking the kiss and manoeuvring her until she was on her back, and I was over her.

I stared down into those pretty eyes, all glittery, gazing up at me like I was her hero for giving her an orgasm. Fuck, I needed to get my dick under control, because I had to give her another one.

If she was going to let me fuck her. Jesus, I hoped she would.

"What do you want now, Honey?" I asked, my voice strained from the tension of holding back my own climax.

She reached up and wrapped her soft fingers behind my neck, pulling me down to her mouth. "I want you inside me."

She licked my bottom lip, and I started counting by sevens to hold the ache in my balls at bay.

"Just let me get a condom," I mumbled, leaning back and planting a tiny kiss on her nose, before standing up and walking to the bathroom. I desperately needed a breather to take control back from my dick. I grabbed two condoms from the packet—probably wishful thinking—but manifested destiny and all that shit. I took a couple of deep breaths and headed back to the bedroom.

She lay, still relaxed in the afterglow of what I'd done to her. Something strangely like pride swelled in my chest. I'd helped her to feel good about herself. So good that she'd fucked my fingers and screamed out her pleasure.

I chucked one of the packets onto the bedside and knelt at her feet, tearing open the one in my hand. She watched with obvious fascination as I rolled it down over my dick.

"Tell me exactly what you want," I commanded, staring down at her beautiful, soft nakedness. My dick throbbed, trying to override my brain as I thought about how our bodies would slide together, those lovely thighs around my hips, those tits bouncing in time to every thrust.

Amanda smiled softly up at me, and I swallowed heavily as she bent her knees and then let them drop to the sides, giving me my first proper view of that beautiful, glistening pink pussy.

"I just want you, Levi," she whispered, and that was enough. I tucked myself between those thighs, lined my dick up with that still dripping entrance, and slowly slid inside.

"So fucking tight and hot," I hissed, inching deeper. She was so goddamned wet, but her muscles were too tense. I stilled, leaning down and taking her face in my hands.

"I want to make this feel good for you," I whispered, stroking my thumbs across her cheeks, feeling them pucker as she smiled. I kissed that smile, fucking absorbing it into myself, as she opened those pretty lips for me and met my tongue with hers.

And slowly, as I licked and sucked and flicked into her mouth, those muscles relaxed and her thighs softened, dropping further apart as I nestled into the cradle of her pussy, my dick sliding deeper, until I was in all the way to the hilt.

A tiny little exhale of breath told me she'd not been quite ready for the size of me.

I didn't move for a moment. Partly because I wanted her to get used to me, but also because if I moved at that second, it would all have been over. Two fucking strokes and I'd have been done for.

Seven, fourteen, twenty-one, twenty-eight, thirty-five …

"It feels … I didn't expect to feel so full," she murmured against my jaw, her hands coming up to grip my shoulders. I shook with a quick laugh.

"You know just what to say to make a guy feel good about himself, don't you?" I replied. "I'm going to move now, okay?"

She nodded, biting that pouty bottom lip. I leaned my forehead against hers and started a slow slide out, then back in. Slowly, in time with my silent counting.

Forty-two, forty-nine, fifty-six …

She started making those little sounds again, her fingers gripping tighter to my shoulders, her heels digging into the mattress to rock her pussy, try and get more, get me fucking deeper.

I leaned back to look down at her, gritting my teeth as she wriggled those hips, teasing my cock with her fucking tightness. "You want me to fuck you hard, Honey?"

Those eyes snapped to mine, her lips parted, cheeks flushed, and she nodded.

"Say it, Amanda," I reminded her.

"I want you to … to fuck me hard." Her voice was throaty, raw from the screaming she'd done only minutes ago.

Fuck. Hold on Levi.

It wouldn't take much, I could feel it in the way her hips moved against me, rocking to find that spot that when my dick rubbed it, would send her over the edge.

"I'm going to touch you, is that okay?" I asked hoarsely. She nodded again, and I slid my palms under her butt, angling her hips just right so I'd hit that spot she was so fucking desperate for.

And then I fucked her hard, kissing and biting at her neck as I pounded my dick deep into that welcoming pussy, revelling in every moan, every cry, as her noises got louder and more erratic, as she clawed those nails into my shoulders.

Sixty-three, seventy, seventy-seven, eighty-four …

The second she started to tighten on me, it was all fucking over. I threw back my head and roared as my orgasm shot down my spine, seared through my balls and shot like liquid heat straight through me.

I collapsed down onto her, wrapping my arms around her back and turning her so we lay side by side, and I wouldn't crush her under my huge body.

"Fuck I'm so glad I was in that bar tonight," I murmured against her hair, planting a little kiss to her temple.

AMANDA

I was still coming down from the second orgasm of the night—and the shock of the little confession he'd made as he snuggled me in the aftermath, before leaving to dispose of the condom.

I'm so glad I was in that bar tonight … I was so glad I'd been there too. My night had gone nothing like I'd ever expected, but it just felt … right.

Except, what did I do now? Should I leave? Did he want me to go? Did I want to go?

Levi sauntered back into the room, and his penis was just as impressive now, laying against his leg, as it had been bobbing against his stomach. I swallowed back a sigh. It was a very nice-looking penis, and the piercing just …

Oh God, I was sore, but I thought I'd like to have that in me again.

He grinned lazily at me, holding up a washcloth. "You're probably a bit tender right now, Honey. Let me cool you down."

He knelt on the bed, nudging one knee to the side. My face

flamed, but I parted them, giving him access to gently swipe that cool cloth over the heated flesh between my legs. Even as he cleaned up the mess of my own arousal, his eyes never left mine.

"Feel better?" he murmured. I nodded, not trusting my voice, and he leaned down to press a kiss to the tip of my nose, before standing and leaving the room again, returning without the cloth.

"You need to use the bathroom?" he asked me, climbing onto the bed without putting a stitch of clothing on. "You probably should pee, you know—women can get UTI's from sex."

A tiny giggle escaped my lips. "I know all about UTI's—I'm a nurse," I replied, but I stood, pausing for a second before crouching self-consciously to collect my discarded clothing.

"What the fuck are you doing? Leave those there, go pee, and come back and spoon me!" he commanded. I flushed, but did as he said, scuttling naked to the bathroom, doing my business with the light off because there was a full-length mirror on the back of the door, and I really just couldn't look at myself.

And then I was back in his dark bedroom. He lay on top of the sheets—it was far too hot to be under them—and he watched me as I sat down and scooted onto the bed, sitting up and hugging my knees to my chest.

"I can go, if you …" I trailed off. I had no idea what was expected of me now that the sex part was over and done with.

"I don't know about you, but that was so fucking good I can barely keep my eyes open. I'm sure you're tired too. So, lie down, let me spoon you, and go to sleep."

And I did. I lay, naked in bed with a man I barely knew, who'd just gotten more intimate with my body than any other man, and he tucked himself up against my body, draped an arm over me, and kissed me on my shoulder.

I fell asleep with his lips still nestled against my skin.

CHAPTER NINE

Somehow Cheapened It

AMANDA

I woke to a ray of sun shining right in my eyes. Blinking in disorientation, I rolled over to avoid the blinding light. And directly into a warm, solid chest.

"Morning, Honey," he murmured, voice gravelly from sleep. His arms circled me, pulling my body against him … and his morning erection.

Woah.

His hands stroked slow, gentle circles up and down my spine. "I like this," he mumbled, and within moments, his breathing had evened out and his hands relaxed. He'd fallen back to sleep. With me in his arms.

Last night had been … God, I could still feel where he'd been. I was tender, but in a way that had me aching for it again. But lying here, in his arms, in the harsh light of morning had nerves thrumming through my stomach. If he woke up, he could see everything —every not so little piece of me.

I needed to get up, get out of bed. I needed to go home, get some space, work out how I felt about all of this. I'd had sex, for the first time, with a guy who … what did I even know about him? I knew his first name, that he had a physical job, that he was into tattoos and piercings, that he lived with his brother. That he could play pool as well as I could. That he was a talented, generous and considerate lover.

That was the extent of it.

There was no way I could regret a second of what had happened. But that didn't mean I wanted to stick around this morning and have the awkward conversation about how this was just a one-night thing, and it had been great, but … see ya.

I slid down the bed, disentangling myself from his arms, crawling to the corner so if he woke, he wouldn't see me naked in the unforgiving morning sun. I sat on the floor, tugging on my underpants and clipping my bra hurriedly. I slipped my tank on and struggled with my shorts, not wanting to stand up until I was fully dressed.

A grinding noise came from down the hall, and I sucked in a breath—the door was open. Was his brother home? Oh God—had he been home last night? Had he heard everything? Mortification burned my skin.

"That'll be Xan," Levi mumbled sleepily, half sitting up. "He always makes a coffee as soon as he gets home on a Sunday morning. He'll make you one if you want."

With that he collapsed back onto his pillow. Okay, so Levi was most definitely not a morning person. I added that to the pitifully short list of things I knew about him.

But … did he want me to leave? Was that my *'get your coffee to go, thanks for the ride last night'* dismissal?

I had no idea. I had literally zero experiences to compare this to. I needed to get home. I needed to talk to Alison.

I needed to be able to take a full breath. For some reason I felt like I couldn't.

I really didn't want to confront his brother, but what choice did I have? He wouldn't miss me walking straight past the kitchen on my way out. Besides, I'd left my heels and clutch discarded under the stool at the kitchen island.

I took one last look at the sleeping, naked man who had been inside me only hours ago. He was so handsome. Just not in the way that I'd always thought of handsome in the past.

Danger Boy. That name suited him to the ground. Dangerously handsome. I could become dangerously obsessed with the way he'd made me feel last night. Like I was sexy, and desirable, and that my pleasure mattered as much as his … like my pleasure gave him pleasure. Not like my pleasure was a chore that was just too difficult to achieve.

I headed down the hallway, trying to pull a deep breath into my lungs, and not quite managing it.

"Morning," a deep, mellow voice remarked from the kitchen as I approached my abandoned shoes, eyes down. I glanced up, and almost gasped to find a slightly less dark, much less dangerous looking version of Levi standing in the kitchen.

"Uh, hi," I mumbled, crouching down to collect my shoes, as my face flamed hotter. I'd been naked on his brother's bed all night … with the door open. Had he seen?

"I'm Xander," he continued as he frothed some milk for whatever fancy drink he was making with his shiny coffee machine.

"Amanda," I replied, taking a tentative step in the direction of the door. He glanced up, a tiny smirk playing on his lips. God, he looked so much like Levi!

"He still asleep?"

I nodded, and the smirk widened into a proper smile that had my stomach fluttering. Because I'd seen that smile on his brother last night, so many times, before, and during, everything we'd done together.

"You must've worked him hard last night."

I turned beetroot. Spinning, I fled for the front door, even as I heard Xander calling after me, "Wait, I'm making you a coffee!"

I wasn't waiting though. I couldn't.

Five minutes—that was all it took for me to walk from Levi's house to mine. I didn't know how to feel about the little thrill that zinged through me, knowing we lived so close to one another. I fumbled in my clutch for my key as I stepped up onto the porch, but just as I went to put it into the lock, the door swung inwards, Levi's friend Theo on the other side. I took a step back as he grinned knowingly at me.

"Up top, fellow walk of shamer!" he chuckled, holding his hand up for a high-five. I was already red from the embarrassment of my encounter with Xander, and from walking in the blistering morning sun, but this just took the cake. My face felt like it was about to melt right off, and I looked down at the silvery, weather-beaten old timbers on the porch.

His hand gripped my wrist, and he dragged my arm up, smacking my limp palm to his. "Own it, Amanda," he muttered. "Honestly, I haven't seen Levi that hot for a chick since high school."

My eyes flicked up to his. "You've known him since high school?" I asked.

Theo nodded, dark eyes sparkling. "Since kindergarten, actually. And we've been teammates since we were fifteen."

I wanted to ask about a million questions: what kind of teammates were they? What was Levi like as a little boy? When did he get his first tattoo? Was I right about the scar on his eyebrow being from a piercing that had grown out?

Instead, I shrugged self-consciously, and stood aside to let him past. He glanced sidelong at me, before turning and calling back through the door, "Thanks for a fucking brilliant night, Alison!"

"My pleasure—literally!" she shouted from somewhere in the shadowy bowels of the house. Theo winked at me and trotted off down the front path and out onto the street.

I took a deep breath and entered the house, bracing for the third degree I was about to get from Alison and Dani.

I was enveloped in a huge bear hug the second I closed the door behind me.

"Oh, my little girl's finally a woman!" Alison cried melodramatically and so loudly right next to my ear that I flinched, wishing I didn't have skin that blushed so easily. She released me, but only to hold me at arm's length and look me up and down.

"You loved it, didn't you?" she asked, her voice dropping to a conspiratorial level. "I knew it—the chemistry between you two last night was off the bloody charts!"

I had loved it. But despite my thought earlier that I needed to talk to her, I just wasn't ready to share it with anyone else just yet. It was too … raw. It had too much power over me. And everything that had been said to me this morning—by other people, not Levi— had taken what had been magical and beautiful in the moonlight last night, and somehow cheapened it.

"I don't want to talk about it right now," I mumbled, shaking her off and heading straight for the bathroom.

LEVI

Sunday mornings were my one chance to sleep in—the other six days I was up before sunrise and already out on the water just as the sun came up. Plus, I'd come so fucking hard the night before that I slept deeper than I usually would. I vaguely remembered half waking at one point and tugging her closer, but it was hazy.

My phone buzzed harshly on my bedside table, snapping me out of my snoozing. I reached for it, knocked it to the ground. With a groan I slid halfway out of bed, stretching and rummaging through my pile of clothes from the night before, finding it nestled inside my underwear.

My eyelids snapped a little wider as I realised that her clothes were gone. Fuck. What time was it? I snatched up my phone. Fucking ten forty-five! I hoped that I'd find her out in the living room, sipping coffee and being schmoozed by the suaver of the two Fox brothers.

The notification on my phone's lock screen was from Theo. I opened his message.

> **Theo:** Was last night as hot for you as it was
> for me?

I shook my head, texting back.

Levi: I'm not gonna kiss and tell dipshit.

I dropped the phone on the bed beside me, rubbing my eyes with the heels of my hands. She'd gone. I fucking knew it, without even having to go check. She'd snuck out while I slept in.

My phone vibrated beside me. For fuck's sake, if this was Theo harassing me for details of the hottest night of cherry-popping that had ever existed in the history of fucking, I was gonna throw my phone across the room.

Mac: The best man won last night Levi.
Congratulations on your pretty blonde prize.

Fucking hell! What was wrong with that dickhead? Had he honestly thought that I had only pursued Amanda out of some competitive urge? What kind of fuckhead did he think I was?

Why did she sneak out?

I climbed out of bed and stalked out to the kitchen. A jolt shot through me when I saw the kitchen stool, askew from the others. That was where Amanda had sat last night, those fucking beautiful thighs on either side of my hips, tits pressed against my chest, tongue in my mouth.

Fuck me. I'd been hoping for sleepy morning sex. Although, given she'd been a virgin last night, and we'd fucked hard, she would probably have been too sore for an encore. But to not even leave a note? Not even wake me up to say goodbye? Fuck, she'd tucked her gorgeous arse up against me and let me spoon her all night. She'd been soft, and warm, and comfortable in my arms. At least, that's how it had felt to me. What if she'd been lying awake all night wishing she could just leave?

"Morning," Xander said, emerging from his bedroom. "Chuck some instant into a mug for me, will you?"

I grunted, adding a tea bag to my cup and a spoon of coffee to Xander's, leaning against the bench while the kettle boiled.

"Was she still here when you got home?"

"Amanda?" Xander asked, which answered my question. "She was very pretty—nothing like what you've gone for in the past." Not like fucking Zilla, is what he meant.

"I think I scared her off," Xander confessed. That got my attention.

"What?"

"Amanda—I made a joke about her wearing you out, and she was out the door faster than lightning."

I scowled at my stupid brother. "Why the fuck would you say that? She …" I stopped mid-sentence. I wasn't about to tell my brother that I'd popped her cherry last night. For some reason that information felt too raw, too fucking personal. "I actually fucking liked her!" I said instead.

Xander rolled his eyes. "Oh, come on, Lev, I didn't do any permanent damage! Just call her, apologise for your stupid big brother, do some of that sweet talking you're good at, and it'll be fine."

I took a giant gulp of my tea, ignoring the too-hot liquid searing my tastebuds off. "I didn't get her number, or her last name, you fucking knob! I know nothing about her."

Fuck. I knew nothing about her, except she had a voice like honey, a body like fucking heaven, and I wanted her in my bed again. Hell. Maybe I even wanted more than that. The way she'd felt in my arms as I fell asleep last night. I could get used to that. I could get very fucking used to it.

What the fuck was I supposed to do with these feelings now?

CHAPTER TEN

Old and Flabby

AMANDA

"I had sex."

They were the first words that came out of my mouth, before I even sat down in my usual chair by the window. Dr Hansen —Gillian—took her own seat, letting my blurted confession sink into the pores of the furniture. I stared out the window of her office. She had such a lovely view out over Rose Bay. She must have been making an absolute fortune to be able to afford this sort of real estate.

I knew how much I was paying her—it was why I'd scaled back to monthly appointments. I couldn't afford that sort of cash on a fortnightly basis, not on a nurse's salary. Especially not when I'd dropped back to part-time hours to be able to finish my Graduate Diploma. Come the end of the year, I'd be a midwife. After everything that happened with Thomas, I felt like it was my duty, to help new life come into the world …

"Would you like to talk about it with me?" she asked eventually.

It had been almost a week since I'd walked out of Levi's house the morning after. And for some reason, all I'd managed to tell Alison about it was, *It was nice, I enjoyed it. Can we not talk about it anymore?*

What a euphemism all of those nonsense words were. 'Nice' didn't even come close to describing what it had been like.

"It was my first time," I confessed, picking at a pulled thread in the cushion beside me.

"Yes, we did establish your views on sex before marriage early on. Did you change your mind about that?"

I shook my head, all the words bubbling up from my chest. "It was never about that. That—the whole keeping myself pure nonsense—that was just the simplest excuse to stop people when they asked me about it."

"So, why *did* you choose to abstain previously?" Gillian asked gently. The thread got longer as I tugged on it.

"I … it was easier to just say no, than to deal with …" I took a deep, shaky breath, "With being told that I wasn't what they wanted."

Gillian paused, scratching something on her notepad. "So, you feel like a man would get close enough to you to want to engage in sex with you, and then decide he didn't want you?"

I shrugged, gave a tiny nod. Her words summed it up pretty concisely.

"Why?" she asked.

"Because I'm not what men want." There. I'd said it out loud. Finally.

"What makes you feel that way?" Gillian was relentless. This is how it always went. I needed to get something off my chest, and within minutes I was regretting it.

She's just doing her job, I reminded myself. *She's just trying to help you get to the bottom of this. She's not invalidating your feelings, she's unpacking them.*

"Look at me." I forced the words out. Gillian said nothing. I sighed. "I don't have the kind of body men want to take to bed." I swallowed around the growing lump in my throat.

"This man who you slept with … did he have an issue with your body that prevented him from wanting intimacy with you?"

I shook my head as a tear fell. I snatched up the tissue box from her coffee table, resting it on my lap and tugging one out, blotting my eyes hurriedly. But the tears kept coming.

"Do you want to talk about this man?"

I shook my head. I was a liar. I wanted to talk about him more than anything else. The words came out almost on their own.

"We met in a bar. Of course, because that's apparently my MO." I was blubbering. "See, this is why I hate it when I drink! I'm not in control of my decisions, and I end up with inappropriate men."

"Why do you feel this one is inappropriate?"

I rubbed at my swollen eyes. "Because he's the polar opposite of my type! Big, muscly, covered in tattoos … he has a pierced penis, for crying out loud!"

I throbbed between my legs at the thought of it. And then felt a rush of guilt for being aroused by the thought of his penis, while sitting in a therapy session, no less!

"Why is that inappropriate?" Gillian persisted.

I couldn't answer that, and I hated that I knew the reason why. Because it wasn't inappropriate at all.

"Do you think that by calling his physical attributes inappropriate, you're judging him the same way you feel that men are judging you?" Gillian remarked.

Damn her, she was right.

"*Did* you find his physical attributes off-putting?" she pressed.

I shook my head. "No. Quite the opposite, actually."

"Did the way he looked have much bearing on how he acted during intimate moments?"

I shook my head again.

"Did he struggle to become aroused by you?"

My face flamed. I shook my head vigorously. Gosh, he'd been hard as stone before he even took his pants off. I'd never experienced that with other partners … well, with the one other partner whose penis I'd touched, anyway. It had taken a lot of work on my part to get him even close to that state of arousal.

"Was everything you did together consensual?"

I nodded.

"Were you under the influence?"

"I'd had a couple of drinks, but I was almost completely sober by the time we …" I flushed an even darker red, if that were possible, as I thought about what we'd done. The way he'd let me ask for what I wanted … and the way he'd given it to me, so eagerly.

"So," Gillian said thoughtfully, "you say that when you drink you make silly decisions when it comes to men. Yet you only had a couple of drinks, and when you made the decision to sleep with this man, you were sober enough to make it rationally."

I shrugged, grabbing a bunch of tissues and swiping at my streaming eyes and nose.

Gillian scratched on her notepad again, and the sound made me suddenly furious. I tried to breathe through the sensation, tried to remind myself that her job was to get me to talk about difficult things with her, that I'd been the one to bring the whole drinking thing up. I only had myself to blame. I'd promised myself never again after the last time I'd raised it in a session. That session had ended with me storming out halfway through because she wanted me to talk about Thomas, and I just wanted to talk about my issues with drinking.

"He's on your mind again, isn't he?" Gillian interrupted my reverie. I shuddered, gave a tiny nod, knowing she wasn't referring to Levi anymore.

"Would you like to talk about him today?" she asked softly. I shook my head.

"Can we just deal with my current man crisis, and not that other one?" I asked.

Gillian gave a reassuring smile. "Do you have plans to see this new man again?"

The lump in my throat swelled to a point where I simply couldn't force any more words out. Grabbing a bunch of tissues, I held them to my face and sobbed pitifully into them.

"I don't have his number and I don't know his last name. I have no way of contacting him," I managed eventually.

Such a lie. I knew how easy it would be for me to walk the few minutes to his house and knock on his door. My biggest fear was that I would just blurt out, *'Can you put your talented penis inside me again please?'* Lie. My biggest fear was that he'd laugh in my face if I said that.

"If you did have a way to contact him, would you want to see him again?" Gillian asked.

I couldn't lie again. I nodded. "But what if it was just a one-time thing for him?" I managed through my hiccupping.

Gillian reached out and patted my free hand, where it lay, still twirling that stray thread on the pillow. "Do you think not knowing at all would be better than him telling you he wasn't interested in anything more serious?"

I couldn't answer that one. Closure was always the goal, wasn't it? But closure, if it meant being told I'd just been a bit of fun for a single night, didn't seem like a goal I wanted to aspire to.

"I think we need to spend some time focusing on self-esteem and body image." Gillian said quietly.

I sighed. I'd known this would come the second I let the words out of my mouth.

"Maybe … probably you're right," I conceded. "But I don't know if I'm really in a state to dive into that worm hole today. Add it to your little list, and we can revisit it when I'm not a blubbering mess."

Gillian actually chuckled at that. "I'm proud of you for not just getting up and storming out when I said it, Amanda. That's progress."

I managed an eye roll as I patted my eyes and cheeks, blotting away the tears that still sluggishly leaked.

"Hooray for me!" I grumbled.

"And we do need to talk about Thomas again at some point, Amanda. You don't have a drinking problem—you're actually a very responsible drinker. Your guilt isn't about the alcohol. It's about him. If we don't talk about him, we're never going to relieve you of these guilty feelings."

I stood abruptly, swallowing back the lump in my throat. She was right, bugger her! But I didn't want to hear about it today. I should be over him; I should be over all of it! But eighteen months of therapy later, and some days it still felt like yesterday.

The memory replayed in my head in horrifying clarity. The way I'd tipsily boasted to him, when the highlights of Mel's quarter-final had started playing on the big screen in the sports bar, "Yeah, you see her? She's one of my bestest friends in the whole world."

Those had been the words that had sealed my fate. And the fate of said bestest friend too. She'd almost died because I'd had a few and decided to use her to flirt with him.

"I think I've had enough for today," I mumbled, staggering for the door. Gillian knew better than to follow me out.

I managed to scrape in enough time to duck home and shower away the tears before I had to race over to the Eastern Sydney Mother and Baby Centre, where I was undertaking my midwifery clinical placement under the very sharp eye of Bethany Logan.

Beth worked for Dr Christopher Bentley, one of the most sought after private OBGYNs in Sydney.

Beth joked and played with a rambunctious toddler and a very uppity four-year-old, until both were giggling and had stopped clinging to their mum long enough for me to do her observations—blood pressure, heart rate, fundal height. She'd have a routine ultrasound during her appointment with Chris once we finished her notes.

"That's a real skill," I said to Beth after she had ushered the mother and her two kids back into the waiting room. "Being able to make everyone feel at ease the way you do—even the little ones!"

Beth grinned, tightening the scrunchie on her messy black bun and passing me an antibacterial wipe to clean down the surfaces. "You've gotta make a strong connection with your patients. After all, chances are you'll be getting up close and personal with their vaginas at some point in the not-so-distant future."

Vaginas didn't ick me at all—you can't be icked by anything when you get into nursing. I'd cleaned up enough blood and excrement and vomit, and had seen enough naked patients in the last couple of years to be totally desensitised. But in my haste to specialise in midwifery, I hadn't really thought too much about getting up close to vaginas right at the moment they stretch, and sometimes tear, to push out a baby.

Oh well, too late to have those thoughts now. I was doing this; I was fully committed. I'd watched dozens of birthing videos in class, and now on placement I was going to get to see it all happen in reality … to help it happen.

A trill of excitement zinged through me.

"Our next patient is new to the clinic—she's only early on. She'll be a great patient for you to partner with, since you can assist in her care from start to finish."

I nodded, grabbing my folder and getting out the consent paperwork. Hopefully this new patient would be happy to have a student midwife follow her pregnancy journey.

"If she consents, would you like to sit in with Chris when he's doing the dating scan?" Beth asked.

"That would be great!" I replied.

"Well, you finish sanitising and I'll go and grab her." Beth stood, rolling her shoulders and sauntering out of the room. I swiped the wipe over the vinyl bed, over Beth's desk and the chairs the kids had been sitting in.

"Umm, I don't know about this," a shrill voice drawled out in the corridor. "I mean, it's a bit much, don't you think? Letting some Uni student stare at my vag?"

Beth opened the door and stood aside as a tall, attractive blonde woman sauntered in. She eyed me with suspicion. I found myself gripping the folder containing my consent form in front of me like a shield.

Everything about the woman who'd just walked into the room said that her entire personality revolved around being gorgeous. From the perfect makeup and hair that looked like she'd just come straight from a salon to the brightly coloured designer activewear that exposed her flat belly, enhanced her big, perky boobs, and showed off her very obvious thigh-gap. Women like this one were the ones who had always looked down on women like me—women with big, round bums, bellies that wobbled, and a thigh-overlap.

She eyed me and my hastily scraped back ponytail, no makeup, and scrubs that pulled tight across my bum. "Oh, she's old!" the woman said, folding herself into one of the chairs, crossing her legs and drumming her long, metallic pink nails on her thigh. She glared accusingly at me as if it were somehow my fault that I wasn't what she'd expected. I glanced up at Beth, who raised her eyebrows behind the woman's back, before taking her seat.

"Emilee, this is Amanda. She's a registered nurse with three years of experience under her belt, and she's retraining as a midwife. She would be an asset to your care team because of her years of medical experience." Beth turned to me with a smile and a nod. That was my cue to launch into my spiel about the benefits of partnering with a student midwife.

"Well," I began nervously, "As a student midwife, my role is to support Beth and Dr Bentley as we all work together to provide you with continuity of care throughout your pregnancy and birth. Most importantly, I am here to support you in advocating for your needs and—"

"Okay, this is getting boring," Emilee interrupted. My jaw clicked as it snapped shut. I glanced to Beth, whose nostrils flared just slightly, the only sign she was angry with the rudeness of this woman.

"Yeah, you can do your, whatever it is, with me. I'm probably going to need all the help I can get." She turned to Beth. "So, I have two super important questions: how do I keep my figure? Like, I know I'm gonna end up with a beach ball out front, but how do I keep my arse from getting all …" she waved a hand in my direction, and I couldn't miss how her eyes zeroed in on my bum, "flabby?"

My stomach dropped as Beth turned to face Emilee straight on, crossing her legs and resting her hands in her lap. "And what was the other super important question?"

I had to bite my lip to stop myself from smiling at Beth's sarcastically pleasant tone, but Emilee didn't seem to notice it at all. She tossed her icy blonde waves over her shoulder and smacked her lips once.

"Okay, so, question two. Is being pregnant going to screw with my boob job? Because I did some Googling, and it's like, I dunno, but sometimes the …" she cupped her boobs through her crop top, "milk ducts, or whatever, can make the implants go out of shape?"

"Alright, let's deal with these worries," Beth said quietly, and I realised that she'd gotten her anger under control, and was ready to be the personality that Emilee needed—someone who would reassure her on every teeny, little worry, no matter how shallow they seemed to us.

"You look like you've been blessed with good genes—I'm guessing your mum managed to bounce back to her pre-pregnancy figure after having you?"

Emilee nodded eagerly, and I realised that these were actually genuine concerns of hers. And then I felt a bit mean for judging her. She was early on in her pregnancy, probably still coming to terms with what she was about to go through. I needed to cut this girl some slack, no matter how unkind she'd been to me.

"Right," Beth continued, "so you're probably going to be the same. And if you continue with your current exercise and nutrition, your body will be just fine. But you do need to listen to your body. If you feel tired, rest. If you feel hungry, eat more. Don't be stingy with the calories—you're growing a human in there! Continue to make healthy eating choices, lots of fresh fruits and vegetables, lean meat … you know the drill."

"And …" Emilee pressed, giving her boobs a pat.

Beth smiled indulgently. "It's very rare that your implants will be impacted by pregnancy at all. But you do need to be prepared that your breast shape will change during and after pregnancy. The good news is implants won't prevent you from breastfeeding your baby."

Emilee shuddered. "Ew, God no! Formula is totally a thing, you know."

I sighed, but I handed her my clipboard with the consent form on it. "If you can just sign this, please, Emilee. And, if you're okay with it, I'd love to sit in while you have your dating scan with Dr Bentley."

Emilee snatched the folder from me and scrawled a signature on it without even reading the consent form, then handed it back to me. Beth passed me the blood pressure cuff, and I took her observations while she sat there scrolling Instagram.

"Are you excited—you'll get to hear the heartbeat for the first time!" I commented as I walked her from Beth's office to Christopher's, trying to sound bright but already feeling exhausted at the thought of spending nine months caring for this woman.

"Yeah, I guess," Emilee said, and her voice sounded a little wobbly. I glanced at her from the corner of my eye.

She *was* worried. I gave her arm a reassuring squeeze. "If you're ever feeling overwhelmed about anything pregnancy related, you can talk to Beth or to me about it. That's what we're here for."

Emilee's eyes slid over me and she shrugged.

"Yep, got it," she said shortly, as Chris greeted her warmly and got her up onto the bed to see her baby for the first time.

"Holy shit, Manda, you look like you need a stiff drink!" Alison exclaimed from the kitchen as I trudged in the door that evening. I dropped my keys on the hall table, managing the last few steps to the lounge and collapsing onto it.

"Rough day?" Dani asked sympathetically, plonking herself down beside me. She too was dressed in scrubs, but unlike unkempt, rumply me, she was looking as fresh as a daisy. She was on nights, so she was having her 'morning' coffee before heading to the hospital.

"You could say that," I muttered. "Emotionally draining, that's more how I'd describe it."

"Gillian put you through the ringer this morning?" Alison called out from the kitchen, and I heard the clink as she put a wine glass down on the stone benchtop. "You want a glass too?"

I shook my head. "Gillian wasn't too bad," I lied, reaching for the remote and scrolling Netflix until I found *Emily in Paris*. I cued up the next episode in my binge-fest. "But I'm pretty sure I got fat-shamed by a pregnant lady today."

"What a fucking bitch!" Alison immediately growled, and she joined Dani and me on the couch. I had to laugh. Exhausted, messy, frumpy me, sandwiched between tall, pristine Dani, her black hair in a perfect bun, her pale blue scrubs neatly pressed, sipping on her latte, and tiny, petite Alison, red curls rioting around her face, wearing hot pink scrubs because her boss liked them all to be individuals, a glass of sav blanc balanced in her delicate fingers.

"What happened?" Dani asked. I sighed, wishing I hadn't brought it up, but also glad that I had two house mates who always had my back no matter what.

"She's a new patient—still very early in her pregnancy. But she was so worried about her body changing, and when she was asking about it, she sort of …" I swallowed, "pointed at my butt and then started asking how to prevent *her* arse from getting 'flabby'."

"Oh, wow," Dani breathed. "Yep, I'm with Alison one hundred percent here—total bitch!"

"Your arse is not flabby!" Alison protested. "It's a perfect, round peach! And your thighs! Holy shit, I'd die to be as cellulite free as you are!"

"Cheers to that, sister!" Dani said, clinking her coffee mug to Alison's wine glass.

"My bum is definitely not tiny though," I mumbled, shifting uncomfortably between them.

Alison snorted. "Who the fuck wants tiny? What you've got would give any self-respecting guy a raging hard-on. Christ, if I were a guy, I'd be ready to blow just imagining bending you over and gripping fistfuls of those gorgeous hips of yours, watching as I slammed my dick deep into you, that sexy butt bouncing with every slap of my hips against it."

"Jesus Christ, Alison!" I protested, a shocked laugh bursting out of me as my cheeks flamed. "That's one very graphic fantasy right there!"

"You know I'm a visual person, Manda," she responded unrepentantly. "And speaking of visual … I need more details than 'it was nice', about what happened between you and Danger Boy last weekend!"

Dani gave my knee a quick squeeze and stood, heading for the kitchen to rinse her coffee mug. "That's my cue to leave for work. Have a nice evening, girls!"

I waved half-heartedly in Dani's direction, studiously avoiding Alison's intense focus. When we heard the front door close, Alison started on me.

"Come on, Manda, I'm starting to worry that something really bad happened. That he forced you, or he was really, really bad in bed. At least reassure me that it was consensual!"

I nodded. "It was." I thought about Levi's method of consent, and heat rushed between my legs. The 'I want' game. Oh God, I wanted to play the 'I want' game with him again.

"And …" Alison prompted, her hand waving as if to spur me to talk.

"And what?" I asked, pretending I didn't know what she was about to ask.

"And did he at least make sure you got yours before he got his?" she demanded.

Twice. I got mine twice. And they had been the two best orgasms of my life.

"Yes, he did," was all I could manage.

Alison slapped her thigh. "Oh, come on! I need more details than that!"

I stood abruptly. "Well, I don't have any more details to share. It was one night. It was … more than nice. But it's never happening again."

"Says who?" Alison's eyes narrowed in my direction. I shrugged, trying to act nonchalant.

"Just … mutual agreement," I lied, and I walked out of the room before she could say anything to try to convince me that I should be going back for more.

There was no way a man like Levi wanted more than a night with a woman like me. Even if that night had been spectacular.

CHAPTER ELEVEN

Moon-Fox

LEVI

"That shoulder's still giving you shit," I muttered to Theo as he puffed away on the rower beside me.

"Nah, it's fine," he growled, wincing but pushing himself even harder.

I huffed, finishing my ten k's and leaning forwards to stretch out my hammies. Theo thought he could bullshit me. He forgot that you can't bullshit a bullshitter.

"Seriously, mate, we're still a few months out from Olympic qualifiers. D'you really think you should be fucking around with this? If you need surgery, you should pull your finger out and get it done now. It'll set your fitness back, sure, but shit … if you have to pull out just before the WRCs, and I have to team up with that dickhead Mac, I'm gonna be pissed off."

"Fuck. Off," Theo snarled, but I caught him massaging his right shoulder. Fucking arsehole. If my best mate's refusal to admit he had a problem ruined our chances at the Olympics …

"Besides," Theo continued, climbing off the rower and heading over to the mat to stretch, "The ARCs are in five weeks."

"Fuck the ARCs!" I snarled, collapsing down beside him and grabbing a roller to smash my glutes and tibial bands. "I can cope with Mac as my partner for one week in Western Australia. But you know what I can't cope with? Having to travel to Serbia with him in September for Worlds, and probably not even fucking qualify for Paris! So, get that bloody shoulder sorted."

I hissed as the roller caned my tibial band. Theo threw me a filthy look.

"Keep your voice down, Fox," he muttered. "I don't want Patto hearing you overreact. It's just a twinge, that's all."

Just a fucking twinge my arse. I saw how tight his face was at the end of a training session. I saw him popping prescription anti-inflammatories even though he thought he was being sneaky about it.

"Maybe Patto needs to hear about it. Maybe he can talk some sense into you."

Alfie Patterson was a fucking legend in the rowing community, having taken gold in three consecutive Olympic Games, the last being Sydney in 2000. Retiring from competition at his peak, he'd been the head coach at Sydney Rowing ever since.

He'd be taking Theo and me to Paris for our second Olympic Games—if Theo pulled his fucking head in and got his shoulder looked at and sorted before the World Rowing Championships in September. The year before the Olympics the WRCs doubled as the first qualifier event, so they were really fucking important this year.

Theo had always been that bloke who liked to pretend he was invincible. In high school, he'd competed with me in the under seventeens double sculls at the Australian Rowing Championships with appendicitis for fuck's sake. We'd won it, too. And then Theo had passed out on the medal podium and had been rushed to hospital for emergency surgery.

I really fucking hoped that this shoulder thing wasn't going to end in a similar way.

"You going to see that chick from the pool bar again this week-end? The big-titted blonde?" Theo asked as we headed for the showers. I stripped out of my sweaty gear, running the water cool.

"Fuck off, Theo. I'm not talking to you about her," I grouched, grabbing my body wash and swiping a soapy hand as quickly as I could over my dick and balls. Theo's mention of Amanda and her glorious tits had put my dick on high alert. If I so much as grazed it the wrong way, I was going to be raring to go.

I hadn't felt so turned on by a woman in fucking years. Even when Zilla and I were in the early stages of our relationship, and she was actually pretending she found sex with me enjoyable, I'd never felt as horny as I did just from the thought of Amanda's soft curves, her round arse, her pink lips and nipples … fuck. I needed to stop thinking about her.

To try and get my raging boner under control, I recalled the last time with Zilla. She'd initiated it—hate-sex in the middle of our break-up fight. It had been rough, and angry, which was the only way Zilla could get off with me for most of our relationship. I'd been shocked that I'd managed to come, to be fucking honest. I think the only thing that had gotten me over the edge was the fact that I knew it would be the last time I'd ever be inside her.

"I'm guessing that's a no? She was a one-and-done for you?" Theo persisted. His words at least helped my dick go completely flaccid once more.

Amanda … whatever her last name was … was not the kind of girl you got out of your system in one night. I was dying for more of the same, but she'd ghosted, and I couldn't work out why. The sex had been off the goddamned charts. I'd pulled her back into bed after and spooned her. She'd slept like a fucking princess in my arms. A soft, delicious princess who smelled like flowers and sex. And fuck me if I hadn't felt the most content I could remember, falling asleep with my lips pressed to her skin.

I had to assume that she wasn't interested in more than one night. I was starting to think that she'd probably seen the tatts and then the pierced dick and thought she'd spend a night taking a walk on the wild side, just to get the 'bad boy' experience out of her system. But she'd been a virgin. Did virgins even think that way?

I wouldn't fucking know—she hadn't even left a note.

I was so stuck in my head about her. I knew that I'd be heading to the pool bar again tomorrow night—a week from our first meeting—in the hopes that she'd be there again. That I could at least talk to her, get some fucking closure.

But was closure, if it meant I never got to spend another night with her again, really something I needed?

"Levi!" Theo snapped me back to the present.

"What?"

"Jesus, you whacking off in there or something? You've been in there for fifteen minutes!"

Fuck, I had been stuck in my head. I turned off the water, grabbed my towel and hurriedly dried myself, dressing and joining Theo as we headed out to our cars.

We passed Patto in his office. He looked up and gave us a nod. I paused for a second, glancing at Theo. Talking to Patto about Theo's shoulder was on my mind, since he clearly wasn't planning to do it himself. But it really wasn't my place to be discussing his injury with our coach behind his back. I'd just have to keep at him to bite the bullet and let coach know it was bothering him.

"G'day guys!" Mac's overly bright voice greeted us as we headed out the door. "What a beautiful afternoon it's turning out to be. Enjoy the rest of your day."

I blinked hard so I wouldn't roll my eyes and gave what I hoped was a friendly tilt of my head in his direction. Mac was always lurking around the facility, even though he must've had a paying job elsewhere. Being a reserve rower, he wasn't getting any sponsor kick-backs, and even us 'career' rowers knew that the sponsorship bucks were thin on the ground. Rowing wasn't a high-profile sport. You were laughing if you thought you could get rich from rowing alone, even if you ended up at the top of the sport.

But Mac always seemed to be around. And he was just so disgustingly eager to please—a real brown-noser. I shuddered. "Kill me if I ever act that fucking happy with life," I muttered to Theo as we reached our cars.

Theo laughed as I pulled a protein bar out of my bag and tore the wrapper off, stuffing half the thing in my mouth. Training had been brutal today; two hours on the water, and then weights and the indoor rower. I was famished. I'd probably stop and grab a pasta on my way back to Xander's, and then have second lunch once I got home.

"You're a free man now, Levi. No woman, no commitment. You can pick up a new chick every weekend if you want to. If a wide and willing variety of pussy isn't enough to make you that happy with life, I don't know what to say."

"You know that's not my fucking style," I muttered, popping the boot of my car. I had to jiggle the handle a bit because it had started sticking a couple of months ago. I had no spare cash to be fixing it, not with still forking out half the fucking rent for the apartment in Coogee that I'd shared with Zilla—the really fancy one she'd insisted we needed because the view of the beach from the balcony was 'Insta-worthy'.

"It was last weekend," Theo replied. I scowled. I'd never picked up a woman and slept with her in the same night. Sex had been a date number three thing for me, up until last weekend.

"Maybe we could go out to that pool bar again tomorrow night?" I suggested to Theo, who rolled his eyes.

"If you wanna go trawling the same places, you're gonna see the same women. And while I had a fucking great night with that redhead, I'm not keen to run into her again. I don't want her to get the wrong impression. I'm not interested in more than one night."

I swallowed around my suddenly dry throat. "Yeah, well, maybe that was my plan."

"What, to try and bang my redhead? Have at it, I say. She's fully into butt-stuff, just to warn you. And not just *her* butt …"

"No, I … Jesus fuck Theo, did you … did she?"

Theo chuckled, tossing his bag into the passenger seat of his car. "Don't knock it until you've tried it, that's all I'm gonna say." I watched with narrowed eyes as he grabbed at his right shoulder, rotating his arm a few times.

"Go home and ice that, dickhead," I mumbled, tossing my own bag into the boot of my car. "I'll see you at training tomorrow."

I climbed into my car, letting her idle while the ageing aircon slowly kicked in. Did Theo seriously assume that I wanted to go out and hit on a girl who was clearly good friends with the one I'd taken home the week before?

Then again, I hadn't corrected him. I'd let him assume that, because the truth was much more pathetic. I was hoping that I'd run into *her* again. And I was hoping I'd be able to convince her that another night together wouldn't be as terrible as she clearly fucking thought it would be.

My phone buzzed far too fucking early for me on a Sunday morning. Especially when it was a rare hungover Sunday morning.

Amanda hadn't been at the pool bar last night. I'd gone down there with Xander and Dom, who had both given up on the place at eleven, heading further into the city in search of women to go home with. I'd played too many games of pool by myself. I'd drunk far too much Scotch—a drink I didn't even like all that much. I'd staggered home at around two and barely managed to strip before I collapsed into bed.

My head hammered, and my mouth tasted like arse. And I still felt as fucking miserable as I had the night before. I swung my legs over the side of the bed, grabbing my underwear with my toes and dragging them over. My phone vibrated again, reminding me there was a message waiting for me.

"Fuck off, whoever you are!" I snarled, but I picked up the phone anyway.

My stomach clenched.

Boobzilla: Surprise, baby daddy to be!

I froze. The three dots flashed. An image came through.

An ultrasound image.

"Levi, are you awake? What the fuck am I seeing?" Xander's horrified voice wafted from the kitchen. I couldn't answer. This wasn't fucking real. This was a fucking joke. A sick joke.

Footsteps up the corridor and Xander's shadow darkening the doorway of my bedroom. "Are you looking at Instagram?"

I turned to him, but my mouth wouldn't work. I shook my head, handing my phone over to him.

"Fuck, Lev," was all he said, in a low, dark voice.

Fuck indeed.

"She's posted on Insta about it too," Xander added. "Tagged you and everything. 'A Moon-Fox baby, coming October 2023—here's what I'll be using on my pregnancy journey'. Looks like she's already lined up a bunch of brands she'll be working with."

My stomach churned, and I leapt off the bed, shoving Xander out of the way and only just managing to make it to the toilet in time to throw up what little there was in my stomach. Panting and gasping, I staggered to the sink, rinsing my mouth and splashing water on my face. I looked up at my pale, horrified expression in the mirror.

This could not be happening. I was finally fucking free. We'd always used a condom. Even that last time, which had been so fast, and angry, and fucking unplanned, I'd still stopped and put one on.

I stumbled out to the kitchen, grabbing a glass and filling it from the tap with hands that shook. I drained it in one long gulp.

"You need to call her, Levi," Xander said softly, his voice totally reasonable, holding my phone out to me. I snatched it, staring down at the picture on the screen. I zoomed in on the words at the top.

Emilee Munro, DOB 12/12/1995, GA 7w2d approx

What the fuck did that last bit even mean?

"Call her, Levi." Xander's voice was more insistent this time.

"Fucking … fuck," I grated, storming back to my room as I tapped on 'Boobzilla' in my contacts.

It rang twice, and then, "Surprise! How excited are you on a scale of one to ten right now, babe?" Her shrill, fake voice grated on every nerve in my body.

"Is it true?" I asked.

"Of course it's true! That's the first ever baby picture—our baby, Levi!" How was she so fucking upbeat about this? She'd never shown even the slightest interest in babies before.

"Is it mine?"

The silence stretched. Xander's eyes were burning fucking holes in my back.

"How dare you, Levi! Things might have been shit between us for a while, but don't you try to make out that I cheated on you. Have you forgotten how you fucked me on the floor the day you walked out! This is as much your problem as it is mine." Her voice started to wobble. "I'm just trying to make the best out of this. I didn't want this —fuck knows I'd never pictured myself having kids. But when I saw that little jellybean on the screen, I knew I couldn't … you know."

I pinched the bridge of my nose, inhaling a long, slow breath. I was about to fucking lose my shit at her, and … fuck … she was right. This *was* my problem. And if she wanted to keep it, then I had to set aside my personal feelings about her and do the right thing.

"What would … what do you expect from me?" I asked her, trying to inject some calm into my shaking voice.

Another long pause. "I … I hadn't really thought that far ahead, Lev."

I saw red. "You thought ahead enough to organise a bunch of brands to spruik online—you thought ahead enough that you fucking posted to Instagram announcing a fucking Moon-Fox baby, literally at the same time you actually told *me*—the fucking father—about it!"

Another silence.

"I should've told you first. That was a mistake. But the prenatal vitamin company have me on a really tight schedule! They wanted first post out immediately. I'm sorry, I was just … excited, and I got ahead of myself."

I sighed. "Look. I need some time to process this, Emilee. Just … hold off on calling it the Moon-Fox baby for the time being."

"Why?" she demanded. "Are you going to try and act like it's not yours?"

I fell back against my mattress, covering my aching eyes with a palm. "No! Fuck, I just—you need to give me time to … to tell my family! Xander found out about it before I did! He saw your post and freaked the fuck out! Just let me break it to Dad, before you start a fucking trending hashtag or something, okay?"

"Yeah, okay Lev." She sighed. "Maybe you could come to my next appointment with the obstetrician? You know, get a better idea about what's going on?"

I mulled on that for a moment. "Send me the date, and I'll … I'll get back to you."

"Okay, babe."

"No," I growled, standing up and pushing past Xander to stalk up and down the hallway. "Look … I'm not gonna shirk my duties here. I'll be as present in this baby's life as you want me to be. But I am not your fucking 'babe' anymore, Emilee. I can be civil, for the sake of a kid, but that's as far as it goes. Got it?"

Another pregnant pause. "Loud and clear, Levi." Her voice shook.

"Send me the appointment date, and I'll be in touch." I hung up before she could say anything else.

"Jesus, that was a bit harsh, Lev," Xander said behind me. I stormed out to the kitchen, grabbed the kettle and filled it, setting it to boil.

"I can't fucking believe this!" I snarled as I pulled a mug and a teabag from the cupboard. "We used a condom every single time for years! And we hadn't had sex for … for fucking months before we broke up. Except for that one last time—and I *still* used one! How the fuck does this happen?"

"They aren't infallible, Lev," Xander reminded me. "Sit down, I'll make your tea."

I grunted, knocking one fist against the benchtop. Fuck. I looked down at the fresh tattoo on my arm, still healing. The one of Godzilla, rampaging through a city, wearing a bright pink bikini top to cover its giant tits.

Apparently I was going to be the father of a child with that monster. And when that child asked about Daddy's tattoo, what the fuck was I going to say?

CHAPTER TWELVE

Like a Fucking Child

LEVI

Training had been literal fucking hell for the last month.

Scratch that. Everything had been hell. Xander had been pussyfooting around the house like I was about to have a breakdown. Except for when he was hounding me about breaking the news to Dad. I told myself I was waiting until after the appointment that Zilla wanted me to go to with her. I hoped that appointment might actually jolt me into realising that this was my real life, not some fucking awful nightmare, and maybe that would spur me into action where Dad was concerned.

I liked kids. I really did. I thought I was pretty good with kids actually. After the Tokyo Olympics Theo and I had done some school visits to talk about achieving your dreams, and the kids had fucking loved me. They'd thought I was hilarious.

But having my own kid? It was a *'maybe one day, when I find the right girl'* type of thing. Not a *'fuck, guess what, you're having a kid with your bitch of an ex who trapped you in a toxic relationship for three years'* type of thing.

I'd cut off my right hand to make it not be true, if I thought that would work. I tried to stop thinking about it, but that left a metric buttload of space in my brain for Amanda.

Tomorrow night it would be five weeks since 'that night'. I'd replayed our scorching hot sex in my head every day since, while fucking my own fist in the shower. Those same scenes were playing in my head when I woke up in the middle of the night thrusting my rock-hard dick into the sheets. The memories forced themselves on me when I looked at Xander's kitchen stool, even though I felt like a complete knob thinking about sex when I looked at a fucking stool.

I'd spent every Saturday night since then lurking by the pool tables in the bar, on the off chance that she would be back there. She hadn't. And then I spent every Sunday morning walking the streets of Bondi, hoping that I'd just … I didn't even fucking know what I was hoping. That I'd happen to walk past a random house, and there she'd be, standing out the front, waiting for me to come find her.

I'd even gone as far as to search 'Amanda' on Instagram, to see if I could find her. With no luck, which in hindsight was a fucking blessing, because if I'd found her, followed her, and she'd seen Zilla's post about the 'Moon-Fox' baby, with me tagged …

Which brought me right back to stewing over the shitty turn my life had taken in the last few weeks.

"Get out of your head, Fox!" Patto shouted through his megaphone. "You're missing water every stroke!"

I scowled, taking a deep breath, trying to shove all the frustrating thoughts out of my head and focus on rowing.

Catch, drive, finish, recover. Catch, drive, finish, recover.

I repeated those four words for the rest of our water time, the way I had when I was a raw beginner at this sport. At the very least it kept the shitty thoughts from my brain. Patto didn't call me out again, so it must've worked.

Theo side-eyed me as we hauled the shell out of the water. I scowled back at him. He couldn't exactly talk—he had much less power in his right arm. His strokes today had felt lopsided. And still he refused to say a word to anyone.

"I'll be in soon, just need to take a dump," Theo muttered as we headed into the building in the direction of the gym. He didn't wait for me to respond, just veered off towards the change rooms.

Fucking liar. There was a toilet in the gym. He was on his way to pop some pain pills. Just like he had every day for the last three weeks. He always looked glassy eyed and spaced when he returned to the gym after fifteen minutes.

Not my fucking circus, I tried to tell myself. Except it was. Theo and I were a team, and if one of us let the team down, we both failed. But shit, I was letting the team down with my shitty attitude and being stuck inside my head. So, I guess we were both failing. Fucking brilliant.

I did some stretches for my hammies and glutes before jumping on the bike for a few minutes while I waited for Theo to show up. He was taking his sweet arse time.

"You want me to spot you?"

Fucking Mac. Just like the rest of the blokes who trained here, he knew all about my predicament with Zilla. The others had made grunting noises of awkward condolence, which I'd been able to shrug off. But fucking Mac … he'd actually come up, slung an arm around my shoulders, and said, "I know this would be the last thing you wanted to happen, after everything with her. But for the record, I think you'll make a brilliant father."

And then he'd patted me on the arm and said, "I'm here if you ever feel like you need to vent about it."

His words made me want to cringe, and punch him, and curl up in a ball and fucking howl in misery all at the same time. Why couldn't he just do the blokey thing like the others did?

"You *are* heading to do weights now, aren't you?" Mac asked, eyeing me oddly. I realised that I'd totally spaced for a moment there. I glanced around. Still no sign of Theo.

I sighed. "Yeah, okay." I really had no choice. It wasn't like I could just sit around waiting all morning. I had a lot of moping around Xander's living room planned for that afternoon.

I was loading plates when Mac spoke again. "Have you seen that pretty blonde again? Amanda, that was her name, wasn't it?"

I almost dropped a plate on my foot when he said her name. My teeth clacked together so fucking hard I saw stars for a moment.

"Nope," I replied shortly, shoving the plate onto the bar and wishing he'd just shut the fuck up. I wasn't in the mood to talk to anyone, let alone Macintosh Graham.

No such luck.

"Oh, I kind of got the impression that you were hitting that."

Jesus! I stopped what I was doing and turned to Mac. He must've seen the murder in my eyes, because he held up his hands and took a step back.

"Sorry, Levi. That was probably out of line. Theo told me you left with her, I just assumed."

"Well, don't fucking assume," I snarled, fists clenching. "And don't ever speak about her like that. I know the boys all seem to think that I only went after her to cock block you, but I …" I stopped mid-sentence. I shouldn't be talking about her with him. I didn't have to justify myself to fucking Mac, or anyone else.

"Fox."

I turned to see Patto leaning against the door frame, his arms crossed over his chest and a look on his face that scared the living shit out of me.

Fuck. Had Theo told him about his shoulder? Was he pulling him? Jesus, we were due to fly to Perth on Wednesday for the ARCs!

"My office. Now," he said before he spun and stalked back out of the gym. I caught Mac's eye. He looked scared for me.

"I'm sure it's nothing too serious," he muttered encouragingly as I walked past him. I sucked air through my teeth, because why did he have to always act like he fucking cared?

The corridor from the gym to Patto's office had never felt so fucking long. I stared at the fake timber laminate the whole way there. It wasn't until I opened the door that I looked up, freezing in the doorway.

"What the fuck is going on here?" I demanded as Patto and fucking Dad stared back at me.

"Sit down, son," Patto said quietly. Dad's eyes narrowed at my coach's use of the term. I took the only seat left in the room, next to Dad, sitting stiffly and staring across the desk at Patto. Dad had never come down to the facility. Not fucking once. So why now?

"Do you want to talk to me about Emilee's pregnancy?" Patto

asked, straightening a stack of papers on his desk and then turning his icy eyes on me. Dad's gaze lasered through me. I swallowed.

Shit. I'd been holding off on telling Dad, but clearly he already knew. This was worse than Theo's fucking shoulder.

"There's nothing to tell. We broke up, almost two months ago, but apparently the fucking condom also broke, the last time we were together. I'm supposed to go to some appointment with her next week, I guess I'll know more then."

"What are your plans for the child?" Patto asked. I glanced at Dad out of the corner of my eye. This wasn't a question Patto would even give a shit about. And why the fuck was Dad here?

"I have no fucking clue! I'm still in shock about it. I was hoping that this appointment next week would shed some light on it all for me." I sighed heavily, leaning forwards to prop my elbows on Patto's desk. "Look, I'm going to do the right thing here. That's my kid, even if I'm on shit terms with its mother. I want to be present in its life. I'll just have to make the best of a fucked-up situation."

"You realise that you'll be expected to pay child support," Dad muttered. My hands clenched into fists.

"I'm not a fucking imbecile," I grated without turning to him. I glanced up at Patto. "What the fuck does any of this have to do with my job here?"

"Your father seems to believe that you aren't financially stable enough to be able to support a child on your sponsorship funds," Patto replied.

Of course he fucking didn't.

"Well, I guess that's a me problem," I muttered, furious heat starting to unfurl in my stomach.

"We've got a busy two years ahead of us, Fox," Patto continued. "ARCs next week, WRCs in September, and all going well, we start Olympic prep. If things don't go well in Serbia, we're back to the drawing board, and a trip to the Asia-Oceania Qualifiers. Regardless, training will get busier, you know that. There won't be time for extra-curriculars."

I looked up at him with a snarl. "Grant's missus is due in two months. Have you had this same conversation with him?"

Patto didn't respond, just kept watching me expectantly. He fucking hadn't. He couldn't care less, as long as we all showed up and put in the effort. This whole discussion was all Dad's doing.

"I'll make it work," I hissed through clenched teeth. "I'm not giving up on my dreams because I accidentally knocked up my ex. I'll reach out to some more sponsors. I'll do some fucking modelling if I need extra cash—I know a few agencies who'd be happy to have me on their books. Shit, I'll take a leaf out of Zill … Emilee's book and do the influencer thing if I have to. I can fit all that shit around training."

I stopped short of outright begging Patto. There was no way I was stooping to that level in front of Dad. He'd see that as validation that he'd known all along I couldn't make a living out of rowing.

"And how will you fit being present for a baby around this packed schedule, and world travel?" Dad's snide voice butted in.

"How do Grant and Harvey fit in parenting? No one's questioning their presence in their kid's lives!" I snapped. I stood up, knocking the chair over.

"This conversation is over. I'm almost thirty for shit's sake, you need to stop treating me like I'm a fucking child!" I glared at the empty air above Dad's head.

"I will when you stop acting like one."

That was all I could take. I left the room, went straight to my locker, grabbed my shit—not even bothering to shower—and headed for the door.

"What happened?" Mac asked as I shoved past him in the corridor.

"I just need some fucking space!" I growled, not looking back as I burst out the doors.

My car was stinking hot. I turned it on and blasted the AC as cold as I could. But I didn't drive away. My hands were shaking too much for that. What the fuck was Dad thinking, coming down here and trying to shit on my career?

I mean, yeah, I definitely wasn't going to get rich from rowing, but I earned enough from sponsorships to get by. Once Zilla got her shit together and either found herself somewhere else to live or got herself a roommate, I'd have a chunk of extra cash at my disposal. Thank fuck Xan wasn't asking me to pay him rent. I was basically my older brother's charity case at the moment. A charity case who had a baby to pay for.

Shit, I actually was going to puke. I opened the door just in time to throw up my pre-dawn breakfast onto the gravel carpark.

"Jesus Christ, kid, your life's not that bad!"

I looked up at Patto and groaned, sitting back into my seat and reaching into my bag for my water bottle. I swished some around my mouth and spat it out on the ground.

"Sorry," I muttered, letting my head fall back onto the headrest.

There was a long silence, and then the passenger door opened. I tilted my head in Patto's direction. He watched me impassively. The man never seemed angry. Just permanently mildly disappointed in everything.

"Listen, Levi, it's obvious there's a whole heap of shit going on in your life at the moment, and that's going to affect your mental health. But, kid, you're a bloody star, okay? You're one of the best I've seen. You and Theo were a split second from gold in Tokyo—a photo finish. It's going to happen for you in Paris, I can feel it. But you need to bring your A-game, and you can't do that if you let your personal life become a distraction."

I grunted. "Cut me some fucking slack, will you? It's been less than a month since I found out I'm going to be a father. It hasn't fully sunk in. And fuck, did you invite Dad here today? Because that was a big mistake, if you want me to be less distracted. That man has been the number one reason every time I've come close to quitting this sport. The only thing that stops me is knowing that it wouldn't fucking make a difference to him, I'd still be the world's biggest disappointment, no matter what I was doing with my life."

Patto was silent for a long moment. I took another swig of water, washing away the last of the burn from puking all over the carpark.

"I didn't invite him. He showed up in my office this morning, demanding that we have a sit down with you to discuss your 'options' in the light of your soon to be changing circumstances." Patto's voice was dry. I managed a snort.

"Yeah, that sounds like something Dad would do," I agreed, turning to face my coach. "I want to be able to put all the shit aside and focus. I want it more than almost fucking anything at this point. But I really don't need my father trying to push his agenda. So if he tries to come down here again, send him packing, will you?"

"Agreed," Patto responded. "Now, I think getting your head sorted today is more important than weights. Go home, think about what you want your future to look like—with rowing, with your kid, with everything. And make a plan. Then be back here on Monday morning ready to train your arse off."

"Yes coach," I replied wryly. He punched me lightly on the arm and climbed out of my car.

"Oh, Fox," he added just before he shut the door. "Don't forget you've got that thing tomorrow morning."

I sighed heavily. "I hadn't fucking forgotten."

Patto chuckled. "Good work, kid."

I went home, and I responded to a few emails I'd ignored from months ago—modelling agencies that wanted to rep me. It had been Zilla's idea, of course. Me being an athlete *and* a model would have looked so good on her socials. I'd thought it was a joke.

Well, it's not so fucking funny now, is it? Now you're about to have a kid to support.

So, operation 'Get More Money' was underway. I couldn't really do much about operation 'Deal With Zilla Being The Mother Of My Baby' yet. We'd have to have a frank conversation about that next week. The thought of having to see her again was horrendous, but then I imagined my child—my own fucking flesh and blood— being raised by a narcissist, without a stable influence to offset all the crazy, and it was enough to make me shudder.

I had to do this right, for the kid.

And what about operation 'Stop Moping About Amanda'? What the fuck was I supposed to do with that? I knew what I wanted to do; door knock every house in Bondi until I found her, dragged her back here, tied her to my bed, and buried my face in that sweet pink pussy, making her come over and over again until she apologised for running out the morning after, and admitted that she'd loved the sex we had and wanted more of it just as much as I did.

Fat chance of that happening.

It'd have to be a problem for another fucking day.

CHAPTER THIRTEEN

Black Speedos

AMANDA

Mel: Lunch tomorrow? I have a photo shoot on Bondi Beach in the a.m. but should be finished by 11.

Amanda: Sounds good. You working this weekend, Brad?

Brad: I'm good—have Fri and Sat off this week! Italian?

Mel: You know I'll never say no to Italian!

Amanda: Is Joel coming too?

Mel: Yeah.

Amanda: I'll book for 4 ppl then. Midday?

Mel: (thumbs up emoji)

Brad: (double thumbs up emoji)

I put down my phone with a little smile and pressed start on the next episode of *Emily in Paris*, nibbling the corners off a Tim Tam and dipping it into my tea, sucking the hot liquid through. I was mildly addicted to mostly melted chocolate biscuits soaked through with milky Earl Grey.

I was on the umpteenth rewatch of season one, and no matter how many times I witnessed Emily's first meeting with Camille, I cringed, knowing what was coming for their so-called friendship. Camille was such a nasty piece of work, the way she manipulated Emily into ending things with Gabriel, only to sneak right back in with him herself. And Gabriel wasn't much better—kissing Emily when he had a girlfriend—what sort of person did things like that?

Although, I supposed what Gabriel did paled in comparison to the things my ex-boyfriend did … but no, I wasn't going to think about him. That was a shame spiral I didn't need to send myself down today.

But of course, to distract myself, my brain conjured up Levi. Danger Boy, with his tattooed body and his wicked smile, and his fingers … and his kisses … and the way he'd made my body feel … and the way he'd found ways to keep me from getting in my head about my insecurities. And the way he'd been so into it.

God, I was aching all over now. I'd never touched myself so frequently as I had in the last few weeks. Every night, in bed, I was fingering myself until I exploded. And then again most mornings too.

It was all Danger Boy's fault. I hadn't this morning, but maybe I should? I was home alone, my shift at the hospital not starting until midday. Could I possibly just … here on the lounge?

I stood abruptly. Nope. I could not in good conscience masturbate on the lounge my housemates shared with me. Just the fact that I'd considered it for a second was enough to calm some of the fire raging in my blood. I flicked off the television. I wasn't in the mood for *Emily in Paris* today.

I checked my phone—I was due at work in three hours. I looked down at the ratty old cotton tights and stained Princes of Lion t-shirt I'd found in an op-shop last year.

I had a sudden, nasty vision pop into my head, of me walking out the front door to check the mailbox, wearing this exact outfit, and Levi happening to be walking past. My body might be far from ideal, but Alison's little shopping trip had showed me that the way I currently dressed made that frumpy body look a thousand times worse. There was no way I ever wanted Levi to see me like that.

I shook myself. The chances of him walking past my house were slim to none, despite us living so close. No one walked the streets of Bondi when they could walk along the beach, or the coastal track. He wasn't going to see me. He probably wasn't even thinking about me.

But still, I badly needed a new wardrobe. And I had a lunch date tomorrow, so that was a deadline to have some new clothes. If even fashion-blind Mel had noticed how dowdy and baggy my wardrobe was, what did other people think?

I sighed, cursing Alison for putting ideas in my head about how different I looked when I shopped outside of my comfort zone, and I headed to my room, bundling my scrubs and shoes into my work bag before making for the door.

I winced as I peeked my head outside, checking both ways along the street that there was no sign of a tattooed hottie, before scuttling to my car. I just hoped that the flattering salesgirl was working again, certain that she'd be happy to help me put a dent in my credit card.

Distraction. It was better than dwelling.

I was cleaning up my breakfast plates on Saturday morning when Alison sauntered into the kitchen, doing an exaggerated double take at my outfit.

"Dani, who the hell is the gorgeous stranger in our kitchen? She's doing the dishes! Did you hire us a sexy maid?" Alison teased, placing her cup into the sink of sudsy water.

I flashed her a wry look. "What's the salary for a sexy maid? I might have to quit my day job!" I retorted, scrubbing the dregs of coffee from her mug.

Alison grinned at me. "Depends on what services the sexy maid is providing. There's a bonus for tongue action." She made a V with her fingers and flicked her tongue between them. I flushed crimson, although I should have known that Alison would take the conversation in that direction.

"Seriously though babe, that dress is fire! I am so proud of you for going shopping for hot clothes all on your own! You really *are* growing up!"

She sat down on a stool and gave me a pointed stare. She was fishing, again. She'd been fishing for details about my night with Levi with increasing fervour for four weeks now.

"I'm having lunch with Brad and Mel … and Joel, today, I thought it'd be nice to have something new to wear," I replied breezily, letting the sudsy water out of the sink and wiping my hands on a tea towel.

Three … two … one …

"Oh, God, you lucky bitch! Joel is so fucking hot! Play footsie under the table with him for me, would you? Or better yet, give him a dick massage with your foot under the table!"

Dani giggled from the living room as I met her eye. Alison was so predictable whenever I mentioned Joel.

I smacked Alison with the towel. "I will do no such thing, because I value my life. Mel would flipping strangle me! She's so possessive of him."

Alison pretended to swoon against the kitchen bench. "I'd be possessive of him too, if I was the one getting off with him every night. Jesus, to be a fly on the wall in their bedroom. Two athletes in peak physical condition, the sex they'd be having would be out of this world."

"People don't *have* to be in peak physical condition to be out of this world in the bedroom," I blurted. Alison gasped, her head snapping up to meet my eyes.

Oh, God, she was never letting up now.

"Yes! You and Levi were out of this world!" She paused, running a finger across her lips. "I totally called it. His thick, tattooed arms sliding around your flawless, pale skin, those big, tanned hands gripping fistfuls of that peachy butt."

I turned to the fridge, pretending to look for something inside it so she wouldn't see how beetroot my face was.

"I think you've thought about Levi and me far more that I have," I remarked. What an utter lie. He'd lived rent-free in my head for over a month.

"Hmm," Alison responded, and I felt that twinge that she was up to something again. But I really didn't want to know.

"Do you think we can go out tonight?" Alison asked. "I mean, it's been five weeks, and 'Immersing Amanda' was supposed to be a monthly thing."

I rolled my eyes. "I think Amanda 'immersed' herself enough the first go around. I'm probably totally cured now."

Alison snorted but said nothing more.

"We could probably go out tonight," I conceded. "Into the city?"

Alison and Dani shared a meaningful glance. "Yeah, we can go into the city if you like." They saw right through me. Avoiding our local meant avoiding running into him again, and they knew it.

I suddenly felt claustrophobic in the house. I checked my watch —it wasn't quite ten. Mel would still be doing this photo shoot on the beach. I wondered what it was for. Maybe some sponsorship thing. Could be fun to watch.

"I'm heading out early," I called to the girls as I ducked up the hall to grab my handbag from my bedroom. I gave myself a quick once over in the full-length mirror in the hallway, willing the nervous butterflies in my stomach to settle down. It was just a dress. There was nothing scary about leaving the house wearing a dress.

The salesgirl had absolutely gushed when she'd seen me in it. It had a ruffle-hem that sat at mid-thigh, and a V-neck that plunged to show off just enough cleavage to be suggestive. The waist cinched in at my own natural waist, highlighting what was apparently an hourglass figure. Even if it was a few sizes larger than 'average'.

I looked pretty. I didn't look hot—I was never going to look hot in anything I wore, that was just a fact of life. But at least I didn't look like I was wearing a garbage bag.

Taking a deep breath, I strode towards the door. Well, if today was the imaginary day that Levi happened to be outside my house, he'd see me the same way he saw me that night four weeks ago—well dressed and appearing to have my act together.

I made my way through the streets of Bondi towards the beach. I was grateful that, despite being sunny, it was surprisingly cool and a little breezy for early March. At least I wouldn't be sweating through my new dress before my friends saw me in it. I wondered what Brad would have to say. He'd never commented, or even seemed to notice my appearance in the past. It was one of the reasons I felt so comfortable around him.

Levi noticed your appearance, and he seemed to like it just fine, a new, sassy voice in the back of my head remarked. I ignored it. Too many voices in my head couldn't be a good sign, even if this one was saying nice things for once.

The water was glistening that cerulean blue than made sunny Sydney beaches such a tourist trap. And today was no exception. The beach was crowded with sunbathers and those pop-up tents that families liked to use, the waves lined with surfers waiting for the next big break. I almost immediately worked out where the photo shoot was taking place, seeing cameras and technical equipment on a cordoned off stretch of beach.

"Amanda!" a familiar, smooth voice called out as I was taking my sandals off to head onto the sand. I looked up to see Joel striding towards me.

Alison was right—he was hot. His eyes were the same colour as the ocean, sparkling out of a tanned face. He was tall, muscular and always impeccably dressed. But he just didn't do it for me. I'd always thought that was because he had a cheeky streak that meant he stopped short of giving off the 'nice-guy' vibe. But that wasn't it at all. Because apparently, I had a thing for the naughty ones.

Oh God, I didn't need to be thinking about Levi.

"Who's that blush for?" Joel asked as he reached me, which only made the blood spread across my entire face instead of just my cheeks. Joel chuckled, but thankfully didn't ask any more questions.

"Mel's almost done—it's a shoot for the paper about local athletes who are hot picks to watch for Olympic Gold next year."

"Oh?" I said, perking up, as Joel led me to a line of chairs, where a few other buff-types were lounging in swimwear, or wrapped in towels. They barely spared me a glance. "I didn't even realise that Mel would attend the Olympics! How exciting!"

Joel beamed from cheek to cheek. My God, he was so in love with her.

"Yeah, well, when she has a coach as good as hers, the sky's the limit, really," he replied, the teasing tone of his voice suggesting that he was just playing. Maybe.

I scanned the area, seeing Mel, looking bored in a black bikini as a photographer fussed with her hair, trying to get it to sit just right. The breeze continued to ruin his plans. Eventually Mel shooed him away, raked her fingers through her long, glossy brown waves, and smirked suggestively at the camera.

"Jesus, Stinky," Joel muttered, scrubbing a hand across his face. I giggled. It was adorable how utterly besotted he was.

I pointed to where another photographer was working down where the water lapped at the sand. "Who's that down—"

I didn't get to finish, because Mel trotted up at that point, wrapping a sarong around her toned body and plonking herself down unceremoniously on Joel's lap.

"Hi Amanda! Is that a new dress? It's cute!" She turned to Joel. "Bet you loved that last little pose I did," she purred, wriggling her bottom in his lap. Joel groaned again.

"You really want to play that game, Stink?" Joel retorted. And yeah, they were in flirty foreplay mode. I sighed, turning my head back towards the photographer down by the water.

I gasped.

Striding out of the surf, beads of water sluicing down defined, tanned abs, a tattooed arm reaching up to tame that slightly too-long hair. He was wearing nothing but a pair of black Speedos. I was sure I could actually see the bump of his piercing where his penis bulged against the fabric—but only because I was staring so hard.

"Copping an eyeful of Fox, hey Amanda?" Joel muttered. I practically jumped out of my chair.

"Fox? Who?" I said, not quite able to take my eyes off Levi as he stood, hands on hips, staring pensively out at the ocean while the camera clicked feverishly.

"I don't blame her—those tattoos are freaking hot!" Mel exclaimed, then squealed. I blinked, tearing my gaze from Levi to find Mel pinned in the sand by her boyfriend, squirming, but not really making a genuine attempt to get out from under him.

"I'll show you hot," Joel growled, nipping at her jaw.

I left them to whatever they were doing—heading towards second base by the looks of it—and flicked my eyes back to Levi. The thought of watching him, all wet and almost naked, without him knowing I was watching, was … exciting.

Except he did know.

My eyes met his. Those light-filled golden-hazel gems widened at the sight of me, and then he was striding up the sand in my direction.

I was glued to my chair. Frozen like a deer in the headlights.

Thank God I went shopping! The silly thought filled the tiny space in my brain that wasn't completely overwhelmed with the sensory overload that was Levi, wet and glistening, and moving towards me so fast I wasn't sure what he planned to do to me. My heartbeat headed south, thrumming below my navel.

"Hello Honey." How had my memory not done that slightly rough, dark voice justice? I shivered, not quite meeting his eyes.

"Hello Levi," I replied shyly. Mel and Joel sat up, dusting off the sand and watching us both with avid expressions.

His cool fingers met my chin, tilting my head up so I couldn't help but look at him, looming over me, dripping water everywhere. His eyes blazed and a small smile lit his face.

"I've been hoping I'd run into you again." Forget shivers—heat blazed over every inch of my skin, before centring between my legs.

"Hold up!" Mel interrupted, snapping me out of whatever trance Levi had put me into. "You two know each other?"

"Yeah," Levi replied, as someone handed him a towel. His gaze never left mine as he ran the fabric over his chest and stomach, before wrapping it around his waist. I stifled a sigh—I'd really been enjoying the view of those Speedos …

"How?" Mel demanded.

"We … ah … we met in the pool bar down the road, about a month ago, maybe?" I replied, as if I didn't remember the exact date and time. Levi moved closer, his shadow consuming me. I stood abruptly, finding myself staring right at his collarbone. Our height difference was so much more pronounced without my spike heels.

"I have to go," I muttered, my voice flustered. "Mel, we have lunch plans."

"I've still got to go and get changed, and probably shower, since this moron decided to roll me around in the sand," Mel said. Joel chuckled. Levi's chest heaved in front of my eyes. Neither of us moved.

"Amanda, fuck, just let me go get cleaned up, please. I'll be right back," Levi said, and something in his tone made me look up into his face. Those eyes were serious as he stared me down, and I found myself nodding.

"Thank fuck," he muttered, "Don't move." He spun, grabbing a sports bag and saying something sharp to the photographer before he raced in the direction of the change rooms. I let out a shuddering breath.

"You're shaking, Mandy-Moo!" Mel said, walking over and taking my hand. "What exactly happened between you two in that pool bar?"

I sucked in air like my lungs had just remembered how to breathe. "I … we slept together, okay? I met him, I went home with him, we … you know … and then I fell asleep in his bed. And snuck out the next morning while he was still sleeping."

Mel was silent. I turned to look at her, realising she was fighting a smirk. Joel's eyes flicked between me, and the direction Levi had gone. Probably wondering what on earth had possessed Levi to take me, of all people, home with him. I turned back to Mel.

"What the hell is that smile for?" I demanded. She stopped fighting it, her lips curving upwards.

"You broke your rule for Levi Fox! Honestly, I don't know what to say first … congratulations? What was he like in bed? Oh my God, I need details!"

I managed an eye roll. "I am not going to kiss and tell, Melanie Black. It's not like I demanded details when you and Joel finally got together!"

Mel shrugged. "Look, it was worth a shot."

"You're still here," Levi panted behind me. I jumped, turning to find him dressed in shorts and another t-shirt with those crossed oars on it. This one was pale blue. The colour looked delicious against his tan.

"I'm still here," I managed. "I think you just broke a world record for getting dressed though."

"Well, from what I know of you, you have a habit of disappearing when I least expect it," Levi murmured.

I blushed, and he grinned, his thumb coming up to swipe across my cheek.

"Pink is really your colour," he murmured.

"Okay, Amanda, you are officially off the hook for lunch today. You and Levi Fox clearly have some catching up to do."

I snapped my head towards her, a pleading expression on my face, but she shook her head slowly, a cheeky grin spreading across hers. Gosh, Joel was really rubbing off on her!

"Let me take you to lunch," Levi said, his fingers skating down my arm, winding through mine.

How on earth was I supposed to say no to that?

"O-okay," I stammered instead. Joel chuckled knowingly, and I desperately wanted to throw a furious glare in his direction, but my heart was thundering, and my face was frozen in a *what the hell is happening to me right now?* expression.

"Let's go," Levi said, "Nice to meet you, Mel. Maybe we'll see more of one another in future."

What was that supposed to mean? I was so confused, as he leaned across and held his hand out for Joel to shake. "You too, man."

"Enjoy your … lunch," Joel said suggestively, and I wanted to strangle him, but there was no time because Levi tugged on my hand gently.

"Come on, Amanda."

I came.

CHAPTER FOURTEEN

Multiple Repeat Performances

LEVI

I was a terrible person. A truly fucking despicable person.

She looked fucking edible. We reached the edge of the sand, and she paused, balancing on one leg and then the other to brush the sand off her feet and slip her sandals on. She leaned against me as she did so, and I sucked in a lungful of that scent. Flowers and clean, warm woman. That smell made me want to fucking devour her.

If I'd thought she looked gorgeous in tiny shorts and fuck-me heels, her in a flirty pink dress that gave me a perfect view of those tits and thighs … Jesus. I was fucking done for with this girl. I was already semi-hard, and we'd barely spoken.

And you're going to be a father to another woman's child.

There was no fucking way that was coming up in conversation though. I'd just found her, no need to scare her off just yet.

"So," I began, trying to adjust my aching dick without her noticing as we headed off towards all the cafes and restaurants of Bondi. "How do you know Mel Black?"

Amanda watched me out of the corner of her eye, her gaze flicking down to our joined hands uncertainly. I smirked, rubbing my thumb against her palm, just to watch that pretty pink stain her cheeks again.

"We, um, we've been friends since high school," she explained, her voice like warm honey, even if it was tinged with nerves. But what the fuck did she have to be nervous about? It wasn't like we were fucking strangers.

Well, yeah, I supposed we sort of were. I planned to change that today.

"Where did you go to school?"

"Saint Bartholomew's at Vaucluse, then Sydney University for my nursing degree. What about you?" Amanda's fingers squeezed mine briefly. My eyes rolled back in my head. Fuck, if she could make me feel like this just from squeezing my hand …

"King Henry's College," I muttered, "And nowhere for uni." I waited for her shock that someone as rough as me came out of the most prestigious private boys' school in Sydney—hell, probably in the whole of fucking Australia.

She didn't though. She just continued to walk beside me, her fingers warm in mine.

"What's your sport?" she asked instead.

Now that was a topic I didn't mind talking about. "Rowing—double sculls. Theo, my mate who was at the bar that night, he's my partner. We've been rowing together since high school."

She glanced up at me, interest sparking in her eyes. "So, you're going to the Olympics next year?"

I shrugged. "Fucking hopefully. We've got to qualify first, and Theo … he's got this shoulder problem, but he won't get it looked at."

Amanda nodded beside me. "I work in the surgical ward at Frankwright Hospital, and I had a guy only last week on the ward for surgery to repair a torn tendon in his shoulder. He's up for several months of recovery. He was not happy about it. It's a nasty injury, if it comes to that."

This conversation was making me feel depressed, and it kept reminding me about Theo and his appendicitis. Just like back in high school, would he act like he was fine, right up until the last minute when his tendon just ripped through? Fuck.

"I remember you telling me you were a nurse … while you were lying naked in my bed," I murmured, to change the subject. Her face flushed.

"What do you feel like eating?" she asked. Apparently there were two of us wanting to change the subject.

I almost replied, *"You,"* but I stopped myself at the last moment. Clearly talking about our sex was flustering her. I'd need to warm her up a bit before we broached the subject of a repeat performance.

"I'm not fussy when it comes to food. What would you like?"

She smiled shyly, glancing up at me from under those fucking perfect lashes.

"They make really good burgers there," she replied, lifting our joined hands to point to a little burger bar across the road. I grinned.

"I fucking love a woman who loves a burger!"

Her smile slipped a fraction, her eyes skittering away from mine, and I remembered how she had wanted the lights out, how she hadn't let me touch her fucking beautiful thighs.

Shit, she obviously has some issues with her size.

I had no idea why—her body was a literal fucking wet dream. Those curves … I wanted to run my hands, and tongue, and teeth over every inch of them, have her writhing under me … on top of me.

Pull yourself together, Levi!

I tugged on her hand and crossed to the burger joint without another word, ordering the biggest burger they had on the menu, adding an extra patty, double cheese and bacon, and a monster serve of fries. I really fucking hoped that would help her feel less self-conscious about enjoying a burger with me. Plus, I was starving, I'd polish it all off in a flash.

She seemed to brighten as she ordered a southern chicken burger. "I'm guessing those fries are to share?" she asked coyly. I smirked at her.

"The first of several things we could share today, Honey," I replied, raising one eyebrow at her. That fucking blush was going to be the death of me. I thought I'd bend over backwards to keep her cheeks that colour pink all day. Or bend her over backwards.

Cool it, dickhead, I told myself firmly.

Over lunch, I learned that Amanda had no interest in sport whatsoever.

"My best friend just won the Australian Open, and all I remember is that the TV was on at home, but I was doing the ironing and thinking about work," she confessed with a wry smile. "I couldn't tell you what 'double sculls' even looks like."

I chuckled. "Do you want to know, or is it too boring a topic for you?"

She giggled. "I'd like to know more about what you do."

Fuck me if that didn't make me feel warm and fuzzy inside. Zilla hadn't even pretended the mildest interest in my rowing, after she'd established that I had an Olympic medal which looked really good around her neck on social posts.

I briefly explained the use of two oars as opposed to one in sculls, the length of the race, and what this year looked like for me with events. When I mentioned winning silver in Tokyo, the surprise on her face forced a bark of laughter from me.

"So, I've been eating burgers with an Olympic medallist, and I didn't even realise?" she said, popping another fry into her mouth. I watched those lips, mesmerised, as she chewed. "I should feel embarrassed, shouldn't I?"

I laughed. "Not at all." I was shocked to realise how much I liked that while she was interested in my sport, she wasn't starstruck by my Olympian status. It was a breath of fresh air after fucking Zilla.

Zilla. Carrying my baby. Jesus. I blew out a long breath, my eyes leaving Amanda for the first time since we sat down. This girl … the thing between us felt like something special to me already, and the reality of my situation was like a bucket of ice water upended on my head.

"Hey, is everything okay?" Amanda asked, watching me with those wide, grey eyes as she dunked a chip into the aioli.

I stifled a wince. I should come clean about my situation with Zilla. I should be honest with Amanda. But I convinced myself that the conversation about my impending fatherhood could wait for another time. This girl deserved more than my shitty baggage.

She probably deserved more than me. But Jesus, I wanted her so fucking badly.

"You got plans this evening?" I asked her instead.

She paused. "I'd told Dani and Alison—they're the two girls I was with in the bar that night …" My mouth twitched as she flushed, and I reached for her hand where it rested on the table, covering it with mine.

She looked down at our hands, releasing a shaky breath, and then she hooked her thumb around mine. My dick jerked in my shorts.

"So, I'd promised them I'd go out into the city with them tonight," she finished, her soft thumb stroking my calloused one.

Fuck. I'd been hoping I could tempt her back to my house for the evening. Probably overnight—I needed time for all the things I wanted to do to her.

"Well, I can't say I'm not fucking disappointed," I replied truthfully, meeting her eyes. I wanted to tell her how nice it felt, to be able to talk about my sport with someone who showed interest without an agenda. Or without shooting me down the way Dad did. I wanted to find out more about her, about her friends and her job, her dreams. Her whole fucking life.

But she'd probably just laugh at how much of a sap I was, if I acted like that. Zilla had always laughed when I'd said or done anything sweet. Laughed, and told me to shut the fuck up and look hot for another photo.

So instead, I kept it light. "But there's still all afternoon, and you're wearing such a pretty dress. I can't let this date end just yet." Her white teeth bit down on that pretty, pouty bottom lip, and I almost groaned.

She sucked in a tiny breath. "This is a … a date?" she asked. I chuckled.

"What else would you call two people who are attracted to one another, sharing a meal and getting to know each other a bit better?" I asked, grinning at the expression on her face. "I'd like another date, too, if you're interested," I added in a low voice, leaning closer to her across the table.

She looked flustered, but she managed a smile. "I don't want this date to end yet, either," she confessed in a whisper.

"I want to fucking kiss you, Honey." She sucked in a tiny breath, as I reached out and captured her other hand, leaning closer still. "Can I kiss you?"

She didn't answer, just pressed those soft, pink, fucking delicious lips to mine. I groaned against them, but before I could work them apart, she pulled back, panting, her blush spreading down from her face to her lush tits.

"Should we go for a walk on the beach?" she asked breathlessly, standing up.

Shit, I needed a minute to get my dick under control.

Seven, fourteen, twenty-one, twenty-eight, thirty-five …

"Yeah, that sounds good," I managed, standing up, hoping my erection had gone down enough that I wasn't turning my shorts into a fucking tent.

Walking with Amanda on the beach was the best sort of torture. The breeze, picking up as it did most afternoons, played havoc with that little dress of hers, blowing it around her thighs. The way she kept smoothing it down over them put filthy ideas into my head about watching her touch herself, dragging those soft fingers over those pretty thighs, and higher, to the prettiest pussy I'd ever seen.

Fuck, I needed to distract myself from the intensity of my desire for her.

"So, you work in a surgical ward? That must be full on."

She flicked me that shy smile that made my chest flip. "It is at times. But I'm actually retraining at the moment, to be a midwife. I'll be fully qualified by the end of the year."

"Oh?" I asked. "What made you change your mind about nursing?"

Her eyes dropped from mine, and I gave her fingers a squeeze. "If it's personal, you don't need to—"

"No," she said, staring out over the waves. "I just had a bit of an … epiphany, I guess. Or, maybe a calling? Anyway, whatever you'd call it, I felt like what I needed to be doing was supporting women to bring new little lives into the world. So, I dropped back to part time hours at Frankwright, and enrolled in a Graduate Diploma."

She was as sweet and selfless as a fucking saint, with a voice that sounded how sex felt, and a lush body that felt like silk under my rough fingers. The wind blew the smell of her flowery hair into my nostrils, and I breathed that shit in like it was cocaine.

When she shivered in the cool breeze, I slung an arm around her, something in my chest tightening like a spring when she nestled into my side. I glanced down at my arm where it wrapped around her. And there was the Boobzilla tattoo, glaring accusingly up at me, like fucking Zilla herself.

I sighed.

"It's getting late, Honey, if you're going out with your friends tonight, you'll probably want to get home soon," I said reluctantly. I wanted to pick her up and carry her home to my bed and never fucking let her out again. But the tattoo was judging me.

I was going to fuck this gorgeous woman again. Shit, my need for her went beyond the purely physical, if I was being honest. But I felt fucking terrible about lying to her about my impending parenthood.

"I don't have to go out with them," she replied, turning until she faced me, peeking up at me.

Fuck. I wanted this to happen tonight … but I needed to sort my shit out with Zilla first. I had to make sure we were on the same page with the baby stuff. Civil co-parenting was my aim—I'd spent enough time Googling to know that was the gold standard for our situation. But I needed to make sure Zilla knew that was all that would be between us.

Don't start anything with Amanda until you've got your shit together.

"No, don't bail on your friends. Besides, I'm not going anywhere. And you know where I live." I chuckled. "But maybe you could give me your phone number, so that if you ever try to sneak out on me again, I can at least get in touch to tell you what a dick move that was."

Amanda looked away. "I … I wasn't sure you'd want to see me in the morning, that's all. I didn't know if it was just a one-night thing."

My nostrils flared. "Honey, even if it had been just one night for me, I'd never kick a beautiful woman out of my bed. Not when she fucked me nine ways from Sunday, and then kept me warm all night." I sighed. "I'm not a player, you know. I've never done casual before. I'm a fucking serial monogamist, and that night was as much a surprise for me as it was for you."

I reached out and dragged her closer, wrapping my arms around her back, caressing up and down her spine. "I'm so fucking glad I broke my rule for you, Honey. I haven't been able to stop thinking about that night since. And wishing I could get in contact with you, because fuck, I want a repeat performance. I want multiple repeat performances."

Her body shook under my hands. Shit, was she crying? I gripped her shoulders, held her at arm's length.

She was fucking giggling!

"I'm sorry," she managed around her mirth. "I just … it's all I've been able to think about for the last month, too, and I kept trying to forget about it because I was sure you wouldn't want me again, and …"

"Not want you again! Jesus fuck, Honey, can you feel this right now?" I pulled her closer so she could feel the bulge of my dick. "I've been sporting a semi the entire time we've been together today!"

Her giggle died in her throat, mouth popping open. She wiggled her body against my dick. Fucking hell. She didn't even realise I was about to go from a semi to a fucking rock-hard erection thanks to her.

"I shouldn't have snuck out," she confessed. "I'm sorry. What we did … what we had together that night was worthy of at least a conversation the next day."

I snorted. "A fucking conversation! The only conversation we would have been having the next day would have been my mouth conversing with your pussy."

Her eyes widened, cheeks going bright red. *Christ Levi, learn to shut your fucking mouth!*

"I think I probably should get going," she said hurriedly, looking down at a non-existent wristwatch. I laughed darkly. Yep, I'd fucked this date up.

"I had fun today," I muttered as she adjusted her bag on her shoulder.

"I did, too," she replied, and she seemed to actually mean it. Her eyes flitted up to mine, and then she dug into her bag, pulling out her phone.

'What's your number?" she asked. I almost laughed. She was getting my number, so she could tell me she'd text hers to me, and then never follow through.

Regardless, I rattled off my number to her, and she typed it in.

"When are you leaving for Perth again?" she asked me once she tucked her phone away. My eyebrows lifted. She'd remembered I was going to Perth for the ARCs?

Honey was full of surprises.

"We fly out Wednesday."

She chewed on that lip again, and I couldn't fucking stop myself. I reached out and dragged my thumb along her lip, pulling it from between her teeth.

"I want to be the only one biting that lip," I murmured. Because clearly I hadn't gotten the memo about not saying every dirty thought that popped into my head.

"Dinner, Tuesday evening?" she breathed against my thumb, her eyes locked on mine.

"Can I have you for dessert?" I asked.

There was a long silence. And then, because this woman apparently liked to shock me, she nipped at the pad of my thumb.

"You'll just have to wait and see."

She reached up, grabbed the back of my neck and pulled my head down, bringing her lips to mine. I let her take control. Soft at first, then firmer, she worked my mouth open and slid her tongue in to meet mine.

I brought my hands up to stroke her cheeks and slip around to tangle in those blonde beach waves of hers. I licked into her mouth, hunger and fire burning through me and shooting straight to my dick.

She broke away, panting. I let her.

"I'll text you about Tuesday," she said breathlessly. "Thanks for lunch."

"Any time, Honey," I managed around a weird fucking lump in my throat as I watched her scurry off up the beach and out of sight.

She wasn't going to text me.

My phone pinged.

Unknown number: Do you like Italian food?

I grinned, and something in my chest loosened as I quickly added her to my contacts before texting back.

Levi: I fucking love it

Honey: The Italian restaurant two doors up from where we had burgers. Tuesday 7pm OK?

Levi: It's a date Honey

The three dots flashed. Disappeared. Flashed again. Disappeared. Flashed again. Fuck, this was torture. I shoved my phone back into my pocket and headed for the lockers back at the surf house where I'd stashed my bag.

My phone buzzed.

> Honey: The way you kiss me makes me ache

> Honey: everywhere

Fuck. I was in trouble with this one.

CHAPTER FIFTEEN

Not the Nastiest Surprise

AMANDA

I lay awake at three a.m.—an hour after we'd arrived home from our night out in the city—thinking about Levi.

Thanks to our 'date' today, the list of things I knew about Levi Fox was growing. Just probably not as fast as I would have liked. On the upside, I actually knew his surname now. I knew what he did for work. I knew that he had an Olympic medal stashed somewhere at home.

I knew he could devour a double bacon cheeseburger from Bright Burgers in record time, and still have room for their beer battered fries. I knew that he was worried about his friend Theo's shoulder.

I knew that he had a dirty mouth … and it made me feel so hot I could barely stand it. I knew that his kisses felt like he was burning himself onto my skin.

'My mouth conversing with your pussy' … Oh God, when he'd said that, I'd almost felt like I might let him try it. Almost. But I knew I wouldn't. Because if there was anything that would stop me from climaxing, it was stressing about whether he could breathe down there given the size of my thighs … there was no way I was letting Levi go down on me.

More sex between us though? I figured it was inevitable. Maybe not tomorrow after our date, but soon. Maybe once he got back from Perth. Maybe once we'd been on a few more dates, and it felt less like hooking up and more like a relationship. Once I had a chance to figure out if that was what he was looking for. Or if it was what I was looking for.

I needed sleep. Dani and I had left the club before Alison—so much for her 'Immersing Amanda' nonsense. At one thirty, when both Dani and I told her we'd had enough, she'd waved us off, telling us she'd happily Uber home, and continued to grind with some random guy on the dance floor. It hadn't been the first time she'd insisted we leave her like that.

I was tired, but wired, and it was such a strange combination. I threw off my sheets and padded out to the kitchen for a glass of water.

"Oof!"

I collided with a semi-naked man in the hallway.

"What the …?" he grunted.

Oh my God. I knew that voice!

"Brad? What are you doing creeping around my house in the middle of the night … shirtless?"

I peered into the darkness at his naked chest, then dragged my eyes up to his face. He seemed lost for words, raking a hand through his blond hair.

"The game's up, Al," he muttered through the cracked doorway to Alison's room. I almost choked, I sucked air into my lungs so fast.

"You and Alison?" I asked. "As in … you and Alison are …?"

Brad sighed and headed for the kitchen. I followed hot on his heels as he reached for a glass—knowing exactly where we kept our glasses—and held it under the tap.

"Um, you can get me one while you're there, seeing as you're just helping yourself, like you live here!" I said, taking a seat on a kitchen stool and watching him as he moved around the kitchen. Clearly he'd done the night-time sneak around in my kitchen before.

"I can't believe this!" I muttered as he slid a glass of water across the counter to me. Oh my God, he was walking around my house in a pair of boxer briefs! This was too weird.

"I have to text Mel!" I said, standing to go and get my phone. Brad reached across the counter and gripped me by the wrist.

"Please don't," he pleaded, eyes serious. "This is … Al and I …" He was clearly still lost for words.

"Brad and I hook up on a semi-regular basis. Mostly we go to his place, but sometimes we come here too, because my toys are here," Alison explained matter-of-factly from the kitchen doorway.

I turned back to Brad, mildly horrified, but also a little amused. He dropped his face into his hands.

"Jesus, Al, I don't think Amanda—who I've known since I was five—needs to know the details of what we do in the bedroom!" he said through his fingers.

Alison shrugged, completely unrepentant as always. "Why not? I mean it's not like we're using my toys on you … unless you think that might be fun …" She waggled her eyebrows at him.

"I think I'm going to head home now," Brad mumbled. I stifled a shocked giggle that was threatening to burble out of my throat.

"Why bother?" I asked. "I mean, we all know what's going on now—down to the sordid toy details. You may as well just sleep here. No need to sneak around anymore."

Brad threw me a withering look, but he shrugged and gave Alison a wry smile. "I guess the cat *is* out of the bag."

I gasped in mock horror. "Don't tell me there's a cat involved in whatever you're getting up to in there!"

"Ha fucking ha," Brad grumbled, taking Alison's hand and pecking her on the cheek before leading her back into her room.

I watched them go, and something twinged inside me. I knew that Alison wasn't exclusive with Brad—she'd had Theo in her bed last month, and it looked like this thing with Brad had been going on for quite some time. But they seemed so … intimate … even if it was just about sex, they were both happy and they were enjoying each other. Not just in the act, but afterwards.

The way it had been with Levi, that night.

Oh God, if he so much as looked at me sideways, we'd end up

sleeping together on Tuesday night. I wanted … needed it too badly to wait for things to develop the usual way.

———

"How are you feeling about seeing Emilee again today?" Beth asked as I made my morning cuppa.

"What do you mean?" I asked, tipping milk into my cup, and wishing I had some Tim Tams to dunk. I knew exactly what she meant, and chocolate would certainly have helped.

"Well, she wasn't the nicest to you last time."

While I composed myself enough to answer, I lifted my cup to my mouth, took a sip, and hissed as it scalded my lips.

"I've been a nurse on a surgical ward for three years, dealing with patients in pain, many of them geriatric. I can handle a patient being 'not the nicest' to me." I said.

Beth could see right through me. "Yes, but they generally just swear and curse, or tell you you're not giving them enough pain relief. She got a bit personal with you."

I blew across the surface of my tea. "It wasn't all that bad. Honestly, I've had much nastier, and much more overt unkindness about my looks than that. One old man refused to refer to me as anything but 'that fat bitch'. I've developed a tough skin." I wished I was as blasé about it as I pretended. Even the little things, like what Emilee had done last time, left a mark. I was just really good at hiding them.

"You are gorgeous, Amanda. You know that don't you?" Beth asked me, dark eyes intense as she tugged her hair out of its messy bun, letting those glossy dark strands fall down her back, before she flipped her head over and began gathering it up again, securing it tighter with her bright orange scrunchie.

"You don't need to flatter me to try and balance things out," I replied. "I'm a big girl, I can cope with it."

Beth was the master of the withering glare. "You're beautiful, on the outside. But more importantly, you're beautiful on the inside— something I'm not quite sure we could say for our friend Emilee."

I took a sip of tea, thankful that it was cool enough to drink now. I had no response for Beth. *'You're beautiful on the inside'* was the classic line everyone told fat girls. I'd heard it my whole life. As much as it was a kind sentiment, I didn't really need to hear it from Beth. And I didn't need to have my weight at the front of my mind when Emilee of the perfect body and the perky fake boobs was due for her next appointment any moment.

"Emilee Munro, ten a.m." Her voice wafted down the hallway from reception.

"Speak of the devil," Beth murmured, a little smirk plucking at the corners of her mouth. I started to put my cup down.

"No you don't," Beth said. "She's early, she can sit in the waiting room for a few minutes while you finish your tea."

With that she bustled off into her office. I took another sip, checking my watch. Nine fifty-seven. Three minutes until we had to call her in. I'd finished cuppas on the ward in far less time than that.

The phone rang, and Florence, the lovely receptionist, answered in her bright tone. I took another sip of tea.

The front door opened, and a low voice mumbled something incomprehensible. My cup shook slightly as I brought it to my mouth. I'd thought a month was long enough for me to put Emilee's throwaway comments about my 'flabby' backside behind me, but maybe it hadn't been. Something had me on edge.

"Late as always," her snarky, high-pitched voice carried down the hallway. Another rumble from the deep voice. She must have brought her partner along this time. She wasn't speaking very kindly to him. Maybe that was just how she was with everyone. Maybe her unkindness to me wasn't personal.

It still felt personal.

I tipped my cup back, draining the last dregs of tea. Briskly rinsing it under the tap, and setting it to drain, I ducked into the toilet off the staff room. There was still one minute before we needed to call her in, and I suddenly felt the need to compose myself.

I peed, washed my hands, and checked myself in the mirror. I'd actually made a little effort with my hair and makeup today. I'd tried to tell myself it was just because I'd woken up early and had the spare time. But I knew it was really because I wanted to give myself that extra little bit of armour.

I left the toilet and headed out to where Beth was standing in the doorway of her office. "Would you like me to go and get her?" she asked. I shook my head.

"It's fine," I replied. I didn't want to be handled with kid gloves over something as trivial as being called flabby. I'd been bringing my patients in for weeks now, there was no need for that to change just for this particular one.

Beth nodded, and I turned, heading down the hallway. Florence bubbled with laughter to whoever was on the phone.

"Emilee," I called out.

I rounded the corner, and the waiting room came into view.

I stopped dead.

My mouth went dry.

My skin prickled.

My eyes burned.

Standing up from the chair beside Emilee Munro, looking as utterly horrified as I felt, was Levi.

How I managed to unstick my feet from the floor, and turn to head back into Beth's office, I'll never know. I was sure I looked like I was fleeing a crime scene. I just wasn't quite sure who had committed the crime.

"Come on, Levi!" Emilee snapped behind me. Her shiny trainers squeaked on the flooring. Behind her, his footsteps were solid. Heavy. The way my chest felt.

Don't cry. Don't cry. Just get through the next ten minutes. Don't cry.

Beth's office wasn't the biggest room at the best of times, but it felt a thousand times smaller with his presence in there.

"Lovely to see you again, Emilee!" Beth said. "How are you feeling? Oh, who's this handsome fellow?"

Oh God, don't faint! I told myself firmly as the attention of everyone in the room went to Levi. I went to the corner and fiddled with the blood pressure cuff, unwinding the cord and then winding it back up again.

"This is my boyfriend, Levi, the father," Emilee explained in that strident tone of hers. My hands shook, rattling the BP monitor.

"*Ex*-boyfriend," his deep voice clarified, putting extra emphasis on the 'ex'. "It was a bit of a shock to me when Emilee told me. Condoms, man … is it even possible for them to break without me noticing?"

There was a thump, and a sharp grunt. I wasn't looking, couldn't look, but I wondered if Emilee had elbowed him in the stomach.

I felt like someone had elbowed *me* in the stomach.

"To answer your question, Levi, while it's not common, it is absolutely possible for a condom to fail and leak without it being obvious to the naked eye. Now, judging by your presence here today, you're planning to co-parent?" Beth asked, turning to her computer and tapping away at the keyboard. "I can print you out some information about it if you'd like. There are also support groups available. Will you be attending the birth and parenting classes together?"

"I think we will, don't you Levi?" Emilee said, her voice dripping like maple syrup. I felt like gagging on the weird, thick feeling in the back of my throat.

"I'll be honest with you, apart from knowing I'll do what's right for my kid, I have no fucking clue about any of the rest of it. I … uh … this is not the direction I'd seen my life taking." God, he sounded so flustered.

Well, join the club, mate. My heart thudded heavily, but also somehow too fast, in my chest. Its beat reverberated in my eardrums.

Don't you dare faint, Amanda McGregor. This is not the nastiest surprise a man has sprung on you. I told myself firmly. The blood pressure cord was wrapped several times around my hand. I unwound it.

Only because your ex-boyfriend turned out to be a serial killer, the nasty voice reminded me.

"Oh, come on, Lev, you were excited when I told you on the phone!" Emilee argued.

"I was in a state of shock, when *I* called *you* to find out what the fuck your text message meant." Levi clarified in a tight voice.

"Okay, I can see there is a bit of tension between you two," Beth said.

Try us three, I thought bitterly. Wind. Unwind.

"That's fairly normal, in situations like this," Beth continued as she turned and gently extricated my wrist from the blood pressure cuff. "Can you go out and grab the leaflets off the printer, please Amanda?" she asked me, her tone soothing. She thought this was about Emilee. She was giving me space.

Holy hell, I'd never needed space more than I did right at that moment.

"Sure," I managed, and without even a glance in Levi's direction, I escaped. The break room still felt too claustrophobic. But I couldn't just walk out of the office altogether.

This is your career, Amanda, I pep-talked myself as I leaned against the bench, trying to focus on my hot chocolate breathing—in through my nose, smell the drink, out through my mouth, blow on it to cool it. It was a technique Gillian had taught me when I first started seeing her, back when the panic attacks had been frequent. *You have to act professionally, no matter what the circumstances.*

Why her? Of all the women in the world, why did he have to have put his penis in her?

The breathing exercise wasn't working. I sank down against the cupboards, bringing my knees up, putting my head down, trying to make a small space to breathe into. To hide myself away from the world. I closed my eyes, and just let the tears come. There was no point in trying to prevent them.

Professional would have to wait for another day.

CHAPTER SIXTEEN

Pins In My Dick

LEVI

F*uck.*

Fuck, fuck, fuck.

I couldn't have told anyone a single fucking thing that happened in Zilla's appointment. Well, I could remember one thing: the way my heart had fucking stopped in my chest when I'd seen Amanda standing there, looking as sick as I felt.

The worst part was, she looked utterly fucking adorable in those light blue scrubs. When she turned and walked stiffly back up the hallway in front of us, the sight of her arse swaying in them had been life changing. Jesus, I was almost positive I would think she looked sexy in a garbage bag.

She disappeared shortly after we were called in, and she didn't return. I tried not to lose my shit, worrying about what she was thinking.

I needed to talk to her. She probably wouldn't ever want to talk to me again.

You're an arsehole, Levi Fox.

I stood at the reception desk when the whole ordeal was over, handing over my credit card—Zilla said that it was only fair that I pay for every second appointment—and not even paying attention to the amount they were charging me.

Where the fuck was Amanda?

"Are you coming?" Zilla demanded. I glared at her, but followed her into the corridor, down the lift and out into the carpark.

"What the fuck, Emilee?" I demanded as she headed for her car. She spun, scowling, her face all red and scrunched up.

"What the fuck yourself, Lev! Could you have been any less engaged in there? This is your child, the least you could have done was to actually switch your fucking brain on for once and pay attention!"

"I guess I got thrown by you referring to me as your fucking boyfriend!" I snarled, shoving my hands into my pockets because I felt like I'd punch the nearest car. "We are not together, we will never be together again. No child is going to change that. You and me? Fucking toxic. I want to do this—I want to be the dad that kid deserves," I dragged one hand out of a pocket to wave vaguely in the direction of her midsection. "But that means us being civil to one another, and having some clear goddamned boundaries around … around fucking everything! And that includes not lying to health care providers about our relationship status!"

Her bottom lip trembled, her eyes started to glisten. I sucked my lips between my teeth. A year ago, I would have felt all the fight go out of me, and I would have pulled her to me, and apologised for being a dick, and she would've perked up immediately.

I wasn't falling for her shit again. Nothing I'd just said was something I should apologise for.

"I think we should talk when I get back from Perth. I want us both to be on the same fucking page with this, Emilee. But I'm not in the head space to have that conversation with you right now, and you're clearly too pissed off to listen."

The lip wobble disappeared, the eyes narrowed. "Screw you, Levi!" she snapped, turning and stomping to her car. I sighed, letting her go. Getting Zilla to see reason at the best of times had always been a fucking chore.

Once she was gone, I turned to go back in and find Amanda. I had to explain to her. I had to …

There she was, sunglasses on and a bag slung over her shoulder, hurrying out the door and disappearing around the corner of the building.

I sprinted after her.

"Amanda!" I shouted. She flinched, but she kept walking. "Fuck, Honey, please, will you just—"

She turned to face me, her cheeks flushed, but not the way I liked them.

"I can't talk to you right now!" she said, her voice raw.

"I need to explain," I said, reaching out a hand to her. She backed away.

"I can't listen to your explanations. I just … I don't need this in my life right now." The defeat in her tone almost broke me. Jesus, I'd really fucking hurt her.

Of course you did, you dickhead! You were kissing her and grinding your dick against her three days ago, but you couldn't tell her that your ex is up the duff?

"Can we still see each other tonight?" I asked, and even to my own ears I sounded fucking pitiful.

She laughed—a frantic giggle that cut the air between us like a knife.

"Are you serious right now? You still want me to go out for dinner with you, while your 'ex' girlfriend grows your baby?"

I groaned. "We don't have to do dinner. Just … can I see you tonight, once you've had a chance to get some distance?"

"A few hours isn't even going to put a dent in the distance I need from what just happened in there. I can't even …" her words faltered, and she brought a shaking hand up to her face.

"I can't go off to Perth tomorrow knowing you're pissed off with me!" I confessed, then balked at my own ridiculous words. Shit. I'd made it all sound way too fucking serious. We'd been on one date— two if you counted the night of incredible fucking. Of course I could leave tomorrow without this being an issue.

Couldn't I?

"I'm going home now," she said, and while I stood there, my thoughts in a bloody mess, with no idea what to say to her, she turned and walked away from me. And I fucking let her go.

I wasn't quite ready to fucking let her go.

"Christ, Lev, you're a mess!" Xander said as I checked my phone for the billionth time. Still nothing. I'd sent her seven text messages. I'd even called her—she hadn't answered—and left a fucking voicemail, even though I hated talking on the phone.

"I fucking know, okay?" I muttered, glancing up at him. He took a swig from his beer. He'd offered me one, but in an ironic twist, right when taking the edge off might have helped, the thought of having a few beers in me when … if she got back to me, was fucking terrifying.

I needed my wits about me if I wanted to fix this.

And why the fuck do you want to fix it so badly? my brain piped up.

As if he had a wire straight inside my head, Xander leaned forwards, put his beer on the coffee table, and asked, "Why is this such a big deal? You slept with her once, went on a date, she found out your dirty little secret, and it's over. Call it a day and move on, Lev!"

I eyed my brother with intense dislike. "I like her, you dickhead! I like her, I did a shitty thing, I'd like to at least make a bit of peace between us, even if it doesn't make a difference to how she feels about me. It's called fucking maturity. I didn't realise that you hadn't grown up a day since high school … although I guess the way you act with women is pretty fucking childish."

Xander's brows shot up. "Don't try to drag me down with you, Levi. You do whatever you think you need to, but … Jesus, take a hint! If she wanted to hear what you had to say, she would've responded by now. The writing's on the wall."

"Oh, is that how it all went down with—"

"Don't you fucking dare," Xander warned. Yeah, I was right about him. He'd never had a real relationship, because the only one he'd ever wanted had ended before it could begin. And he still wasn't fucking over it.

"You're right," I agreed, backing off. "I can't force her to hear me out. But Jesus, I don't think what I did was all that fucking terrible—I mean, if you'd screwed a girl, and taken her on one date, do you think you would've felt like it was time to spill your stupidest mistake to her?"

Xander sighed. "I know what you're saying. I mean, I can see how it would've been awful for her, finding out the way she did … but I think it wouldn't be a conversation I'd be having until things looked like they might be getting serious."

I nodded. "Fucking exactly! You don't vomit out a bombshell like that on a first date!" I sighed, running a hand through my hair. "I just need to explain that to her, so she doesn't think it was—"

"Levi!" Theo called from the door. I jerked my head at Xander, and he got up and let Theo in.

"What the hell is wrong with you?" Theo asked as he collapsed into a seat. Xander headed for the kitchen to grab him a beer. "You look like shit, mate!"

"Yeah … you know Amanda?" I began. Theo nodded, smirking. I hadn't told him a fucking thing about the night I'd spent with her, so of course his mind had gone to the darkest, dirtiest places imaginable. "Guess who is one of the midwives looking after Zilla …"

Theo's jaw dropped. "No fucking way," he hissed.

"Yes fucking way." I leaned back against the lounge. "So, after our fantastic date on Saturday, she had a 'Moon-Fox Baby' sized bombshell explode in her face, at her place of work."

Theo closed his mouth with an effort. "That's … you couldn't make this shit up, Levi."

"I tried to catch her afterwards, to apologise, to fucking explain—just to try and get her to understand that I hadn't intended to hurt her—but she wouldn't have a bar of me. She won't respond to text messages. I even called her, for shit's sake! And it went to voicemail, and I actually left a fucking message for her."

"Jesus, Levi, you *do* like this one, don't you?" Theo muttered. I stared up at the ceiling, and the room lapsed into an uncomfortable, judgemental silence.

"You could just go to her house, hammer on the door and refuse to leave until she listens to you," Theo suggested.

I scowled. "Aside from that making me look like a fucking insane person, I don't have the first bloody clue where she lives."

"Yeah, well, I can help you with that," Theo said smugly.

I sat forward in my seat, hands clenched into fists against my knees. "Are you fucking serious? You know where she lives?"

Theo hissed out a laugh. "I banged her housemate, remember? Alison—the redhead? I saw your buxom blonde nail and bail doing the walk of shame the next morning, as I was leaving."

I surged to my feet, roughly grabbing Theo by his shoulder and dragging him out of the chair. "Don't fucking speak about her like that!"

"Ow! Fucking hell, Levi, watch the shoulder!" Theo winced.

I dropped him like he was a hot potato. "Shit! Sorry mate! Fuck." I collapsed back onto the lounge. "I'm really not in a good way right now." I dropped my head into my hands.

"Mate, take a few deep breaths, work out what the fuck you want to say to her, and I'll text you her address." Theo pulled out his phone and tapped something in.

My phone pinged.

I stood, slowly this time, and walked into the kitchen, grabbed a cold bottle of water from the fridge, and sculled the entire thing. It burned like ice on the way down, freezing off the worst of my agitation.

"Okay," I said, shoving my feet into my thongs and heading for the door. "Wish me fucking luck."

Theo and Xander raised their beer bottles in my direction.

"Good fucking luck," they chorused.

"Who are you?" a male voice asked when I banged on Amanda's door for the third time. He wasn't wearing a shirt, and his pants were scrubs. I hated him on sight. Was this some 'friend' of hers, parading around her house half fucking naked?

"I'm Levi. Who the fuck are you?" I grunted. The other guy eyed me up and down, his gaze lingering on my tattooed arms. His eyes narrowed.

"I don't think she'll want to see you," he eventually said.

I ignored him. "Amanda! Will you please, just fucking let me in, and hear me out?" I shouted. The shirtless guy walked off down the hall, and I peered through the screen door at his retreating back.

And then the redhead appeared, gave shirtless guy a quick kiss, and sauntered towards the door, wearing an oversized t-shirt and nothing else.

"You've got a nerve, coming here," she snarled. "How did you get her address anyway?"

I barked out a laugh. "You banged my best friend." I wondered if Shirtless McFuckingScrubs knew about that. He'd disappeared into the room the redhead had appeared from.

"Theo," she muttered, before pasting a false smile on her face. "Well, it was lovely to see you, Levi. But I think you should just piss off home now. You've done enough damage today."

I swallowed back my fury, letting out a calming breath. "I've got no fucking expectations, okay? I just want to talk to her, explain … even if all I get out of this is some closure, I'll walk away satisfied."

Fucking liar.

Redhead snorted. "Closure? What drugs are you on? You screwed her, and you took her on one date. What kind of closure do you think that warrants?"

"The kind where she doesn't get a fucking voodoo doll made of me so she can stick pins in my dick," I retorted. "It's none of your business. I'm not relaying what I need to say through you.

"Amanda!" I shouted again, banging on the screen door so it echoed through the house. "Just let me talk to you!"

A door in the hallway opened, and the shirtless guy came out.

"Al, I think we need to get scarce."

The redhead threw me a murderous glare and sauntered off

down the hallway, spanking shirtless guy lightly on the arse. They both disappeared through another door.

And then she appeared, and I nearly choked.

She'd been hot as fuck in tiny shorts and a tank top. She'd been sweet and sexy in that pink dress. But this girl – the one wearing a stretched out old Princes of Lion t-shirt and a pair of yoga pants.

She made my heart fucking stop.

She approached the door, not meeting my eyes, and unlocked it. "You'd better come in—our neighbours are elderly; they'll have the police here in a flash if you keep yelling like that."

She turned and headed back down the hallway. With a hand that was suddenly shaking, I opened the door and stepped inside, following her, not seeing anything, not registering one fucking thing about her home, because all I could see was that soft t-shirt. And all I could think about was gripping that fabric in my fists, dragging it up her insanely gorgeous body and kissing everything it revealed.

I followed her into a room—her fucking bedroom—and she closed the door behind us. The room was all soft light and pale, calm tones. A cosy looking purple blanket sat in a pile on top of her comforter, like she'd been huddled up in it until a moment ago.

I wanted to wrap myself in that blanket, feel the warmth her skin had left behind.

"Honey, I—"

"No, you're going to be quiet. It's my turn to talk," she interrupted, her voice so fucking calm, but her eyes wide, and her cheeks flushed, and her fingers knotting in the bottom of that t-shirt.

She was fucking beautiful.

I stood silently waiting. Her gaze flicked around the room, grazing everything but me.

"Did you … how long ago did you and Emilee break up?" she asked.

"Over two months," I replied honestly. Her eyes flicked to mine, and then away again, her top teeth chewing on that bottom lip. I wanted to remind her of what I'd said to her on the beach on the weekend. But now was not the right time. The right time might never fucking come.

"And … you think that the condom failed?" she continued, shifting from one foot to the other. I nodded.

"The last time we were together was the day we broke up. I was … distracted and angry. I wasn't paying enough attention to the state of the condom after. This whole shitshow with Zi—Emilee … this is never something I wanted with her."

Her shoulders relaxed down from her ears just enough to give me a tiny sliver of hope that she wouldn't fucking hate me forever. "When did you find out about … about the baby?"

Fuck. My shoulders slumped because I knew I couldn't lie about this.

"She texted me a week after …"

A little crease formed between Amanda's eyebrows. I wanted to run my thumb over it, smooth it out. And then replace my thumb with my mouth.

"A week after …?" she asked, her voice thick with confusion. I almost laughed, only managing to choke it back because this was too fucking important.

"A week after you and I …" I explained. Her eyes went wide, and she took a step away from me.

"So, you knew on Saturday that you were going to be a father?"

I closed my eyes, massaging my temples. "Yeah."

"And you didn't think that was an important piece of information to share with someone you want to date? 'Hi, I'm Levi Fox, Olympic Danger Boy and father-to-be'—that's all you needed to say!"

"Danger Boy?" I repeated, cocking my eyebrow.

"That's the thing you want to focus on? Not the 'father-to-be' part?" Her voice was louder and shriller. "Why her?" She clapped her hand over her mouth, as if she hadn't meant for those words to come out. But they were there, in the room.

"Why her?" I asked. "Would it make you feel better if I'd knocked up some random girl, and not a woman I was in a fucking relationship with when it happened?"

Amanda's blush drained from her face, and her eyes fell to the floor.

She's obviously fragile, Levi. You are so shit at handling female emotions.

"How can you …?" Amanda stumbled on the words, scrubbing at her cheeks. Fuck, she was crying.

"Honey, I …" I began, reaching for her. She stiffened when my palm brushed her shoulder, but she didn't flinch away. Instead, her body started fucking trembling.

"How can you want me after you had someone like her?" she sobbed.

"What the …?" I couldn't even wrap my head around what she was trying to say. Her shoulder shook under my hand.

And then I realised what she meant, and I let out a grunt. Why the fuck wouldn't I want her? She was like a breath of fresh air after the fakeness of Zilla.

"Fuck, Honey, I want you …" I tucked two fingers under her chin and lifted it until she was facing me. Wet lines streaked her face. Without thinking, I leaned down and kissed them. The salt of her tears, the flowery smell of her skin.

"I want you so fucking bad," I rasped against her cheek, "because you're so sexy, and … Jesus, you smell amazing." I was rambling, but I didn't care, because the tension in her body was melting away.

I tilted her chin up and before she could stop me, I kissed her.

CHAPTER SEVENTEEN

Follow Me Into Oblivion

AMANDA

I *should stop him. We haven't even talked this through properly yet …*

But his lips were warm, and firm, and they pried mine apart, and before I knew it, his tongue was lapping against mine, and my fingers were clawing in his hair, and his hands gripped the bottom of my ratty old t-shirt and snaked underneath, stroking the skin at my waist. And God, it felt good.

"Wait," I gasped, breaking away from his mouth, gripping his wrists and moving them away from my flabby bits.

"No," he disagreed, the word right against my ear. I shivered as he nipped my earlobe, and with too much ease, he pulled free of my grip and his hands resumed their exploration of my squishy hips. And at that moment, I just couldn't care.

"You know the rule, Honey," he murmured, nibbling and licking and sucking his way down my throat. My head fell back, giving him more access to my neck. The stretched-out neckline of the t-shirt slipped off my shoulder, and Levi groaned against the skin there.

"Rule?" I breathed, as his mouth moved further south.

"If you don't like it, what do you have to say?" His teeth grazed my collarbone, and my hands were back in his hair.

"I … I want you to stop," I replied before my brain went completely offline.

"And do you want me to stop?" he asked, his voice dark as his hands slid up my sides, and with a groan he thumbed the curve of my braless breasts. "Please don't make me stop," he begged.

"I want you to …" I broke off to gasp as his thumbs skimmed over my nipples. He paused, waiting for me to finish. "I want you to fuck me," I blurted before I could think too hard about whether or not it was a good idea.

The grunt that rumbled from his chest caught me off guard, and then I was on the bed, Levi's calloused hands pushing up my t-shirt to reveal my breasts. I sat up slightly so he could drag it off me entirely.

"It's too bright in here," I muttered, stretching my arm out towards the lamp on my bedside. He grabbed my hand and pressed it to the pillow above my head.

"I want to see you, Honey."

I swallowed, not quite meeting his eyes as his hands came down on either side of me, and his mouth resumed that slow, sensuous exploration of the dip at the base of my throat, his tongue laving the sensitive skin there until I was gasping, self-consciousness leaving my body as I suddenly wished those lips would move lower, my nipples tight and achy for his attention.

His eyes met mine, amber and hungry. "Your tits want my mouth all over them." It wasn't even a question, but I nodded.

In the glow of my bedside lamp, he moved down my body, his eyes never leaving mine as he cupped both breasts in his rough palms, squeezing gently even as his lips descended, sucking one tingling nipple into his mouth.

I bucked, my hips lifting off the bed and grinding against the rock-hard length of him jutting against the soft fabric of his shorts. He groaned around the pebbled skin of my nipple, releasing it with a pop, only to lick and flick at the gratuitously pointy peak.

"Hmmm," he murmured as he leaned back, and together we looked at how red and wet and straining that nipple had become under his tongue. He thumbed it again, grazing that calloused pad back and forth over the skin. Heat and wet and aching pulsed between my legs, and I squirmed, coming into contact with his erection once more. He reached down, pressing my hips into the mattress, his thumbs resting in the crevices where my hips and thighs met.

"Don't worry, Honey, I'm working my way down there," he mumbled, taking my right nipple into his mouth and sucking hard enough that I trembled. It wasn't until his lips started moving further south that his words sank in with a sickening flutter to my stomach.

Oh God. He wanted to … to converse with my …

I grabbed him by the waist, pulling him back up my body so his penis was nestled between my legs. "Just … I don't need you to do that. I just want this," I muttered against his cheek, rocking my hips so that my centre rubbed against the length of him.

"What if I want to?" he asked, his eyes flicking between mine, a little furrow marring his forehead. My body trembled in disgust.

He'll never want to be near you again if you let his face down there, the nasty voice piped up.

"I just want you inside me," I whispered, trying to sound sexy, but probably failing miserably. I rubbed against him again, and he groaned, his forehead dropping to my shoulder.

"Fuck, you're making it very hard to take this slow," he complained, even as he rocked his hips against mine, the thickness of him grinding against my clitoris through our clothes.

"Does it need to be slow?" I asked breathlessly. He chuckled, leaning down to take a nipple between his lips again, nipping it just hard enough that I squeaked and wriggled under him.

"That depends," he responded, soothing the sting from his teeth with his tongue. "If I fuck you hard and fast now, I'm still going to want to take you slow after. And you might be too sore for more, if I fuck you as hard as you liked it last time."

Oh my God. Just those words had me clenching emptily, needing him inside of me.

"Finger me, then," I mumbled, inhaling sharply as his teeth found my nipple again, sending an electric current straight between my legs. "Finger me now, and then you can take me as slow as you like."

"That's what you want?" he asked, leaning back to take in my expression. I nodded mutely, not trusting my voice. The way he'd done it last time had been so incredible, the memory alone was enough to force that fear about his face muffled by my flabby thighs to flitter away.

"Say it, Honey," he commanded, pinching one of my nipples. I huffed out a breathy moan.

"I want you to finger me, and then fuck me."

His mouth took mine in a possessive, searing kiss, before he broke away, eyes dark.

"Your wish is my command." His voice rough as his hands gripped the waistband of my yoga pants and pulled. I lifted my hips so he could get them all the way off.

My heart thundered raggedly as he sat back, just looking at me, naked in the muted glow of my lamp. I was completely bare to him, and he was completely clothed. My clitoris pulsed even as my cheeks burned at the scrutiny as he dragged his gaze over my nakedness. My body tensed under his stare. No one had ever seen me this way—naked and utterly vulnerable with the lamp spotlighting all my flaws—and I wasn't sure what to do with the conflicting feelings warring in me.

Cover yourself—he's looking at your gross body, the nasty voice hissed.

He seems to not hate looking at me this way, I argued with it uncertainly.

He knows he's getting some tonight—he's not about to look a gift horse in the mouth now ... but later, once he's had what he wants ... he's going to remember what you look like ...

But I didn't have a chance to absorb that, because he ran one finger down through my curls, and along the soaked flesh beneath them.

"Legs wider, Honey. I want to watch you come on my fingers."

Oh my God. My knees fell wide of their own accord, and the nasty voice fell silent.

LEVI

Thank fuck she'd let me keep the light on.

The sight of her lying there, the lamp casting shadows over her pale, soft skin, her big, beautiful tits heaving as she panted. Trimmed curls surrounded her pussy, and the wet, pink flesh beneath … fuck, she was dripping for me. I'd been a little worried when she'd stilled beneath me, when her eyes had looked fucking frightened when I'd started to kiss lower than her tits.

It looked like the 'I want' game was going to be an ongoing one. I wanted her to enjoy this. Even if my jaw was aching, my mouth salivating to be buried in that slippery perfection. I craved it, but not if she wasn't into it.

I had nothing to complain about—my dick was so fucking hard it hurt. I wanted to take it out and stroke it while I thrust my fingers into her, but if I did that, she'd end up with her stomach covered in cum. There was no way I was lasting in that situation.

I traced my finger up and down the length of her slippery, swollen flesh, circling the entrance with one finger, but not quite breaching it. She rocked to my finger, trying to get me to slip it inside.

I chuckled. "Not yet, Honey. I'm playing for a bit first."

I was teasing myself as much as I was her. And it was the headiest fucking thing I'd ever done. Her clit was rosy and so swollen. I gathered wetness and dragged it up to that spot, circling a few times to make sure it was nice and wet, then flicking it, gently at first, then faster, until she was writhing, her body tensing.

"Fuck, don't come yet," I warned her, taking my finger away and watching as she wriggled, looking for my touch, tucking her feet up close to that gorgeous arse and thrusting off the bed.

My dick throbbed, but I rode it out, until she was back from the brink enough that I could start touching her again.

"You're such a tease!" she muttered, trying to sound cross but only managing fucking adorable. I grunted out a laugh.

"When you go off like a fucking atomic bomb, you'll thank me," I replied, my finger finding its way back to her pussy again, circling the wetness, then breaching her just to my first knuckle.

The sneaky minx, she took her chance and rocked to me, my finger slipping deep. She moaned loudly, and I groaned as her pussy gripped my finger. Wet, hot, tight.

"You want me to fuck you hard with my fingers, then slow with my dick, do you Honey?"

She nodded, eyes bright and bottom lip trapped firmly between her teeth. I wanted to kiss that mouth until that fucking lip was between my teeth, while her pussy squeezed my fingers with her climax. But I wanted to watch her pussy more, so I stayed put, adding a second finger and moving them inside her, stirring, thrusting, curling.

Her hips shook, her head thrashed against the pillow, and the short, sharp moans that escaped those bitten lips? Made me fucking crazy.

I thrust faster, curling my fingers to reach her g-spot. I wished I could lean down and lick that swollen clit as I fingered her. But clearly that was not on the table tonight, so instead, I ground the heel of my palm against her clit as I pumped into her tight little pussy with two … then three fingers.

"Jesus! Levi!" she cried out, half levitating off the bed as her pussy tightened, tightened, and then clenched my fingers in waves of pulsing energy as she gasped and moaned through her orgasm.

I watched those muscles contract around my fingers, pushing more wetness out to soak my hand. Fuck me. How was I going to make this last? Fuck her slow? It wouldn't matter. Just being gloved in that tight heat and I was going to explode.

As the fluttering of her pussy slowly subsided, I slipped my fingers from her, and brought them to my mouth, sucking every drop of her off them. Jesus fuck, my eyes nearly rolled back in my head at the taste of her. She watched me with wide, fascinated, mildly horrified eyes.

A chuckle burst from deep in my chest at her expression. "I knew I called you Honey for a reason." She panted through slightly parted lips as I cleaned the last of her off my fingers, and knelt back, dragging off my t-shirt and struggling out of my shorts and underwear. My dick jerked against my stomach when I saw how fucking ravenous she looked as she stared at it.

"Let me touch you," she begged in a fucking sexy whisper, reaching out towards my dick. I pulled back.

"You touch me, Honey, I'm not going to last," I muttered, grabbing her hands and moving them away from me, above her head. I settled myself over her, careful not to let my dick touch her skin, and kissed her, letting go of her hands to tangle mine in her fucking beautiful golden hair. I was almost positive she had never dyed it.

"You are so ... so incredible," I murmured against her lips, before pressing my tongue into her mouth, making her taste her own arousal still lingering, sweet and musky. She moaned around my tongue, and a sneaking little hand suddenly gripped my dick.

"Fuck," I grunted, leaning back to eye her darkly as she thumbed the head, fucking toying with the barbell.

"I really ... really like this," she confessed in a whisper.

"I really fucking like it, too," I hissed, too busy focussing on counting to really give her much more.

Seven, fourteen, twenty-one ...

"What if ... what if I took the edge off with my hand. And then we'll be able to take it slow?" Her words broke through the numbers and my eyes snapped to hers.

"Christ, Honey," I managed. "You're trying to fucking kill me."

She gave a tiny, shy smile, and while I propped myself over her, elbows either side of her, she tightened her grip around me. I dropped my head, watching. Her arm between our bodies, her hand wrapped around me, stroking firm but slow, fondling the jewellery every time she got to the tip.

"Jesus fuck," I cursed, thrusting into her hand. Her breath was hot against the side of my face; she was watching this too, panting into my ear. She picked up the pace, stroking me faster, harder, her fingers gripping me almost as tight as her pussy.

"I'm gonna come on your stomach, Honey," I groaned.

"Please," she begged. That was all it took.

I roared as I watched my orgasm explode all over her stomach. It went on for far too long, lash after lash of cum over her pale, soft skin. I collapsed beside her, kissing her on the shoulder.

"You needed that, didn't you," she mumbled as we both gasped for breath. Her matter-of-fact words, said in that fucking sexy purr of hers … it undid me.

"I don't think *need* is a fucking strong enough word," I replied, sitting up. My eyes rolled back in my head for a second, but I breathed through it, looking around her room.

"You got any tissues in here Honey, so I can clean you up?"

I looked over at her, finding her blushing and not meeting my eyes. Shit.

"There should be some in the drawer," she mumbled, gesturing to the bedside table where the lamp was. I climbed off the bed and walked around there. Yep, tissues in the drawer. Grabbing a few, I sat down beside her, but before I could touch her, she snatched the tissues from my hand, still not looking at me as she mopped up the enormous amount of cum I'd spilled on her.

I cleared my throat, trying not to feel offended that she'd gone from hot to cold in seconds.

"Fuck, Honey. You had me so fucking riled, I didn't know which way was up anymore!" I murmured, taking the sopping mess of tissues and lobbing them into the little bin I spotted under a desk in the corner. I handed her another few, noticing there was still a glistening streak of it just below her navel. We repeated the weird, awkward process in silence.

Fuck.

I turned back to the bedside and clicked off the lamp. I climbed over the bed until I felt her warm hip against my groin. My cock twitched. Jesus, there was no way I could get fully hard again that fast. Not even with the soft warmth of this fucking beautiful woman next to me. But my dick was trying its best.

"Come here," I said, gathering her into my arms. She rolled onto her side, facing away from me, but she did scoot back against me, her round arse tucking up against my dick.

"Was that weird for you? Watching me come on you like that?" I asked quietly, reaching up to tuck a strand of hair behind her ear so I could press a little kiss to her cheekbone.

"No, I've seen guys come before," she replied, and my jaw tightened. "Well," she continued, "I've seen one guy come before."

One too fucking many, some dark, primitive voice growled in the back of my skull.

"So, what's eating you, Honey?" I asked, forcing myself not to picture her wringing an orgasm out of another man's dick.

"I … nothing," she mumbled, and I knew instantly that she was lying. I just didn't know how to get the truth out of her. I smoothed her hair off her shoulder and pressed my mouth to it. She sighed and wriggled her body closer to mine.

And … my dick twitched again. It wouldn't be much longer before that gorgeous arse of hers was being prodded with my boner.

"What do you … what are your intentions with Emilee and … and the baby?" she asked haltingly. My heart stuttered. Yeah, this was probably what she was freaking out about.

Honesty, Levi. Just be fucking honest, and it will all be good.

"I want to be there, for the baby," I replied, and before I could stop them, more and more words forced themselves out. "I mean, fuck, this was the last thing I would've wanted for my life right now —especially not with her—but these are the cards that fucking fate has dealt me. I'm not going to shirk my responsibilities just because it wasn't planned. I want to make sure my kid gets love, and affection, and one steady parent, because I highly doubt Zilla is capable of that."

"Zilla?" Amanda asked. I snapped my jaw shut. Fuck me and my stupid fucking mouth.

"Is that what you call her, like a nickname or something?" she asked, and there was so much vulnerability in her tone. Jesus. I'd opened a can of worms here.

"Honey, you have to understand," I began softly, pausing to kiss the side of her neck, wrapping my arms tighter around her as she tensed. "Emilee and I were not good together. And we spent three years not being good together. It was … it was fucking toxic, but I took the easy way out and went with the flow, rather than trying to rock the boat."

I took a deep breath, inhaling the flowery smell of her skin, and somehow, it calmed me. "All my mates saw what it was like early on. For ages, I defended her. I downplayed how shitty she was to me in public. I told them nothing about how much worse it was when no one else was around. But they knew I was lying. They started to call her Zilla—short for Boobzilla. They said she was like a fucking monstrous reptile with a boob-job."

"Your tattoo …" she mumbled, lifting my wrist and turning my arm until she could see it. She stroked at the green scaled monster with its pink bikini and screaming sound-waves erupting from its maw.

"Yep," I confessed. "I got it the day I moved the last of my stuff out of our apartment. It's my freedom tattoo." I laughed bitterly. "Except now I'll never be free. We'll have a kid keeping us together for life."

Amanda rolled over until her front pressed up against mine. Jesus, those tits against my chest—fucking heaven.

"You keep surprising me, Levi Fox," she whispered against my collarbone. "And for the record, I think you'll be a wonderful dad." She leaned back, gazing up at my face, her grey eyes sparkling. "I mean, your child will probably be swearing like a sailor before they can even walk, but other than that …"

A deep laugh burst out of me, even though the whole fucking mess was no laughing matter. Amanda giggled, her fingers sliding up my arms to my shoulders. She leaned back, taking in my tattoos.

"Well, I've solved the mystery of this one," she murmured, nails gently scratching down to the freedom tattoo on my forearm. She swept her hand back up that arm, over the crashing waves that covered my bicep and shoulder. "I think this one doesn't need any explanation."

I stopped breathing, waiting for what I knew was coming next. Wishing it would never fucking come.

"But this … this one I just can't figure out. It's so pretty though, these pink and red flowers." I froze as her attention went to the clock on my deltoid. The one with four hands. "But what does this mean, right here?" Her thumb swiped over the hands, and I shivered.

"That is a very long story," I managed shakily.

"We have time," she murmured, nuzzling her nose against mine. Time wasn't the problem though. The jolt of pain I felt whenever I thought about that tattoo was.

I silenced her with a kiss.

AMANDA

I tasted a touch of myself on his tongue as he flicked it against mine. I'd been shocked when he'd licked his fingers clean—there had been so much of me on them—but the sight of it had done something to my insides. It had been so unexpectedly hot … but something about it had also made me feel all squishy in the chest, too.

God, hearing him talk with so much conviction about how he wanted to care for his baby, make sure they knew love, even though it meant he couldn't leave behind what sounded like a downright abusive relationship … that squishy feeling tripled.

And just because he might not want to tell me about his tattoo, that didn't mean anything. It might be super personal. It might be embarrassing, or upsetting, or bring up bad memories. And I didn't want the tight look on his face when he'd shut my questions down to be the thing I dwelt on.

So, I deepened the kiss, locking my hands behind his neck and holding him to me. Ignoring the tiny stone of worry in the pit of my stomach, focusing instead on his warm, hard chest, the rippling of his abs against my skin. He reached around and grabbed fistfuls of my bottom, squeezing and kneading and grinding me against him. He wasn't hard—well not fully—but it wouldn't be long, judging by the way he groaned as he broke away from my lips, trailing kisses along my cheek, my jaw, and down my throat.

"Can I sleep here tonight, Honey?" he asked, his tongue darting out to lick the pulse point in my neck. I nodded, not trusting my voice.

"Good, coz I have to leave for Perth tomorrow, and the last thing I want to see tonight before I fall asleep is you, in my arms, exhausted and smiling because I've fucked you into oblivion."

Heat flooded my cheeks and my chest at his words, and as he stroked the sensitive skin around the cleft of my bottom, I was so ready for him to do just that. I was hot, and achy, and so wet, from before, and from what he was doing to me.

I reach between us to stroke his semi-hard penis, my body thrumming as I felt the piercing again. I honestly couldn't get enough of it. I almost wished that I could have him in me naked, so I could really feel it inside of me …

Thankfully my rational brain won out on that score. "Do you have a condom?" I mumbled against the stubble on his cheek as I ran my fingers along the vein in the underside of his penis. He groaned, his penis swelling more against my palm.

"Fuck. No."

I giggled breathily as his hands swept up my back, into my hair, down to cup my breasts and thumb my nipples. "I'm sure Alison has some."

"Oh, I'm fucking certain she does," Levi replied wryly, and I shook with laughter, resting my forehead against his pec.

"Do you want me to go grab one?"

"Well, I don't want you to get up, because this feels too fucking good, having you in my arms when I don't immediately need to blow a load from the feel of your body." He sighed. "But off you go."

I scrambled towards the end of the bed, feeling about on the floor for my t-shirt. It was long and baggy enough that I could just pop it on and scurry into the bathroom to where I knew Alison kept a bulk box of condoms.

I stepped on something just inside the door. Leaning down, I picked up the strip of foil packets. Face flaming, even in the dark, I turned back to Levi, tossing them at him.

"Apparently my housemate pre-empted us," I said, caught between utter mortification and amusement.

"Well, she's redeemed herself then. Now get that shirt off and get back on this fucking bed," Levi demanded, tearing one of the packets off the strip and tossing the rest on the bedside table.

I couldn't help the cackle that burst out of me at the thought of my 'fucking bed', even as I threw my shirt on the floor and crawled back into his arms. He wrapped me up in them again, kissing my cheek, my nose, and then my mouth, nibbling at my bottom lip as his hand skimmed down my side and around to the front, fingers teasing between my legs.

"Still so fucking wet," he groaned, his penis fully hard and pressing against my hip. I plucked the packet from his free hand and tore it open, gripping him and rolling the condom down his length.

"Fuck me, that is the hottest fucking thing I've ever seen," he growled, staring down at where I rubbed at his piercing through the latex.

"So, me putting a condom on you trumps you licking your fingers after they've been inside me?" I asked. He grunted and dragged me closer, until we lay side by side. He rubbed the tip of his nose against mine.

"That … that was in fact the hottest fucking thing I've ever tasted," he murmured against my mouth, and then his palm gripped my thigh, dragging my leg over his hip, and he reached between us, stroking my clitoris with the tip of his penis.

"Are you ready for me?" he asked, his tongue tasting the seam of my lips as he fitted the tip of his penis against my entrance. I nodded.

Slowly, so excruciatingly slowly, he inched into me, one hand tangled in my hair, the other gripping the flesh at my hip, his movements controlled, precise. And as he stretched me, any thoughts that lingered about how much fat he was able to grab on my hip, or whether the weight of my leg on his body was hurting him, fled to the furthest corners of my mind, until all I could think about was the size of him, inching forwards, filling me.

"You are so fucking tight," he grunted against my cheek as he wedged himself all the way into me. I cupped his face in my hands and brought his mouth down to mine.

"Please move, I need you to move," I whispered against his lips before I kissed him. His moan vibrated through his chest, and he withdrew, a slow, measured withdrawal. And as he thrust again, he rolled his hips, gripping my butt and hitting every single nerve ending inside me.

I gasped, clutching at his neck as he repeated the movement. This time I rocked my hips in sync with him.

"Fucking heaven," he muttered, nibbling at the skin on my neck as we continued this hip rolling dance that sent tingling pleasure zinging out from between my legs to every part of me. I hitched my leg higher on his hip, and with his next thrust he hit deeper. A thin sheen of sweat coated our bodies, and as the sensations built, he picked up the pace, his hips slapping against me, my heel digging into his butt, dragging him in every time he withdrew.

He suddenly rolled me onto my back, his thumb reaching between us, circling my clit as he continued that hip-roll in and out of me. "Come for me, Honey," he begged, his thumb pressing against that sensitive flesh, his penis stroking in and out in such agonising slowness. But it was building. The pressure on my clitoris combined with his measured thrusts, sent electricity pulsing through my veins, the ache in my abdomen tensing, my legs falling wider to get him deeper, give him better access to my clitoris.

"Harder, Levi, I need it harder!" I cried. I was on the edge, but I needed more.

"Jesus," he groaned, pumping quickly into me, and I could feel the peak, only seconds away. My toes curled, my fingers gripped the sheets.

He pulled out. Without a word, he flipped me until I was on my stomach, looming over my back and nipping my earlobe as I turned my head to the side.

"You want it hard? I'm going to make you come on my dick so hard you'll forget your own name," he growled in my ear, and I clenched around air at his dirty, commanding words.

Who knew I'd like being spoken to like that so much?

Without another word he hitched my hips up until my butt was in the air. I blushed at what it must look like to him, but thought fled when he sighed out a little breath.

"I will have wet dreams about this view for the rest of my fucking life."

His fingers slid up the backs of my thighs, the skin there—never touched like this by anyone, not even me—quivering under his touch. He reached my bottom, parting me, rubbing the tip of himself up and down my swollen, aching flesh. I moaned into the pillow.

He thrust inside me, gripping my bottom as he dragged his hips to meet me. Oh God, I felt so full this way. He slid out and back in again, torturously slow.

"Fuck, Honey, watching my dick disappear inside that tight little pussy …" he didn't finish that sentence, just punctuated his words with a hard, quick thrust of his hips, filling me so suddenly that I cried out.

"More?" he muttered.

"Yes!" I begged, and he did it again. And again, and again. My muscles tightened, my head thrashed against the pillow. Sweat dripped from him onto me as he fucked me hard, just the way I'd begged him for.

"So fucking tight!" he hissed, spreading me wider. I rocked my hips back to meet him, our bodies slapping, the ache building, my vision blurring, his groans so loud.

And then I was screaming his name as I came apart on him.

"Fuck, Amanda!" he shouted, pushing deep into me as he followed me into oblivion.

CHAPTER EIGHTEEN

Phenomenal

AMANDA

"I have Vegemite breath," I complained.

"I don't give a fuck," Levi replied, kissing me hard, his hands at the small of my back, pressing me closer to him. His lips worked mine apart until our tongues tangled, and my knees weren't holding me up properly.

"Jesus, get a room!" Alison said from the kitchen doorway. She eyed Levi with an unreadable expression as we broke apart, and I stuffed another bite of toast into my mouth. I was showered and dressed for a day shift at Frankwright, and Levi was showered and dressed in the clothes he'd been wearing the night before.

I was also sporting a very bright blush. Levi and I had just 'gotten a room' in the shower together, because apparently my body with water dripping down it was not something he could resist. It made zero sense to me, even as my skin heated thinking about his hands, gripping my hips, my hands pressed to the tiles. The slapping sound our bodies made …

"Coffee?" Alison asked, heading over to the espresso machine she and Dani had spent months saving up for.

I shook my head. "You know I'm not a coffee drinker."

Alison turned and winked. "Yes, but you're not the only person here this morning, are you?" she reminded me. "Plus, I thought after such a sleepless night, you might suddenly see the benefit of caffeine."

My face was about to melt off. I turned to the kettle, flicking the switch. "There's plenty of caffeine in tea, thank you anyway," I said.

Alison chortled. "Levi? Coffee?"

"Nah, thanks anyway. I'd love a tea, though, Honey." Oh my God, the way he called me Honey with such casual affection made my insides flutter. I grabbed two cups.

"Earl Grey okay?" I asked. "It's my favourite."

His warm body crowded against my back, and he reached over my head, snagging the box of tea bags off the shelf, plucking out two. "It's my favourite, too," he murmured against my damp hair. I shivered. Why did I feel like he wasn't just talking about tea?

His hands came to rest on my hips, and I tried not to feel weird about all this PDA when I honestly had no idea where things were going with him. The more I discovered about him, the more I felt drawn to him, which, considering the revelations of the last day, seemed unfathomable to me. Despite the fantastic sex, and the cuddling, and the kissing, and all of it, I still didn't know how I felt about his situation with Emilee. Or how Levi felt about … anything really, except how he felt inside me, that is.

But this thing didn't have to be serious—it could just be for fun. I'd never really done 'fun' before. Things with Thomas had been so full-on so quickly, and look how that had turned out. Maybe I just needed to play this day by day, and not worry about step ten, when we really were still on step one, and might never leave there.

That thought left my insides icy. I reached for my toast, but Levi snatched it out of my hand, took a bite himself, and then held it to my mouth. Blushing furiously, I nibbled at it, and he put it back down on my plate.

"Milk for your tea?" he asked, turning away from me and opening the fridge, for all the world like he lived here.

Squishy feelings intensifying!

"Um, yes please," I mumbled, pouring boiling water over the

teabags. He was back behind me again, warm and close and so male. He poured milk into both cups.

Alison watched this whole pantomime avidly from the other side of the kitchen bench as she sipped at her coffee. "Naw, you two like your tea the exact same way! How adorable!" Her tone was overly sweet, but there was an edge to her words. Her gaze flicked to mine, and her eyes narrowed.

"Shit!" Levi said suddenly, looking at his phone. "I've gotta run. Flight leaves in two hours and I haven't packed yet."

I almost choked on a sip of tea. "Two hours?" I screeched. "You won't make it to the airport in time!"

Levi chuckled, downing his tea like it wasn't scalding hot, and quickly rinsing his cup under the hot tap. "Honey, I can pack in about two minutes flat. Patto—my coach—has a car picking me up in half an hour. I'll be fine."

"Well …" I began, meeting his eyes and then dropping my gaze. That glowing greenish-amber colour was too intense for me this morning. Especially after last night. "Let me walk you to the door," I finished lamely.

"I'll be back late Monday," he said, taking my hand as we headed up the hallway. Tingles zinged up my arm. God, my body reacted to him far too easily. He turned me to face him just inside the screen door. "Can I come here when I get back?" he murmured, brushing a stray strand of damp hair from my cheek.

"I … I'll have to get back to you, I need to check what my roster looks like next week," I fibbed. I was almost certain it would be fine, but I needed to breathe for a second. His presence was intoxicating, but there was so much baggage that came along with him. Emilee shaped baggage. Pregnant Emilee baggage.

He shrugged, taking my words at face value. "I'll text you when we land in Perth, okay?" I chewed on my lip, nodding. His thumb stroked my chin, tugging gently until my lip popped free of my teeth.

"This lip is mine, Honey," he growled, leaning closer, eyes gleaming as he nipped at it. I gasped and he followed that nip with a lick, pulling me against him, his tongue dipping into my mouth.

My body turned to flames, curving against him as his hands gripped my bottom and pulled me even closer. The world narrowed until it was just my soft body melting against his warm, hard one.

He broke away, panting and resting his forehead on mine. "Fuck, I really have to go. Text me about Monday. Don't forget."

And with that, he let himself out and strolled off, hands in pockets, down my street. I practically collapsed against the wall, gasping for air.

"Get your peachy arse in here, Amanda McGregor!" Alison called from the kitchen. I took a deep breath and walked back down the hallway, trying to act like I hadn't been completely ravished at our front door.

"He's intense," Alison commented wryly, biting into a crumpet.

'He's got a lot going on," I retorted, heading back to my tea and drinking it quickly before it cooled too much more. My toast was a complete write off now, cold and tough as a rock. I stuck my head in the pantry and came out with a muesli bar, grabbing a tub of yoghurt from the fridge too.

"Yes, which is exactly why I need to talk to you," Alison said, sliding her empty plate in my direction. Wordlessly I took it to the sink. Something uncannily like worry unfurled in my stomach as I washed it up.

"What's that supposed to mean?" I asked, attempting, and probably failing, to sound unconcerned by her words.

"Manda, he's got a pregnant ex-girlfriend. Someone you really don't want to have to associate with. Do you really want to tie yourself to him when he's 'got a lot going on'?"

I huffed shakily. "Tie myself to him! What? We're barely even dating, it's just … fun, for now. It might never be more than just fun."

That cold feeling trickled through my veins again.

Alison sighed. "Manda, you're not capable of 'just fun'."

I bristled at her condescending tone. "I thought you'd be advocating for the 'just fun' style of relationship."

She laughed. "For me—just fun works for *me*. But, my gorgeous sweetie, 'just fun' isn't your style. And I'm going to go out on a limb here and say that I don't think that Levi is a 'just fun' sort of guy, either."

I shook my head. "There's no way in the world he's looking for more than just fun with me. I mean, you've seen what he just had. He was in a serious relationship with every man's wet dream of a woman. I'm just … I'm probably just a rebound. Someone so totally different to his ex that he can get her out of his system entirely."

I wasn't sure I believed those words, but they stuck in my head once I'd said them. And I didn't need that today. Not when I was staring down the barrel of an eight hour shift full of helping elderly patients to the toilet, and changing antibiotic bags on IV lines, and arguing with grumpy post-surgery patients when they insisted they were due another dose of pain relief.

I didn't need to think about how Levi Fox was working his way under my skin, and I didn't need to think about whether he felt even a smidgeon the same way.

And I certainly didn't need to think right now about step ten— what would happen if things did become more than just for fun, when before the end of the year he'd be a father to another woman's child. To Emilee Munro's child.

"I have to get to work," I mumbled, grabbing my water bottle and heading towards the door.

"Just don't jump headfirst this time, okay?"

Her words echoed in my brain all the way to work, where those words rapidly dropped out of my head. An elderly patient recovering from a hysterectomy developed a fever and declined rapidly, necessitating a rush to Intensive Care, and a temporarily short-staffed ward.

Two other patients managed to soil their beds during that drama, and I was lucky enough to end up looking after the meaner of the two.

"Oh, Miss Piggy's here to change my shitty sheets!" the old man grouched as I walked into his room and clicked off his call button. I helped him out of his bed, ignoring the stench, and walked him to the ensuite shower room, settling him in the chair and getting the temperature right as he grumbled and complained the whole time.

While he was rinsing off under the warm water, I grabbed an orderly to sort out the bedding for me, then went back in and soaped him down.

"Jesus, if I'd known I'd get a rub and tug from a nurse today, I would've requested the *hot* blonde, not the porky one!"

I chose to ignore him, even if I kind of wished I could shove the entire shower head right up his backside.

That evening, tired and cross, I stepped into the shower, grabbing my body wash. The scent immediately transported me back to that morning. To the way Levi had soaped up his hands, cupping my breasts, the bubbles sliding over my nipples as he'd played. The way he'd bent me over, rubbing his piercing over the swollen flesh between my legs, until I was mindless, begging.

The way he'd reached out of the shower for a condom, and moments later he'd filled me, his pace slow, punishing, until I saw stars, biting my lip but not able to fully suppress my cries as he took me over the edge, following me soon after.

I was so intensely aroused from just the memory that I found myself going to my knees on the shower floor, my fingers rubbing my slippery, swollen parts until I was shaking, writhing and coming undone, shocked at how fast I'd orgasmed.

Levi was well and truly under my skin, in a raw, physical, sexual way. A way no other guy had ever gotten under my skin. Not even Thomas. No, I'd thought we had a strong emotional connection, which was why I'd given him so much more than he'd been prepared to reciprocate. And then he'd completely betrayed me. Or more to the point, his betrayal through the whole of our relationship finally came to light.

With Levi, it was the opposite. So physical … but would the emotional come with time? Was that even what he wanted from me? With everything else going on in his life, I almost wouldn't blame him for just wanting something no-strings. His life was a tangle of strings everywhere else, did he just want me to be that one thing that didn't tangle it more?

And how would I feel about that?

I dried and dressed, my body relaxed from my climax but my mind whirring. I checked my phone. Messages from Mel, who was in California, and from Levi. Heart thrumming, I read the messages from Mel first.

> Mel: I need much more detail on the you and Levi Fox situation
>
> Mel: Like, stat
>
> Mel: Because Joel said that Emilee Moon is pregnant with Levi's baby. I NEED to know what the hell is happening!

I chewed on my lip. Emilee Moon? Did she mean Munro and her autocorrect had a moment? I flicked over to my browser and Googled Emilee Moon.

Oh My God.

The first result was an Instagram account. Emilee Moon. Nine-hundred *thousand* followers! I clicked through, and it took me to the app. I steered clear of social media usually—for someone like me, apps like Instagram were a minefield of inferiority and self-loathing —but I had set up an account years ago.

Emilee was a yoga instructor turned 'influencer'. She worked with fitness and lifestyle brands that even I knew the names of. Her profile was full of pictures of her in bikinis or teeny activewear, contorting her body on beaches, in forests, on high-rise buildings overlooking the ocean.

Her most recent ones showed her drinking green juice with captions about prenatal vitamins and pregnancy nutrition, or in yoga poses with 'yoga workout for the busy mum-to-be' emblazoned across the reel. One with her wearing a gorgeous body-con dress, claiming she'd be partnering with the brand to create her own range of maternity wear 'that will feel like you're wearing a cloud, while looking like you're heading for the red carpet'.

Then I came to a post of her in skimpy lace underpants that did nothing to cover her toned bottom, making a heart symbol with her hands over her flat belly and looking down lovingly, her breasts absolutely centre stage, naked but covered artfully with her long, straight hair. The caption read: 'A Moon-Fox baby, coming October 2023—here's what I'll be using on my pregnancy journey'. I scrolled through the images on that post, showing a variety of supplements, vitamins, and maternity wear.

That post was dated a week after I'd first slept with Levi. The day he'd told me he found out about the baby. Had she really, truly posted to Instagram the same day she'd dropped this news on him? Or had he known about it longer than he'd admitted?

I didn't want to think about that too deeply, even as anxiety swooped through my stomach. I thumbed the screen again, scrolling for quite some time, until I found what I was looking for and dreading in equal measure.

Posts with Levi in them. Attending a new product launch. A movie premiere. Her clinking a glass of champagne to his schooner of beer in some tropical locale. I didn't read any of the captions. I felt like I was going to be sick. They looked phenomenal together. So perfectly matched. Him with his intense eyes and bad-boy looks. And Emilee, with her tall, toned body, gorgeous mane of silvery blonde hair and blue eyes, and pouty, bee-stung lips.

I imagined what photos of Levi and me would look like and cringed. Tall, muscular Levi next to short, frumpy, chunky me, who barely reached his shoulder and was twice the width of him.

The world would laugh.

And I still had a whole bunch of text messages from the object of my intrusive thoughts to go through. Taking a deep breath, I clicked on his name.

Levi: Just landed

Levi: Can't stop thinking about last night

Levi: And this morning

Levi: Never jerked off on a plane before

Levi: Guess there's a first time for everything

I almost fanned myself thinking about him stroking that thick, pierced penis of his in an airplane bathroom, because he was so worked up thinking about me …

But it didn't quite erase the misgivings that were laying down roots deep inside of me. He had a beautiful ex-girlfriend, who was having his baby. And even if he claimed their relationship had been toxic, how long would it take before he got bored of plain, chubby Amanda McGregor, and went looking for someone who fit him better?

CHAPTER NINETEEN

Double Fucking Fuck

LEVI

"You're in a bad mood," Theo said just before we took to the water to warm up for our semi-final. Light rowing, a few bursts of speed, and then back to land for a rest before the race later in the morning.

I was in a fucking terrible mood. I grunted incoherently as we pushed the shell into the water. My brows furrowed as Theo flinched from the movement. We were sharing a shitty motel room while staying here, and he thought he was being sneaky, but I saw how many fucking painkillers he was popping just to get through a training session.

And it wasn't just Theo and his fucking shoulder that was pissing me off—although really that should have been the most worrying thing on my mind.

Amanda hadn't responded to my text messages. It was Saturday. I sent them on Wednesday. I'd stopped myself from calling her—just —and only because we'd been full on with training and races and equipment maintenance.

Maybe I went too far, telling her I'd stroked one out on the plane. But fuck, I'd tried to close my eyes, get some rest, and the first thing that popped into my brain was the sight of her round, bouncy arse, bent over in the shower, and the way my dick had looked when I'd rubbed it up and down her slippery pussy until she was fucking begging me to impale her.

How was I not supposed to take the edge off after that?

You're the only guy she's been with, the sane part of my brain reminded me. *Maybe just take it down a notch or fucking seven, until she's used to your filthy mind.*

Well, my filthy mind was a safer thing to introduce her to than the needy, desperate part of me that wanted to say things that would freak her right out. Things like *'your smile makes my insides feel like they've turned liquid'* and *'I fucking love knowing how you take your tea, so I can make it just right for you every morning,'* and *'fucking Christ can I permanently move you into my life?'*

You know, the shit that would send any sane woman running a mile from someone like me, someone who had nothing worthwhile to offer.

I forced Amanda and my intense feelings for her to the back of my mind. I had a race to prep for, and a teammate who was dropping the ball, which meant I had to pick it up. No time for me to be dropping my own ball.

Our warmup went okay, but as we pulled the shell out of the water, Patto's expression was strained. I wasn't sure how much—or even if—he knew about Theo's shoulder. I hadn't told him. I fucking should have. But then I'd be here, warming up with fucking Mac, and that would've been a nightmare. A small part of my brain knew that was why I hadn't ratted Theo out to our coach.

Theo would push through. I knew he would. He was a tough bastard. I just hoped that after this he would listen and go get it looked at. We had six months until the WRCs in Serbia. That was hopefully enough time to get some rehab done on it. Our Olympic place relied on our performance in Serbia. And I had shit to prove.

We headed for the marshalling area, to rest, have a snack and wait for our race to be called. Mac plonked himself into a seat next to me.

"Good warm up?" he asked, his tone so fucking pleasant it set my teeth on edge. I grunted at him.

"He's in a shitty mood, Mac," Theo said beside us, massaging his shoulder. "His girlfriend won't reply to him."

"She's not my fucking girlfriend," I growled. Fuck, I wished she was my girlfriend.

"Isn't she? You're sure acting like she is," Theo scoffed.

"Is this Amanda? I didn't realise you guys had reconnected after that night in the bar! Good for you, Levi!" Mac patted me on the back. I shoved his arm away.

"We're just having fun," I grumbled under my breath. Well, I thought we'd been having fun. So much fun I never wanted it to end. Maybe she'd come to her senses, and realised that my future was fucking bleak, permanently tied to my ex. Maybe the reality of that had scared her off.

It should have scared her off.

"Good idea, Levi," Mac agreed. "Take it slow, you just got out of a serious relationship. You need time to heal after everything you've been through."

Where the fuck did he get off saying shit like that? What a dick.

Before I could cuss him out in reply, they called our race, and tight-lipped, I got the fuck out of there.

The weather was perfect the day of our final. Sunny, still, the water like glass.

"Good weather is a great omen for today!" Mac commented. Theo stared out at the water, rotating his right shoulder and looking pensive. I threw Mac a withering glare.

"It's as good a fucking omen for every other team as it is for us," I reminded him. He leaned closer.

"No chop and no headwind mean less drag on the oars for Theo's shoulder," he muttered. I gaped at him. Even Mac knew about it? Had he told Patto? Was this common knowledge and everyone was just fucking pretending nothing was wrong?

You've been doing exactly that for months, dickhead.

I turned away from Mac, heading towards Theo. "People are noticing that your shoulder is fucked," I hissed.

Theo shrugged with his left shoulder, still massaging his right. "I've been going easy the last few races, saving the juice for this one. You don't have to worry about me, Fox—keep your shitty opinions to yourself."

"Okay, arsehole. No need to get your panties in a bunch," I grumbled as they called the teams for our race to come to the marshalling area.

***

"Aaargh, fuck!" Theo screamed, dropping his oars to grip at his right shoulder with a hundred and fifty metres still to go.

"Fucking … fuck!" I grunted. Flashbacks of the under seventeens, of Theo collapsing on the podium, flooded my brain. Only this was a billion times worse. Because the race wasn't over.

And I really fucking wanted to win.

"Pull your oars in, Theo!" I roared, and then I rowed like a murderer was after me. We'd had a fucking monstrous lead on the other teams until that point—Theo had pushed himself harder than I'd seen in months. Was it going to be enough with him out of action? Probably fucking not, but I had to try.

The other teams gained as I checked the markers. One-hundred metres to go. The Australian National University team pulled closer. Theo was doubled over now, barely managing to stay in the shell.

"Not today, fuckers," I muttered, my muscles screaming. Fifty metres. They were almost neck and neck with us now. Thirty … twenty … I didn't look to see where they were. I pulled us across the line, my ears roaring, and I signalled for a boat to come and help Theo to shore.

Then, exhausted and alone in our shell, I manoeuvred it to the dock. Mac was waiting there to drag it out with me.

"That was some superhuman feat there, Levi!" Mac said. I shook my head, too out of breath and head-fucked to answer. I collapsed onto the grass and squinted up at the sky.

What the fuck had just happened? Had we won the race? Did I even care anymore? I felt like something inside my brain had fucking exploded.

A race official approached me, blocking the blistering sun from my face.

"You're needed at the podium, Fox," he said quietly. "You'll have to accept Drysdale's medal on his behalf."

I grunted, and stumbled to my feet, shaking out my limbs. I needed to do something before the lactic acid took hold in my arms, my glutes and quads. I was going to be totally fucked for anything physical for days otherwise.

"Where is he?" I asked, but the official had already headed off towards the podium.

"They've taken him by ambulance to the hospital," Mac replied. "Patto's gone with him. He was utterly ropable."

I had no fucking words. This was my fault as much as it was Theo's. I'd let him deal with his shoulder by popping pills and pretending everything was fine. I'd let him do that for far too long. And now, who the fuck knew what damage he'd done to himself?

The medal ceremony went by with my ears still ringing, and my head somewhere else completely. It only broke through when I realised that they were slipping a fucking gold medal over my neck, and handing me one for Theo.

"Shit," I muttered, doing my bit and standing there as photos were taken. When a news crew got up in my face as I walked off the stage, Mac was there.

"No interviews," he said sternly to the reporter sticking a mic in my face. "You'll get a statement from Alfie Patterson tomorrow."

I didn't want to admit that I was just a tiny bit grateful to Mac for helping me out. But then again, that was what he lived for. He was probably getting a boner over being able to help out.

"Let's get to the hospital," I mumbled as we headed away from the crowds.

"His pec tendon is completely detached from the bone." Patto swiped a hand over his exhausted face. I stood frozen, my sweaty palm clutching Theo's gold medal. "The scans show a lot of bone shards and wear and tear around the joint in the shoulder too. This is not a new issue."

"Nope," I replied in a monotone. Patto made a sound that was part sigh, part groan.

"How long have you known he had an issue?" he asked me. I glanced towards Mac, who was looking everywhere but at us.

"Too long," I mumbled, collapsing into one of the plastic seats that were bolted to the wall. "Far too fucking long."

"Why the hell didn't you say something?" Patto growled. My temper flared to life, and I surged to my feet, adrenaline burning away the exhaustion.

"Because it wasn't my fucking place to say anything!" I snarled. "Believe me, I thought about telling you every fucking day since I started to suspect something was wrong. I told him multiple times to tell you, to have it looked at, to make sure that whatever it was, it got fixed before Serbia!"

Patto put a hand on my shoulder and shoved me back into the seat. "Well, there'll be no Serbia for Drysdale now. He's lost all strength in that arm. Could barely even move his fingers. They're talking about nerve damage. He's gone in for surgery now, but at the very least we're looking at six to twelve months of solid rehab before he can even look at an oar again."

"Fuck." I ran my fingers through my sweaty hair.

"Fuck is right, Fox. So, if you want to qualify for the Olympics," Patto turned and gestured in Mac's direction, "you're looking at your only chance."

Double fucking fuck.

Back at our crappy motel, I collapsed onto the single bed like it was a fucking cloud. In reality, it was as hard as a board, and there was a spring that stuck me right in the middle of my back every night.

It was a tiny fucking room, but it suddenly felt empty without Theo there. I stood, and without thinking too hard about how invasive I was about to be, I went to his suitcase and rummaged through until I found a little black zip-bag that rattled. I opened it and looked inside.

Fuck me.

Valium and prescription anti-inflammatories. So there was a doctor somewhere who knew he had an issue. But the one that scared the shit out of me the most was the bottle of Endone.

Endone was a fucking banned substance in competitive sport.

I checked the bottle and breathed a sigh of relief. It was still sealed. Hopefully that meant he hadn't been taking them. But fuck, he'd definitely been taking them back in Sydney—I could picture the glassy eyes, how spaced he'd seemed some days. How long did that shit stay in your system? Hopefully whatever they gave him in the hospital would mask it.

Not that it mattered anyway. Even if he got banned, by the sounds of it the ban would be over long before he could get in the water again. Either way, there was no chance for him in Serbia.

My phone rang and I jumped guiltily. I zipped the pills back into the case and shoved it deep into Theo's bag, racing over to my bed and snatching up my phone. My heart leapt into my throat when I saw the caller ID

Honey.

"Hey," I answered, totally lamely, a sudden bubble inside my chest preventing more words from coming out.

"Levi, hi." She sounded nervous. "I just saw you on the news."

I pinched the bridge of my nose. "Yeah," I managed.

"Are you … are you okay? How's Theo?"

"You didn't reply to my messages."

There was a long pause. "I know, I'm sorry. I had a rough day at work that day, and I just … I'm sorry. There's no excuse."

I sighed heavily. "No idea how Theo is. They were prepping him for surgery when I left the hospital. Patto's—my coach—he's staying with him. The pec tendon tore right off the bone."

Amanda hissed sharply. "That's … Levi, what does that mean

for your Olympic chances? He won't have recovered enough to compete in Serbia in September!"

I rubbed at the ache in my chest. She'd remembered so many of my rowing details from one throwaway conversation.

"If I want to compete in Serbia, I need to take Mac on as my partner." Fuck I sounded so bitter. The thought of having to work with him, to train with him. To celebrate or commiserate with him, when he'd just plaster that goofy smile on his face and act like everything was fucking hunky dory no matter what.

"Mac?" Amanda asked, confused. I couldn't help the grin that spread across my face then.

"Oh, Honey, you just stroked my ego big time. The blond guy with the puppy-dog eyes who tried to hit on you in the bar the night I found heaven inside your pussy."

She giggled nervously. "Oh, yeah, I remember now. So, are you going to team up with him?"

I huffed out a breath through my nose. "I really don't have a choice. He's the reserve, this is the reason he's around. I just … fuck, this is turning out to be a really shitty year for me." I flopped back against the bed, grunting when the spring jabbed me in the back.

She was quiet for so long I started to wonder if the service was patchy. But then she cleared her throat. "Tomorrow night. I'll come to your place. Text me when you're home, okay?"

"You don't have to do that," I murmured. "I can—"

"I want to," she interrupted me. "I want to be in your bed … with you."

Fuck if that didn't make me ache in odd ways.

"Okay, Honey," I conceded. "Thank you."

"Take care of yourself, Levi," she said quietly before hanging up.

***

"He's not just being left here alone, is he?" Mac asked as we boarded our flight back to Sydney, concern drawing his eyebrows together. I bit back a sigh.

"His mum flew in on a red eye, got here first thing this morning," Patto reassured him. "She'll fly home with him once he's cleared to travel. I'll check in on him daily. But my first priority is you two now."

He turned and glared at me. I scowled back at him. "Lose the attitude, Fox. Graham is your only hope for the Olympics now. And I hate to admit it, but this might have been the best thing for you."

I gaped at him. "How do you fucking figure that?"

"Because Graham is hungry. Just like you are."

I shook my head. He wasn't hungry, unless it was to have everyone tell him what a good boy he was.

I slept on the flight. The seat on the plane was more comfortable than the fucking motel bed. When I woke, bleary eyed as they were bringing snacks around, Mac grinned goofily at me.

"Hungry?" he asked, holding a bag of pretzels out. "I know I am."

"Are you making a joke?" I asked, genuinely mystified. Mac shrugged, smirking lopsidedly at me. I guffawed, shocked that it had actually been kind of fucking funny. Maybe I was still half asleep. Everything was funny when you were still half asleep.

Patto turned to me as we waited at the luggage carousel.

"No training tomorrow. You get home, get a good night's sleep, get your head right and be at training Wednesday at five-thirty on the dot," Patto said, eyeing me. I gave a brusque nod. "Mac, that goes for you too."

"Aye aye, Captain!" Mac said with a salute. He flicked me some wicked side-eye, and my lips twitched, but Patto just nodded, because Mac was a fucking dorky people pleaser who said dumb shit like that all the time and actually meant it.

Which was true … wasn't it? I didn't know what the fuck to think anymore. All I knew was that I had to spend six mornings a week for the next six months with him. And it was going to be hell.

CHAPTER TWENTY

Not a Single Red Cent

AMANDA

The second time I woke up in Levi's bed, naked and wrapped in a warm man with morning wood, felt different from the first.

I didn't feel the immediate need to wriggle from his arms and hightail it out of there. And this time, thankfully, the door was closed, so no chance of Xander walking past and catching an eyeful of my flabby backside. My face heated as a sleepy Levi rolled his hips, the underside of his erection rubbing between the cheeks of said flabby backside.

"I could get too fucking used to this," he rumbled sleepily, his hand trailing over my hip and across my belly. I swallowed, wrapping my fingers around his wrist and gently moving his hand back to my hip. My stomach was … it was a no-go zone for me. It was the part of my body that I most hated looking at. Hated even acknowledging.

The thought of it brought back all the misgivings I'd had while he'd been away in Perth. My body was not anything like the kind of body he'd found desirable in the past. No one in their right mind would find this wobbly thing desirable.

And suddenly the need to escape was almost overwhelming. Levi must have felt me tense, because he pulled me closer, enveloping me in his arms, pressing a kiss to my shoulder.

"Don't you dare fucking run on me again … I know where you live now, remember?"

"I …" I blurted but had no idea what I wanted to say to him.

I needed to talk to Gillian.

The fact that I even felt that way made me pause. Normally I dreaded talking to her, because she made me face things I wasn't prepared to look at in too much detail. But I realised I *wanted* to look at this. I wanted to not feel … less … when I compared myself to others … to Emilee.

"I have a very good way of keeping you from running …" he continued, moving the hair away from my neck and nibbling at the sensitive skin there. I shivered, and his hand left my hip, avoided my belly but reached between my legs, tracing circles in the curls there. I let out a shaky breath and parted my thighs for him, forcing my inner turmoil to wait until he finished whatever he was starting.

His fingers dipped, and he grunted in satisfaction to find me wet. How could I not be, when he played my body like a fiddle?

"So ready for me, Honey," he mumbled, removing his hand. I moaned in disappointment, that quickly turned to a sharp hiss of pleasure, as he parted me from behind and rubbed that pierced head across my flesh. This was quickly becoming my absolute favourite foreplay move of his.

"When are you due at work?" he whispered, rocking his penis against my clitoris. I wriggled, and he groaned into my neck.

"I have clinical placement from ten today."

"Can I finally fuck you slow then? While we're both sleepy enough for it to maybe stay that way?"

I clenched around nothing, wishing he'd just slip inside me.

"Okay," I managed, and he leaned away, the tell-tale rip of the condom packet priming my body, my arousal coating my inner thighs.

And then he slid inside me, slowly, from behind, rocking himself in and out of me. His hand slipped between my legs, fingers circling, pressing, flicking at my clitoris, as he punished me with gentle, slow strokes of his penis.

"You feel so fucking good this way, Honey," he confessed. "Fuck, you feel so good every way." He trailed kisses along my neck, my shoulder, as his fingers and his penis worked in synchronisation, stoking the fire inside me.

It did feel good this way. But something about it also felt … different, somehow. I ached, but it wasn't just the aroused parts of me that ached. Pressure built behind my ribcage with each thrust, each kiss and nip at my neck. Each hot breath against my cheek.

I arched my back slightly, and he hit me from a different angle. We both moaned together at the feeling.

"Keep doing that," I begged him. "Don't go any faster, just … keep doing exactly that."

He rocked, and thrust, stroking me inside with his penis, and outside with his talented fingers, until I was panting, gasping, and the build that had been so slow, began to peak … gradually … so the deep, hot ache of sensation started inside me, and bled out along my limbs to my fingers and toes, so prolonged that when it finally tipped me over the edge, it was like a freefall through an ocean of pleasure. I moaned loudly into the pillow.

"Fuck, Honey, you come so fucking hard, I can't … fuck yes!" he gasped against my ear as he followed me. We lay there, his front against my back, as we came back to earth together, chests rising and falling hard.

"What about you?" I eventually asked, rolling over in his arms, pulling the sheet up to cover my stomach and breasts. "What does your workday look like?"

Levi grunted, smoothing sweaty strands of hair off my face. "I've been given the day off today. So, I'll go for a run, maybe a swim … anything to keep my mind off the shitshow that is the next six months."

I traced my fingers along his stubbled jaw. "So … what happens if you qualify with Mac? What then? Can he and Theo interchange if Theo improves enough to compete next year?"

Levi shook his head. "Nope. If Mac and I qualify, Mac and I go to Paris."

"And how do you feel about that?"

Levi pressed a kiss to my forehead. "Fucking conflicted, Honey, that's how I feel. I … Theo and I have been rowing together since we were in high school. I can't even imagine how he would be feeling, knowing he's fucked his chance at the Olympics. Hell, rowing at a competitive level might not ever be something he can do again— who knows?"

"But … you wouldn't consider sitting it out, would you?"

"Fuck no. I've got to make it to Paris."

There was something in his voice that stopped me from probing further. So, I changed the subject, to one that was probably even more fraught with danger for both of us.

"Will you be attending all of Emilee's appointments from now on?"

Levi stilled, then extricated himself from the tangle of bedsheets, tugging off the condom and dropping it into the waste bin in the corner. He bent to pick up his boxer-briefs, stabbing his legs into them and sitting down on the edge of the bed, resting his forehead in his hands.

"I didn't mean to …" I began, but he turned and rolled back onto the bed, dragging me to him.

"You didn't do anything, Honey," he said against my hair, hands sliding up and down my back. "I'm just being a fucking baby, that's all. Emilee hasn't said anything about coming to the next one, but I probably will. I need to get used to the fact that she's growing a baby that's half mine. I need to connect with it.

"Why do you ask?" he added, pressing me back and eyeing me with those crazy light-filled eyes, his scarred brow drawn over them. "Will it be too awkward for you? I mean, I know last time was shit, but now you know that she's … that I'm … fuck, maybe I shouldn't come to the appointments."

I shook my head, reaching up and linking my hands behind his neck. "No, you should definitely come. Now that I'm not going to get the shock of my life seeing you there, I think it's important for you to be involved this early on. If you want to have an active role in the baby's life, then that starts now. You should talk to the baby …" I giggled when he rolled his eyes, "No, I'm serious, Levi. Talking to a baby in-utero is important. The baby can hear you from about twenty-seven weeks. Let that little baby hear your voice, so that they already know you when they're born."

"You're a goddamned angel, Amanda," he muttered, before leaning in to take my mouth, pushing me back on the bed and plundering me until I was gasping, before hopping up and heading for the door.

"You want to shower first?" he asked, hand on the doorknob. "Or …" he waggled his eyebrows at me, "do you want to shower together?"

I flushed, but gathered my clothes. "I have to get to work, and I didn't bring any of my things with me. I should probably just head home and shower there."

Levi's cheeky smile slipped slightly, and he left the room, closing the door behind him, leaving me alone to dress, and to wonder whether I'd just said something terribly wrong.

LEVI

I didn't know what had put me in such a fucking bad mood. Was it the constant reminders that both my career and my personal life were a steaming pile of shit? That I was now reliant on a reserve rower, who annoyed the living shit out of me, to get through to Paris? Or the fact that if I wanted to be a hands-on dad, that meant having contact with Emilee when that was the absolute last thing I wanted?

Or the fact that there was no fucking way on earth that anything more than mind-blowing sex with an expiry date was on the cards for Amanda and me. If she was sane, she'd run a goddamned mile.

If I were in her shoes, I'd run a fucking marathon to get away from my shitshow.

I changed into swimwear and went for a run on the beach, throwing myself into the waves at the end to cool off. I grabbed a bacon and egg roll at the burger joint we'd had lunch at—shit, had that only been just over a week ago? I had too much going on in my life.

I smashed my breakfast down on the walk home, and while I boiled the kettle for a cup of tea, I stared at my phone, tossing up whether to send a text to Theo. Not knowing what the fuck to say. Was he out of hospital yet? How had his surgery gone? What were the doctor's saying about his recovery? Or was it too early to know? Was he going to be pissed at me for competing with Mac? I had a billion fucking questions, and none of them felt right to ask.

So, I didn't text him. I decided I'd wait and find out what Patto had to say tomorrow first. Theo couldn't possibly feel shittier than I did about having to team up with Macintosh Fucking Graham.

Taking a slurp of tea, I checked my emails. Holy shit. My inbox had sixty unread messages. Modelling agencies begging to have me on their books. Ripley Eyewear wanting to sponsor me personally, cash and product, could I get back to them to organise a time to come in and sign a contract asap? Same with Christian Kane, asking me to be the face of their new fragrance, 'Utopia', and Amphibian Watches, who wanted to partner with me to launch their 'Ocean to Evening' range.

And then dozens from newspapers, magazines, podcasters and TV news breakfast shows, wanting to interview me.

And every fucking email started with some version of, "We were blown away by your heroic act of strength and sportsmanship at the Australian Rowing Championships …"

I didn't know how the fuck to respond to any of those enquiries, so I just ignored them for the time being. But, out of morbid curiosity, I opened Instagram—something I'd barely done since Zilla and I broke up.

If I'd thought my emails were a goddamned circus, social media was even worse. I'd been tagged in over five thousand posts, all showing aerial footage of the race. I hadn't watched it until now, but the way Theo's entire body spasmed as he dropped his oars sent chills down my spine.

#rowinghero was trending, as was *#athleteoftheyear*.

And then I got far enough down my notifications to the first posts that happened just after the footage would have dropped on the news. And there she was.

Emily Moon: OMG you guys, that's #mybabydaddy right there, winning #gold with a critically injured teammate. If my ovaries hadn't already given it up for him, they would be right now! #moonfoxbaby #ovariesexploding #levifox #rowinghero #athleteoftheyear

My gut churned so hard that I almost threw up all over my phone. I swallowed back the bile and sipped at my lukewarm tea, hoping it would wash the bitterness from my mouth. What I wanted to do was call Zilla and ream her out for that utter bullshit, for capitalising on Theo's injury. For using that fucking 'Moon-Fox Baby' hashtag when I'd told her not to. For making it sound like we'd somehow planned this pregnancy, that we were still a fucking couple.

I didn't want to act like a hero just for getting to the end of a fucking race. I didn't want to take credit for the gold medal, when we only managed it because Theo had pushed so hard that he'd torn his pec tendon to get us the lead we'd had.

I didn't want to sit there and force a fake laugh with vapid breakfast talk show clowns, or anyone else who wanted a piece of this story.

I went back to my emails, and I deleted every single one asking for interviews. And then I responded to all the ones that were offering me a pay day.

I had a baby to support … and a father to prove wrong.

I hadn't even gotten out of my car properly before he was on me.

"Levi!"

I climbed out, slamming the door and heading for the boot to get my gear. "This is a fucking early start for you, Dad," I muttered, slinging the bag over my shoulder and heading towards the clubhouse.

He didn't reply, but he fell into step beside me. My skin crawled—I hated being this close to him.

"How's Theo?" Dad asked as I reached the door to the clubhouse and stopped. There was no way I was going inside, because he'd only follow me, and standing at the front door was already further than I wanted him to go.

"No idea," I said. "I've got to get to training." I turned for the door.

"What's the point, son?"

I froze, my hand on the doorknob. "Did you seriously just fucking ask that?" I said, my fingers clenching into a fist around the handle. "Worlds are in six months, and it's an Olympic qualifier year. That's the point."

"You've got no partner. What's your plan? To re-train for singles? At what point do you recognise that you've been pursuing a dead end. This stupid obsession was starting to look desperate and pathetic years ago. You're almost thirty, for crying out loud! If you do the right thing now, there's still time to head to uni, get a real qualification. Actually make some decent money, so you're not driving around in a second-hand car, barely scraping by to pay rent on a unit you can't even live in because you gave it to your pregnant ex-girlfriend."

Every word was like a fucking cheese grater on my spine, but I let him say his piece. Sometimes it was just easier to let his ranting peter out on its own.

"I'll take that under advisement, Dad."

"You're never winning Olympic Gold now, without Theo to prop you up."

My jaw clenched.

"Well, we don't know that yet, do we Levi?" another voice piped up from behind Dad. He turned, and there was Mac, smiling that 'I'm goddamned sunshine all the fucking time' smile.

I didn't groan, because I didn't want to give Dad any more

fodder to bang on about my wasted life. If he knew how much I disliked Mac, that'd just be one more reason I was a stubborn fuck-up.

"Who are you?" Dad asked, and Mac approached, his own gear bag in one hand, the other held out for Dad to shake. His smile didn't falter, even though the tension was so thick I could've choked on it.

How he put that face on I didn't know.

"I'm Mac Graham—I'm one of the reserves here. Levi and I will be training together for the WRCs. And I feel pretty confident that we have a great chance of qualifying for Paris, wouldn't you agree, Levi?"

I grunted, because I was nowhere near as sure as Mac seemed to be. I just wanted Dad to fuck off, I wanted to talk to Patto, find out how Theo was doing. I wanted to get out on the water and lose myself in the rhythm of the strokes. Even if I had to do it with fucking Mac in the shell with me.

Dad glanced between Mac and me, eyes narrowed. He turned back to me, leaning close.

"I'm going to give you one chance, Levi. If you don't qualify for the Olympics, you give this pie in the sky dream of yours up. You enrol in a degree. I don't even care at this point what it is, as long as it's something you can walk out of with a job. I'll pay all your uni fees. I'll even pay you for rent and board with your brother. But this is a one-time only offer. You turn it down, you continue with all this —" he gestured to the building, to the river behind, "—this bullshit, and you'll get nothing out of me. Not a single red cent. Are we clear?"

"Crystal," I snarled. "But it's a moot point, Dad. Because I'm … we're," I pointed to Mac, who stood to the side, pretending the conversation wasn't happening. "We are going to Paris. And you can take every single one of your red fucking cents and shove them right up your arse."

Dad straightened, his mouth tight. Without another word he turned and strode back towards his fancy fucking black Audi. I turned back to Mac.

"I don't particularly like you, Graham," I said. "I'd go as far as to say that you annoy the shit out of me more often than not. But you and I are going to fucking qualify for Paris if it's the last thing I do."

I turned and opened the door, holding it for Mac to walk through.

"I'm hearing you loud and clear, Levi. And for the record … I get it."

He headed off for the change rooms, leaving me wondering what the fuck he supposedly 'got'.

CHAPTER TWENTY-ONE

A Complicated Unicorn

AMANDA

"I hope it's not so fucking weird this time," Levi grunted as he slipped into his clothes in my dark bedroom.

"What's that?" I mumbled sleepily, wincing up at him.

"The whole, 'we don't know each other, we're just two strangers who happen to see each other once a month for my ex-girlfriend's pregnancy check-ups'."

"It's sort of necessary though, it would be so—"

"Yes, un-fucking-professional. I get it, Honey. I really do. I don't care that we have to do it, but I'm a shit actor."

I chuckled roughly. "I don't know, that transition reel you did on Instagram for that ocean-to-evening watch, where you come out of the waves all dripping and shirtless, and then next second you're in a tuxedo sipping a glass of Scotch at a fancy bar—that was an Oscar-worthy performance."

"Smart arse," he grumbled, then leaned down and planted a kiss to my cheek. "I'll see you at midday."

"Today you can find out the baby's sex, remember?"

Levi's low growl echoed around the room long after he'd left for training. We were so practiced at the dance we'd been doing for almost two months now. We got home from work, ate dinner together, either at his house or mine. We had very good sex, we spooned in our sleep. We got up, went about our days.

If I asked him how things were going with Mac, I got an, "Okay." I left it at that, although I was sure 'okay' meant that things were a real struggle between the two. I didn't want to push him to talk about it. He didn't mind discussing the other work he'd been taking on—brand ambassadorships and modelling—topics that didn't require either of us to put our tightly held cards on the table.

On the surface it was simple. Underneath … the undercurrents of everything we didn't discuss were tossing about in my brain.

We hadn't talked about the baby since I'd told him he should continue to attend appointments with Emilee. The appointments were just another dance, one of us being polite strangers in the clinic. We'd only had to do it once so far, but as Emilee's pregnancy progressed, those appointments would get closer and closer together. And as her belly grew, so too would the elephant in the room. And it would become impossible to ignore the fact that any future I might imagine with Levi wasn't just the two of us. It was another tiny being too … and that tiny being's mother.

There was absolutely no way I was getting any more sleep. I got up, grabbed my bed socks from the floor and padded out to the kitchen. The sky was still dark. I huffed out a laugh, remembering how I'd assumed Levi wasn't a morning person, that first 'morning after'. Turned out, he just had to get up before five a.m. every day except Sunday to train at the crack of dawn. He earned that Sunday sleep in.

"You're up early," Alison said with a yawn, walking into the kitchen and stretching.

"I couldn't get back to sleep after Levi left," I admitted, putting on the kettle.

"Things getting serious between you two?" she asked, grabbing a pod for her coffee machine.

"Still just having fun," I replied, as breezily as I could manage. I wasn't quite ready to admit out loud to the seeds of doubt burrowed deep in the back of my mind. Voicing them would make them all too real.

Alison shot me a look from the corner of her eye that told me she didn't believe me for a millisecond. "So … hypothetically, if Levi decided that he wanted to 'have fun' with another woman while you and he were also 'having fun' … how would you feel about that?" she asked.

My stomach roiled at the thought. I tried to ignore it by focusing on making my tea. "People can just have fun, and still be monogamous," I eventually said. "I mean, if I wanted to sleep with another guy, I'd talk to Levi about it, end things first. I feel like he's the kind of guy who would do the same."

"Yes, but you're *not* thinking about other guys, are you?"

"Do you think he's thinking about other girls?" The words came out before I could call them back, and Alison must have noted the distress in my tone, because next minute she was wrapping an arm around me.

"Oh, sweetie, of course not. I was just trying to make a point that you're in this deeper than you're admitting. Besides, if the sounds you guys make on the nights you sleep here are anything to go by, he's got nothing left for anyone else. You're literally stealing every single one of his boners."

"That's … creepily reassuring," I muttered with a watery laugh.

"So …" Alison began, keeping one arm around me as she pressed buttons on her coffee machine and the kitchen filled with the bitter scent of espresso. "I'm going to go out on a limb here and guess that you guys haven't had the 'what happens when the baby comes' chat."

I almost choked on my tea. "That's … we've been hanging out for seven weeks for crying out loud! We're not even close to a place where that would be a discussion either of us would initiate!"

Lie. That exact question was on a constant loop in the anxiety-riddled part of my brain.

"Whatever you say," Alison said, making it clear she thought I was completely full of crap. "But, just out of curiosity, if he said to you tomorrow, 'Amanda, Honey'," she put on a terrible impersonation of Levi's voice, "'I want you to be the stepmother to my accidental baby with my evil ex'… what would your response be?"

I gaped at her. "I … I would probably say, let's just see where we are in another five months when that baby is due."

Alison raised a disbelieving eyebrow at me, but thankfully she dropped the subject.

"So, is the sex as good as it sounds?" she asked instead, flustering me for a completely different reason. "Or are you just a really enthusiastic faker?"

"Oh my God!" I groaned, before taking another sip of tea to try and hide the blush staining my cheeks. "I'm not going to answer that!"

Alison chortled. "Yes, you are! Because now you have to defend his honour! Seriously, Manda, if you don't tell me, I'm going to assume he's shit, and you scream and moan the way you do just so that he'll finish, and you can get a break!"

Well, there was absolutely no way I could have her assuming that about Levi.

"It's all real," I said in a low voice. "It's like he has a … a magic penis."

Alison guffawed, then saw how serious I was. "Oh my God, you actually mean that, don't you?"

I nodded, red-faced, but warming to the idea of being able to confide in her about how good the sex part of what Levi and I had together was. Even if the other stuff was confusing as hell.

"But he also … we mostly don't even get to sex until he's made me come at least once."

Alison fanned herself. "Are you telling me that he gets you off once, *or more*, before he even puts his dick in you?" I nodded.

"Jesus, you've got yourself a unicorn! He must have some grade A oral game!" she sighed. "I need to know details, please."

If I could have gotten redder in the face, I would have. "I … um … I don't … we haven't …" Alison's brows drew together as I stuttered.

"Are you saying that he's never gone down on you? Shit, please don't tell me he's one of *those* guys!"

"One of what guys?" I asked, but the sinking sensation in my stomach told me that I knew exactly what type of guy she was talking about. I'd had firsthand experience with one of them.

"You know, the ones who happily accept a blow job, but when it's time to reciprocate, they come up with some utter bullshit excuse why they can't eat you out. You know, they'll say something like …" she paused, thinking.

"Like, 'your thighs are so big, I'm worried I might suffocate between them," I mumbled. Alison looked at me sharply.

"Tell me he did not seriously fucking say that to you!" she snarled.

I shook my head. "Not Levi … Thomas," I barely whispered. Alison enveloped me in a huge hug, no mean feat for such a teeny person. I quickly put my tea down on the counter so it didn't spill, and sank into the comfort of her embrace.

"That arsehole! Jail isn't bad enough for him! I'm guessing this is the reason why you haven't let Levi down there?"

I nodded, screwing up my face, hoping that I wouldn't cry. I'd shed enough tears for that creep over the last two years. More than he deserved.

"And I haven't offered to … for him, either. Because he's the kind of guy who wouldn't let a blow job go unreciprocated …" I coughed around the lump in my throat.

"Of course he is. He's a fucking unicorn. My God, Levi is a complicated guy, isn't he?"

I nodded again. "And the worst part is," I said, then let out a weird half laugh, half sob, "he has such a nice-looking penis, I really want it in my mouth!"

Alison laughed as she hugged me tighter. "Then that's the new goal. Let's set aside worrying about what's going to happen when that skank ex of his pops, and instead work towards you getting a taste of that unicorn penis."

This new goal definitely seemed more attainable than the other. Just as long as I could work out a way to ensure he wouldn't try to return the favour. That was a conversation I just didn't want to have with him.

Why did I have to blush so easily?

The second I walked out into the waiting room to call Emilee in for her appointment, and saw Levi sitting there, his light-filled eyes raking over me knowingly, his lips tweaking up on the same side as his scarred eyebrow, heat crept up my neck to my face.

Was he trying to get a rise out of me? If so, it was working. I cleared my throat.

"Come on in, Emilee. You too," I made a show of looking down at her folder, as if I was double checking I had his name right, "Levi."

Emilee sighed dramatically and flounced into Beth's room. Her belly was just starting to show, and today she was wearing a stretchy knee-length dress that emphasised her adorable little bump. I wondered if there was a post of her in that dress on Instagram today. I wondered if some maternity brand was paying her to wear it.

As Beth asked Emilee all the standard questions about her general health, I checked Emilee's blood pressure. Levi's eyes followed me. He watched avidly as I strapped the blood pressure cuff around Emilee's arm, as I popped the stethoscope buds into my ears. I tried not to feel hot and bothered by it … and failed utterly.

I grabbed a tape measure, waiting for Beth to finish her review. When they stopped talking, Beth nodded to me. Emilee sighed and turned in my direction. Levi, of course, was already looking at me.

"What now?" Emilee huffed. Beth made a tiny noise that sounded suspiciously like a snort, which she quickly covered up with a sneeze.

"You're at twenty weeks now, so we need to start taking a fundal height measurement. It helps us to track the baby's growth."

"Isn't that what an ultrasound does?" Emilee asked, folding her arms and resting them on her rounding belly.

I nodded. "It is, but it's always best to measure in a variety of ways. Ultrasounds can sometimes be misleading when it comes to baby size, but if for instance you were showing ahead or behind on both an ultrasound and on fundal height, it's a good indication that we need to monitor you accordingly."

I went and stood by the door. "We need to take the measurement on an empty bladder, so if you want to duck out and wee for me, please Emilee?"

She got up and shoved past me. Levi's eyes burned into me as I busied myself, fluffing up the pillow on the vinyl bed, and a low sound rumbled from his throat. I paused, realising I was leaning over the bed, my backside pointing directly at him in my very fitted scrubs.

"You sound so fucking knowledgeable," he said, voice raspy. I turned back to him, a pleasant 'you're a stranger but I'm at work so I'll be friendly' smile on my face. I almost swallowed my tongue to see him scrubbing his hand over his mouth, as if he was barely containing himself from pushing me up against the bed and dragging my scrubs down just enough to get inside me.

Hot and bothered, I threw him a quick warning glare, and replied mildly, "Thanks, I've studied hard." Then, with a sudden, quite uncharacteristic desire to flirt, I added, "*Very* hard."

Beth's eyes snapped between Levi and me, and I knew then I'd made a mistake. So much for being the one who constantly insisted on professionalism. One heated look from Levi and I was throwing it all out the window. His eyes darkened as I bit my bottom lip—a warning that it belonged to him.

Ping!

Levi glanced down to where Emilee had left her phone and car keys on the chair, rolling his eyes.

Ping! Ping! Ping!

My God, how popular was she? I guessed with almost a million followers she got her fair share of DMs.

The door opened and Emilee slipped back in. *Ping! Ping! Ping! Ping!* Emilee practically dove for her phone, snatching it up and tapping frantically at the screen, catching her bottom lip between her teeth. I knew that when I did that, I never looked even a scrap as sexy as she did. My stomach flipped.

"Instagram emergency?" Levi asked while Emilee giggled as she typed. She glanced up at him, as if she was only just realising that she was in the middle of a prenatal appointment, and three other people were in the room with her.

"Did you seriously check my phone?" she retorted, swiping and tapping frantically at the screen.

Levi huffed. "No, but it was kind of fucking hard for us all to ignore it constantly going off. Do you need a minute to respond to your rabid fans?"

Emilee rolled her eyes, "It's just this one random weirdo, okay? He keeps sliding into my DMs."

Levi huffed out a sarcastic laugh. "I'll bet you fucking *hate* that, don't you?"

"Jesus Christ, Levi! You think I enjoy having a stalker?" Emilee turned her sly eyes to me, a smirk pinching her mouth. "Amanda knows *all* about how much fun stalkers are, don't you hun?"

My windpipe clenched and I coughed at her words. *She knows about Thomas.* Turning away from her I glanced wide-eyed at Beth, who pursed her lips and stood up.

"Okay, please save domestic situations for after the appointment. Emilee, hop up on the bed and pull your dress up so your belly is exposed. Amanda will take your fundal height measurement and then you can head back to the waiting room until Doctor Bentley is ready for you.

With shaking hands, I stretched the tape measure over Emilee's belly, reading out the measurement to Beth. Emilee hopped up, wiggling her bum suggestively in Levi's direction as she tugged her tight dress back into position over the tiny black G-string she was wearing. I glanced sidelong at Levi, but he hadn't even spared her pert bottom a glance. He was staring at the floor like it held all the secrets of the universe.

When Beth opened the door, Levi leapt out of his chair and was gone before Emilee even got out of her chair. She flicked me a smile that didn't touch her eyes and followed him.

"I don't want details, Amanda," Beth said, quietly but firmly. "But I will say one thing … just be careful. He might be single, and he might look at you with hungry eyes, but those two clearly have a lot of history, and a very volatile relationship. Don't risk your professional career for someone like that."

She walked out of the room, leaving me frozen, nausea swirling through my chest.

CHAPTER TWENTY-TWO

Envy

LEVI

"Okay, so I have a shortlist of names picked out. It's going to be either Destinee, Fayte, or—"

"Lily," I muttered, rubbing at my tattooed shoulder. A daughter. I was going to have a daughter. When the doctor had said the words, "That's a little girl in there," it was like a fucking bolt of electricity shot me straight in the chest. I didn't believe in God, or Heaven, or any of that bullshit, but for a split second, it'd felt like some higher power was sending me a message.

Zilla scoffed at me. "There's no way I'm naming our baby something as common as Lily!" she snapped. "I don't care how special the name is to you. There'll be five other kids in her class with the same name. I want our little girl to have a name no one else would ever have."

"You want a name so fucking terrible that no one in their right mind would ever choose it," I said under my breath. She didn't hear me, because she was too busy gasping.

"Oh, I've got it, Levi! Emvi!"

I gaped down at her. "You want to name our daughter Envy? What the actual fuck?"

"No, idiot! EM-vee. Like Em, the first two letters in Emilee, and V.I., pronounced vee, the last two letters in Levi."

"Do I get a veto?" I asked, but I already knew what the answer would be.

"I have to push this baby out of me, I get final say. Emvi. I *love* it. So unique. I'm gonna post about it now."

I snatched her phone out of her hand. "Sleep on it before you go around announcing our unborn child's name to strangers on the Internet, okay?" I growled. She shot me a look of malice and snatched her phone back.

"Okay, Levi, if it'll keep you from getting your fucking underwear in a knot, I'll leave it until tomorrow." She went to walk off to her car. I wrapped my fingers around her elbow, turning her back to me.

"I think you should hold off on posting any shit about her. If that arsehole who keeps DMing you really is a stalker, do you want to be giving him personal details about our baby? I feel like I should have a say in this shit too, and I am not okay with randos on the Internet knowing all about her!"

"You jealous, Levi?" she snarled. "Did you try to read my DMs?"

I suppressed the urge to strangle her. "Your phone was going off like crazy, I glanced down, that's all. But you're saying he's a stalker, and you want to advertise intimate details of our child for thousands of people to see, including this freak?"

She wrenched her arm out of my grip, rubbing at the spot where I'd held her, bottom lip trembling. I fell back a step.

"Fuck, I'm sorry, Em," I mumbled, pumping my fists by my sides.

"Do you want me to lose my income, Levi?" she asked shakily. "Because I've got agreements with a huge babywear brand, a skincare brand and a cloth nappy brand, and that's going to require me to post photos of her. Those deals are worth tens of thousands of dollars to me."

Shit.

"Of course I fucking don't Emilee," I sighed, rubbing my forehead. "What about a compromise. First, we don't decide on a name until closer to the birth. And second, you can post photos of her, but let's give her a nickname on socials—real name is for family and friends only."

Zilla flicked her hair over her shoulder. "Whatever makes you feel better," she said, like I was the one being ridiculous. "You can pick whatever nickname you want for me to use on socials. But her real name will be Emvi; it's a done deal, Levi."

She was just too fucking ridiculous to argue with at that point.

"See you in a month," she said, turning towards her car. It was only then I remembered that there was something I had wanted to ask her, before she'd side-tracked me with all the ridiculous talk of 'unique' baby names.

"Hey, Em!" I called out. She turned, shielding her eyes from the sun. "Why'd you say that the midwife in there would know all about stalkers?"

Zilla's face instantly transformed from morose to sly, and I realised I'd been fucking played by her crocodile tears. Again.

"Oh, Levi. I always do a background check on anyone who's a chance of getting up close and personal with my vag. And that fat cow's search results were insane! You should take a look, if you want a good laugh. Google Amanda McGregor."

Fury misted my vision. Clenching my jaw, I forced myself not to lose my shit at the fake bitch as she turned and flounced off to her car. How fucking dare she speak about Amanda like that? I wanted to rage at her, tell her that Amanda's curvy arse and beautiful, soft tits, and those smooth, creamy thighs of hers got me hard just thinking about them. I wanted to roar to the skies how everything about Amanda was so much more fucking arousing than bony hips and tits that felt like overfilled water-balloons.

Hell, I wanted to wax lyrical about how Amanda was smart, and kind, and sweet, and playful, and fun and … and fucking *everything*. The only thing that stopped me was knowing that Amanda wouldn't want me to say anything. She didn't want anyone at her work to know about us.

I stood in the parking lot for a long while after Zilla left, struggling to get the rage under control. There was no fucking way I was going to Google Amanda. There was no way that whatever came up was anything I needed to know about, unless Amanda decided to tell me herself. But shit, I knew it was going to fester away in the back of my brain now.

My phone vibrated with a message, and I looked down, hoping it would be Amanda. It wasn't.

> Mac: I'm going to visit Theo this arvo. Want to join me?

Fuck no, I thought, and then instantly felt like a piece of shit. I hadn't seen Theo since they'd pulled him out of the water in Perth. I'd texted a couple of times, asking how he was. I got single word answers.

> Theo: Shit

> Theo: Fucked

> Theo: Screwed

I never knew how to respond to them, so I hadn't. But I knew I couldn't avoid him forever. And having Mac there as a buffer might make things a bit less fucking awkward. Even if after seven weeks of far too much Mac time I was burning out from his constant fucking sunshine. No one could be that happy all the time, could they?

> Me: Yeah, okay. I'll meet you there in an hour

"Well, you two look cosy!" Theo sneered as we sat down in the living room of his parents' house. I hadn't been in this house since the graduation party Theo had hosted at the end of high school. Eleven fucking years ago.

The house hadn't changed one bit. It was a typical upper-crust

North Shore home—modern, light-filled and minimalist. Photo-shoot ready at all times. Theo's parents had a full-time housekeeper, even though they were empty-nesters, and it wasn't like they made a lot of mess. But with Theo staying with them while he recovered, the housekeeper probably had her work cut out for her—he'd never been the tidiest guy.

Ingrid, Theo's mum, brought us all glasses of fresh home-made lemonade. Theo, whose arm was still in a sling, glared at her until she handed his cup to him so he wouldn't have to struggle lifting it off the table.

"My meds," he grunted, which sent Ingrid scuttling off to the kitchen. I watched her go, frowning. Theo had always been babied by his parents. It had never bothered me before, but his attitude to his mum pissed me right off.

"How's the new dream-team shaping up for the Olympic quali-fiers?" Theo asked, his voice bitter. Ingrid hurried back and dropped a couple of pills into Theo's hand. He tossed them into his mouth and downed them with a long slug of the lemonade.

"I think we're making progress, don't you, Levi?" Mac answered, sitting very straight on the lounge and taking a sip of his lemonade. I stared down into the yellow liquid.

"Yep, progress is happening," I agreed.

Theo snorted. "You don't sound too convinced there, Levi."

I looked up at him, raised one eyebrow. "It's an … adjustment," I managed. "Things on the water are going okay." Mac wasn't as strong a rower as Theo, maybe he never would be. But he wasn't nursing an injury, something that Theo had been attempting to hide for fucking months even before Perth. The rest we were working on.

"It's just all the shit off the water that's driving you nuts, isn't it, Fox?" Theo said with a dark chuckle. "Having to spend time with Mac when you hate every fucking thing about him."

Ingrid gasped into the silence that followed Theo's words. I glanced over at Mac, who shrugged, a half-smile plastered over his face as he took another sip of lemonade.

What the fuck was Theo's problem? Sure, I'd told Mac at the start that he wasn't my favourite person, but we'd sort of reached an uneasy truce. Well, it felt uneasy for me—for Mac everything always seemed to be sunshine and fucking rainbows.

"I don't know Mac well enough to hate everything about him," I replied through gritted teeth. "I just want to focus on getting through the next few months, getting to Serbia, and getting the job done there."

"That's the goal!" Mac chipped in. "I might not be as good as you, Theo, but I'm going to do my best to give Levi a red-hot go at making the Olympics again."

My lips twisted, along with something in my chest at how fucking selfless Mac acted.

Theo glared between the two of us. "You're wasting your time, Levi," he growled. "You would've been better off retraining for singles at this rate … but even that you probably would have fucked up too."

Everything went still. I pressed my lips together so tight because I was worried what would come out of my mouth if I didn't. I took a deep breath and stood up. My control slipped as I headed for the door. "You know who you sound like?"

Theo grunted sarcastically behind me, and I didn't bother to elaborate. He knew he sounded like my dad, and he didn't give a fuck.

"I'm so sorry, Levi!" Ingrid said, following me out onto the driveway. "He's not in a good place, mentally, right now. He's in pain, and he can't see a light at the end of the tunnel. And he feels like he let you down. Not to mention he's envious of you and Mac, heading off to Worlds without him."

"I get it," I muttered, taking my key fob out of my pocket and unlocking my car. "I really do. But I can't deal with that shit from him right now. I'm not in the best place mentally either."

Fuck. That was the first time I'd admitted it out loud. And now that it was out there, I had no clue what to do with it. Ingrid gave me a pitying look, which made me want to punch a dent in my car, squeezing my hand before returning to the house.

I climbed into my car, starting the engine, but I didn't drive away. I stared at the steering wheel. As much as Mac drove me close to fucking insane with his always-on positivity, Theo's shit in there had hit home for me that the two of us—Theo and I—had always had the potential to be emo together.

"You okay, mate?" Mac asked, opening the passenger door and sticking his head inside. I gripped the steering wheel until my knuckles went white.

"Yep, fucking fantastic," I muttered. "I'll see you at training tomorrow."

Mac watched me for a long moment, instead of getting the fuck out of my car.

"You know, Levi, you can always—"

"I'll see you tomorrow!" I grated. Mac nodded, as if that was exactly what he'd expected, and closed the door. I didn't wait around another second. I sped off down the road.

CHAPTER TWENTY-THREE

My Friend Amanda

LEVI

> Levi: Come straight to my place after work. Keep your scrubs on. I haven't been able to think about anything else but your arse in them all fucking afternoon

I grabbed a beer out of the fridge, feeling a tiny twinge of guilt about my little lie to Amanda. Sure, I'd thought about her arse—it was always on my mind—but I'd had so much else in my brain all afternoon that my head felt like it was about to spin off.

I needed her. I needed to lose myself in that sexy, curvy body of hers. I needed to have her screaming and moaning in my ear, I needed to slide my dick along her wet pussy the way she really fucking loved.

Hell, I needed more than anything to bury my face between her sweet thighs and lick an orgasm out of her … but the one time I'd tried to kiss lower than her tits she'd frozen, begged me to finger her instead.

I figured she didn't like oral. Some girls weren't into it, I got that. But I was really good at it, and I really, *really* fucking enjoyed doing it. I wondered if the asshole whose dick she'd touched in the past had been shit at going down on her, and had ruined her for oral for life.

The doorbell rang and I put my beer down.

"Hey." Her sweet, sexy voice echoed down the hallway as I approached. She looked worried. I didn't want to think about why that might be. Had what Zilla said to her earlier struck a nerve? I'd managed to avoid Googling her, but only fucking just. Twice I'd had my phone out opening the browser before I came to my senses.

"Hi, Honey," I said, my voice low. I opened the door, and as I eyed her up and down in those scrubs, I shot hard as a poker. I didn't move aside, and as she tried to squeeze past me in the narrow hallway, I snapped.

Pinning her to the wall, I took her mouth, forcing her lips apart and licking deep inside. She moaned, her body melting against mine, her hands gripping the back of my neck, nails clawing into my skin.

"Everything about you makes me so fucking hard," I murmured against her mouth, grinding my hips against hers so she'd feel my boner. I turned her, walking her backwards towards the kitchen. "Those fucking scrubs, I couldn't stop staring at your arse in the appointment today."

"I noticed," she whispered against my stubble. "We need to be more careful."

"Not right now we don't!" I growled. "I'm going to fuck you so fucking uncarefully right now."

"I don't think uncarefully is a word," she said, squeaking when I spanked her arse. "What about Xander? Is he home?"

I shook my head. "He does after hours appointments on Tuesdays. Don't worry, no one is here to witness me screwing you into oblivion. Now, tell me you want me to fuck you on the kitchen bench."

"What?" she asked breathlessly, as I pressed my thigh between hers, grinding it against her pussy.

"Say, 'Levi, I want you to fuck me—uncarefully—on the kitchen bench.'"

She licked into my mouth, rubbing her pussy against my thigh until I was groaning on her tongue.

"I want that—even the uncarefully part," she mumbled between presses of her lips to my jaw.

We reached the kitchen island and I turned her, bent her, pressed her chest down against the cold stone, until she was on the tips of her toes, that arse right where I wanted it. I stood back and just admired the view for a second, letting the anticipation of dragging her pants and underwear down just enough that I could slide along that wet pussy of hers … into that wet pussy of hers.

"Levi, what are—"

"Be quiet. I'm looking at my fucking muse."

She wriggled her butt, trying to get better traction on the floor. Jesus fuck. I dragged my dick out of my shorts and gave it a few quick pumps, stepping closer and stroking a hand over the curves of her arse, then cupping the heat between her legs. She rocked back onto me.

"So fucking responsive, Honey," I groaned, stroking myself slowly. "You're going to be ready for me, aren't you?"

"Yes," she breathed, sliding her arms along the stone until she was gripping the other side of the counter.

I slid my fingers up under her top, just far enough that I could grip the waistbands of her scrubs and her underwear. I dragged them down just past the curve of her arse, so her legs were still pinned close together. With one finger, I traced the crease of her arse, all the way from the small of her back, down to where it met the slippery heat of her pussy.

She bucked back against my finger until I was coated with her arousal.

"Fuck me, you really are ready," I grated, bringing that finger to my mouth and sucking it. My eyes rolled back. I wanted to eat her pussy so fucking badly. Maybe I'd have to tie her to my bed to stop her from escaping just so I could do it.

That thought made my dick jerk, and I gripped it, sliding just the head against her entrance.

"Oh!" she cried, her fingers clawing at the counter. "I can feel the metal of your piercing!"

"You could feel it inside of you," I suggested, circling her entrance with the head of my cock. "I promise it would feel so fucking good."

Amanda panted against the counter, her arse jiggling. I gave it a light slap, pulling a sharp cry from her.

"Put it in, Levi!" she begged. "Just don't come in me like that."

"Are you fucking serious?" I choked out. She turned her head so I could see her face, nodding.

"Just for a minute, and then you can put a condom on. Okay?"

"Fucking yes, that's okay!" I gritted, rubbing my dick along her pussy until it was wedged between her pinned legs, the head rubbing on her clit. I pumped my hips a few times, grinding it over her sensitive nerves. Her panting got louder, hoarser.

"Are you sure?" I whispered, stroking my hands across the soft exposed skin of her arse.

"Levi," she said, her voice sharp. "I want you to fuck me with your bare penis, just for a minute. I want us both to feel that together."

I closed my eyes for a second, willing my balls to stop tightening before I even got inside her.

Seven, fourteen, twenty-one, twenty-eight, thirty-five, forty-two …

"Christ," I cursed, pulling back and finding her entrance again, lining myself up, and pushing into her. She gasped, and I moaned.

"So fucking tight this way, Honey!"

I pumped in and out, her wetness coating my dick. The sight of it, glistening on my bare skin each time I withdrew, had my balls drawing up again. I'd never been naked inside a woman before, and fuck me, it was heaven.

It might have also had something to do with the fact that she was so fucking beautiful, so goddamned sexy. I wasn't going to last if I kept this up. I pulled out of her, and she cried out in disappointment. I replaced my dick with my fingers, pumping them, curling them to stroke her G-spot, gripping a fistful of her arse as I fucked her with two fingers, then three. Fuck, she was so tight around them.

"Listening to you talk medical shit today made me so fucking horny, Amanda," I muttered, groaning at the wet sound my fingers made as they thrust into her. "You're so fucking smart, and so fucking sexy in these scrubs."

"Levi, oh my God!" she cried, her back arching as her pussy spasmed around my fingers. She went limp against the bench.

"I'm not finished with you yet," I warned her, pulling my hand away and tugging her pants down and off her legs entirely. I lifted her, turning her until her back was against the counter, her butt hanging just off the edge.

Her nipples were so hard they strained visibly through her shirt and bra. I pinched one, and her head thrashed as I reached into my pocket, pulling out a condom and quickly rolling it on.

Sliding my hands up the backs of her thighs, I lifted her legs until her ankles rested on my shoulders. Fuck, she looked divine, her ponytail half fallen out, her face misted with sweat from her orgasm. Staring up at me with that half-lidded starry-eyed look that told me she was so fucking pleased with me right now.

Well, I was about to please her some more. I lined myself up and thrust.

"Yes! Oh God, Levi," she mumbled, arms above her head, which made her tits push up towards me. I let my hands drop from her ankles to knead those fucking gorgeous mounds as I stroked inside her.

"Next time I do this, I'm going to plan it better so I can have your tits naked in my hands, so I can pinch and stroke these gorgeous nipples properly," I grunted as I thrust, bringing one hand between her legs, thumbing her clit and circling as I jacked my hips to meet hers.

"Please," she begged breathlessly, her legs quivering where they rested against my body. I pinched her clit, rolling it as she tightened, her pussy quivered, and pleasure shot down my spine, heat searing my balls and shooting along my dick as she squeezed around me, whimpering and sobbing out my name as I thrust into her one more time, and my orgasm ripped through me.

Panting, my hands dropped to the edge of the bench to hold my shaking legs up.

"Fuck, you make me come so hard!" I grunted, turning to press a kiss to her ankle before helping her move her limp legs off my chest. She lay there on the kitchen bench, panting and pants-less. And I fucking wanted her again.

I wanted her in every fucking way.

"Well, that was … unexpected," she mumbled as she sat up, slipping off the bench and looking around for her pants, which I'd tossed halfway across the room. They were draped over a lampshade.

"Unexpectedly fucking amazing, you mean," I chuckled, sauntering into the kitchen to dispose of the condom, as she went to retrieve her pants.

"Unexpectedly … dirty," she replied, but her voice sounded so satisfied that I took it as a compliment.

The front door rattled.

"Shit!" I grunted, adjusting my still semi-hard dick in my shorts. Amanda sucked in a breath, racing for her pants. She tugged them, but they were tangled, and instead of them coming loose, the whole fucking lamp came tumbling down with a crash.

"What's going on?" Xander's voice called from the hallway, getting closer. Amanda's horrified eyes met mine, and she ducked into a crouch behind the lounge chair, out of sight. I vaulted over the kitchen bench and untangled her pants from the lamp, tossing them to her.

"Levi," Dad's voice said. I froze halfway through lifting the lamp back to its original spot.

Fuck.

"Uh, I thought you had late appointments on Tuesdays," I said lamely, setting the lamp upright and moving to stand by the chair, trying my best to shield them from catching a glimpse of Amanda as she struggled back into her underwear and pants from the floor.

"I usually do, but I had a … different commitment today," Xander replied, and he looked away shiftily. I wondered what the fuck that was about for all of a split second before Dad interrupted.

"I'd like to know who the woman behind the chair is," he said in that haughty voice of his. I struggled not to grimace and glanced down at Amanda, who was dressed, although looking very fuck-rumpled.

She stood up, gave a wan smile and waved sheepishly. If they hadn't already figured out what we'd been up to, the look on her face gave the game up entirely.

"This is my … friend, Amanda," I said, not looking Dad in the eyes. "Amanda, this is Charles, my dad."

"Oh!" Amanda squeaked, then moved forwards, her smile turning bashful as she stretched her hand out to him. "It's lovely to meet you, uh … Mr Fox."

Dad didn't take her hand. His eyes raked her, taking in her crumpled scrubs, her mussed hair. Her kiss-stung lips. His ever-present fucking frown deepened.

"You a nurse, are you?" he sniffed. Amanda's smile faltered, and she dropped her hand to her side, wiping it on her pants.

"I am, yes," she replied, glancing my way before taking a deep breath to continue. Fuck. My eyes flicked to Xander's and he stepped forwards.

"Did you want that drink, Dad?" he interrupted smoothly. Dad gave Amanda the once-over again, before turning and ignoring her entirely.

I watched with a sick sense of satisfaction as Dad sat down at the kitchen island, resting his elbows right on the spot where we'd just fucked. I turned to Amanda, smirking, to find her wide-eyed, pale and looking like she was about to puke.

"Are you okay, Honey?" I murmured, low enough that Dad and Xander wouldn't hear. Her eyes flicked from Dad to me, and she shook her head, just slightly.

"I think I should go home."

"Oh, right," I muttered, but she'd already turned and fled down the hallway. I followed quickly, grabbing her hand before she opened the door. "What's wrong?"

She shook her head again, eyes on the floor. "Nothing … just a bit embarrassed, I guess. I don't think that was the best way for your dad to meet me."

If I had my way, she would never be subjected to the nasty old fuck.

"Can I come to yours later?" I asked, reaching out to stroke her cheek. She leaned into the touch for just a second before she shook her head.

"I just … I'm not going to be good company tonight," she mumbled.

I pinched her chin gently. "That makes two of us. So maybe we could be shitty company together?"

She blinked. "I'm pretty tired, Levi. Go, spend time with your dad. I'll talk to you tomorrow." She tugged on the handle and let herself out, slipping her feet into the shoes she'd left on the front porch. I watched in silence, feeling like I needed to say something … fucking anything, but nothing would come out.

I stood at the door for far too long after she'd driven away.

"Levi, you having a drink?" Xander called from the kitchen. I pinched the bridge of my nose, willing away the burning feeling in my sinuses, and stalked back to the living room.

"Nope. Training early tomorrow," I managed to grate out, collapsing into a chair with a huff.

"Since when has something important ever stopped you from having fun?" Dad muttered. Even with my eyes closed I could feel his glare like fucking icicles in my skin. "Oh, that's right, that rule only applies to the things that are important to *you*."

I stood up. "I'll be in my room."

"Running away when things get difficult, as always."

I spun on my heel and stared him down. "I'm working so fucking hard right now to do well at Worlds with a new teammate. I'm taking on extra work so that come October I'm in a position to support a baby I never expected to have, because I recognise it's my responsibility. Don't you dare fucking suggest that I run away when things get difficult."

I stormed down the hallway and crashed into my bedroom.

He'd be out there telling Xander that I still acted like a teenager, stomping off to my bedroom and slamming the door in a tantrum.

He was the worst tantrum thrower of them all, but he would never fucking acknowledge it.

I collapsed onto my bed, rubbing at the scar on my eyebrow, hating my life. I couldn't help but feel like I'd done something to piss Amanda off. I never did anything but piss Dad off. Theo had the shits with me, Zilla was … fucking Zilla, and still in my life.

"He's gone," Xander said from the door. I snapped awake.

"Jesus, how long …?" I asked groggily. Xander leant against the door jamb and crossed his arms.

"You've been in here over an hour. Mr Cranky Pants needed his little boy nap, did he?"

I stood up, scrubbing at my face. "Fuck you," I grouched, pushing past him and to the kitchen for water. "You know that Dad's bullshit fucking exhausts me."

"It exhausts me, too," Xander admitted.

"He thinks the sun shines out of your arse!" I argued before chugging a full glass of water. Xander eyed me incredulously.

"I walk on fucking eggshells, Lev. Mixed with broken glass. That's what it feels like to stay on his good side. It's no stroll in the park."

I sighed. "Yeah, I know. I don't want to fight with you about him. It's probably what he wants—to drive a wedge between us."

"Okay, so let's not talk about him. I'd like to address the elephant in the room, however."

I raised an eyebrow. "Oh, yeah?"

"You screwed her in the living room? Seriously? I have to watch TV in this room knowing you've fucked on my lounge."

I managed a smirk. "The kitchen bench, actually. Right where Dad sat."

Xander looked equal parts amused and disgusted. "Go and clean the bench down. I don't want to think about your sweaty balls anywhere near where I prepare food."

I huffed out a laugh and went to get the cloth and spray.

"She couldn't have gotten out of here fast enough," Xander commented. I stared at the bench as I sprayed cleaner over it.

"Yeah. Well, I think she was fucking mortified. I'd told her you worked late on Tuesdays. Where were you this arvo anyway? And with Dad?"

Xander cleared his throat. "I, uh, I'm considering a new opportunity. But I don't know if it's going to be my cup of tea. I took Dad along to look over the contract with me."

"What sort of new opportunity?" I asked.

"I can't talk about it. I had to sign an NDA."

I gaped at him. "What the fuck?"

He shrugged. "If I decide to go ahead, you'll find out what it's about soon enough." He slapped his knee. "Now, stop trying to distract me. I want to talk about Amanda. Lev, I think you upset her."

I turned away to put the spray back in the cupboard. "I know I upset her. I just don't know what I did to upset her."

Xander snorted. "Oh, I don't know, I think introducing her to Dad as your 'friend' might've had something to do with it."

I squeezed the cloth under the water, my knuckles going white. "I don't … I mean, we haven't had that conversation."

"Do you need to have that conversation? You've been sleeping over with each other for two months now," Xander reminded me.

"I don't want her to feel pressured. I'm a shit deal for any woman right now, let alone one like her. Up the duff ex girlfriend, can't even afford my own place, probably won't make it to the Olympics next year."

"I don't think she sees you the way you see yourself."

I sighed, draping the cloth over the drainer. "Besides that, I was caught off guard by Dad. The thought of introducing her to him … fuck, when she was about to tell him about her job …"

I glanced up at Xander who was as fucking pale as I felt. "Yeah. Close call. And it gets worse … he told me to remind you that Mum's birthday dinner is coming up in a couple of weeks, and his exact words were, "Tell Levi to bring his 'friend' with him."

Shit.

"I can't bring her. I don't want her anywhere near him."

"I'll prepare him in advance, so that it doesn't come up in conversation and take him by surprise," Xander offered. I nodded.

"I couldn't just not bring her, could I?" I mumbled, knowing exactly what Xander's answer would be.

"Well, if you want him to rant at you all evening about how you can't even get a girl to be serious enough to come to an important family event with you, then go right ahead."

Yep, his response was to the fucking letter exactly what I'd expected.

"How come he never rants at you about not having a girl-friend?" I asked.

"Probably because I've never had one. You on the other hand are always in a relationship. Even if you're not prepared to admit it to yourself … or to her."

Shit.

"What should I do about Amanda? I don't want her to feel like she has to put a label on this … but I also don't want her to think I'm just in it for the sex. It's … much more than that." I rubbed my aching forehead.

Xander stood up and walked in the direction of the bathroom. "I'd have a think about that overnight. Don't go banging on her door like a nutcase again—she'll start to think you're a stalker."

Stalker. I did not need to hear that word again today.

"Calm down, think it over, and talk to her tomorrow. That's my advice." Xander closed the bathroom door, and seconds later the shower was running.

I took my phone out, staring at the screen for a long time before typing out a message.

Levi: You okay Honey?

I waited for what felt like fucking forever, drank another full glass of water, turned on the TV to watch the news, before a reply buzzed.

> Amanda: Yeah, just tired. Big day at work today

> Levi: What happened at work today?

> Amanda: Well …

> Amanda: I got sexually harassed

What the fuck? I dialled her number.

"Hey," she answered warily.

"What the fuck do you mean, you got sexually harassed at work today?" I demanded. "Did Dr fucking Bentley put his hands on you? I'll rip his fucking dick off."

"No! God no, it wasn't Chris, he's very professional …"

Her words trailed off as I paced the lounge room floor, pent up rage heating my blood.

"It was one of the fathers," she mumbled eventually. "He was leering at me, and … and talking to me in a dirty way when he thought no one else could hear."

My nostrils flared, rage flooding me with heat. "Was it that guy sitting in the waiting room when I left? He looked like a fucking pervert. If he's in again next time, I'll explain to him what will happen if he so much as fucking blinks in your direction again."

Amanda giggled. "No, it wasn't him … it was the guy who came in before him, actually."

"Who the fuck was in before …" I stopped pacing, my angry heartrate slowly returning to normal as a smile pulled at my mouth. "Oh, yeah … him. Total creeper, that guy. He was definitely thinking about bending you over the examination table and fucking you until you screamed."

Another breathy laugh came through the phone, making my dick twitch. "I'm pretty sure he acted that fantasy out this evening. Gosh, you got a bit alpha male then, Levi."

My voice darkened. "Don't act like you didn't love it."

I could almost hear her cheeky eye-roll over the phone. "Goodnight, Danger Boy. I'll talk to you tomorrow, okay?"

"Okay," I agreed, so fucking relieved that she was happy enough to tease me. "Bye, Honey."

CHAPTER TWENTY-FOUR

Casual-Sex Friendship

AMANDA

"How are things with your male friend?" Gillian asked.

"It's funny you should use that word," I mumbled, winding the strap of my shoulder bag around my hand and unravelling it again. "Because we've been spending more nights together than apart for almost two months now, but he introduced me to his father the other day as his 'friend' Amanda."

Gillian watched my face. I wasn't going to cry about this. I felt kind of numb about it to be honest. Numb enough that when Levi had texted to check on me later that day, I'd teased and distracted him rather than bring it up.

"Do you feel like that definition is inadequate for the relationship you have?"

My finger got caught too tightly in the bag strap, and I shook it free with a hissed curse. "Well, I kind of feel like … maybe in my head at least, I'd been thinking of him as my boyfriend."

"Have you discussed this with him?"

I shook my head. "I know this is all my fault. I assumed, because, you know, two months of sleeping together exclusively—on my end at least—and I feel like I can't bring it up, because I don't want him to feel pressured, to call this something he's not ready for.

He has so much going on in his life. And that's not an excuse, I promise." I moved on to the zipper of my bag, zipping it open, then closed. "I don't know if a commitment is something he's really in the right place for at the moment."

"Well, if you feel like you're in that place, you do have a right to raise it with him, to work out where you both stand. Communication is the cornerstone of any healthy relationship, whether it's a romantic one, a sexual one, or a platonic one."

I nodded. "I know … I just … we haven't even really dated, you know? We met in a bar, we've been out to lunch once. Everything else has been at his house or mine. Mostly in the bedroom." I blushed, thinking about the kitchen bench. It had been so very sexy, until everything with his dad had sullied it.

"Is going out for dates something you want to do?" she asked. I found myself nodding before I'd really given it any thought. And then immediately realised that it was exactly what I wanted. Everything was backwards with us. Maybe 'dating' might bring some clarity to the situation. For both of us.

"So," Gillian continued, eyeing me squarely. "Ask him out. Go out for a nice meal together—somewhere you can spend time talking, that isn't in the bedroom." I blushed at her words, but if she noticed, she ignored it. "That will be a good start to working out where things are headed for the two of you. It doesn't have to begin with a frank conversation about the future, but moving things in a direction you would like to see them go, that's a healthy start."

I let out a shaky breath.

"How is the intimacy between you?" Gillian asked, catching me off-guard. Heat blossomed all over me.

"It's … um … it's very good."

"Has intimacy with him changed how you feel about your body?"

I stopped, thinking about that for a moment. "Uh … maybe a bit. I mean, to begin with, I couldn't handle him seeing me with the lights on. But he's seen it all now. I still don't want him touching my stomach or … or my inner thighs, but I can ignore the other feelings to a degree, when we're in the moment."

"What about at other times? Do you feel there are other things that trigger your dislike of your body?"

I chewed on my lips. "Sometimes I'll put a piece of clothing on, and somewhere in the back of my head I'll be thinking 'you can't go out in public looking like that'. Or … well, sometimes when I'm in bed with Levi after we've been intimate, that same part of my brain tells me that I can't lie a certain way or let him see me in a certain position or from a certain angle, because it will disgust him. I compare my appearance to … to his previous partner, and I wonder why he chose me after he had someone like her."

"So, there are intrusive thoughts around your body image."

I nodded. Zip … Unzip.

"A colleague of mine, who is both a talented photographer, and an experienced psychologist, has just started trialling a new therapy style. I think it's something you should consider doing."

She turned and leaned over to her desk, rummaging through some folders until she came up with a pamphlet. She handed it over to me. A woman, larger than me, posed candidly in red lingerie.

"Boudoir Photography as Therapy?" I read aloud, my incredulous gaze flicking up to Gillian. "You mean posing for sexy photos in my underwear is supposed to cure me of hating my body?"

Gillian's smile was patient. "It can be quite cathartic. And the photos don't need to be provocative. It's about showing you that your body, just the way it is, is beautiful and should be celebrated. My colleague would see you for a consultation to begin with, and of course I can write a referral with my thoughts to provide further context. But she's had a number of women speak very highly about the process, and how it has changed their attitude to their bodies. There are testimonials on her website."

"I don't know …" I said, sweat prickling along my spine. It was one thing to get undressed for Levi in the heat of the moment, when my own desire wiped away some of my anxiety. But to strut around in lingerie for a stranger … with a camera? Nausea rolled in me.

"Just give it some thought. There's no judgement if you decide it's not for you. But you know it's my job to present you with options if I believe they will be of benefit to you. And I believe this is one of those options."

Zip … Unzip …

I stuffed the pamphlet into my bag. "Alright, I'll think about it."

Levi: Can I come over tonight?

Amanda: What time? I'm in a class until 5

Levi: Not until 7, I just booked a job, it's a photoshoot at a warehouse somewhere in Randwick, but I can bring dinner with me?

Amanda: I'll cook. Text me when you're on your way

I tucked my phone back into my bag and tried to pay attention to the lecturer once more, but the thoughts battering back and forth in my brain distracted me. The conversation with Gillian today had me trying to formulate plans for Levi and me to 'date' without it seeming weird that I suddenly wanted the date stuff after two months of being satisfied with sex and snuggling at home.

And then there was the boudoir photography. I couldn't help but compare me doing a photoshoot like that, to the sorts of photoshoots Levi had started doing since he began taking modelling jobs. I knew, rationally, that making these comparisons was ridiculous, but I also knew that the little, nasty voice that blurted out all the cruel things inside my head didn't care one teeny bit about rationality.

When I got home, I made a cup of tea and plonked myself on a kitchen stool. As I blew the steam from the mug, I scanned the pamphlet Gillian had given me, and then grabbed out my phone and typed the URL into my browser.

Beautiful Bodies, Beautiful Minds: Boudoir Therapy came up in big letters, with a scrolling bar below showing women of all shapes and sizes wearing a variety of different lingerie styles, from cotton boy shorts and crop tops to G-strings and barely-there demicup bras, or even just covering their bare breasts with their hands. There was even an image of a topless woman, post a double mastectomy, grinning fiercely at the camera.

I skimmed the text. Lots about empowering women to find the beauty in their bodies, working with each client to determine how much and which parts of their bodies they were comfortable with showing. A note that images were never touched-up, never photoshopped, that real bodies should be celebrated. Time was spent with each client focussing on the parts of their bodies that they love, and parts that make them feel uncomfortable. That seeing the whole picture can help women to fixate less on 'zooming in' on the parts of themselves they view as undesirable, and instead focus on the whole of themselves as a real, beautiful person.

The gallery was full of women with so many different body shapes, sizes and colours. And every single one of them looked lovely. I wondered if she'd be able to make me look that lovely.

I was about to tap on the 'testimonials' tab when a hand shot into my vision and snatched the pamphlet off the bench.

"Oh, you are definitely doing this, my modern-day Marilyn!" Alison exclaimed, eyes sparkling as she scrolled the pamphlet. "Are you booking in now? Is that what you're doing?" She snatched my phone out of my hand.

"Give that back," I said, stretching for it. Alison held it out of my reach, scrolling through the gallery.

"You are hotter than ninety percent of the women on this page," she commented. I stood up and grabbed my phone back, closing and locking the screen.

"Comparison isn't the point of the therapy," I argued, as she went back to checking out the pamphlet. "It's to celebrate our own unique bodies."

Alison shot me a withering look. "Yes, you're so right, Miss 'I compare myself to Instagram models who use filters on every part of their bodies, and feel ugly in comparison'. We shouldn't be comparing ourselves to other people. But you are a hot, sexy peach, and you should totally show off that killer body in the skimpiest lingerie possible."

I was distracted from rolling my eyes at her by a text from Levi telling me he was just finishing up and would be on the road soon. I headed for the kitchen, rummaging through the fridge for ingredients to make something for dinner. Levi ate like an absolute horse—of course he did when he trained six hours a day—so I opted for chicken, bacon and mushroom pasta.

"You cooking for an army?" Alison asked as I piled ingredients onto the kitchen bench.

"No … Levi."

Alison guffawed. "That beast *is* a one-man army. Do you think there'll be enough left for Brad and me?"

I glanced up from where I was dicing onion. "Brad's coming over tonight, is he?" I smirked. "Hope you bought fresh batteries."

Alison laughed, completely unconcerned by my teasing. If the roles had been reversed, I would have been scarlet and sweating at the thought that someone knew what kinky things I was getting up to in my bedroom.

"Hey, Al," I began tentatively, transferring the onion to a bowl and getting started on crushing the garlic. "You and Brad … that's been going on a little while, right?"

Alison glanced up from the pamphlet she was still perusing, a slight smile tickling the corners of her mouth. "Yeah, over a year, now."

I gaped, the knife slipping on the garlic clove I was about to crush and almost slicing my finger. I put the knife firmly down. "A year? How did I not know about this earlier?"

"We mostly went to his place in the early days. And it wasn't as frequent as it is now." Her voice was soft, her usual brashness muted. I watched her for a moment before picking the knife up and continuing with my prep.

"So, is it still just a casual, sex thing?"

Alison started to shake her head, then paused. "It's … it's like a very special friendship. I mean, I know you and Brad have years of friendship behind you, but this is different."

"Because you get naked together?" I asked.

Alison chuckled softly. "Because we know each other in a different way. But we're not together. Or exclusive."

My brow furrowed. "Do you mean … he's got other women too?" I just couldn't imagine it of Brad. He'd pined silently for Mel for so many years, hadn't even looked at another woman. To picture him sleeping with Alison one weekend, and another woman the next … it seemed out of character for him.

"Not right now, he doesn't," Alison said, worrying at the corners of the pamphlet. "He has in the past, just one-night things, though."

"Like you and Theo were a one-night thing?"

Alison cleared her throat. "Yeah." A little rip formed on the pamphlet, and she pushed it away.

"So," I felt suddenly awkward asking her about this, but pushed on anyway. "It's not going to go any further than a … a long-term, casual-sex friendship?"

Alison picked at a fingernail. "Nope."

"So how do you stop yourself from developing … feelings?"

"You don't," Alison muttered. "You just learn to keep them under wraps."

I walked to the sink, washed the onion and garlic off my hands, and headed around the bench, wrapping her up in a hug.

"I had no idea you felt that way," I admitted, letting her fall against me and settle into the embrace.

"Yeah, refer back to the 'learning to keep it under wraps' statement," she replied quietly. She wasn't crying, but there was sadness in her tone that broke my heart just a little bit.

"Does he have any clue?" I asked. She shrugged.

"I did once sort of half-heartedly suggest that maybe we could go public with it. He seemed confused about why we would need to, when everything was so good the way it was. I didn't want to rock the boat any further because … well, the sex is next level. And he spoons me. And he likes hanging out and just, I don't know, being himself with me. It's enough … for now."

"Oh, God, Al. How do you cope when he's off with another woman?"

Al sighed. "The last time I knew he was going on a date was the night I brought Theo home here."

I looked at Alison through new eyes. Brad must be completely blind or stupid not to want to lock her down. Sexy, petite redhead, clever, funny, apparently into all the same kinks as him in the bedroom, whatever those were … what was he thinking?

"Why the interest?" Alison asked, catching me off guard. "Are you finally going to acknowledge that you're catching feelings for Danger Boy?"

"I … Gillian suggested today that if I want … more, we should try to do some things that take us in that direction. Like dating properly, not just hanging out at each other's houses and sleeping together. But I'm so afraid to bring it up, because what if that's not what he's looking for at all? What if he's like Brad, and he's happy exactly how things are?"

Alison flicked me a genuine smile. "My darling Manda, your Danger Boy is not Brad Jacobs. Anyone can tell he's absolutely besotted with you."

Can they? I wondered. I couldn't. Yes, he seemed insatiable when it came to sex … and he did love to put my enjoyment first in bed … and the shower … and on the kitchen counter … But it could just be that he was a very generous lover. Sexual intimacy and true intimacy were very different things, and while we were definitely going well with the first, I wasn't sure about the second.

"Well, I think he'd be delighted if you asked him out to dinner. I don't think you've got anything to worry about on that score. And hey, you've got that voucher your parents sent you for your birthday last year that you haven't used yet—the one for that Spanish fusion place?"

"*Comida Orgasmo?* Jesus, you have a better memory than I do, Al. I'd totally forgotten about that voucher!"

"Well, you've got a good excuse now. Just tell Levi you totally forgot you had a restaurant voucher, it's about to expire, and would he like to come with you."

I nodded, nerves jangling in my stomach. He might like going out to eat, but would he place the same significance on it that I was?

But Gillian was right, I had to start somewhere, and going on a proper date seemed like as good a place as any.

I popped a frypan on the stove to heat, swirling some olive oil into it. "Hey, Al," I said, keeping my back to her.

"Yeah?"

"If … and it's still a big if at this point … If I decide to do this boudoir thing, will you help me pick out some lingerie to take with me?"

"Uh, hell yes! How about we go shopping for lingerie, and you can decide about the boudoir stuff after. Even if you don't go ahead with the shoot, Levi will appreciate you hard in the lingerie. And I mean *hard*."

I giggled. "Okay. And … it says you can bring a friend along to the actual session, for support. Would you …?"

"I'd be honoured, Marilyn Manda."

I rolled my eyes, but my chest felt suddenly full.

Laundry was the bane of my existence. Between my scrubs, which often needed more attention than just a quick go around in the washing machine, my leisure clothes, and my heavy-duty underwire bras, laundry was constant and annoying.

I'd just psyched myself up enough to go out and get the latest load off the clothesline before the sun went down and it got damp again, when there was a knock at the door.

"Well, hello there, Honey," Levi greeted me, leaning against the doorframe, the long sleeves of his polo shirt rolled up, exposing the tattoos on his muscular forearms.

"Oh!" I exclaimed, wrenching my eyes from those lovely arms to focus on his face. "I didn't … I wasn't expecting you this afternoon!"

I opened the screen door and let him inside. He gripped me around the waist and pulled me against him, kissing me hard and fast. My legs quaked, and he pulled back, smirking at me and pressing his lips to my forehead.

"I hope I'm a good surprise," he murmured against my skin. I shook my head, my lips tilting upwards.

"You're always a good surprise, Levi. But I was just about to go and get my washing off the line."

He straightened, heading down the hallway towards the back door. "Well, let me help you, and then I thought you could cue up that weird French show you keep talking about."

I stumbled slightly. "You want to watch *Emily in Paris* with me?"

He flashed his sexy grin over his shoulder. "Honey, I'd watch paint dry if it meant I could do it sitting next to you."

The squishy feeling in my chest that I seemed to get so often around Levi was back with a vengeance as he strode out to the line, not even needing to wind down the old Hills-Hoist to be able to easily reach my clothes. I flushed as he unpegged one of my work bras—the heaviest of heavy-duty underwear I owned. But he didn't even comment, just folded it neatly—and correctly—and placed it into the basket.

"You ... uh you don't have to fold things for me, I can do that later," I mumbled, heat lingering in my cheeks. Levi lifted that scarred eyebrow in my direction.

"Don't you fold your washing as you get it off the line?" he asked, not a hint of irony in his tone. I blushed even redder.

"I ... I usually just chuck it all in the basket and then fold it once I'm sitting in front of the TV," I confessed. I didn't tell him that could sometimes be two days after I got it off the line, and in the meantime, I would rummage through the crumpled clothes to find what I needed.

"Trust me, Honey, my way is so much better." He eyed me up and down, then reached over and turned the rusty old crank on the Hills-Hoist until it was at a height where I could easily reach it, but he had to crouch to get under it.

I couldn't help myself. I giggled, the squishy feeling becoming something warmer and softer, and I joined him under the line, grabbing a pair of my granny-panties and folding them.

"Besides," Levi added, folding one of my old t-shirts more

precisely than I ever would, "I have more important things to do with you than the folding while we watch TV this afternoon."

"Like what?" I asked. Without warning, he scooped me into his arms, nuzzling into my neck and inhaling deeply.

"Like smelling your fucking delicious skin," he murmured, his lips nibbling at my earlobe. I shivered, knowing my underwear was going to be soaked if he kept it up.

"Well, I suppose we'd better get the chores done," I replied breathily. "I wouldn't want to keep you from the important business of sniffing me."

Levi's dark chuckle only made the dampness between my thighs worse, as he reached for another item of clothing.

"That French chick is a massive bitch!" Levi muttered in disgust, leaning back against my pillows and putting his hands behind his head.

I grabbed a Tim Tam from the packet beside my bed and dunked it into my tea. "Yes, that's sort of the point. Emily needs to feel … foreign, and out of her depth, and unwelcome. Her first days … weeks in Paris are supposed to make her question what she's doing. You'll understand it better the more you watch."

"She's nothing but super nice to them, and they're all so fucking awful to her! I mean I know the French have a really bad rep when it comes to politeness to foreigners, but this is next level shit!"

I leaned back beside him, balancing my tea on my chest and licking a smear of chocolate from the corner of my mouth. "It's cute that you're so invested already," I murmured around another mouthful of Tim Tam. "Just wait, you haven't even seen a scrap of the drama yet."

"Am I going to want to punch someone?" he asked, turning to kiss my forehead. "Well, someone other than the French bitch, and that weird, skinny guy with the fucking creepy hair."

I laughed aloud at that. "You mean Sylvie and Luc. And yes …

you are going to want to punch other people in this show too, by the sounds of it."

"Shh," he hissed. "Okay, so this has to be the new love interest. She's not going to cheat on the dickhead back in Chicago, is she? I mean … he seems like a total fucking wet blanket, but I don't want to have to punch Emily too."

"You won't want to punch her. Several other people, definitely. You'll want to cringe on her behalf so many times instead. And maybe cry a couple, too."

"How many times have you watched this?" he asked, reaching over and plucking my cup of tea from my hands, sitting it on the bedside. He took my Tim Tam covered fingers and sucked them into his mouth, licking the last of the chocolate from them, before trailing kisses up my arm, without his eyes once leaving the screen.

I let my free hand slip up under his t-shirt, dragging my nail over the rippling muscles of his stomach. He made a low noise, his fingers digging into my hip.

"A few," I admitted.

"Don't spoil anything for me, promise?"

I laughed, trying to ignore the increasing hammering of my heart. If there was ever a time to ask him about going on a date, this was it. But I couldn't make my mouth form the words.

He's going to say no. Why would he take the cow out in public, when he's already getting the milk for free? the nasty voice whispered in my mind.

I swallowed back the bitter taste that voice left in my throat and lifted my head to rest my chin on his pec. "Hey, Levi …"

"Yes, Honey?" His voice was thick, like golden syrup. He reached out to pause my laptop, swivelling his body to face me. "You have my full, undivided attention."

"Do you think that we could … I was thinking that maybe … if you want to that is …" Oh my God, I was royally stuffing things up.

"Take a breath and start again," he suggested, those amber eyes locking on mine, his hand moving from my hip to slide comfortingly up and down my back.

I did as I was told. *Deep breath in … and start again.*

"I'd like to go out for dinner sometime … with you," I whispered.

Levi's eyes widened just fractionally, and I watched as they flickered, focusing on one of mine, and then the other.

"I'd fucking love that, Honey. It's just …" He flopped onto his back and covered his eyes with his arm.

Okay. I should have been expecting this exact reaction, so why was worry pummelling the inside of my stomach? I had to backtrack, and fast.

"No, it's okay, really, it was just a suggestion. I don't want you to feel like you have to do something you don't want to do," I blathered, sitting up so fast that my laptop slid off the bed, falling onto the carpet with a *thunk*.

His warm, tattooed arm slid around my shoulders, pulling me back down onto the bed.

"I can't believe what a prick I am," Levi murmured against my hair. His touch, the warmth of his breath on my neck, was comforting. His words were the complete opposite. "Of course you would want that, and you fucking deserve it …"

He lifted my hair and pressed a kiss to the nape of my neck. Oh God, was this him letting me down easy? I couldn't breathe.

"I just … this is embarrassing … I can't afford to take you to the sort of places you deserve to go. I … shit … being a rower is not a lucrative career, Honey. And, as my father has reminded me on more than one occasion, raising a baby and paying child support is expensive. I've been taking on these modelling jobs to supplement the crappy income I get from sponsors, but I need to have a bit of a savings buffer when the baby comes. Still, that's no fucking excuse. I should be wining and dining you properly."

Oh.

Oh my God.

I rolled over in his arms, nestling my nose into the hollow at the base of his throat.

"For starters, I don't have expensive tastes when it comes to dates. Fish and chips on the beach, a cheap bottle of wine and takeaway Chinese on a picnic blanket. I'm easy pleased." I planted a kiss on his collarbone.

"Secondly, Alison only just reminded me the other day that I have a voucher that's going to expire soon, to a Spanish fusion restaurant. I thought maybe we could go there. My treat ... well, my parents' treat—they're the ones who sent the voucher to me."

He was silent for a long moment, the only sound the hiss and puff of his breath.

"Honey, I'd be fucking delighted to go on a date with you. Even if I feel like a massive fuckwit for not being the one to offer in the first place."

I looked up into his eyes, giving his stubbly cheek a stroke. "Don't you dare feel that way. You have so much on your mind."

He leaned down and nuzzled his nose against mine, tilting my head to the side until his lips were brushing mine. "I've got you on my mind twenty-four-seven, Honey."

Then he plundered my mouth, nipping, licking, sucking, and I knew that we wouldn't be finishing our episode of *Emily in Paris* any time soon.

CHAPTER TWENTY-FIVE

Slay Me

LEVI

"**S**till one point five seconds off qualifier time, Fox!" Patto called through his megaphone as we cut past the two-kilometre mark.

"Fuck," I muttered.

"Sorry, Levi," Mac apologised in front of me. "How do we fix this?"

I breathed deep through my nose. We'd managed to cut three full seconds off the time that Mac and I could manage over a full race, but we just couldn't shave off that last second-and-a-half. Mac was fit, but he was lacking the extra quad and glute strength that would give his strokes that powerful edge they needed.

"More time in the gym," I replied. "Starboard turn."

Together we turned the shell. Returning to the start point of our course was active recovery, but to be honest, I didn't think another fucking go at the race length was going to do anything to help either me or Mac right now. Patto pulled up beside us in his boat.

"I think you've both had enough water time this morning," he said, as if he'd read my fucking mind. Mac's shoulders slumped almost imperceptibly. But I'd been staring at his back for weeks now,

I knew enough about how it moved that I could picture it in my sleep.

I was learning that Mac was really good at burying just about everything underneath his fucking rainbows and lollipops exterior. And just as I suspected, by the time we'd stowed the shell and our oars, his 'I'll do anything to be helpful' smile was firmly in place.

"We need to up your weight on squats and deads, Mac," I grunted, handing him a protein drink as we headed for the club house. "We've got your form pretty much perfect, but we need to work on your power. It's the only thing now that we can do to shave those last seconds off the time."

"Okay, that's doable. We've got time."

Not enough, I thought. Patto had calculated the average qualifying time from the last four WRCs, and we were working towards beating that. If we could stay above average, that should get us into Paris. And then we had months to work towards bettering that time before the Olympics.

I hadn't worked this hard at my sport in years. Theo and I had really been cruising. Maybe that hadn't been such a good thing. Maybe it wasn't just Mac who needed to up his game.

"I'm going to work towards increasing my lifts by ten percent over the next month," I said to Mac. "You should do the same. Also, we need to allocate more time to powering your strokes." I threw a smirk his way. "Bet you fifty bucks that you can't beat me over a kilometre on the indoor rower. I'll give you a week. Next Saturday, it's on."

Mac held out his palm, and after a second's hesitation, I shook it. "You're on, Fox," he said, before chugging the rest of the protein drink, and lobbing the bottle into the bin at the door. "Weights room?"

I nodded.

Mac and I didn't talk much about anything other than rowing. Not from lack of trying on his part, though. He was always asking me shit, about Amanda, and the modelling work I'd been doing, and the baby. It was becoming almost fucking impossible to avoid his questions—I was starting to realise how much of a rude prick I seemed for doing it.

I just didn't want to talk about any of it. When I was with Mac, I just wanted to think about rowing. I didn't want to think about the fact that the clock was ticking down until I'd be a dad. Which meant the clock was also ticking towards the expiry date on whatever the hell Amanda and I were doing. She was a fucking saint, but even saints have limits, and tying herself to a man with a baby to another woman—a woman who could well be Satan incarnate—was a step further than I could ask of her. She deserved so much more than me. We didn't talk about it, because I think we both knew what was going to happen when D-Day hit.

The thought was fucking depressing.

"Got any plans tonight?" Mac asked in between sets on the squat rack.

"Yeah, Amanda and I have a dinner date," I replied.

"Eating in?" he asked, and I glanced up to see him waggling his eyebrows wickedly at me. I clenched my jaw.

"Fuck off," I grumbled. I wished I was eating in the way Mac was insinuating. Christ, I was getting to the point where I'd get on my hands and knees and fucking beg Amanda to let me go down on her.

"I've got a date tonight, too," Mac added. I shrugged, managing a half-smile.

"Where'd you meet her?" I asked as I added another lot of plates to the bar. Mac didn't answer right away, stepping under the bar and working through his set.

"On a dating app," he puffed, quickly taking a slug from his water bottle.

"The good old right swipe, huh?" I said. "She good looking?"

"Tall, blonde, likes the outdoors."

"Jesus, you looking for a clone of yourself?" I joked, adding more weight to the bar. Mac remained silent, which was so fucking unlike him I actually looked at him properly. He was pale, which was weird since he was squatting heavier than he had yesterday, and he was staring off out the window.

"What's up, man?" I asked before wondering why I actually cared. Because I realised that I sort of did care.

Mac's eyes snapped to mine, and for a second he looked like he was about to say something really important. But then his eyes flicked away.

"Just a bit nervous," he mumbled. "I haven't been on a proper date for a very long time."

I sighed. "Yeah, me either. I'm a total shithead. Amanda had to ask *me* on a date. We've been together for over two months, and in that whole time I haven't once thought she might like to go out."

I'd just assumed she didn't want that. Her words the day she found out about Emilee, still echoed in my brain … *Are you serious right now? You still want me to go out for dinner with you, while your 'ex' girlfriend grows your baby?*

Who the fuck would want to tie themselves to my fucked up mess of a life in any public way?

Maybe Amanda did. And maybe I shouldn't get my fucking hopes up.

"Well, she's a modern woman, Levi," Mac reassured me, clapping me on the shoulder as he stepped under the bar. "Good on her for taking the initiative when you didn't."

I sighed. I should be giving her far more credit than I was. I didn't deserve her brand of fucking perfection in my life. I'd only drag her down with me, into the shit that was co-parenting with Zilla, and never having enough money to spoil her the way she deserved. And my piece of shit father who would hate her no matter what, just for what she did for a living, and because she was with me.

I would never be able to give her what she deserved.

We finished the rest of our training in silence, apart from a grunted, "Good work," from me when Mac finished a session ending each exercise on the highest weight he'd lifted so far.

I showered, dressed, and stuck my head in with Patto on the way out. "See you Monday."

He looked up from his computer and beckoned me into his office. I swallowed and took a seat, wondering what the fuck I'd done this time. Patto clocked me with those beady eyes of his. Sweat trickled down the back of my neck.

"I'm proud of you, son. You seem really focused, you're helping Mac out and you're not letting your personal shit get in the way. You're in top form, and we have enough time to get Mac there before Serbia. It's great to see you taking him under your wing."

I sat there speechless.

"I'm not … I haven't …" I stuttered eventually, not knowing where the fuck to look.

"Listen, Fox, I know you aren't used to hearing praise, even when you more than bloody deserve it. So just say, 'thanks coach', and get on with your day." He turned back to his computer, and I scrambled to my feet, my head spinning.

"Thanks coach," I mumbled.

"Oh!" Amanda gasped, the pink of her lovely cheeks matching the colour of the bouquet of roses I held out to her. "I wasn't expecting …"

"Honey, you're taking me out to this fancy fucking place," I replied, gesturing to the restaurant behind me. "A bunch of flowers is nothing in comparison."

She took them from me, pressing her nose into them and inhaling deeply. "They're lovely! The colour is spectacular."

I grinned, reaching out and stroking her jaw. "I thought you'd like them. I've told you pink's your colour." I pinched her chin before releasing her and scratching at the back of my neck.

"I also thought they kind of looked like the ones Emily bought from that bitchy florist in your show," I admitted.

"But we're not up to that episode yet," she muttered, her eyes meeting mine and then glancing away, the pink spreading across her face.

"I might have gotten curious and watched a couple of episodes on my own." Fuck, I was a total sap. She'd laugh in my face.

Amanda beamed, reaching out and winding her fingers through mine. "You're a trickster, Danger Boy."

I raised a questioning eyebrow at her until she giggled.

"You put on this tough exterior, but you're just a sweetie on the inside."

A slightly embarrassed laugh erupted from my suddenly aching chest. "Just don't tell anyone, okay?" I murmured, before opening the door to *Comida Orgasmo*, and ushering her inside.

We were greeted by a smiling maître d. My eyes roved over the wood panelled walls, the deep green upholstered leather chairs, hardwood tables and slate floors.

"You know, *Comida Orgasmo* roughly translates to 'Foodgasm', right?" I breathed against her ear as the maître d gestured for us to follow him.

"Well, it better live up to the name, then, hadn't it?" she muttered back. "If I'm not moaning in delight from every bite, I'll demand our money back."

I chuckled. "Don't worry, Honey, if this place lets you down, I'll make sure you get some moaning in before the night is over."

I moved her ahead of me as we made our way through the tables, my eyes trailing down her swaying curves. I'd never seen the dress she was wearing before. It was some sort of silvery, shimmery, silky fabric that slid along every perfect fucking inch of her lush body like butter.

Her blonde waves swayed against the bare skin of her upper back, and without thinking, I reached up, brushing it aside and swiping my thumb over the smooth, creamy skin of her neck, mesmerised by the softness of her.

"Fuck, your skin is perfection," I murmured against her hair, inhaling its flowery scent just before she turned to sit at our table. She flushed my favourite shade of pink, a shy smile tweaking the corners of her lips. My chest felt suddenly tight and I cleared my throat, taking my own seat and picking up my menu. I tried not to choke when I saw the prices.

"Jesus fuck! I hope you know I'm not an expensive date either,

Honey," I muttered, eyes scanning down the mains. The cheapest one was sixty bucks.

"It's okay, I was expecting prices like this. I figure we could have some tapas to start, and a main each, and a bottle of wine to share. My voucher will cover all of that," Amanda replied, her own eyes unconcerned. "Or we can skip the tapas and share a dessert after."

A sudden, fucking vivid picture popped into my head, of feeding her spoonfuls of some rich, overpriced fancy dessert across the table. Wondering if her eyes would roll back in her head at the taste. As much as I liked the image, fancy dessert wasn't Amanda's thing.

"I've got a packet of Tim Tams with our names on it in my bedside drawer," I said, reaching out and grazing my fingertips across her knuckles. She sucked in a tiny breath, and that tight feeling in my chest intensified. "Let's wait until we get home to have dessert. And I'm paying for the wine."

"You don't have to do that, Levi," she protested, eyeing me over the top of her menu.

I smiled. "I want to. You pick the wine, it's on me. What sort of boyfriend would I be if I let your parents pick up the whole tab for our first proper date?"

And there was my favourite pink again, spreading across her cheekbones.

"You're my …" she began, her tongue darting out to taste her bottom lip as she flipped her hand, winding her fingers through mine.

I cleared my throat again, rubbing at my chest with my free hand and staring down at the menu. "There's a kilo ribeye on here for ninety bucks. Think the budget can stretch for that?"

If she started getting all emotional about me using the 'boyfriend' word, I was going to start spouting all of the things that I kept pushing from the tip of my tongue—things that would absolutely have her running a mile if I said them out loud.

Your eyes remind me of the waves at Bondi on a cloudy morning … Touching your silky hair is like therapy for me … When you talk in medical jargon, it makes me ache all over at how fucking smart you are … You're so goddamned beautiful, it makes me want to cry … I'm terrified to tell you how fucking strongly I feel about you, because what I can offer is so much less than you deserve …

Amanda laughed lightly. "I'd pay extra to watch you polish off a kilo of steak." I shook myself, focusing on the menu once more.

"Challenge accepted," I grated, my voice suddenly thick.

"Levi Fox?" a deep, heavily accented voice asked from behind my left shoulder. Amanda looked up curiously as I turned. A guy in a chef's uniform stood smiling behind me. I narrowed my eyes.

"Yeah, that's me."

The guy smiled wide, swiping a hand through thick black hair. "Welcome to *Comida Orgasmo*! It's so exciting to have a celebrity athlete dining tonight!"

I raised an eyebrow before turning back to Amanda who was smirking behind her hand.

"I'm not …" I began, but the dude waved away my protests.

"You're an Olympian who managed to win a race singlehandedly with an injured teammate. That's celebrity in my books. Can we get a photo of you for our wall of fame?"

My neck heated with embarrassment. "I don't …"

"I'm so sorry, you're obviously here on a date." He turned and eyed Amanda up and down. There was something about the way he looked at her that made me want to stand up and punch the absolute shit out of him.

"Yes, this is my girlfriend, Amanda." I watched her over the menu as she flushed and waved shyly at the guy. I felt a pang of rage that he got to witness that pinkness on her face. That was *my* fucking blush.

He beamed at her. "I'm Mateo, owner and head chef here."

"Nice to meet you," I said dismissively, hoping he'd get the hint and piss off. Instead he glanced down at the flowers.

"These are lovely! Can I put them in some water for you?"

"Thank you," Amanda replied, giving him a smile and picking them up to hand to him. He sniffed them and made a weird little noise.

Thank fuck the waitperson arrived to take our order. Mateo murmured some instructions to the staff member to bring a vase and water for the flowers, then excused himself back to the kitchen.

"So, I have a celebrity … boyfriend?" Amanda asked, not quite meeting my eyes. My jaw twitched as I reached over and took her hand. Fuck I hoped she wasn't pissed at me for making things official.

Our moment was interrupted by the server bringing our wine over. I gestured for Amanda to taste it. She barely let a drop touch her lips before she was nodding, and the server poured and finally left us alone again. I took a breath, squeezing her fingers.

"Is that a label you'd like to put on us?" I asked.

Her eyes finally flicked up to mine, and the sweet smile that lit up her whole face flooded me with relief. My chest ached harder.

"Tell me about your dad," Amanda said suddenly, catching me off guard with the sudden subject change. I lifted the wine to my mouth, taking a good slug to try and steady myself.

"I … why?" I managed, stalling and thanking fuck that the server interrupted once more with a vase for the flowers. Why did we have to talk about that arsehole and ruin our dinner?

"Children were never on my parents' agenda," Amanda blurted as the server retreated, her fingers caressing the stem of her wine glass like it was the most fascinating thing she'd ever seen. "They were both very career-minded, but when they found out they were having me—after they got over the shock of it—they knew they didn't want to be those parents who sent their kid to day-care from six weeks old so they could both keep climbing the corporate ladder. It was my dad who decided to leave his job and be the stay-at-home parent, mostly because Mum earned more.

"Dad and I always had a special relationship because of that. He was the one who taught me trick shots on the pool table. He was quite a shark back in the day. He's got bad arthritis in his hands now, though, so he can't play the way he used to."

Her grey eyes flicked up to mine. "When they retired, they moved up north. They bought a townhouse in Cairns, and they live the tropical retiree life now. I try to visit them once a year, but I haven't managed it since …"

Her words faltered, and her lips pulled down at the corners.

"Since what, Honey?" I prompted gently, reaching out and squeezing her hand. She took a deep breath, her expression unreadable.

"Since I decided to go back to uni, get my graduate diploma. I've been too busy juggling work and study. But I'm hoping I might be able to get up there for Christmas."

I wasn't sure I was getting the whole story, but I wasn't about to push, because my whole story was far too depressing for our first fancy date.

"So, now you know about my parents, it's your turn. Tell me about yours."

I sighed. I hated sharing my fucked-up past. But a split-second gazing into those open, non-judgy grey eyes of hers, and I found the story spilling out of me. Well, the abridged version anyway. Some things were just not dinner date fodder.

"My dad and I have never gotten along great. I'm not academic, the way Xander is. But I've always been good at sport. It pissed Dad right off—he tolerated sport only as an accompaniment to good grades … that just wasn't me.

"My mum died when I was seventeen."

"Oh, Levi, I'm so sorry," Amanda breathed. I squeezed her hand again, rubbing my thumb over her knuckles.

"It was a long time ago now, Honey. But it happened right at the start of my final year of high school. I … Mum and I were always close. She was the one who made me want to pursue rowing in the first place, and she stood up to Dad when he was being a fuckwit about it.

"Anyway, I sort of went off the rails, for months after she … after she passed. And my already sad grades became fucking pathetic. I didn't score high enough to get into any university course. But I didn't care, because I'd won gold at the ARCs that year with Theo, and I knew that I wanted to be an athlete.

"Dad's been on my back ever since to quit rowing and get a real job, to get into uni another way … to make something of myself, be more like Xander. He loves comparing me to my brother, and Xan the successful vet is a yardstick I can never measure up to. Rowing is a hobby, according to him. Something you do to wind down after sitting in an office sixty fucking hours a week."

Amanda's brows furrowed. "But you won silver in Tokyo—you're an Olympic medallist! You won in Perth even when Theo was injured! How can he not see that you've achieved so much while doing what you love?"

I snorted, picking up the wine and taking a big swallow. "Because I'm never going to make six figures from rowing. Money is the only valid measure of success, in Dad's eyes. Ever since he found out about the baby, he's been a thousand times fucking worse than usual. He sees it as leverage to hold over my head, because parenting, and child-support, are expensive. That's why I've been taking on modelling work. I don't need any qualification for it, I can fit it around training, and the extra money'll give me a bit of a buffer when this baby comes."

And there it was again. The fucking elephant in the room.

"That little baby will be lucky to have you," Amanda murmured, her eyes flicking away as the waitperson delivered our tapas plates. I rubbed at my chest again, focusing on the clatter of the plates onto the timber table.

"Emilee wants to name her Emvi," I mumbled as the waitperson retreated.

Amanda's eyes shot to mine. "What? Did you say she wants to name your baby Envy?"

I laughed humourlessly. "That's what I thought when she told me, too. But apparently, it's spelled E.M.V.I—like a mix of her name and mine."

The look of horror on Amanda's face forced another bark of laughter out of me. "Yeah, this is the woman I'm dealing with." I smacked my hand on the edge of the table. "Okay, my ex and her crazy baby-name ideas are officially banned from date-night conversation!" I said, trying to sound jovial, and failing fucking miserably. I shoved a cheese-stuffed pepper into my mouth to try and mask my distress.

Amanda weaved her fingers through mine. "It's okay if you

want to talk about it with me. I can tell that you have … big feelings about this situation, but do you ever talk them through with anyone?"

I shoved in another mouthful of pepper. "I don't want to burden you with this."

Those grey eyes of hers burned straight into my soul. "It's not a burden, Levi. I want to help you. I care about you."

I bit my tongue because the words I wanted to say to her just weren't fair. I wanted to tell her that she was already more than I could ever have fucking hoped for. I wanted to tell her that her just being there was enough to make things better. If I was selfish, I'd say them, do anything to tie her to me more permanently. But I couldn't bring myself to do it. I didn't want her to get sucked into the shit my life would be once I had to co-parent with Zilla. I wanted to fucking rant at the universe for letting me meet her just as my life turned to shit.

Instead, I leaned across the table, gripped her chin between my thumb and finger, and drew her closer, kissing her deeply. Surprise froze her, but soon her lips parted to dart her tongue out to tickle mine.

I broke away, panting, and she leaned back in her seat, taking a sip of wine and watching me over the top of the glass with eyes that gave nothing away.

"You slay me, Honey," I muttered, pressing a hand to the fucking intense ache in my chest.

"You're going to have to roll me home, Amanda," I groaned as I held the door open for her. She chewed on her bottom lip, eyes sparkling.

"I told you that you didn't need to eat the entire cow on your plate," she admonished teasingly.

"I'm an athlete, Honey. I thrive on competition. I wasn't about to let that juicy steak get the better of me. Besides, that chef guy was watching me, like he was hoping I'd fail. Did it seem to you like he was staring at me a lot?"

"Well, you are a celebrity," she replied with a grin, linking her arm in mine. We headed down the footpath towards her car.

I took a deep breath, then blew it out. I still hadn't told her about Mum's birthday dinner, but it was only two nights away.

Fucking grow a pair and do it now, Fox.

"So … every year on Mum's birthday, Dad makes us come over to his place for dinner. He wants me to bring you this year," I said before I lost my fucking nerve, adding quickly, "You aren't obligated at all, so don't feel like you have to say yes."

"When is it?" she asked. "I'm going to be moving to night shifts next week. But if I'm free, I'd like to meet your dad under less awkward circumstances. Am I … am I invited as your girlfriend?"

I tried to smile, but couldn't, because she was so wrong if she thought there was any way to meet Dad that would be anything but awkward, and that was putting it fucking mildly.

"It's on Monday night," I told her. "And yes, you're my girl-friend. You have no idea how good it felt, me introducing you that way earlier to that weird chef. This isn't just a …" I trailed off, but she seemed to get what I was blathering about. She nodded, wrapping an arm around my waist.

"I can come then—I'm off Monday night."

I slung an arm across her shoulders, and she snuggled closer to my side. Conflict roiled in my gut. If I had my way, we'd never see Dad. She'd never have to spend time in his toxic presence. She'd never have to witness him treat me like shit. But selfishly I was glad she'd agreed to come. She made shitty experiences so much more bearable.

———

"What's going on?" Amanda groaned sleepily beside me. I cracked an eyelid.

BANG! BANG! BANG!

"Levi Fox! Get your fucking arse out here!"

Shit. That was Zilla at Xander's front door, making enough noise to wake the entirety of fucking Sydney. I sat up so fast the room spun, tapping my phone to check the time. Just after two.

I turned to Amanda, sitting up in bed, holding the sheet up to her chin. Her eyes were like saucers, her lips parted and her skin the palest I'd ever seen it.

"Stay in here, I'll deal with her," I told her firmly, scrambling into a pair of shorts as I left the room, closing the door behind me. Whatever the fuck Zilla was here for, Amanda really shouldn't have to witness it.

"What the fuck is wrong with you?" I hissed as I opened the front door. "Someone'll call the cops on you if you don't shut up."

Zilla glared at me through the security door. "I don't give a shit, Levi. Let me in or I'll scream some more."

Swallowing back apprehension, I unlocked the screen door. She snatched it open and flounced through, heading immediately down the hallway as if she was going into my bedroom.

I grabbed her by the arm and redirected her into the living room.

"What the fuck are you doing here? Is everything okay with the baby?"

Her eyes blazed as she dragged her arm from my grip, wheeled back, and slapped me.

"Fuck!" I grunted, staggering back.

"What kind of man-whore are you, Levi? Ever heard of the saying 'don't shit where you eat?'" Damn she was ugly when her face was all screwed up with rage.

"What the hell are you talking about?" I asked. She waved her phone erratically in front of my eyes. I couldn't tell what I was supposed to be seeing, I was too busy avoiding it smacking me in the face too.

"I know you struggle to go a full week without getting your dick wet, but honestly? Not only do you go and bang a fucking fatty, but you have to pick one who watched me get an ultrasound probe stuck up my vag?"

I gripped her wrist, held her phone still long enough for me to focus on the image on her screen.

"How the fuck did you get this?" I asked, staring in shock at the picture of Amanda and me, kissing across the table in the restaurant earlier in the night.

"A friend saw you, thought I'd like to know that the father of my child was out sucking face with a fucking whale!"

My vision blurred with the need to hold back on losing my shit at her. Losing it at Zilla had never gotten me anywhere.

"She's not a fucking whale," I said through gritted teeth.

"Don't think I haven't noticed the way she's been eye fucking you at every appointment we've been to together! Honestly, are you that hard-up that you're chubby chasing now?"

"Shut your mouth," I growled. "She's goddamned beautiful to look at, and a beautiful human being too."

Hysterical laughter bubbled out of Zilla. "I'm guessing you didn't take my advice and Google her then. She loves the fucking psychos. Probably gets off on them. Who knows if she wasn't helping him slice people up?"

My insides turned to ice. "What fucking bullshit are you—"

"I bet she puts out like a whore, doesn't she, Levi? I bet she fucks you dirty, the way you like it. The fat, desperate ones always do like to fuck dirty."

Red washed over my vision, but I forced back the rage. The only outcome of yelling back at Zilla was her taking her crazy to eleven. If I wanted to get her out of the house, I had to try and keep my cool. I just needed her gone, so I could go back to Amanda and apologise for everything she would have overheard. I kept my voice as even as I could. "Emilee, you and me … we're not together anymore. And you being pregnant doesn't fucking change that. I want to be there for my little girl, but I'm allowed to be with another woman. I'm allowed to try and be fucking happy."

Zilla snorted. "You're never going to be happy, Levi. You'll never be anything but a miserable shit, and a flabby cow with a willing pussy isn't going to change that."

"Get the fuck out."

"Are you going to keep seeing her?" she asked, eyebrows raised. I gripped her shoulders and steered her down the hall.

"I'll worship her for as long as she'll fucking have me."

Zilla paused by the hall table, and before I had a chance to react, her hand flashed out and snatched up the vase with Amanda's roses in it. She turned and hurled it against the wall, where the glass exploded, the flowers falling limply to the floor in amongst the shards of broken glass.

With a smirk, she made sure to tread on every single blossom as she walked the last few steps to the front door, leaving me staring down at the ruined flowers and knowing that this was what my life would be like forever—every beautiful thing I tried to do, tried to have, crushed by my vindictive ex.

CHAPTER TWENTY-SIX

Bubble of Denial

AMANDA

Something large and jagged was lodged in my throat. I clung to the sheet, holding it against my collarbone. I barely dared to breathe after I heard smashing glass. Shock had frozen me in place on Levi's bed.

Silence. For a long time, nothing but silence. And then the muted sounds of Levi cleaning up whatever Emilee had just ruined. I wanted to get up, put on a t-shirt and help him to fix it. But I couldn't move. My hands were shaking and clammy, and I felt like I might faint. I fell back against the pillow, trying to concentrate on my hot chocolate breathing.

Eventually his footsteps echoed up the hallway and the door opened. His face was a mask of exhaustion as he plonked himself down on the edge of the bed, dropping his head into his hands.

"I'm so fucking sorry you had to hear all of that," he muttered thickly. His tone was so defeated, my hammering heart shuddered for him, knowing his past with her was traumatic. I knew enough about traumatic ex-partners to know it still impacted you months … years later.

He needed me, right now, and despite the churning in my stomach, I managed to crawl across the bed, reaching a shaking hand out to his shoulder. He covered my hand with his, squeezing my fingers before falling back onto the bed, flinging one arm over his face.

"You know that none of the shit she just said is true, don't you?" he said, the words muffled by his arm.

Some of it is, the nasty voice insisted. *You are a whale. And you did get off with a psychopath.*

I didn't know he was a psychopath at the time! I argued, shaking my head to try and dislodge the awful thoughts.

"I think you're gorgeous, Honey," Levi murmured, removing the arm from his eyes to stroke at my hair, running his fingers through the length. My skin rose into goosebumps at his touch.

"You're so fucking lovely that sometimes when I look at you, I can't breathe, Amanda," he continued, his fingers toying with my earlobe. "Everything Emilee said was a total fucking lie."

I didn't want to be reminded about what she'd said. It was nothing more than I'd said to myself on repeat for as long as I could remember. I just wanted Levi to stop talking about it, to stop saying nice things, to stop trying to undo Emilee's vicious words.

"You're so beautiful, Amanda. On the outside, but on the inside as well. You're smart—fucking brilliant, really, and you … you actually care about …" His words choked off, his hand tangling in my hair.

'Beautiful on the inside'. Those words were going to break me one day. I was overwhelmed with the need to stop him from trying to explain away the things she had said. Without thinking further, I pushed him down on the bed. I planted kisses along his jaw, his collarbone, and down his utterly perfect chest, and the words died on his lips. The lump in my throat eased in the near silence that replaced them. I reached his nipples, darting my tongue out to flick them, taking them into my mouth the way he did to mine and sucking, nipping.

"Fuck, Honey, what—"

I silenced him with a squeeze of his penis through the soft fabric of the gym shorts he'd hastily put on before. He was already semi-hard, and as I dragged my palm over his length he grew until his shorts were completely tented and he was groaning wordlessly.

I continued to kiss down his abs, nibbling and sucking at his hipbones, running my tongue along the V that disappeared under his waistband.

"Jesus," he managed hoarsely as I lifted the waistband up, over his penis, and tugged the shorts off entirely. I knelt between his legs, nudging his knees further apart to fit my wide bottom between them, looking down in the dark at the way his penis bobbed against his stomach, jerking up and down with his want, the little light that filtered in through the blinds glinted off his piercing.

"You … you don't have to do this," he muttered, eyes dark, jaw clenched. "I don't need you to … I don't deserve … I just need to hold you …" His penis jerked as I lightly stroked it.

"Levi. *I want* to do this." My voice was hoarse, and I hoped he interpreted that as me being overwhelmed with desire, and not that I was a hairsbreadth from choking on the lump in my throat. I leaned down, pressing a chaste kiss to the tip of his penis, before taking the silver ball on the end of his piercing into my mouth and tugging on it gently. His hips practically levitated off the bed. I held him down, swirling my tongue around the head, flicking at the barbell, tasting a tiny drop of precum that leaked from the tip.

"Fucking Christ," he grunted, his hands reaching down to fist in my hair, knees spreading wider in surrender. I stroked down the crease either side of his groin, until my fingers found his testicles. I fondled them, ran my nails over them.

I opened my lips wider, and took him into my mouth, slowly moving down the length of him, relaxing my throat until every inch of him was inside me.

"Fuuuuuuck," he hissed, his hands tightening in my hair. A throb started between my legs just the way it always had every time I'd given Thomas oral. He'd conditioned me to see his pleasure as mine. To give to him, while giving to myself. Giving, never taking.

Because he'd been so disgusted by my size, unable to bring himself to give me pleasure.

Just stay in this moment, with Levi. Squeezing my eyes shut to drown out those memories, I hollowed my cheeks on the way back up his shaft, then took him in deep once more. As I withdrew this second time, I gripped the base of him, teasing his head with shallow little sucks, running my tongue and just a little hint of teeth against his piercing as I stroked the rest of him slowly, torturously.

"Please, Amanda," he begged, his hips shifting, fingers tightening in my hair. Heat flared between my legs. I wanted him to take control, to push my head down on him again. I hated that I wanted him to. I hated that the thought of him using my mouth like that turned me on so much, because it was what Thomas had always done. Arousal and shame were so intertwined with this act for me. I wondered if they always would be.

I gave him what he wanted though, gripping his hips and sucking deep, breathing calmly through the urge to gag as he filled my throat. And finally, he did what I'd been both longing for and dreading. He used that hand fisted in my hair, pulling me up, then pressing me back down, his hips lifting to meet my mouth at the base of his penis.

I couldn't help myself. I moaned around him, sucking harder as he thrust himself in and out of my mouth. The ache between my legs was so intense that there was no way I could deny myself. I reached between them, finding my thighs slippery with my arousal.

Thrusting two fingers into me, I moaned around his penis again, spreading my knees wider so I had better access, curling my fingers inside me as I sucked him, hard, deep, fast.

"Fuck yes, are you fingering yourself? You fucking beautiful girl." His hip movements became more erratic, sweat broke out on his stomach, his muscles tensing. "Don't fucking stop. Make yourself come, please Honey," he begged. "Fuck, I'm trying to hold off until you come."

He eased the pressure on my head, only allowing me to suck halfway down his shaft. But I was so close, slipping my fingers out of me to frantically circle my clitoris. I broke free of his control and sucked him deep again as the ache built between my legs. I keened around his penis, my fingers returning to thrust into me as I tightened, squeezing around them as my orgasm barrelled through me.

"Yes, Honey, will you drink me down?" he growled, his hips bucking to my mouth. I gave a moan of acquiescence as I pressed the flat of my tongue to the ridge on the underside of his penis, rubbing it along that sensitive length.

"Gonna come so fucking hard!" he gasped, and with one final thrust to the back of my throat, he shouted incoherently as hot, salty spurts of semen jetted into my mouth. There was so much I couldn't swallow it all fast enough, and some leaked out the corner of my lips.

I didn't stop to wipe it away. I kept gently licking and sucking and kissing his softening length as he came down from his orgasm, his stomach muscles spasming from my touch, until he hooked me under the arm and pulled me up his body, nestling me in the crook of his arm. I reached up to wipe the dribble of semen from the corner of my mouth, but he got there first, gathering it on his thumb and feeding it back to me.

"Well, that was ... unexpectedly fucking amazing," Levi murmured with a sleepy smile. "Now, let me clean those fingers up."

I couldn't meet his eyes as he took my slippery fingers, licking and sucking my arousal from them. The momentary lust that had overcome me at the feel of him hitting the back of my throat had kept that insidious lump at bay, but now it was over, the lump, and the threatening tears that accompanied it, were back with a vengeance.

"Come here, my beautiful girl" he murmured, turning me so that my back was pressed against his front, stroking two fingers up and down the length of my arm. "Thank you. I feel like after everything that just happened, it should have been me giving to you, and not the other way around. I ... I don't deserve you, Honey. I fucking hate that you had to hear all of that. I hate that she said such toxic bullshit about you."

"I don't want to think about it," I managed to choke out. "I just ... I need to sleep."

He pulled me closer, tucking me right up so that every inch of my back was pressed against every inch of his front as he pulled the comforter up over us. His skin was warm, and should have felt comforting, but all of the energy I had left in me was holding my tears at bay.

"I'll be your hot water bottle," he murmured sleepily against my shoulder. "When you wake up, I'm going to worship you properly. And if I have to fucking tie you to the bed so I can feast on that pretty pink pussy, I will. You deserve to be worshipped. Fuck, you deserve so much more …"

He broke off, peppering light kisses on my shoulder, my neck, my earlobe. His kisses became sleepier, softer, slower, as his body relaxed, and sleep took him. I didn't need to worry about him noticing the hot, shame-filled tears that dripped down my face and onto the pillow beneath me. I didn't need to feel nervous about his promise for the morning.

Because I wasn't going to be in his bed when he woke up.

As I stealthily extricated myself from his embrace, and rummaged in the corner for my overnight bag, taking it to the bathroom to dress, I wondered with a choked back sob if a goodbye blowjob was considered good etiquette.

No, what I'd done was cowardly. I'd used oral sex to stop him from trying to talk about things I didn't want to open up about. I was a complete hypocrite. Hadn't I just earlier that evening told him I wanted him to talk to me about the things he considered a burden? That I wanted to help him with them?

Yet here I was, not sharing my burdens but running away from them, from him. But I couldn't voice out loud to him—a man who could have any stunning woman he set his sights on—my disgust with my body, the fact that Emilee was only saying things I told myself; that she wasn't lying. I would rather run from him than remain in a situation where someone like her would be a part of my life, would have power over me, would echo out loud things about myself that I tried to hide away in that dark part of my mind.

Her words had the power to break me. Had already done their damage. And not just about my size, but about Thomas, too. What he'd done … what I'd unknowingly enabled him to do … Levi would find out about it soon enough. Emilee already knew so much about it. It would only be a matter of time before he gave in to those little barbs and searched online to see what she was talking about, or she got impatient and spilled the whole sordid story.

And how could he want me then? He'd see me as nothing more than a fat, stupid woman who had been naive enough to be sucked in by a psychopath, so that he could stalk her much more attractive, much more desirable, friend.

If I didn't end this with Levi now, I was going to fall in love with him. And when their baby came, co-parenting with Emilee would become a huge part of his life, and the bubble of denial we were living in would burst … and I was going to end up with a broken heart.

As I shut the front door quietly behind me and hustled to my car, tears gushing down my face and silent hiccupping sobs wracking my body, I wondered if I hadn't already ended up with one anyway.

Through streaming eyes, I managed to tap out a message, hitting send, hoping he was so deeply asleep that it wouldn't wake him. Then, grabbing a tissue from the glove box, I swallowed back the ever-present lump as best I could, wiped most of the wetness from my eyes and cheeks, and started the car.

It would be a very careful drive the whole three streets home, because all I could see was a blur.

CHAPTER TWENTY-SEVEN

The Me Problem

LEVI

I woke to a tongue sliding up my cheek. Bleary-eyed, I rolled over.

"Honey, licking my face is fucking hot, but …" I trailed off when I realised that it wasn't Amanda in bed with me, but a bundle of shiny black fur with terrible puppy breath.

"What the …" I grunted, rubbing at my eyes and sitting up. Xander was standing in the doorway, arms folded across his chest and a sheepish smile on his face.

"What the fuck, Xan?" I demanded as the little lump bounced across the bed and clambered into my naked lap. "It's going to try and nibble my dick off!"

Xander chortled. "Well, wear pants to bed, Lev, and that won't be a problem. But fair warning, her teeth are bloody sharp!"

Picking up the puppy, I held her up to my face, squinting into her inky eyes. She licked my nose.

"Okay, I'm confused. Why is there a puppy in my bedroom at …" What time even was it?

Where was Amanda? Sometimes she got up earlier than me and made herself a cup of tea while she waited for me to have Sunday sleep in. Fuck. I'd promised her that I'd eat her out first thing this morning. That was probably why she was scarce. I shouldn't have run my fucking mouth about something I knew she wasn't keen on.

Thoughts of Zilla's outburst last night flooded back into my half-awake brain. Shit. I hoped Amanda hadn't gone home to freak out in private about my ex's bitchiness. I had to figure out how to get Zilla to back the fuck off if there was any chance for Amanda and me.

Did I actually believe there was a possibility we could make it work? No … but was I starting to hope? Maybe. Fuck.

I reached for my phone, finding a message from Amanda. I navigated to the message app with a puppy nudging its way under my arm, snuffling at the phone.

> Amanda: I can't do this anymore. I know this sounds sickeningly clichéd, but this is 100% a me problem, not a you problem. I'm sorry

The phone slipped from my hand, thumping to the carpet. The puppy nosedived off the bed after it, trying to pick it up in its little teeth and tumbling arse over tit in the process. I stared down at the growling little lump rolling about on the floor, numbness flooding every part of my body.

"Lev?" Xander collected the puppy into his arms and picked my phone up off the floor. He glanced at the screen and sighed.

"Want to talk about it?" he asked quietly, as the puppy panted happily, oblivious to me hitting rock bottom.

"Zilla showed up here last night," I muttered through what felt like a boulder lodged in my throat. "She'd somehow gotten a photo of Amanda and me at the restaurant … kissing. She went off her fucking tree at me, said some of the most hurtful things she could possibly say about Amanda. I sent her on her way, but …"

"Oh, shit. Was Amanda here?" Xander sat down on the bed beside me. The puppy snuffled at my shoulder. Without thinking, I reached out and plucked the little fuzzball out of Xander's arms, cuddling her close to my chest, wishing that her warmth could unfreeze the fucking ice in my heart.

"Yeah. She heard everything. I apologised the second I got rid of Zilla, but she didn't seem to want to talk about it. Shut me right up with the best fucking blowjob of my life. When we fell asleep … well, when I fell asleep, I'd thought everything was okay. Or at least, it would be a conversation for the morning."

"What do you think she means about it being a 'her' thing? I mean, if my partner's ex came around screaming abuse about me in the middle of the night, I'd feel like I was well within my rights to say, 'your ex is too fucking much, I'm out'."

I shrugged. "Probably just letting me down easy," I muttered. "I don't really want to talk about it." The puppy licked my cheek, and I realised there were tears there.

Fuck.

"I'll make you a cup of tea," Xander said, standing, giving my shoulder a brotherly squeeze before leaving the room. Leaving the little puppy snuggling in my arms, its coat getting damp from the tears that just wouldn't stop.

I stumbled out of my room late in the afternoon, with an empty teacup in one hand and a snoozing puppy tucked under my arm.

"There she is!" Dom's voice boomed from the lounge. I looked up to see Xander and Dom relaxing in front of a game of footy on the TV.

"Just because I've spent all day crying about my breakup doesn't mean I've lost my man card," I mumbled in a pathetic attempt at humour. Dom eyed me sympathetically.

"I meant the new addition to the Fox family. Little Princess!" Dom stood and scooped the puppy out of my arms, adding, "Real men cry, Lev." He patted me on the shoulder and plonked himself back down next to Xander.

"You know I'm not calling her fucking Princess, right?" Xander grumbled. Dom chuckled.

"Beach Vet, with Dr Fox and Princess. I can just see it now."

"Shut the hell up, Dom!" Xander hissed. I wondered vaguely why Xander was acting so touchy about this. But I couldn't find enough energy to really care as I collapsed into the lounge chair—the one Amanda had hidden behind the day Xan and Dad had walked in on us.

And there was the fucking boulder in my throat again.

"Did you try to get in touch with her?" Xander asked, taking the puppy out of Dom's arms and scratching her between the ears.

I shook my head. Words were stuck in my throat. I'd picked my phone up every five fucking minutes all day, about to dial in her number, or open the text app and type, before stopping myself. Not knowing when to give up was how I'd gotten into this fucking mess in the first place. I'd harassed her into a relationship, knowing I had a cargo plane full of baggage. Clearly that baggage had made itself too bloody unsavoury for Amanda last night.

I couldn't cut ties with Zilla, because I couldn't abandon my child. But neither could I expect Amanda to have to put up with the sort of abuse Zilla had dished out last night either. If she got that fucking nasty over one kiss, how would she feel when I asked Amanda to move in with me? Or when I asked her to marry me?

Fuck.

I was in love with Amanda.

And there was nothing I could do to un-fuck the situation enough to make the idea of us worthwhile for her.

"Levi?" Xander said sharply, and I blinked, glancing up at him.

"What?"

"I just asked if you think it would be okay for me to call her Lily," Xander said. I rubbed at the clock tattoo on my shoulder.

"I … I don't know. I kind of feel like naming a dog after her would be a bit … crass," I managed.

Xander nodded. "Yeah, I think you're right. So, not Lily then."

"What about Ebony?" Dom suggested.

Xander side-eyed his friend. "Did you seriously just suggest that? Why, because she's black?"

"Why'd you even get a dog?" I asked, trying hard to keep up with the conversation and not slip back into the misery that was lurking so fucking close to the surface.

Xander and Dom exchanged a loaded look, and I wondered for a moment what the fuck that was all about.

"All good vets need to have a pet," he replied eventually.

I snorted. "Does that mean until now you've been a shit vet?" I asked. Dom hid his laughter behind a cough as Xander rolled his eyes.

"It was … it was time." I watched the way Xander gazed down at the little bundle currently gnawing at the hem of his t-shirt. He may as well have had fucking love hearts for eyes.

"She's got you by the balls already," I said, standing and heading for the kitchen. "I think you should call her Georgie."

Both Xander and Dom stiffened as I said it, glancing at one another in the weirdest fucking way.

"Molly," Xander mumbled, watching Dom carefully. "Could I?"

Dom's eyes slid to the floor as he shrugged. "I mean, it's not like she'll ever find out, is it?"

I watched them both in confusion, as Xander's shoulders drooped. He scratched behind the little pup's ears as she nibbled on his thumb.

"Molly it is."

AMANDA

I woke to Dani lying beside me on my bed, scrolling through her phone and sipping on a cup of coffee. My head felt like someone had hammered nails into my temples and between my eyebrows.

"She's awake!" Dani called out. "Bring tea and Advil!"

I sat up, starting to protest that I didn't need pain meds, but the throbbing in my head was so horrendous that the words died in my throat. My sandpaper throat. And then everything came back to me in stark clarity.

I'd stumbled through the door at four a.m., thinking I was being quiet. In reality I'd been sobbing loud enough that I'd roused both Alison and Brad, who were asleep … or maybe in the middle of kinky sex-toy fun, for all I knew. They both came running. Alison had gotten me into bed, Brad had brought me water. Neither of them had asked what happened. I think Alison probably guessed that something had gone bad with Levi.

But they didn't know the full story. I didn't think I wanted to tell them the full story. They hadn't pressed for information; just tucked me into bed and held me as I sobbed myself into an exhausted sleep.

It seemed that when Dani got home from night shift, she'd been put on 'keep an eye on the crazy heartbroken woman' duties.

I really loved my roommates.

Alison tiptoed in with tea, water and a sheet of painkillers. "Tea, or drugs first?" she asked. I sighed and reached for the pills, popping two and dry swallowing them. Alison frowned and pressed the water into my hand.

"You're probably dehydrated, my gorgeous girl," she murmured. "Drink that, and I'll get you some Tim Tams to dunk in your tea."

I felt a bubble of hysterics forming in my diaphragm, and with an effort I swallowed it down with a gulp of water. Mum had always told me, "Tim Tams make everything better, sweetie." I was about to put that sentiment to the ultimate test.

I hadn't seen Mum and Dad in almost two years. I still felt like I couldn't face them after everything that Thomas had done came to light. Not that they'd been anything other than completely under-standing and empathetic, which only made it worse.

"So, do we ride at dawn?" Alison joked as she returned with a whole packet of chocolate biscuits and plonked herself down on my bed. Dani sat up and snagged one immediately, dunking it into her own coffee.

I shook my head, picking up a Tim Tam and just staring at it. I wondered if he'd tried to text me, or call me, while I'd been asleep. That would be just like him. He was never a quitter, he'd want to talk, he'd expect me to justify why we couldn't keep things the way they were. I looked around for my phone.

Dani noticed and shook her head. "You don't have any messages, Manda. No missed calls."

Well, it appeared he was a quitter. I hadn't really wanted him to try to contact me, but the fact that he hadn't cut me deep.

"What the hell happened for you to go from loved-up sex-bunny to complete breakdown at four in the morning?" Alison asked, never one to beat around in the bush.

"His ex-girlfriend happened," I managed. Dani gasped, and Alison leapt from the bed, pacing the room.

"We are sooo fucking riding at dawn! He fucking cheated? And with that rotten garbage smell of a human being?"

I choked on a sob-laugh that popped up my throat at her description of Emilee. "No. She turned up at his house last night, started screaming, called me a whale and a fat bitch, said I was desperate and told him I get off on psychopaths, and that I'd probably …" I cleared my throat, tears prickling again, "that I'd probably helped Thomas slice up his victims." The Tim Tam in my hand had melted to a sticky mess, but still I tried to eat it, hoping the sickly-sweet chocolate might be able to slide past the sharpness in my throat.

"Well, you know everything you just said is a complete load of bullshit!" Alison huffed, as Dani ducked out of the room, returning with a wet cloth, that she used to clean the remnants of the ruined biscuit from my hand. "But I understand why that would've made you upset."

A sob escaped me, and I hiccupped it back at the last minute. "It did upset me. But Levi stood up for me, and he got rid of her, and he was as upset … maybe *more* upset than I was about it all."

Alison and Dani shared a look. "Unicorn," they said in unison. I wanted to roll my eyes, but my head was still too sore.

"It just made me realise that I'm not … I'm not strong enough to handle everything once the baby comes. Now, I see Emilee when she's in clinic. When that baby comes, everything changes. They have to be in each other's lives in a much more meaningful way. And I … I need to get my head right. I need to work on the things that are making me unhappy about myself. And I can't do that with her in my life. Which means not having him in my life either."

"You've got to be kidding me!" Alison exclaimed. "You're going to let that bitch win? She's so fucking jealous of you, she came around in the middle of the night to try and bad mouth you to Levi. She's pathetic and desperate."

I shook my head. "It doesn't even matter what her motivations are. If I can't … if I keep thinking about myself the same way she thinks about me, then I'm the loser no matter what. I really hate the way a part of me was nodding along to every awful thing she said about me. I'm not …"

I took a deep, shuddering breath. "I'm not happy in myself. And unless I can change that, then how can I be happy in any part of my life?"

Alison looked like she wanted to argue. She opened her mouth a few times, furrowed her brow, then closed her mouth again. Dani was the one who pulled me close and gave me a tight squeeze. "You're so right, Manda darling. What can we do to help you be happy?"

Alison left the room. I thought she was too disgusted to participate in the conversation, but she returned with a notepad and pen.

"Project Happiness for Marilyn Manda," she said as she scrawled the words across the top of the page, her tongue poking out one corner as she wrote. I let out a watery giggle.

"Well, you can put down, 'Book in for the boudoir therapy' to start," I suggested.

"Yesss," Alison did a little fist pump and scribbled it down.

So, for the rest of the afternoon, my beautiful roomies did their best to keep my mind off Levi, and on sorting me out.

CHAPTER TWENTY-EIGHT

Happy Birthday, Mum

LEVI

"Y ou ready for this?" Xander asked as we pulled up in the driveway at Dad's place. The house was too fucking big for one man to live in alone, but there was zero chance of Dad ever moving. We'd be carting him out in a box. The whole place was a shrine to Mum, a fucking mausoleum of happy memories that had turned sour the moment she was gone.

"I'm never fucking ready to see him," I grouched, but I clambered out of the car anyway—what was the point in delaying the inevitable? Tonight was going to be a clusterfuck anyway. No Amanda, Xander had brought his fucking dog along with him, because God forbid she be left home alone for even a millisecond.

Dad was going to have a fucking field day.

My feet felt like lead as we hauled ourselves up the steep path to the front porch. Before Xander could extricate a hand from under his bloody dog to ring the bell, the door opened, and there was Dad, looking immaculate as ever, and sporting the same bitter twist to his face that had been there since Mum died.

"Well, I see you brought a bitch with you … just not the one I was expecting."

"You piece of—" I started, but Xander gripped my arm, pulling me behind him. My hands curled into fists. If I made it through the night without bloodying Dad's nose, it'd be a fucking miracle.

"That's a pretty low thing to say, Dad," Xander replied. How he managed not to lose his shit I'd never know. If Xander hadn't stopped me, I would've said things so fucking awful he'd refuse to see me ever again.

Maybe I should've just let loose, saved myself the misery of these visits. But the thought of Mum stopped me. She would hate to think how things had ended up for us.

"Levi and Amanda broke up. It's a long story, maybe Levi can tell you over dinner," Xander continued, stepping into the foyer and putting Molly down on the floor to sniff around. "I might just take her out back for a wee."

And with that my brother threw me completely under the fucking bus, heading off into the bowels of the house in the direction of the back door.

Dad's eyes landed on me, still standing on the front porch. "So, you couldn't even keep her long enough to bring her to a family dinner. Doing well, son."

I clenched my jaw and pushed past him into the house.

"Do I even want to know the reason why?" he continued, "Got bored, perhaps? Even screwing her in the living room where anyone could walk in on you lost its appeal? A bloody nurse, Levi."

I couldn't keep my mouth shut a second longer. I rounded on him, scowling at the sour smirk on his face.

"You know nothing about me or about her! You've shown zero fucking interest in my life for the last decade, except to shit on every single one of my life choices. What makes you think you get to comment on anything about me?"

Dad grunted. "Because you haven't changed at all since you were seventeen, Levi. Still playing house with women who you know will never last long term. I was shocked that things went as far as they did with Emilee—but it was easy for you to let it continue, you knew she was wrong in every way. Always taking the easy way out. Always pretending you're being mature, or responsible when really, you're just shirking the real responsibilities of life."

I stormed up to him, and before I could stop myself, I had my hand wrapped around the stupid fucking tie he insisted on wearing even when he was in his own home. I tugged him closer, feeling a stab of satisfaction that he looked a little frightened. Good. He could finally have a taste of his own medicine.

"You just proved again that you know nothing about me. The only thing I'll agree on was that Emilee *was* wrong for me. But I didn't stay with her because it was easy. I stayed with her because she broke every single part of me, until I felt like I was fucking nothing without her. I was stuck in an abusive, manipulative relationship for three years, and my own fucking father did nothing to try and support me, to help me get to a place where I could leave. No, you just heaped your own abuse on top of it.

"No wonder it took me so long to recognise that my girlfriend was emotionally abusive, when I'd copped the same thing at home for so long that I'd started to believe that was how I should expect people to treat me."

I shoved him, letting go of his tie, turning away because my face felt tight, like it had too often in the last week. I'd learned that meant I was on the verge of another round of bawling my fucking eyes out.

"I finally thought I'd found someone who would be right for me. She's everything I ever wanted in a woman. Kind, caring, smart, fucking beautiful, inside and out. In a lot of ways, she reminds me of Mum, because she wants to do what's right for everyone else around her.

"But of course, I'm not allowed to be happy. I have a baby on the way with an ex who is determined to drive every chance of happiness away from me. All I have to look forward to now is a little girl who I plan to love with every fibre of my being, because she doesn't deserve anything less. And I just hope to fucking God that Emilee doesn't try to poison that as well."

My eyes were stinging. I pinched the bridge of my nose to try and stop the tears. "And you know what? I wasn't 'playing house' with Christa when I was seventeen. Her parents wouldn't let me come home after they saw what you'd done to me."

I started for the stairs. "I'm going to pay my respects, but then I'm leaving."

I didn't wait for a response from him. I took the stairs two at a time and headed down the hallway. The door was closed, same as always. And like always, I found myself tapping so quietly on the door before entering, as if she was in there. As if I might wake the baby.

The baby that never came home.

When Mum and Lily died, Dad had turned Lily's room into a museum. He hadn't touched any of the baby furniture that they'd painstakingly built together. The pink crocheted blanket that Mum had spent weeks making was still draped over one side of the cot. The batteries in the mobile that dangled above had long since died.

The walls were filled with photos. Dad had gone through all the old family albums and had framed dozens of pictures of her. I inhaled the musty air deeply, starting at the door and moving around the room, peering at every photo. I paused at the one of Mum and her rowing team when they'd won the ARCs back in the late eighties. She'd won under seventeens then too. Quad sculls had been her event.

I couldn't look at that photo for too long. That photo was the thing that had made me want to give rowing a shot in the first place. Seeing Mum on the podium with her team, looking so bloody happy. Looking like she belonged.

I moved on, around the room until I came to the last photo. Mum, cradling a big belly, with Xander and me on either side of her. I was wearing the stupid, poncy pinstripe blazer, boater hat and tie that we were forced to wear at King Henry's. Xander looked much less dickish, since he was already at uni by then.

Mum's sunken cheeks and hairless head were at total opposites with her beaming smile.

"You okay, Lev?" Xan asked from the doorway. He took a couple of steps into the room, a squirming Molly in his arms.

"I wanted to name my baby Lily," I choked out. "I wanted to honour their memory. Mum loved that name. She was so excited about little Lily."

"She was," Xander agreed, slinging an arm around my shoulder and tucking Molly in so she could snuffle at my t-shirt. "We all were. She would have been so excited to be a grandparent soon, too."

I couldn't hold it in anymore. A sob exploded from my chest. Xander gripped my shoulder tighter as I lost my shit there in front of the last photo we ever took with Mum. There were none of Lily. Dad had said no at the hospital to having stillbirth photography done.

"She'd be horrified if she was here. She never would have wanted someone like fucking Zilla in our lives. If she … if she'd been here, I might've been strong enough to …"

"The 'what if' game is dangerous," Xander murmured, as Molly clawed her way up to lick the tears from my chin. She seemed to have developed quite a taste for them. "What if you'd never spent three years with Zilla? What if you hadn't ever moved in with me, and gone out that night and met Amanda?"

I barked out a bitter laugh. "Well, then I wouldn't be so fucking heartbroken now, would I?"

"I've been thinking," Xander began. "She said it was a 'her' problem. And Amanda is nothing if not honest. Maybe she's got something going on that is nothing to do with you or the situation with Zilla. Maybe she just needs to sort herself out. Maybe, once things are more settled with the baby and all, you might be able to talk with her."

"Maybe the fucking sky will turn yellow tomorrow," I scoffed, shrugging out of his grip and turning to face him. "Even if that was the case, I don't think I could beg for her back, knowing that meant putting her in Zilla's fucking crosshairs. That night was shit, but I know from experience that Zilla is capable of so much worse. I couldn't put her into that situation. You don't knowingly do shit like that to someone you love."

Xander took a step back, jaw dropping. "You love her?"

I nodded miserably. "Yep. Figured it out a whole day too late to tell her."

Xander's shoulders slumped. "Fuck, Lev. I'm sorry."

"Nothing to be sorry for. I'm just going to have to deal with it.

Get on with my life. Give Emvi, or whatever fucking dumb name Emilee insists we call her, all my love instead."

"Or you could be like me and get a puppy to try and fill the gaping hole in your life," Xander joked, holding a wriggly Molly out to me. I took her and hugged her close.

"I'll bring my little girl around to visit Molly, and her Uncle Xander, as much as I can, and we can be two miserable pricks together."

"You know what?" Xander said as we headed for the door, "I don't think I need to stay for dinner either. Let the old man stew by himself."

I shrugged. "Don't feel like you need to leave on my account, Xan."

Xander shook his head. "Nope, it's high time that I stood up for you, instead of tiptoeing around trying to keep the peace with Dad."

"Happy birthday, Mum," I whispered as we closed the door behind us, before heading straight down the stairs and out the front door without a backwards glance to see if Dad even knew we were leaving.

CHAPTER TWENTY-NINE

Retail Therapy

AMANDA

Project Happiness for Marilyn Manda

Book in for smoking hot boudoir photos (priority #1—go shopping for sexy lingerie with yours truly)

Tell Beth you're not working with the pregnant garbage human anymore

Call Gillian—talk about the arsehole properly FFS

Extra shifts at Frankwright? (Bad idea—all work and no play make Amanda go crazy)

Repeat this mantra daily: I have a smoking hot body, I have a fucking beautiful mind, I have a sexy heart

Get a mind-blowing vibrator! I have recommendations ...

I managed a snort of laughter—a sexy heart, and a mind-blowing vibrator were such Alison things to say. I sipped my tea early Tuesday morning, preparing myself to continue cracking on with my list—the one Alison had written down on Sunday afternoon, adding her own distinctive flair while I choked down an entire packet of Tim Tams.

First cab off the rank had been to email Beth and let her know that I would no longer be working as a student midwife for Emilee Munro. I hadn't gone into any detail, just advised that I would not be able to continue with face-to-face with Emilee moving forward, and that as a result I would like to be removed from her care team. Beth would immediately know what it was about; she wasn't stupid, and she already suspected that something was going on with Levi and me.

When I'd clicked send, my heart throbbed. This was real. I was really cutting ties with Levi and his toxic ex-girlfriend. I knew rationally that I needed to do this. Gillian always said to me that distancing myself from the triggers for my own negative self-thoughts was the first step. It was why I never got on social media. And what was Emilee, if not a very real, very vocal, very vindictive, trigger?

She didn't deserve Levi, but she'd have her claws in him forever now. Having a child together linked people profoundly. And I would never want to come between him and his daughter. He needed to be there for her. He needed to be the adoring, doting father I knew he would be, to balance out the narcissism of her mother.

I blinked—Alison's note was smudged with tears. I was expected at placement at ten, and I was still a teary mess over the whole thing. The thought of never seeing him again—or worse, seeing him months down the track with a new girlfriend, one who would be slim and fit and capable of riding him like she was a rodeo cowgirl … and who didn't have weird hang-ups that made her freeze when he touched her belly or inner-thighs.

I guzzled my tea like it was a stiff drink, and picked up the phone, dialling in Gillian's mobile number. It went to voicemail. I took a deep, shuddering breath.

"Hi, Gillian. I was wondering if you might be able to fit in an extra session for me this week. It's … I'm ready to talk about him. Properly."

I was about to hang up when I gasped, shoving the phone back to my ear. "It's Amanda McGregor, by the way."

I had no idea why I felt so nervous as I lifted my hand to knock on the bright yellow front door.

It's just Mel and Joel, I told myself firmly. *This is not a scary situation.*

The door swung open, revealing Joel. I craned my neck to meet his eyes. *Levi's taller,* the heartsick little voice in my head whispered. I swallowed back the thickness in my throat.

"Well, hello there," Joel greeted me, his trademark cheeky grin showing off his perfect teeth as he held the door open for me. "Gotta be fast around here—Connor's decided he's got a taste for the outdoors, and Mel won't let him roam the streets."

As I squeezed past him, a grey and white blur zoomed down the hallway. Joel slammed the screen door just in time, Connor coming to a skidding halt, not quite fast enough to stop himself from smacking his head on the screen.

"Oh, poor poppet!" I cried, scooping him up into my arms. He glared disdainfully at me but tolerated me scratching behind his ears and cooing to him.

"That cat is too bloody pampered for his own good," Joel grumbled, leading me down the hallway to where the house opened up to an open plan living and kitchen space. Joel and Mel had moved in here eighteen months ago and had done some renovations since then. I had no idea how they made time for it, with all the travelling they did for Mel's tennis.

"He's missed you, Mandy-Moo," Mel greeted me from the kitchen, where she was pouring hot water into mugs for tea. I glanced down at Connor, who had basically fallen asleep in my arms, purring softly.

"I've missed him, too," I admitted. "How's it working out, with him going to Sandra's house when you're away?"

"Mum dotes on him more than Mel does," Joel grumbled, "Julie thinks the sun shines out of his arse, and Shaun feeds him far too many treats. I think he gets annoyed when he has to come back home with us, because I barely give him the time of day."

Mel snorted, bringing three mugs to the table and sitting down. "Get over yourself, Joel. I've seen you when you think I'm not watching, smooching all over him. And don't blame your little brother for feeding him extra treats, I know it's really you. No wonder he's getting so fat!"

She leaned over and pressed a kiss to Joel's shoulder. My heart shuddered. The way they were just so … domesticated … together. It made me want what they had.

It made me want it with Levi …

"So," Joel interrupted my maudlin thoughts, rapping his knuckles on the table. "You wanted to talk about Thomas?"

I cringed. Even thinking his name made me feel icky but hearing it out loud—spoken by someone who had almost been murdered by him—was still so confronting to me.

"Uh, yes," I stumbled over the words, sitting down and busying myself settling Connor onto my lap before taking a deep breath, ready to blurt it all out. "I've been making some progress with therapy. It's taken a long time, but I've finally started talking about everything that happened with him. My therapist suggested that I put together a … sort of a letter, I suppose, detailing all the ways that he hurt me. Which made me think about how you both had to write victim impact statements for the trial. I wanted to ask you about them, about how it felt when you did it, and how you managed to put it all into words."

Mel leaned back in her chair, flicking her long, brown ponytail over her shoulder, and picking up her mug to take a sip of tea. She and Joel shared a long look that spoke volumes.

"Well, you know me, Amanda," she began, "I'm the one to just blurt things out without thinking about them too much. I remember sitting down with a notebook, and just letting all my feelings about it out onto the paper. It was a bloody rambling mess, to be honest."

Joel chuckled. "I had to help her go over it and make some sense of the nonsense before we gave it to the prosecutor."

Mel threw him a withering look. "I actually found it quite healing, to just let out all my anger and hurt onto the page. I think up until that moment, the shock hadn't quite worn off enough for me to properly feel everything that had happened."

I knew what that felt like. Even now, so long after the shock had worn off, I'd avoided talking about him, opening up about all the things that had happened between us, because that also meant opening myself up to the feelings.

But if I wanted to make progress towards my happiness, I needed to do this. I needed to let myself feel it all. Gillian said that if I let myself feel it, I stopped giving so much power to those feelings.

It didn't stop it being super frightening, though.

"I can give you a copy of what I wrote, if you think that will help you," Mel offered. I took a sip of my tea, shaking my head.

"I think I just need to stop procrastinating and let it all out," I sighed. Mel reached over and squeezed my hand.

"Yeah, sometimes it's the only way." She drained the last of her mug and eyed me, a smile tickling the corners of her mouth.

"So, we haven't had much of a chance to chat since I saw you on the beach back in March … you and Levi Fox … what's going on with you two?"

I pretended that Connor needed readjusting in my lap, so I wouldn't have to look at her. My fiddling only annoyed him, and with a grumpy yowl, he leapt off my lap.

Thanks for throwing me under the bus, cat.

"Yeah, that's … we're not a thing anymore," I managed, hiding my face behind my cup. Both Mel and Joel gaped at me.

"No fucking way!" Mel said. "The way he looked at you on the beach that day … I thought I was about to burst into flames, the chemistry was so scorching! What happened? I thought you guys were having fun?"

I ran my fingers up and down the curve of the mug handle. "We were having fun. But then I realised that the fun we were having has an expiry date."

"I'm guessing that expiry date's somewhere in early October?" Joel asked quietly. I glanced at him briefly. His blue eyes were sympathetic, which wasn't helping me to keep the throat lump at bay.

"What are you talking about?" Mel demanded.

"The Moon-Fox baby is due in early October." That was all Joel needed to say for that look of sympathy to spread over Mel's features too.

"Oh ..." she began, before her face scrunched into confusion. "But why would that mean you couldn't be with him? He's not planning on going back to her, is he? I've heard she's a massive diva."

"If only that was the worst of it," I mumbled. "And no, he's not going back to her. It's ... she's not a nice person, and she said some things about me to him that made me realise that I wasn't ... that I've got some things I need to work on, in myself."

"But why does that stop you from being with him? I mean, Jesus, the guy looked like he would crawl around kissing your feet if you let him!"

I shook my head. "I don't want to talk about it," I mumbled, willing the prickling in my eyes to subside. "I just need to focus on me right now. I know that sounds kind of selfish ..."

"It absolutely doesn't," Joel interrupted, his eyes serious. "We can't be what other people need from us, until we can be what *we* need from ourselves."

Mel's gaping mouth turned to her boyfriend, and seconds later she was off her chair and climbing into his lap.

"Fuck, I love you, Joel," she muttered as she wrapped her arms around his neck. He grinned at her, kissing the tip of her nose.

"I know you do, Stink."

I cleared my throat. Mostly to try and rid myself of the sticky feeling in there, but also to remind them that they couldn't just start making out at the dining table like they were home alone. Mel glanced over at me sheepishly. Joel winked.

"I think you're going to be fine, Amanda," he said, his serious tone at odds with the twinkle in his eyes. "I think you've worked out what you need to do, and you're taking steps to get there. Honestly, that's the hardest part over."

I managed a little laugh. "It feels like all I've done is figure out that I have a Mount Everest to scale."

Joel reached over, one arm around Mel's waist, holding her in place on his lap, the other giving my shoulder a squeeze. "But before you worked out where your summit was, the distance was so unimaginable you couldn't see that it *is* actually possible to scale it."

"Christ, you're so corny!" Mel teased, but she ran her hands lovingly through his dark hair as she said it.

My God, I wanted what they had.

"I'm pretty sure this counts as therapy in itself," Alison said, piling a plum-coloured lace G-string and matching bra onto the already teetering pile of skimpy, sexy, and just plain slutty ensembles in my arms.

"Yeah, they call it 'retail therapy'," I joked through the sick swirling in my stomach at the thought of squeezing into some of those teeny stringed things and then letting Alison look at me in them. But really, I'd rather her take a look and give her opinion now, than me show up for photographs in something that looked hideous. "My God, Al, some of these things would be more at home on a porn set than in a therapy session."

"You don't have to buy all of them," she replied, flicking through the stack I held. "We've got a good variety of flirty and dirty in this pile, I think it's time to head for the change rooms."

"Hooray," I mumbled, following reluctantly as we headed for the back of the store. Halfway there, a salesgirl approached us, looking harried and apologetic.

"I can take these for you and pop them into a change room, but you might be waiting a while to get in there, I'm sorry," she said, reaching for my pile.

"What's going on back there?" Alison asked, craning her neck. There was a line of women waiting at the entrance to the change-rooms, with varying degrees of impatience.

"A brand ambassador needs the full-length mirror outside the fitting rooms for a little while, and she can't have other customers in there while she's filming."

Alison flicked a raised eyebrow in my direction, just as a strident … and all too familiar voice echoed from the changing rooms.

"Seriously, can everyone out there just fucking shut up for like fifteen minutes so I can focus in here?"

Alison grimaced, but my stomach dropped into my toes … or launched itself into my throat. Maybe both.

"She wouldn't be trying on maternity bras, would she?" I asked. The salesgirl threw me a tight smile.

"How'd you guess? Apparently, she organised it with head office weeks ago, but no one decided to tell us that she was showing up on a Saturday during business hours." The salesgirl punctuated her words with an eyeroll. Meanwhile, my stomach rolled.

"Oh … shit …" Alison muttered, glancing at me, realising what was going on in that fitting room. I must have looked as sick as I felt. She tapped the salesgirl on the shoulder.

"Do you think we could just get those items set on hold for an hour or so? We'll come back once the commotion has died down."

The salesgirl gave a grateful smile. "I'll do you one better," she said. "Give me your mobile number, and I'll text you when the coast is clear."

Alison rattled off her number, while I stood there like a deer in the headlights. And before I knew it, she was whisking me out of the store. I barely registered where she was taking me, until I was pressed into a chair.

"Tim Tam iced chocolate? You look like you need some sugar." I nodded numbly as Alison ducked to the café counter and ordered.

Slurping morosely on my sickly-sweet drink several minutes later, I finally started to get over the shock of what had almost happened.

"Oh, God," I groaned. Alison reached out and squeezed my hand.

"I know," was all she said.

"I almost … if she'd seen me …"

"If she'd tried to so much as glance twice at you, I would've bitch slapped her!" Alison said darkly. "What a fucking mole, taking up a whole changeroom on a weekend! The poor sales staff, I hope they don't cop too much abuse from cranky customers!"

I nodded along, numb to the plight of the salesgirl.

Imagine if she'd seen you holding all those skimpy sets, the nasty voice said. *Imagine how much she would have laughed at the thought of you wearing them, trying to be sexy.*

I didn't want to imagine that at all. I just wanted to go home and climb under the blankets, which I'd been doing far too often in the month since I'd left Levi's house in the middle of the night.

Alison looked up from her phone. "She's packed up and left the building. We're safe to head back there."

I sucked up the last of my drink and stood. There was no point in trying to tell Alison that I wasn't in the mood anymore. She would be more determined than ever to get me into lacy things if I admitted I was suddenly in a very dark place about it all. Besides, my boudoir appointment was less than a month away, so I really had no choice but to get cracking with my lingerie selections.

I swallowed back my own self-loathing and decided on the spot that no matter what I thought about each ensemble, I'd pick Alison's top three. I was in no state to be judging my body today, but I did trust Alison. She hadn't steered me wrong with the flirty denim shorts after all.

Thinking about those shorts sent a fresh pang of misery through me. I shoved it away as we headed down an escalator towards *Laced With Love*.

"Oh, for fuck's sake," Alison muttered as we reached the bottom of the escalator. I looked up, straight into the glimmering amber eyes of Levi. I staggered back a step, almost knocking a man behind me over.

"Watch where you're walking, fat bitch," he snarled as he side-stepped me. Alison, eyes blazing, stuck a foot out and I watched in slow motion as the man tripped, lost his footing and went sprawling flat onto the tiles with a grunt.

"Watch where you're walking, stupid fuck!" she said, loud enough that he, and a number of people still getting off the escalator behind us, heard. One woman actually laughed. Red-faced, the man got up, glared at us both and walked stiffly away.

"Jesus, Alison," I said, my cheeks flaming but my traitorous eyes straying back to the poster of Levi outside the jewellery store. God, he looked so handsome in a tuxedo, his chin resting on his fist, showing off the Amphibian Ocean to Evening watch. I glanced to the other poster, and sure enough, it was Levi, in swim trunks, walking out of the surf, checking his watch.

"Just think, Manda—you've tapped that, multiple times." I bit the inside of my cheek hard enough for it to sting, willing the tears away, but Alison continued. "That impressive package got rock hard for you, my gorgeous peach. And when you see yourself in sexy lingerie, you're going to wish he could see you in it too."

"This is not helpful, Alison," I grated, grabbing her arm and tugging her away.

"Oh my God! There he is! My baby daddy!"

I groaned, tugging at Alison's arm harder as Emilee sauntered up to the beach poster of Levi, thankfully too distracted with her phone in her hand to notice me. She was clearly filming something, and she turned and leaned against the poster, holding her phone out in selfie-mode and puckering her lips as if she were kissing him.

"That woman is absolutely pathetic," Alison said with a shake of her head, as Emilee continued to take shot after shot of herself in front of the poster, before moving to the other poster and doing the same. "Levi would never agree to pose for Insta for her again, but she wants to hitch her wagon to his star in the only way she knows how. By making sure the world knows it's his baby batter baking in her oven."

"I need to get away from here," I muttered, turning and escaping the ridiculous scene in front of me. Emilee, with her perfect baby bump, and her perky breasts, and her complete lack of muffin-top made me want to shrink to nothing.

But a tiny little part of me noticed how harried she'd looked. How manic her voice sounded as she'd gushed over the poster of Levi. And I thought about how it must feel, knowing that the only thing you had keeping you afloat was the fact that people liked looking at pictures of you. How stressful that must be, knowing how fickle social media was, how quickly she could go from Instagram star to completely obsolete.

And I realised with a sudden jolt that I didn't want what she had. That I'd rather be me, with my flaws, and my beautiful friends, and a fulfilling career, than have a body like hers, and nothing else.

CHAPTER THIRTY

Did You Google Her?

LEVI

"You need to fucking fix this!" Zilla snarled.

I winced as the poor midwife who was running the prenatal class blew out a long breath and trained her eyes on my ex.

"This is an educational seminar, Ms Munro. It's not a gimmick for your own amusement. I have several other couples who are here to actually learn something tonight, and I'd like to start teaching them."

Zilla turned to me, expecting me to intervene. I pinched the bridge of my nose, wishing I was anywhere but fucking here right now. I actually seriously considered just walking out, knowing the tantrum that was about to unfold.

"Levi, fucking stand up for me!" Zilla hissed. I turned and glanced around the room, at the other couples seated in a loose circle, all staring at Zilla like she was completely insane. They weren't far off the mark.

"Let's just take our seat, yeah?" I said, trying my best to stay calm. "I can hold your phone for you if you want some pictures to post."

Zilla stomped her foot like a fucking child, and I knew that nothing I could say would prevent her from exploding.

"You are such a weak shit, Levi Fox! You never could stand up for me. All I asked was that there be a double space allocated for us, with room for me to set up my tripod and lighting so I can film a reel. It's not that big a fucking deal!"

I sighed, folding my arms across my chest. "Yeah, it kind of is a big deal, Emilee. You heard the midwife—she needs to start teaching. Your equipment will get in the way of everyone else. Do you really need to post about tonight anyway? You're not contracted by anyone to post this."

Zilla snarled, reaching out and poking me hard in the chest. "You have no fucking clue, do you? You don't get that I can't just post sponsored content! I need to engage my audience with real shit too. And this is just the sort of real shit I need to be posting about!"

I ran a hand through my hair, feeling the familiar sensation of all the strength leaving my body. Fighting with her was exhausting. Copping the brunt of her fury was exhausting. I'd done it for close to three years. And I shouldn't have to do it anymore.

"You don't need a reel, though, Em. Just take a couple of selfies on the mat, write a bit of content, and be done with it. Simple."

I knew the second that last word came out of my mouth that I'd said exactly the wrong thing.

"You're such an arsehole! You get the shits when anyone questions your fucking rowing 'career', but you put down my career like it's not even worth bothering about! I put so much time and effort into my content, and you're telling me to phone it in? Fuck you, you're such a piece of shit!"

"I'm going to ask the both of you to leave now," the midwife said. I blinked, remembering that we were in a room that was fucking full of other people, all watching us with horrified expressions on their faces. One of them even had a phone out, recording Zilla's meltdown.

Shit.

I grabbed her by the arm and tugged. "Come on, let's go," I muttered, leading her towards the door. I hissed as she kicked at my leg.

"I have to get my equipment, you fucking moron!"

I bit down on the inside of my cheek so I didn't lose my shit. Stopping her beside the door, I said, "Stay here. I'll get the stuff and help you take it back to your car."

Zilla scowled at me, but I ignored her, walking back into the circle and picking up the two large bags of equipment she'd brought in with her. I glanced around the room.

"Sorry for fucking up your class," I said to the teacher. She gave me a tight-lipped smile.

"*You* have nothing to apologise for, Levi," she replied. I fucking hoped Zilla hadn't heard that.

Wishful thinking. The second we were out in the carpark Zilla snapped. "That midwife was a bitch! She better not be on duty when I go into labour."

There was so much I wanted to say, but there was no point. She'd never been able to see anyone else's side but her own. Instead, I gestured silently for her to pop the car boot, and I packed her things away.

"See you at the next appointment?" I asked. Zilla sniffed.

"I fucking hope we aren't missing anything important tonight."

I couldn't help myself. "Well, if we are, it's your own fucking fault, Emilee! You can't just live a moment in your life without wanting to make sure you catch it on camera for the hundreds of thousands of people who really don't give all that much of a shit about you."

She slapped me. The sound of it echoed around the hospital buildings that surrounded the carpark.

"They give more of a shit than you do about the mother of your fucking baby!"

"Go home, Emilee. I'll see you at our next appointment. We can ask Beth if there was anything important we missed, she should be able to fill us in."

"No wonder that fat cow Amanda was so into you—you really are a complete psychopath." With a last sneer in my direction, Zilla climbed into her car and screeched out of the carpark. I watched her leave, letting the sting of my cheek melt into all the other fucking hurts I was nursing.

I turned, but instead of heading for my car, I walked back towards the steps leading into the maternity hospital and sank down, resting my head in my hands, digging my fingers through my hair, willing away the headache that was brewing at the base of my skull. The headache I always got after dealing with one of Zilla's outbursts.

She'd been the one who had insisted I needed to attend this class with her. Because I'd been the one who had begged her to let me be in the delivery room with her when the baby came. I'd felt like the biggest fucking tool trying to plead my case to her, but I kept reminding myself that I was doing it for my little girl.

It was all for her. I'd read that skin-to-skin in those first few hours could make a huge difference to how well the baby bonded to her father. Given I hoped that I would be able to have her with me, without Zilla around, fairly early on, I figured I needed to be there in the birthing suite to start that bonding process.

My phone rang. I reached into my pocket, pulling it out.

"Mac," I grunted.

"Hey, Levi. You okay?"

My brows drew together. "Why the fuck wouldn't I be?" I wasn't, but I didn't feel like sharing that little pearl with him.

There was a long pause while I sat there, wondering what the fuck was going on.

"Oh, I forgot you barely ever get on social media. You've been tagged in a post that is kicking off … well, it's mostly of your ex, but you're clearly in there too."

I massaged my temple with my free hand. "Zilla going rank in the middle of a prenatal class?" I asked.

"Yeah."

"I should've seen it coming a mile away—one of the mothers there was filming the whole thing. She worked fast though, the class isn't even over yet. Fuck, Zilla's going to be even more impossible to deal with after this."

"Don't worry, you come off looking like a saint. Apart from the sailor's mouth, that is," Mac said. "The caption actually says something like, 'are these two still a couple? If so, someone save Levi Fox from this harpy!'"

I chuckled without a scrap of humour. "That will make my life even more fucking difficult. I'll be blamed for making her look bad."

"She does that all on her own, Levi," Mac said.

I shook my head—Mac didn't understand. No one really understood. In Zilla's mind, nothing she did was ever wrong. When things went bad, someone else was always to blame. And nothing anyone said could ever change her mind about that.

"Are you going to be okay?" he asked.

I huffed. "No better or worse than usual. I've dealt with her rage before, I'll do it again."

"This isn't your cross to bear, though, Levi." Mac's voice was quiet, reassuring, and I wanted to punch the fucking brick wall beside me because it sounded like he really did care, not just that he wanted to be the 'nice guy'.

"It is when that little baby inside her needs me," I muttered, more to myself than to Mac. But he grunted as if agreeing with me anyway.

"Levi?"

I almost dropped the phone at the honey sound of the voice saying my name. I looked up and into Amanda's bewildered face.

"I've gotta go, Mac." I hung up the phone before he could say anything else, scrambling to my feet.

"Hey, Hon … Amanda. What … uh, what're you doing here?" I stammered, staring way too fucking intently at her beautiful face. She was in scrubs, her hair pulled back in a messy ponytail, no makeup. She was the most gorgeous thing I'd ever seen. I swallowed, rubbing my knuckles against my sternum to try and ease the sudden ache there.

"I work here. Remember?" Her voice was cautious, and it cut me deep. I cleared my throat, but it did nothing to rid me of the lump there.

"Yeah, but it's eight thirty at night," I said, letting my eyes rove over her pink lips, her gorgeous curves, and then back to her wide, grey eyes, drinking her in like a thirsty man. She blushed and I itched to reach out and stroke my knuckles across her pink cheek.

"I'm on placement overnight in the birthing suite."

Fuck, now I remembered her saying something about that the night we went out for dinner. It had slipped my mind with everything else that had gone down in the hours following. I tugged at my hair, hating the tension between us. Wishing I could just grab her to me and kiss her senseless, until the last two months apart mcltcd into fucking nothingness.

"I … I should probably be going in. My shift technically started five minutes ago."

I gritted my teeth, because if I didn't, I was sure I would throw myself at her feet, begging for her to take me back. Begging for her to pretend that Zilla and the baby didn't exist, and just go back to that happy bubble we were in.

She tapped her keycard against the panel and the automatic doors slid open for her. I stood frozen as she walked through, not even glancing back at me once.

"Fuck, I miss you, Honey," I muttered as the doors closed. Her shoulders stiffened, but she didn't turn. She just walked away past the empty reception desk and through another door, disappearing from view.

***

"How's the puppy?" Mac asked as we prepared to launch the shell for warmup. I couldn't be more grateful that he hadn't said another word about our phone conversation the night before, or why I'd ended it so suddenly.

"Molly's teething like an absolute terror, tearing half of Xander's furniture apart … and sleeping in his fucking bed every night. He hasn't even been out picking up of a Saturday night. He's like a besotted father with a newborn."

I winced as I said the words, and Mac noticed, giving me a sympathetic smile, reaching out to squeeze my shoulder before turning away. Together we launched the shell, manoeuvring away from the bank.

The first week after Amanda had broken things off with me, Mac had tried to get me to open up about it. He was fucking tenacious; I'd give him that much. But I was an iron vault when it came to my feelings about it. At least at training I managed to keep them locked up nice and tight.

So now, when I slipped and said something that made me remember the fucking mess my life currently was, Mac just offered a silent show of support. And as much as I hated to admit it, I appreciated the hell out of it. Because the two months since Amanda had left in the middle of the night had been a total shit-fight of emotional turmoil for me. And seeing her last night had just fucked me right up all over again.

I'd been a wreck leading up to the first OB appointment with Zilla after the breakup. I'd even gone as far as to call Zilla and explain that things between Amanda and me were over, and that she needed to back off the bitchiness and keep things professional in appointments. She'd been a smarmy bitch to me on the phone, all syrup and, *"I'm sure I'll be able to contain myself … now."*

I'd thought she was just satisfied that she'd managed to scare Amanda away from me. But when I'd shown up for the appointment, and the other midwife, Beth had been in the room alone, I'd realised the truth. Amanda wasn't working with Zilla anymore. She wasn't even in the building, and not from a lack of me looking. I'd pretended I needed to piss and had taken a good sticky beak around the back areas to see if she was lurking somewhere. Not that I would have had the first fucking clue what to do if I *had* run into her. Two months later and when she'd snuck up on me last night, I still hadn't known what to say. Except I miss you … which was the most truth I could handle.

"Get out of your head, Fox!" Patto's voice echoed across the water. I ground my teeth together, forcing myself to focus on the swish of the water around my oars, the pull of my muscles as they moved through the stroke. The crisp air hissing in and out of my lungs.

And very fucking slowly, as Mac and I worked through our on-water warmup, I let go of all the bullshit thoughts, and found some peace for a short time.

"Good work today boys, you're beating the average qualifier time by more than a full second consistently now," Patto said, clapping us both across the back as we stowed the shell. "Just keep that up for the next two months, and that spot in Paris is yours."

I managed a wan smile at coach and headed in the direction of the gym, flipping the lid of my water bottle and taking a long slug. Mac caught up, handing me a protein bar. I took it with a grunt of thanks.

"We've got this in the bag, Levi!" Mac said with a grin.

I shrugged. "Yeah, probably."

"Everything okay? I thought you'd be over the moon."

Entering the gym, we both grabbed a towel from the shelves just inside the door. I headed straight for the bike to work out a bit of the lactic acid before I moved to weights.

"Yeah, I'm fine," I muttered, knowing he was waiting for me to answer.

"I'm gonna call bullshit, Levi," Mac replied. I glanced up to find that for once his face was totally fucking serious—no sign of a goofy grin or that eager to please eyebrow tilt.

I snorted. "You can call bullshit all you want. We don't need to talk about it. Rowing is going great, we're on track for the WRCs. Just gotta keep the momentum."

Mac reached between my legs, grabbed hold of the bike knob, and twisted. I went to smack his hand away, but he evaded me, twisting again, and again, until the tension on the bike was too much for an easy recovery ride. I sighed and stopped trying to pedal.

"What the fuck do you want from me, Mac?" I demanded, folding my arms across my chest and glaring down at him.

"You're bloody miserable, Levi. And that's a problem. Patto said this would work for us because we're both hungry for it. But since you and Amanda broke up, you've been a Debbie Downer to be around. You don't even seem to care that we've shaved another two seconds off our best time in the last fortnight. You didn't seem pumped at all when we both managed PBs on the squat rack. And when I finally beat you at a one k indoor row, you didn't even care either way."

"If you have a point, fucking hurry up and get to it!" I grumbled, my jaw clenched tight to try and keep the stinging in my eyes at bay. Fuck, I'd never cried so much in my entire life—not even when Mum and Lily died.

Which told me everything I needed to know about my feelings for Amanda, if I hadn't already worked them out.

"Talk to me, you twit!" Mac said, glaring at me with those brown puppy dog eyes of his. "Or if you won't talk to me, talk to someone! You can't just be a misery guts for the rest of your life!"

"Fuck off I can't." I clambered off the bike, since he wasn't going to let me use it properly, and headed for a treadmill instead, setting it to a light jog. Mac stormed over and hit the emergency stop button.

"Fucking seriously?" I snarled, storming off the treadmill and sinking down onto a bench. "We're going to play it like that, are we? Okay, you want me to talk? I'll talk. I fucked up with Amanda, big time. I didn't treat her the way she deserved to be treated. I fell into cohabiting with her like we were an old couple, without doing all the dating and getting to know each other stuff. I … I just felt so comfortable with her, so quickly, and everything about her was a breath of fucking fresh air after Zilla.

"God, just coming home knowing she'd be there, that we'd be sitting at the kitchen bench to eat dinner together, that she wanted to climb into bed with me after a crappy shift at the hospital … those little things meant fucking more to me than every tropical holiday and fucking celebrity red carpet and restaurant opening that Zilla and I went to.

"But I didn't do the things that women want. I didn't spoil her with flowers and jewellery, I didn't take her out to fancy restaurants.

I didn't fucking show her properly how much I cared." I clawed my fingers through my hair.

"I saw Amanda last night," I confessed. "I was sitting outside the hospital after we got kicked out of the prenatal class. She was heading into work. And I made a complete dick of myself."

"In what way?" Mac asked.

I grunted. "I argued with her when she said she was there for work. Completely fucking forgot she'd told me she was starting night shifts. Then I told her I missed her, when there was no time for her to reply. Not that she did anyway. Just walked off without a back-wards glance."

I stood and paced the floor. "I was so stuck in my own head about everything last night. Zilla being a total fucking psycho …"

I stopped, looking up at the ceiling until the burning in my eyes pissed off again.

"Why does she keep saying that shit?" I muttered, turning and pacing the floor again.

"What shit, Levi?" Mac asked.

"Fucking Zilla. Keeps saying shit about Amanda loving psychopaths. She told me to Google her, hinted that she had dealt with a stalker at some point. Then on the night we broke up she said some really nasty shit about it, said she'd helped some nutter slice up his victims. And again last night, she called me a psychopath, and said it was no wonder Amanda wanted me so bad."

Mac's brows dropped over his eyes. "Amanda … Jesus, Levi, is her last name McGregor?"

I nodded. "Yeah, so?"

Mac took out his phone. "*Did* you ever Google her?" he asked.

I shook my head. "I felt dirty even thinking about it. Zilla loves to stir shit, I didn't want to play her bullshit games. I figured if there was any truth to it, Amanda would tell me eventually." I laughed bitterly. "It doesn't even fucking matter now anyway."

"You know she's good friends with Melanie Black though, don't you?" Mac continued. I nodded, confusion creasing my brow.

"Yeah, but—"

"And you remember that Melanie's coach and his brother were murdered?"

"Of course I fucking remember—that was what, the year before last?"

Mac held his phone out to me. "This guy was the murderer. Thomas Blackthorn. He met Amanda in a sports bar two nights before he killed Steve Herbert. And then he dated her for months, used her friendship with Mel to get close to her, used her to have access to Mel's apartment when she was traveling. And when he confessed, the cops interrogated Amanda because they suspected she was an accessory."

I leaned in to look at Mac's phone, cold swirling through my gut and trickling up my spine. Result after result of newspaper articles talking about his confession, his stalking of Mel, the way he'd used Amanda to gain access to her apartment by 'helping' her feed Mel's cat while she was away.

"Was she an accessory?" I asked, barely fucking breathing. I turned away from the phone, wishing I'd never looked.

"Nope. Not from what I remember. He made a full confession, she had absolutely no clue what he was doing. She was genuinely in love with him, I think. I do remember reading an article that was very sympathetic to her, that talked about how partners of murderers are often extremely traumatised and are demonised in the media even when they're completely blameless."

"Did they demonise her?"

Mac shook his head. "She was lucky. He made a full confession, so there was no big trial. I think it could have been so much worse for her if he'd tried to plead not guilty, and it had gone to a full trial. She would have had to stand as a witness. They would have targeted her then."

I scoffed, gesturing to his phone. "Are you telling me they didn't anyway? I mean there were dozens of results of stories mentioning her." I dropped my head into my hands. "Jesus fuck, the things Zilla said about her that night. No wonder she fucking left."

There was no way she was ever coming back to me. Not that I'd really held out much hope, but if she really did have trauma over what this Thomas dick had put her through—fair chance she did—why would she want to be in a relationship where she'd have no choice but to associate with someone who was going to throw it in her face at every opportunity?

"I fucking hate my ex," I muttered, rubbing at my temples. "I hate that she's pregnant. I hate that I can't just walk away, because my little girl is going to be completely consumed by Zilla's narcissism otherwise."

Mac sat down on the bench beside me, patting me on the shoulder. "That little girl is going to have the best daddy imaginable. And, you know, Uncle Mac is surprisingly good with kids—my sister has three under three."

I glanced up. "Really? I didn't even know you had a sister."

Mac guffawed. "There's a lot about me you don't know, Levi." He stood, reaching out a hand to help pull me to my feet.

"I'm always here, you know, mate," he said as we headed back to the bikes. "Talking helps, even if we can't solve anything on the spot, a problem shared is a problem halved."

I sighed. Mac was wearing me down, little by little. "Why are you so fucking nice to me? I've been a dick to you for years," I mumbled.

"It's just who I am," Mac said.

"Molly!" Xander called down the hallway. "Wee-wee time!"

I turned to the shiny black terror sitting at the foot of my bed, gnawing on my toes. "Your dad is a complete fucking lunatic, you know that don't you?"

Her inky eyes met mine, her tongue lolling from the side of her mouth. I sighed. "You're just as much of a lunatic as he is. Off you go—you heard him, it's 'wee-wee time'." I picked the puppy up, kissing her on the head before setting her down on the floor. She galloped off down the hallway in the direction of Xander's voice.

I turned back to my phone, and the research I was suddenly obsessed with. Thomas Blackthorn had been such a piece of shit.

The only good thing he had going for him was that he made a full confession, which had kept Amanda off the witness stand. What that fucker had put her through was sickening enough.

I wanted to text her. To tell her that I understood why she'd needed to leave after hearing the things that Zilla had said about her. Hell, I wanted to go to her house, wrap her up in my arms and tell her how fucking sorry I was that I hadn't been able to protect her from those words … or from the arsehole who had hurt her in the first place.

I wished I could be what she needed. I wished I could be enough to help her heal from the shit in her past. I wished that she hadn't felt like it was easier to run than to let me help her.

But I only had myself to blame. I'd had time to tell her how I really felt—to show her how I really felt—and instead I'd just floated along, expecting it all to blow up in my face. Anticipating the fucking expiration date.

But maybe, if I'd done more to show her, there would have been a slim chance there might not have been an expiration date.

I sighed, standing and tossing my phone on the bed. I could think myself into a fucking knot, and it wouldn't change anything. Amanda and I were over, and there wasn't anything I could do about it.

CHAPTER THIRTY-ONE

The Power to Hurt Me

AMANDA

"He said he misses me."

Alison chortled. "Of course he fucking misses you! Who wouldn't miss you? You're a goddamned catch, Amanda McGregor!"

I pressed my hands between my knees, grateful that I'd asked Alison to drive today. I was nervous enough just thinking about what I was about to do, let alone with the memory of the look on Levi's face last night. The way his eyes had felt like they were caressing every inch of my body.

I didn't need to be thinking about him right now. I tried to think instead about the appointment I'd had a week ago with Gillian's colleague, Margo Sinclair, the boudoir therapist. I tried to remember what we'd spoken about, to remember what I'd said I wanted to get out of the photo shoot we were on our way to.

But it all just blurred into nothingness, and instead, my mind showed me those hungry amber eyes, conjured up the way his voice had cracked just slightly on his words.

"Fuck, I miss you, Honey."

Just the memory sent shivers up and down my spine.

"Christ, you're blushing, Manda. What is going on in that head of yours?" Alison asked as she flicked on the indicator and turned us into a narrow side street, lined with bare limbed plane trees and terrace houses in a variety of colours. She pulled into a parking space.

"Too much," I mumbled, opening my door and climbing out. I reached into the back seat for the bag of 'costumes' I'd brought along with me. My hands shook. "I'm probably just nervous."

Alison rubbed a comforting hand up and down my spine. "You look like a wet dream in every one of the sets we bought. Don't you worry about that."

I sighed. "Thank you for your enthusiasm."

Alison gave me a sharp look. "I know that seeing him last night has thrown you. But this, today, is all about you. You're doing this just for you. Don't let what he said get to you today."

Easier said than done, I thought, but I nodded, threw her a small smile that I hoped was enough to reassure her, and we headed down the footpath towards the white terrace with the plaque out the front that read *Beautiful Bodies, Beautiful Minds*.

Nice and subtle. No one who happened to see us as we opened the creaky wrought iron gate and took the worn steps up to the black front door would have known that I was about to strip down to my underwear and pose on a bed in front of a camera.

The doorbell chimed deep within the terrace, and we waited. I'd been here a week ago when I had the initial chat with Margo, and she'd shown me through the three different styles of room she offered her clients. It had felt a bit like I was touring a brothel, but I'd tried not to let myself make that comparison.

In the end, I'd selected a room with a four-poster bed, draped with sheer white curtains. I liked it because the window faced towards the back of the property, rather than out over the street, and Margo had mentioned that she often took photos in the window because the natural light was so beautiful.

There was no way I wanted some random passer-by glancing up to see my bottom filling the window frame.

Margo opened the door, smiling warmly as she pushed a pair of bright red glasses up her nose.

"Lovely to see you again, Amanda. This must be Alison?" She held out a hand to my friend, who shook it with a grin, before we all moved off the front step and into a narrow hallway.

"The makeup artist and hair stylist are set up in the bathroom upstairs for you. I'd suggest you hop into the first outfit you'd like me to photograph beforehand. The changing room is next to the bathroom, up the stairs, first door you come to. You can leave all your clothes in there, and pop on the robe that's on the back of the door once you're changed. There's a glass of champagne up there for each of you. I'll come and chat with you once you're in with the stylists."

Margo gestured towards the stairs and on trembling knees I climbed.

"This place is gorgeous!" Alison exclaimed, taking in the lovingly restored historic terrace, with its grey walls, dark timber floors and ornate ceilings. "She must be raking it in to afford real estate like this!"

"She's a therapist," I said. "But I'm pretty sure she also lives here. You should see the bedroom I'll be using for my photos. It looks like it belongs in a luxury hotel."

"I feel like I'm on a holiday, just walking up this staircase, knowing there's champagne waiting for me at the top!" Alison giggled.

I swallowed back my nerves and tried not to think about stripping out of my clothes.

"What are we putting on first?" Alison asked as she closed the door behind us. The 'change room' was actually a smaller bedroom, with sheer curtains over the window, a dressing screen in one corner, and a comfortable love seat and a fluffy rug on the floor, all in shades of dusky pink.

I put my bag down, reaching immediately for the champagne on the side table, taking a good swig of my glass.

"Well ..." I began, stalling by taking another sip. "The room has white linen, so I was thinking ..."

"Definitely the red then! It'll *pop*!" Alison said, snatching my bag and rummaging through it, pulling out a lacy, merlot coloured teddy.

I shook my head. "I think we should go with the white first," I said with conviction. Alison's jaw dropped.

"Adventurous! I thought you'd feel more comfortable in the one-piece to start with. It's got more bum coverage too."

I shrugged. "Nothing like jumping in the deep end, right?" I replied, trying to sound blasé while I chugged the remainder of the champagne as Alison pulled out the white lace bra and matching panties. They were somewhere between a G-string and a bikini brief, which was much less coverage than I'd ever worn in the underwear department.

"I hope that Margo can get some shots of something other than me trying to pick a wedgie—I'm not used to such skimpy undies," I said as I grabbed the items from Alison and scuttled behind the screen, dragging my tights and t-shirt off with hands that shook.

"Margo is going to lose her shit when she sees you. She's going to want to use you on her promo materials. And then modelling agencies are going to start knocking on your door, babe!"

"Don't be ridiculous!" I scoffed. "I'm not even close to what modelling agencies are looking for."

"You have no idea, my lovely Manda. The world's moving away from that awful, outdated concept that all women should be a certain shape. And you are an absolute specimen of feminine beauty!"

I managed a nervous giggle as I adjusted my boobs in the bra. "I wish I could just download your attitude into my brain, to combat the little voice that's always telling me I'm a fat hag."

Alison was quiet for a moment. I waited for a response, not wanting to walk out in lingerie while that little 'fat hag' remark still hung in the air.

"My little voice tells me that no one wants a freckled 'ranga for anything apart from wild sex," Alison said. "Who would want to commit to this—to subject their future kids to teasing and taunting just because of their complexion and the colour of their hair?"

I let out a shaky breath and stepped out from behind the screen.

"You don't really believe that, do you Al?" I asked gently. She glanced up at me, a hint of sadness in her eyes that she quickly hid with a sly grin.

"Of course I don't. Just as you shouldn't believe you're a fat hag. I mean, you had one of the hottest guys in Sydney sporting a giant boner every time you so much as walked into a room."

I flushed. Nerves, misgivings, and the memory of said 'hot guy' staring at me last night made my heart pound. "I thought we weren't supposed to bring him up again today?"

Alison shrugged. "Don't try to tell me for a single second that he isn't on your mind constantly!"

I sighed, because she was right.

***

"Now, Amanda, I'd like you to take a look at yourself in the mirror properly, please, and tell me something positive about what you see," Margo said, as the stylists packed up their makeup and curling wand. Alison helped me out of my chair and stood me in front of a full-length mirror beside the door. I took a deep breath and forced myself to rove my eyes over my reflection—something I didn't ever do, especially not in such a state of undress.

"My boobs look nice in this bra," I managed, wishing I was allowed another glass of champagne.

"What else?"

I swallowed, letting my eyes focus on the bare skin between the bra and lacy panties. "Uh, my skin looks … the shade of the lingerie makes my skin colour look lovely." I'd always been pale, but it was true that the white fabric gave me a peachy glow, almost like a tan.

"Run your hands over your stomach, tell me what the skin there feels like," Margo said. I flushed beneath the minimal makeup the stylist had put on me, doing as I was told.

"It feels … soft."

There was a pause. "That's a nice word, Amanda. When you think the word soft, what other words do you associate with it?"

I thought, absently stroking my fingertips over the skin around my navel. "Uh … squishy?"

Alison coughed lightly beside me.

"Oh, um … maybe …" I stroked my skin once more, feeling a little shiver at the sensation. I never touched myself there intentionally, and it was far more sensitive than I'd imagined. A sudden image jumped into my brain. Levi, leaning over me, his tongue sliding down my belly. Something that I'd never allowed to happen, but I was beginning to wonder if I should have, judging by how responsive my skin was there.

"Smooth," I blurted. "Silky. Sensuous."

I glanced at Alison, finding her smirking at me. My face burned, and I let my hands drop to my sides, hoping that Margo wasn't going to make me stroke my thighs in the same way. I was suddenly feeling a bit pent up.

"Those were some lovely words to associate with your body. I want you to keep them in your head as we move into the boudoir." Margo said, opening the door and gesturing for Alison and me to follow.

"Bet you're wishing you'd ticked 'get a mind-blowing vibrator' off your list right about now," Alison muttered in my ear as we headed down the hall towards the white bedroom.

"Stop it!" I hissed, hoping Margo hadn't heard. But damn her, Alison was right. The feel of my own fingers on skin I never touched had woken something in me. Something I wasn't sure I wanted to acknowledge just yet.

***

Thomas

When I met you, I immediately felt like you were someone I could trust. You made me feel safe. Looking back, I realise that you were just very good at manipulating a naïve, insecure young woman into a commitment that you didn't feel, because it suited your agenda.

I didn't recognise until after your confession that the intimacy you showed me in public, especially when we were around my friends, and Mel, of course, was very different to the way you went about intimacy when we were alone. I thought at the time that this was because you had needs that weren't appropriate for you to express in public.

But now I've had two years to really think about everything that happened between us, and I can recognise that you wanted people to see you as the affectionate, besotted boyfriend when we were out together. But things were very different when we were alone, because you didn't feel so much of a need to act, to put on a show so that everyone else was sucked in enough to trust you the way I'd been sucked in.

Quite apart from the horrific crimes you committed, you conditioned me to believe that receiving love from another meant giving them what they needed, and never expecting or asking for my needs to be met in return. I thought that you offering me praise when I pleasured you was what love was meant to feel like. I thought that me showing you love meant not questioning when you expressed disgust at the thought of reciprocating the pleasurable acts I performed for you. You conditioned me to find pleasure in pleasuring you alone.

You tore down what little self-esteem I'd managed to build up around myself, and I wasn't even fully aware that it had happened until I found someone else recently who showed me what I deserve from a romantic relationship.

Aside from our personal relationship, you betrayed the trust I placed in you. You used the love I thought I felt for you to hurt one of my best friends in so many ways I can barely begin to count them. I still feel guilt to this day about my part in your crimes, however unknowing that part was. I have received unconditional support from Mel and Joel, who have more reason to hate you (and me by association) than I do. They realised that I had nothing to seek forgiveness for long before I did. To be honest, I'm not sure yet that I have properly forgiven myself. I don't know if I ever will.

Gillian, my therapist, told me that writing down my feelings can help me stop giving them so much power. Judging by how much I'm crying right now, all I can say with any surety is that it has unleashed a lot of things that I've had bottled up for two years now. It's hurting, but it's a start. A start I intend to finish because I don't want to keep giving you the power to hurt me anymore.

Amanda

CHAPTER THIRTY-TWO

Girl. Singular.

LEVI

The house was empty when I arrived home from training. Xander was still at work, and he took Molly with him, like a little yappy shadow. I dumped my bag on my bed, and before I could think too hard about it, I was out the door and walking.

I didn't know what I thought I was going to get out of this … hell, she probably wouldn't even be home. But something Mac had said a week ago when I had my meltdown in the gym kept resonating in my head. And it reminded me too much of her.

He was nice to me because that was just who he was. Amanda and Mac had a hell of a lot in common. Both of them had spent more time than they should have putting up with my shitty moods. They were both givers. I'd thought I was a giver too, after everything I'd been through with Zilla. But I wasn't. Not in the same way.

I had no expectations that this gesture would mean anything important to her, but I needed to tell her I was sorry. That I'd taken while she gave.

Her car was parked out the front of her house. I paused, my hands suddenly clammy and my heart going a mile a minute. This was a bad fucking idea. I needed to go home, to leave her the hell alone.

But my feet wouldn't move—not to take me to her front door, not to hightail it the fuck out of there. Before I could get my brain into gear enough to make a decision, the door opened. I forgot to breathe as I looked up.

"Oh, it's you," I said, trying to mask my disappointment as the redhead with the riotous curls sauntered through the door and down the path, meeting me by the letterbox.

"Lovely to see you too, Levi," Alison replied with a smirk. "What exactly are you doing here?"

I tugged at the back of my neck, looking anywhere but at her. "I don't even fucking know."

She chuckled. "Is lurking creepily outside our house something you've done regularly these last couple of months?"

I shook my head, eyes wide. "What? Fuck no! I haven't … this is the first time."

She raised a hand to shut me up. "Okay, I believe you. Besides, I was joking … partly." She leaned against the brick letterbox and folded her arms across her chest. "She can't come out right now anyway."

I swallowed, glancing at Alison. "Does she know I'm out here?" I asked. The thought of her hiding from me stabbed me right in my stupid broken heart.

"No, she's asleep. She's on nights now, remember? She's got a shift on the surgical ward tonight at Frankwright."

My panicking heart took it down a notch.

"Come on, there must be a reason you're here today," Alison said.

"I just … I realised something. And I wanted to apologise."

Alison raised a sardonic eyebrow. "Oh, really? What for? Because if you apologise for that rotting garbage ex of yours, I'll have to reduce the size of your penis quite significantly in my imagination."

"I … you imagine the size of my penis?"

Alison laughed. "Do you imagine girls naked?"

I huffed out a breath. "Girl. Singular. The one who's asleep inside right now."

Alison's expression softened. "Good answer. So, what are you apologising for then?"

"I don't think I should tell you. This is between Amanda and me."

Alison pursed her lips. "Look, I'm gonna be straight here. She's still a mess over you. I don't think seeing you right now is a good idea. She's working through some stuff, and she needs space. But …" she leaned closer, "I'm secretly team Levi," she whispered with a wink. "I think, if you give her some space to work on herself, then you might be in with a shot in the future—with my help, of course."

I shot her a dark look, but my heart started trying to punch its way out of my chest. I managed to keep my voice calm when I replied, "Of course. So, what are you suggesting?"

"Tell me what you're apologising for. I can relay the message to Amanda, when I think the time is right. I'll let her know you're thinking about her. I'll plant some seeds. But if you want her back, you're going to have to do some work on keeping the garbage human's toxicity out of Amanda's life. I don't know if you're going to be able to juggle it."

My head dropped. I knew exactly who she was referring to. "Probably not. I can't just abandon my kid to her."

Alison eyed me angrily. "No one would ever expect you to! But you can set expectations around how she treats you and your partner—any future partner you have—because you have a right to be treated with respect by your co-parent. You have rights too, Levi. Don't forget that."

"Look, I didn't come here with any expectations. I just wanted to say that I'm sorry that I always took, and never really gave, in the time I spent with Amanda. I realised recently that she's a person who gives beyond what is necessary. I think she probably gives more than she has, sometimes. And … I just wanted her to know that I wish I'd given more, when we were together."

Alison took a step back, eyeing me thoughtfully as I stood, feeling miserable and nervous and fucking broken.

"From what I've heard, you were pretty 'giving' yourself," she said eventually, a twinkle in her eyes. "You gave multiple times, is what I've been told."

I gritted my teeth, even as heat pooled in my groin, just at the memory of the things I'd 'given' to Amanda. "That's not what … I didn't give her enough of me … I kept fucking waiting for the penny to drop, for her to realise that I wasn't worth the baggage I come with. I kept it all back, because I was sure she wouldn't want anything I could offer her, in the long run."

I grunted in frustration. "I've never been that good with words. But when I said giving, I didn't mean 'fucking', alright?"

Alison laughed. "Oh, I'm aware. And while yes, you definitely 'gave' in bed, you gave her a lot more than that. You helped her forget about some of the things that she's hung up on. You made her feel desirable—something she's struggled with feeling within herself for as long as I've known her. And … you gave her love, in all the little ways that matter … even if neither of you were aware that was what you were doing."

Fuck. My eyes were stinging. I pinched the bridge of my nose, because there was no fucking way in the world I was going to start blubbering in front of Amanda's best friend. I clenched my teeth because I could feel the confession rising up—the need to say out loud that I did love Amanda. But I couldn't say that to Alison, even if I wanted Amanda to hear it more than fucking anything.

"I'm going inside now," she said as she backed up the path. "I think you should go home. But think about what I've said. And remember—actions speak louder than words."

Finally my feet unstuck and I escaped up the street before I heard the door close.

I wasn't sure what had just happened, or if it made any difference to anything between Amanda and me. But I really needed to put it out of my head, because I had a flight to Serbia and Olympics qualifiers in less than a week.

I took the long way home, heading towards the beach to see if the salty breeze could clear my head. No fucking luck. I huffed and headed home. Xander's car was parked in the driveway. Walking in the front door, I headed straight for the kitchen, opening the fridge and staring in without really seeing anything.

I had no fucking idea how long I'd stood like that when Xander pulled me out of the fridge, reaching in and then pressing a beer into my hand. He had Molly tucked under the other arm. He planted a little kiss on her silky black head before putting her gently on the floor. She immediately galloped off to find her favourite chew toy—the leg of Xander's dining table.

"How're you feeling about Serbia?"

How I fucking wished that was the thing that had me stuck in my own head. I tried to focus on his question.

"It's surprised the fuck out of me, but I think I feel good about it. Mac and I … we actually work well together. He's very different to Theo, but it's been refreshing. Annoying as shit some days, with the way he loves a chat, and wants to talk feelings all the time, but I'm kind of getting used to him."

Xander chuckled. "Wonders will never cease."

"Xander!" Dom's voice echoed down the hall. Xander headed off to let his mate in. They reappeared, Dom carrying a very expensive bottle of Scotch.

"Jesus, what are we celebrating?" I asked, gesturing to the bottle. Dom glanced at Xander, who looked sheepish.

"What the fuck is going on here?" I asked, raising an eyebrow at my brother. "Is this like the anniversary of your epic bromance or something?"

"You need to tell him, Xan," Dom said, resting the bottle on the kitchen island and heading around to grab glasses and ice.

"Tell me what?" I demanded, rounding on Xander. "What the fuck, Xan?"

"I'm … I've accepted a new job," Xan said under his breath. I gaped.

"Huh? As in you're moving to a new practice?"

Xander shook his head.

"You're changing careers?"

Another shake.

"Then fucking what? Don't leave me hanging like this!"

Xander collapsed onto the lounge, and in a flat voice, without even glancing in my direction, said, "I'm still going to be a vet. I just … I'll have my own TV show."

My jaw hit the floor. When I managed to process what I'd just heard, I said, "Like, as in a TV show about a vet?"

Xander nodded, still not looking at me.

"Like, a reality show?"

Xander shrugged. "Uh, more like a documentary series, I think. The full concept hasn't been hashed out yet. They wanted to cast the vet before they worked out exactly what the show will entail."

A grin split my face, and it felt fucking foreign. I couldn't remember the last time I'd so much as cracked a smirk. I looked over at Dom, who was fighting off his own grin.

"Dr Fox … Jesus, is that why you got Molly? Because they wanted a cute puppy sidekick for the show?" The look on his face told me everything I needed to know. I reached down and grabbed Molly from under the dining table, prying her off the timber leg.

"My poor niece, your daddy just wanted a showbiz baby!" I crooned.

"See, this is why I didn't want to tell him!" Xander groaned to Dom, who barked out a laugh.

"What's the show going to be called?" I asked. Xander managed a shrug.

"It'll all be worked out over the coming weeks. They're not planning to start shooting until the summer. They've told me they're keen to utilise the beach vibe of Bondi."

I snorted. "I'm picturing lots of slow-mo shots of you shirtless down at the dog beach? Mummy porn on primetime TV." I could barely contain my mirth.

"I'm so glad that ridiculing me is the one thing that could pull you out of the shit mood you've been in lately," Xander said, snatching the glass of Scotch that Dom held out. Dom passed one to me, and I clinked it to his.

"I live with a fucking celebrity!" I said as I took a sip of the liquor.

Xander scoffed. "You're the fucking celebrity here, Mr Olympian Model. I'm just a vet."

"Foxy Dr Fox, the vet every middle-aged woman dreams about. Fuck me, there's going to be some epic pussy jokes to come out of this!" I said to Dom, who clinked glasses with me again.

"Fuck you both," Xander muttered, and I laughed, for the first time in months I actually fucking laughed.

"Is that *Emily in Paris?*" Mac asked, leaning over to peer at my iPad. I grunted, taking my headphones off.

"So what if it is?"

Mac grinned. "I would never in a million years have picked you for a fan of a dramedy about the messy love life of a budding Instagram influencer slash advertising guru. Sounds a bit too close to home for you. Jesus, they even have the same name!"

I paused the show with a sigh. Mac clearly wasn't going to let me enjoy it in peace.

"Emily is nothing like Zilla," I grouched. "For starters, Emily is sweet, kind of naïve, caring and wants to help others, even if sometimes she doesn't go about it the best way. Zilla ... well, she just doesn't care who she shits on as long as she's getting herself in the spotlight."

Mac chuckled. "Clearly you've thought deeply about this character."

I turned away, scratching the back of my neck. "This is the third time I've watched it."

"Oh, wow. You're a die-hard fan!"

I turned back to Mac, just as the plane jolted and my iPad fell off the tray table and into the aisle. Leaning over to grab it as the seatbelt sign dinged overhead, I said, "It's Amanda's favourite show. We'd just started watching it together a week before ..."

"You're in deep with her, aren't you?" he asked quietly. I bit the inside of my cheek before answering.

"Too fucking deep, considering she wants nothing to do with me and my crazy baggage."

"But, is it really you, or is it just the baggage that's the problem?" Mac asked.

I shrugged. "Wouldn't fucking know. She never gave me a chance to find out. All I got was an 'it's not you, it's me' text, and then she ghosted."

"You didn't take no for an answer when she first found out about the baby. Why did you this time?"

"Because she doesn't need to be subjected to Zilla and her special brand of bitch."

Mac raised an eyebrow. "But *you* do?"

I shook my head, pinching the bridge of my nose. "Well, I don't have a fucking choice, do I? She's the mother of my child."

"That's nonsense," Mac replied, his eyebrows furrowed. "You do have a choice. Just because things didn't work out between you and her doesn't mean that she has the right to speak to you the way she does—the way she did in that video going around social media."

"If you think that's bad, you should've seen the texts that I got from her for days afterwards," I grunted. "If I'd just supported her, 'none of that would have happened'. Because of me, she had to 'make a damage-control post' about how she and I were 'going through a rough time, pregnancy hormones, stress', blah blah fucking blah. I'm apparently the worst person on the planet for not helping her ruin a childbirth class for a whole bunch of people."

Mac didn't respond for a long time. I was about to press play on my show again when he spoke. "She has no right to blame you for her morally repugnant actions. And she certainly doesn't have a right to be abusive towards your new partner."

I felt suddenly fucking exhausted. "I'm caught between a rock and a hard place here, Mac. Almost always things don't go well for fathers who try to put their foot down with the ex. I'm walking on eggshells, trying to make sure that Zilla doesn't lose her shit and refuse me any rights to see my daughter. And fuck … if I can't be in that baby's life, provide some sort of loving, stable influence …"

"But how much stability can you really provide right now?" Mac asked. The plane shuddered again as if to highlight his next words. "You're a mess, man. You're heartbroken over Amanda. You're verging on depressed. And don't try to tell me that the way you feel will change when the baby arrives—that's a hell of a lot of pressure to put on a newborn, and on yourself. You can't be what other people need you to be until you're what *you* need to be for yourself."

"Jesus fucking Christ, Mac," I grouched. "This is far too heavy a conversation for thirty thousand feet in the sky."

Mac grinned. "Nah. This is the best way to talk. You're stuck here with the seatbelt light on, a captive audience. I can say whatever I want to you, and you can't walk away!"

I groaned, letting my head fall back against the seat. "Fuck, Mac, you're right. I am a mess. But I don't know if there's anything I can do to make it right."

"What would make it right? If the world was perfect, what would your life look like?"

"Well, I wouldn't have a pregnant ex who thrives on my misery, that's for fucking sure."

Mac huffed. "Okay, so maybe the world isn't perfect. But what would make you feel … content, even with the whole pregnant ex situation?"

I closed my eyes, and all I could see was Amanda, in my arms. Her soft, beautiful skin warm against mine. In this dream, she was asleep, her cheek resting against my bicep, her arse tucked against my groin. My free hand cupped one of those perfect, full tits, and I just watched her sleep.

"If I could change just enough to make me feel content, I wouldn't have fucked things up with Amanda. Zilla would be polite towards me, and towards Amanda. She'd be reasonable with custody of our baby. Amanda would be happy to be a stepmum." I opened my eyes, glancing over at Mac. "See, even the things that could make me content are fucking out of reach."

Mac chewed on his lip for a moment. "Maybe not."

I started to scoff, but he held up a hand. "If we could make all of that happen …"

"If we could make all that happen, I'd be able to look out the window right now and see a fucking pig flying past. Honestly, Mac, I just need to get the WRCs out of the way. I need to know if I'm … if *we're* working towards Paris next year. Let's just get one crucial event out of the way before you start trying to work your fucking positivity magic on the rest of my life."

The seatbelt lights flicked off with a ding, and Mac chuckled. "Look, you're off the hook now. You can get up and escape me and my positivity. But once we're back in Sydney, we're going to work on a plan to help you get some happiness back into your life."

I unbuckled my seatbelt, but I didn't stand. "Why are you so fucking nice to me, Mac? Why do you want to help me with … with Amanda? I mean, you were pursuing her that night too, but you always seemed so happy for me … for us."

Mac was quiet, and when I looked over, he was staring out the window. "I was never pursuing her. But I saw the way you looked at her, and I thought that maybe you needed a little … motivation … to go over and talk to her."

I had nothing to say to that, because it made no fucking sense.

CHAPTER THIRTY-THREE

Me in my Knickers

AMANDA

"You're a natural in the birthing suite," Beth said, patting me on the back as we clocked off for the morning. I'd assisted in the delivery of two babies overnight. Both had been smooth sailing for the mothers, but one of them had been particularly eye-opening for me.

"All props to her, but there is no way in the world I could … masturbate … in front of two midwives, a doula and my own mother!" I whispered.

Beth chuckled. "Each birthing person is different. She was definitely on one end of the spectrum. She'd been clear from the start that her birthing plan included clitoral self-stimulation as her first method of pain relief."

I shrugged. "Well, it obviously worked—her baby was born with so little effort from anyone else, really."

"They aren't all that simple, though," Beth said. I nodded as we headed out the doors and into the watery August sun. "So much of how the birth goes rides on the attitude of the mother to labour and delivery."

A sudden image of Emilee flashed through my mind. Screaming at everyone, trying to get just the right angle for a selfie for her

Instagram, making sure she included whatever product she was spruiking. Definitely not relaxing into her labour.

"Do you know if Emilee is letting Levi into the birthing suite with her?" I asked suddenly. Beth's eyes were hard when she glanced at me.

"You're no longer working with her. I can't divulge that information," she reminded me sternly. I bit my lip to stop it trembling. Beth was lovely, but she could be intimidating too, when she wanted to be.

"I'm sorry I asked," I said. "I just … I think it will be better for me to be prepared, in case they happen to come in while I'm on placement."

Beth shrugged. "Well, even if they do, you've excluded yourself from Emilee's care team, so she would need to give permission again for you to be present."

I sighed. That was highly unlikely to happen, knowing Emilee.

"Well," I said. "For Levi's sake, I hope that she lets him be involved. He's really going to make a wonderful father." My voice was thick by the time I'd gotten all the words out.

"That he is," Beth agreed, which only made me choke up more.

I miss him, too, I admitted to myself as I climbed into my car.

"I wish you were here with me!" I grumbled over the phone to Alison as I sat in the car later that morning, procrastinating my walk up the steps into Margo's townhouse so that we could look at the photos together.

"I know, babe. I'm sorry. Stupid job, getting in the way of the important stuff!" Alison replied through a mouthful of food.

She was on break at work, but she and I knew well that nursing breaks were practically a myth. She was probably scoffing a muesli bar behind the desk at the nurse's station. She'd had to take on a double shift, meaning she'd bailed on me. Her manager had all but begged her to stay on—she'd had two nurses call in sick, and another was on leave, so she was running on a very skeleton staff.

"You're going to be fine—the photos are going to be absolute fire, I can't wait to see them when I get home tonight!"

"You'll be falling into bed after a double, you won't have the energy to sit through a slide show of me in my knickers," I argued.

Alison laughed. "Manda, babe, you in your knickers is more than enough motivation for me to stay awake."

I laughed nervously as I hung up, checking the time, knowing that I couldn't put this off any longer. With a deep, shaky breath, I climbed out of the car.

I was still crying four hours later when Alison walked in the front door.

"Manda! What's wrong?" she asked, climbing onto my bed and rubbing my back. I handed her my phone. Alison knew all my secrets, including my phone password, so she made short work of unlocking it and seeing exactly what had me blubbering.

"Oh … Manda, sweetie," she murmured, scrolling through. "You look beautiful."

I blew copious amounts of snot from my nose and wiped my streaming eyes as she continued to browse the gallery of my boudoir photos.

"Did you cry like this when she showed them to you?" Alison asked.

I shook my head. "I … I think I was in shock."

Alison's hand moved up and down my back soothingly. "You were shocked that you look beautiful?"

I choked on a watery laugh. "I was shocked that I thought I looked beautiful. I've never thought of myself that way. It didn't feel real. I accused Margo of lying—told her she must be using photoshop."

"My beautiful, gorgeous, sexy friend, I've been telling you for years now that you have the smoothest skin I've ever seen. No computer program could do it justice."

I coughed. "I think I'm beginning to see that. Not that I couldn't look better with some editing … just that I agree that maybe she didn't doctor these photos."

Alison snorted. "Of course she fucking didn't. It would go against everything she's trying to achieve if she did that. What I see in these photos is exactly what I saw when you walked out from behind that screen in that sexy white lingerie."

I wiped once more at what I hoped were the last of my tears and sat up next to Alison as she thumbed through the gallery.

"I think …" I began, not quite knowing how to describe what I was feeling. "I think that these tears might be starting to wash away some of the negative things I see when I look at myself in the mirror."

"So, you're cured now?" Alison asked, flicking from one picture to the next, and then back again, focusing on one where I was sitting on the end of the bed in the white set. It was one of the photos where my belly was really visible. "I love this one—I think it's my fave. Might have to send it to myself for the spank bank."

I let out a gurgling giggle. "Don't be ridiculous. But … yes, I kind of liked that one best, too. And God, I wish being 'cured' were as simple as liking some photos of myself. But I think it's kicking off the process of me reframing how I think of my body."

"That sounds really positive, Manda. Hey, you know who else might like a copy of this for their spank bank?"

I shrugged. "No idea."

"Danger Boy."

I gaped at her, snatching my phone back before she did something crazy like text it to him. "That is not happening, Alison! Oh my God. No one is seeing these except for you and me."

Alison waggled her eyebrows. "That's a damn shame, because I can guarantee he'd be heading straight for his bedroom with a supersized bottle of lotion and a mega pack of tissues if you sent him one of these."

"We are not allowed to discuss Levi," I said, standing and pacing at the end of my bed. "We are *especially* not allowed to discuss Levi … pleasuring himself to pictures of me!"

Alison chortled, standing herself and reaching for her work bag that she'd dropped in my doorway.

"Okay, no discussions about Levi stroking his magic penis, thinking about your amazing rack," she teased, dragging a black plastic bag out of her bag and handing it to me. "I got you this today."

Automatically I reached out and took it from her, sticking my hand into the bag and pulling out a long, thin box. Looking down, I gasped, heat flooding my cheeks.

"What did you do, Alison?" I demanded. She let out a little chuckle as she squeezed past me and out the door.

"Just helping you tick that last thing off your Project Happiness list. We might not be able to talk about Levi doing dirty things to himself. But you sure as shit can think about them, while you make use of your new toy. Once you're … ready … I think we could maybe sit down and brainstorm part two of Project Happiness. I have some ideas floating around in my head."

"… Do they include anal beads?" I asked dubiously. Alison cackled, but said nothing as she waltzed out, leaving me staring down and through the window-fronted box at a bright purple vibrator. 'With clit stimulator', the box advertised.

"It should have enough charge to use straight away," Alison called from halfway down the hallway.

Oh my God.

PING!

"Who's that?" Alison asked as she sat on my bed in a pair of skinny black pants and a green top that made her look like a sexy Christmas decoration with her red hair spilling over her shoulders. She was perusing my wardrobe for something for me to wear out.

I grabbed my phone. "It's … I forgot to delete an event from my calendar," I said under my breath.

"Oooh, this sounds interesting, what is it?"

I swallowed around the lump in my throat. "It's telling me that the first round of the World Rowing Championships starts tonight. Well, technically today, in Serbia, but I had … I found a sport streaming site that will show all the races, and I was going to …"

"You still can, you know. He'd love to know you were supporting him, even from the other side of the world."

"But we're not a thing anymore," I argued.

Alison scoffed. "Oh, you're a thing! You're an 'obsessed with a man you've convinced yourself you shouldn't have, even though he wants you more than life itself' thing."

"That's complete crap!" I argued.

"He came here last week, looking for you, you know," Alison said, turning and fixing her green eyes on me.

"He … what? Why didn't you say anything?"

"You were asleep. And I didn't think you were ready to hear what he had to say."

My heart thrummed. "Oh, and I'm suddenly ready now?"

Alison shrugged. "He came to apologise for taking and never giving."

"He *what?*" I shrieked. Alison silenced me with a look.

"See? Clearly not ready."

I threw my hands in the air. "How could he possibly think that he took and never gave?"

Alison shrugged. "Beats me. But I think what you really should be taking from this is that Danger Boy is absolutely not over you, my lovely Marilyn Manda."

Before I had a chance to even process what she'd just said, she tossed a recently purchased pair of jeans and a black blouse onto my bed.

"Well, we can go down to the pool bar tonight now—you're safe. No chance of running into Danger Boy, since he's on the other side of the world." Alison practically threw my black pumps at me —the ones I'd worn *that* night. The night I'd gone home with Levi.

Everything reminded me of him. I blushed, recalling how last night, only half an hour after she'd given it to me, my curiosity had gotten the better of me. I'd unpacked the vibrator and I'd given in.

And holy hell, the orgasm that had ripped through me less than three minutes later had been the most intense one I'd ever given myself. But not the most intense one I'd ever had. That title still belonged to Levi. I wondered if it always would.

And technically, the one I'd had last night belonged to him as well. As I'd pressed it inside me, I'd been picturing his strong, tattooed arms, muscles flexing as he thrust into me while teasing my clitoris with his thumb, those light filled eyes of his intense on mine as I came apart.

I shook my head, trying to dislodge the memories that even now were making me throb between my legs.

"Okay," I agreed gruffly, snatching up the clothes she'd put out for me and shooing her out the door. "A couple of drinks at the pool bar will be fine. But only because I know he won't be there."

Alison fixed me with a glare. "Would it be so bad if you did run into him?" she asked pointedly. I pressed my lips together, letting a long breath out through my nose.

"I'm … I don't trust myself not to—"

"Well, that's telling, isn't it?" Alison interrupted. "You clearly still have feelings for him!"

I scowled at her. "I've made no secret of the fact that I still feel something for him."

"Something?" Alison asked slyly. "Or *all* the things?"

I threw my pillow at her. "Let me get dressed in peace!"

"This one is my fave!" I shouted over the cacophony of the bar to Dani, scooting around the booth until I bumped into my raven-haired friend. I fumbled through my phone until I found the boudoir shot that Alison and I both loved. "I should save it to my favourites folder so it's easy for me to show ev-er-y-one!"

"Uh, I'm not sure you want to show that to everyone," Dani said, "I mean, you look hot as fuck, but let's not go around waving your sexy pics at every random in the bar, okay?"

I snatched my phone back, squinting down at the strangely blurry image on my screen. "I do look hot as fuck, don't I?" I glanced up at my friends, who both looked at me oddly. I giggled. "You know who would like this picture for his spank bank?" I asked.

"Amanda, I don't think that drunk-texting Levi your semi-nudes is such a good idea right now," Alison said carefully.

I sneered at her. "Oh? You were the one who thought it was the *beeeeest* idea ever yesterday!"

Alison shrugged, her lips twitching. "Fine. Go for your life."

"You're not seriously going to let her—" Dani started, but Alison put a hand on her arm, and they stared intently at each other. I ignored them, clicking into my messages and attaching my favourite pic.

"Done!" I crowed, setting my phone down and taking another long slurp of my cocktail. "Oh! I should probably say hi—it's kinda weird to just send him pictures of my cleavage with not even a 'how are you', isn't it?"

"Yes, *that's* the weird part of all of this," Dani said dryly as I opened my text app again.

Amanda: hi there danger boy

Amanda: did you have a safe flight?

Amanda: did you masturbate in the plane toilet again?

Amanda: do you like the photo I sent?

Amanda: Alison and Dani said I look hot as fuck in it

Amanda: I agree

Amanda: maybe it could be your good luck charm for the rowing racing thing?

Amanda: Alison bought me a vibrator

Amanda: it has this clit stimulator on it

Amanda: it's purple

Amanda: I came so hard

Amanda: not as hard as when you touched me tho

Amanda: and I did imagine that pierced dick of yours stroking my insides while I did it

Amanda: well, goodnight, sleep tight, don't let the serbians bite!

With a satisfied sigh, I set my phone down, sucked up the final dregs of my cocktail and leaned my head back against the booth, watching as the room swayed pleasantly.

CHAPTER THIRTY-FOUR

Blow Your Load Early

LEVI

I squinted, snatching up my sunglasses and shoving them on. The early afternoon sun glinted blindingly off the water of Sava Lake in the heart of Belgrade. Our heat was up in about half an hour. We waited in the relative cool under the Rowing Australia tent for our race to be called.

"You doing okay there, Levi?" Mac asked, bouncing from one foot to the other. He'd been a ball of nervous energy all morning. It was nothing like the surly, straight-faced way Theo had always gone into a race meet. It was fucking contagious. I shook out my hands, needing to expel some of my own jitters.

"You boys have this under control," Patto reassured us, clapping a hand on each of our shoulders. "You've worked hard together to get to this point. I'm proud of you both." With another hearty smack on our backs, he walked off.

I glanced down towards the marshalling area. It wouldn't be long now. Heats today, a break, then semis, and the final the following day. Three races between us and a spot in Paris.

"We should probably get started on our warmup," I said to Mac, gesturing towards the line of indoor rowers towards the back of the tent.

Ping! Ping! Ping! Ping! Ping!

"Jesus Christ, Levi, do you have a fan club I don't know about text-bombing you to wish you well?" Mac asked as I frowned, reaching into my bag and pulling out my still-pinging phone.

What the fuck? Fifteen messages from Amanda. With shaking hands, I unlocked my phone. Was something wrong? My heart leapt into my throat as I navigated to the messages app.

My breath gushed out of me, and I swallowed around my suddenly parched mouth when the first one—a photo—loaded on the screen. I stared down at the image. Amanda, wearing the sexiest white lingerie I'd ever fucking seen, sitting on a four-poster bed, sheer white curtains billowing around her. She was glancing towards a window, the light spilling through illuminating a wistful smile.

Fuck. Me.

And then I read the other messages. Fuck. Me. Sideways.

"Who is it?" Mac asked, leaning across. "Is everything okay?"

I fumbled my phone out of his sight. "I think Amanda might have had a few drinks," I explained, fucking cursing the skin-tight Lycra I was wearing that left nothing to the imagination as my cock swelled. I glanced down, willing it to go limp again.

Mac followed my eyes, his widening. He quickly glanced away, his cheeks red. "Okay, that kind of drunk-text," he muttered. "I'm just gonna … I'm gonna go start my warmup. I'll leave you to … take care of that."

With a vague, mortified gesture towards my dick, he escaped, and stupid me, I dragged my phone out and looked at the photo once more. Then I saved it to my camera roll. Then I took screen shots of the filthy hot texts she'd sent.

In the morning when she sobered up and realised what she'd done, she'd definitely unsend those messages. And I never wanted to fucking forget them.

But I was going to have to sort out my boner. And I didn't think anything other than blowing a load was going to help.

Fuck.

I checked my watch. Marshalling time for our heat was twenty-five minutes from now. Judging by the ache in my groin, it wouldn't even take me five minutes to sort out my throbbing hard-on.

"Just gotta use the loo!" I called out to Patto as I strode past. "Back in five."

I practically raced up the hill to where a bunch of porta-loos had been installed. They were fancy ensuite-style ones for competitors only, so that we could shower on-site if needed.

Locking the door behind me, I wrenched my Lycra shorts down fast as lightning, freeing my dick, which sprang straight up. Yep, there was no way I could've gotten this down without a stroke.

Holding my phone in one hand, the picture of Amanda on-screen, I widened my stance and gripped my dick, thumbing over the head. It was already damp with precum. Jesus. This wouldn't even take thirty seconds.

That fuck-worthy cleavage of hers. I couldn't get enough of it. I tugged on my piercing the way she always used to, then gripped myself tight and pumped. Her tits were insane. I wished I'd had a chance to fuck them, to rub my dick between those soft mounds until I blew all over her chest and neck.

"Fuuuuuck," I groaned as my balls started to tighten, and I thrust my hips forward, fucking my own hand. Wishing it was her hand … her pussy … that fucking talented mouth of hers, sucking me deep.

With the intense memory of her warm, wet mouth taking me all the way into her throat, my orgasm raced down my spine and I exploded. Cum spurted in rope after rope against the shower wall, leaving me gasping, legs shaking, with my pants around my ankles.

I didn't have time to come down from the hardest orgasm I'd had since she left me. I wiped my dick clean with some toilet paper, turned the shower head on to rinse the evidence away, washed my hands and left the bathroom, ready to hightail it back to the tent. But before I did, I found myself looking down at my phone, tapping out a reply and hitting send before I could think about it too deeply.

I was still shaking when I jumped on the rower.

"Feeling a bit less tense now?" Mac teased. I grimaced over at him as I set the rower and started an easy five hundred metres to begin.

"Why the fuck would she text me out of the blue like that? I mean, she was obviously drunk, but …" I muttered as I moved.

"Drunk people text for one of two reasons," Mac began, before falling silent as he started a sprint in his warmup. When he was done and back to active recovery pace, he turned his head to me. "They either say things that if they were sober, they would never even think … or they say exactly what they're always thinking, but are too inhibited to say when they're sober."

My heart lurched. "Oh, fucking great. So, what you're telling me is the best-case scenario is that she might be thinking about fucking me again, but would only act on it when she's drunk?"

Mac threw me a withering look. "Or she's thinking about *you* all the time, and we just need to find a way to get her to want to act on it when sober."

Fuck. Maybe I shouldn't have replied to her message. If I wanted to play Mac's long game, then what I'd just sent to her had probably been a bad idea.

I shook my head. "I can't think about this right now." I picked up the pace for my first sprint of the warmup, effectively stopping the conversation in its tracks.

We didn't just win our heat. We absolutely caned the competition, recording a personal best time. Patto was fucking beside himself, but the pressure was on.

"I hope you boys didn't blow your load early," he said seriously as we tucked into our meal in the hotel restaurant that evening.

I glanced up, meeting Mac's eyes. His were sparkling with humour, and I couldn't help myself. I snorted, putting my knife and fork down and pressing my fist against my mouth to try not to lose my shit.

"I have faith in Levi," Mac said, completely fucking straight-faced, as I went redder and redder trying to hold in my laughter. "I'm confident he could blow his load like that every single day we're here."

"Fuck you, Mac," I grunted with a chuckle, elbowing him in the side. He let out his own snort and took a bite into his Karadjordjeva schnitzel.

Patto looked between the two of us, a bemused smile on his face as he took a sip of his beer. "I'm not entirely sure whether it's a good thing or a bad thing that you two have developed your own in-jokes."

"We're all good, coach," I reassured him, forking up a huge bite of my own schnitzel.

"Have either of you spoken to Theo lately?" Patto asked. That brought the mood down like a tonne of fucking bricks.

"I … not for a while," I hedged, glancing at Mac, who wasn't looking amused anymore. I hadn't talked to Theo once since he spouted all that shit at his house, months ago.

"I've reached out a few times over the last couple of weeks," Mac said, startling me. "But he's not … he's in a bad place, and he's pushing everyone away. He said some pretty hurtful things to Levi last time we went to visit. I honestly don't blame Levi for keeping his distance."

Fuck. Mac, who Theo and I had shit-canned on an almost daily basis for years, had been trying to keep in touch with him. Whereas I, Theo's fucking best friend since forever, had ghosted him after he lashed out once.

Well, that made me feel like a total piece of shit.

"I'll make more of an effort when we're back in Sydney," I muttered, suddenly having no appetite for the Serbian cuisine in front of me.

Patto shook his head. "You don't have to put up with abuse, Fox, even if it's from a fellow teammate. If you don't want to have contact while he's acting out, that's totally your decision."

I found myself glancing over at Mac again. He'd spent years copping passive aggressive bullshit from Theo and me … hell, mostly from me. And yet here he was, having been nothing but super fucking supportive through all the shit I'd dealt with this year.

I nudged him in the shoulder, and without meeting his eyes, mumbled. "You're a better man than I am, Mac."

He smiled tightly, but nudged me right back. "Nah. I'm just better at putting on a face."

CHAPTER THIRTY-FIVE

We Need To Talk

AMANDA

"How's that head of yours?" Alison asked softly. I rolled over, wincing at my pounding temples and sandpaper tongue.

"It's been better," I grunted, trying to sit and then falling back against my pillow with a groan. "Oh my God, I haven't gotten that drunk since …" I didn't need to finish the sentence. Alison knew it hadn't happened since Thomas.

"I've got some Advil and a big glass of water, and Dani's just come back from a Macca's run. She's got a McMuffin with your name on it."

"Does she want me to put her hash brown on the muffin?" Dani called out from the kitchen. I nodded, flinching at the pain and accepting the pills and water from Alison.

Minutes later I was propped up in bed, both of my roomies still in their PJ's snuggled up with me, as I tentatively tucked into the hot bacony, eggy goodness.

"How do you feel, having re-popped your 'getting drunk cherry'?" Alison asked around a mouthful of hotcake. I wrinkled my nose and crunched through a bite of hash brown.

"I'd forgotten how godawful hangovers are, that's for sure," I grumbled. "But … well, nothing terrible happened to me last night.

I didn't go home with another psychopath. I didn't sleep with a random stranger … I didn't embarrass myself in any irredeemable way, so I suppose it's a win?"

I glanced up from my food to see Alison and Dani eyeing each other in a way that made nerves suddenly swarm to life in my stomach. Which, given the alcohol still swirling around in there too, was not ideal.

"What's that look for?" I asked. Alison and Dani looked like they were having a silent battle of wills. Dani shook her head. Alison's jaw jutted.

"What? Tell me now. Did I do something that I've forgotten about?" I demanded. Dani sighed. Alison turned to me with a wicked grin.

"Well, it seems you have forgotten. But if you ask me, it's not embarrassing, it's awesome."

I fell back against my pillow. "Al, what you call awesome nine times out of ten I would call utterly mortifying," I groaned. "What did I do?"

I wracked my brain, remembering vaguely that I'd been banging on about my boudoir photos. I swallowed dryly, reaching for my water.

"Oh, God. Did I show that photo to someone in the bar?"

Alison shook her head, reaching to my bedside and unplugging my phone from the charger, handing it to me. "No … you showed it to someone even better."

I unlocked my phone with shaking hands. "What …?"

"Check your messages."

Oh God. It was coming back to me in dribs and drabs now. The swirling in my stomach intensified as I opened the messages.

Levi's name was at the top. I winced as I clicked through.

"Oh my God!" I moaned as I saw what I'd sent—what I'd *written* to him!

But there was a reply from him at the bottom of the chat. I tried not to read it, as my heart raced. He was probably disgusted with me for being so forward. We weren't even together anymore, and I'd told him that I'd orgasmed on a vibrator while thinking about him!

But I couldn't stop myself in the end. My stupid, traitorous eyes scanned the lines of text.

> Levi: Twenty minutes out from my first race, and I just came harder than I have in months, in a porta-loo while staring at your sexy tits. I miss you and your beautiful boobs Honey. I would love you to be my good luck charm

My heart pounded. My head swam. My stomach rolled, and I dropped my phone and leapt out of bed, racing out the door. I barely made it to the toilet in time to vomit up my breakfast and what remained of the clearly far, far too much alcohol I'd had the night before.

Dani's cool hands pulled my hair back as I continued to retch, even after every skerrick of stomach contents was in the toilet bowl.

"I don't think it's as bad as all that, Manda," she murmured as I sat back, hiccupping pathetically and leaning my head against the cool wall tiles.

"It's actually amazing," Alison interjected, handing me some water. I swished some and spat into the toilet, then drank the rest.

"How is it amazing?" I demanded weakly. Alison passed me my toothbrush, already loaded with paste, as Dani flushed the toilet.

"Because he's still thinking of you."

I almost choked on my mouthful of toothpaste, glaring at her while I brushed.

"I don't think you guys are over," Alison persisted. "I think there is something there—something really fucking good—and I think you're an idiot if you let your own self-doubt, or his fucking psycho bitch ex, get in the way of giving that something a proper chance!"

"And I've said to Alison, multiple times," Dani added, "that it's not her decision to make, whether you and Levi try again!"

I stood up, leaned over the sink and spat my toothpaste, cupping water in my palm and rinsing, then splashing my face. Turning and dripping to my towel, I patted it dry.

"And I think that neither of you actually talked to me about how

I feel about any of this," I muttered, stalking to my room and climbing back into bed. Alison followed me.

"I'm sorry, Manda, that you feel that way. And maybe I should've stopped you when you sent those texts last night. But seriously … I wish I had half of what you two had together with someone!"

I tried to roll my eyes, then thought better of it when my head swam. "What did we have, really? We had physical intimacy. You have that, with Brad. I don't really see the difference."

Alison smacked the end of my bed. "You both fucking love each other! Sure, you mightn't have had the fairy tale romance, like *Emily in Paris* would have you expecting! But he loves you! And I *know* you love him! Love isn't just grand gestures. It's the little moments. Sitting down and enjoying a home-cooked meal together. Cuddling while watching your crappy TV show. Chatting while getting your washing off the line. Having someone who will hold you when you feel like shit."

Alison took a deep, shaky breath and sat down next to me. "I know Levi comes with a tonne of baggage. And I know that he probably hasn't shared all of that baggage with you. But you have baggage too, Manda. And I think he would be someone who would help you get over that baggage … I think he'd already started helping you get over it."

"And what about Emilee and the baby?" I asked in barely more than a whisper.

Alison reached out and gripped my hand. "Well, that's something that you should have talked about. Together. Instead, you both let it be the elephant in the room, casting a big fat elephant sized shadow over your future."

"I don't know, Al," I muttered.

"And you never will, if you don't give things another shot."

"I can't think about this now," I mumbled. "I need more sleep."

"Okay," Alison sighed, giving my shoulder a squeeze and standing. "Just … think about what I've said."

She left the room, closing the door quietly behind her. I lay back, closed my eyes, and … didn't sleep. Because all I could think about was that he hadn't been disgusted by my inappropriate texts. He'd been turned on. So much that he'd had to go and relieve himself, just before an important race.

Before I could think too hard about what I was doing. I tapped out a message.

LEVI

"Is that the fan-club-of-one again?" Mac asked, rubbing his eyes. I picked up my phone. It was just after midnight in Belgrade, which meant it was probably around mid-morning back in Sydney.

> Honey: I'm so sorry about those messages. I'm mortified. And my timing couldn't have been worse! Twenty minutes before your race! I hope my drunken stupidity didn't throw you off your game. I'm too hungover to check the results right now, but if you're not too mad at me, can you let me know how you and Mac did, please? I just need to know that I didn't ruin your chances at Paris. I know how much qualifying for the Olympics means to you

Fuck.

"Is everything alright?" Mac asked. I grunted, reading over the text from Amanda again. She was mortified. She thought she'd ruined my race. She wanted to apologise.

"Mac, while you will abso-fucking-lutely not be looking at any texts prior to this one, how the fuck do I respond to this?"

I climbed onto his bed beside him, holding my phone so he could only see the most recent message. He read it, then stared at the ceiling for a moment.

"I think you just need to do what she asks and nothing more."

I gaped at him. "You're not fucking serious! You're the one who's been telling me we can fix this. She's freaking out that what she sent me was wrong. It was the polar fucking opposite of wrong!"

Mac rubbed at some sleep in the corner of his eye. "To you it wasn't wrong. But you have to look at it from her perspective. She probably thinks that you don't respect her now, because she sent some … clearly thirsty messages while drunk, and you guys aren't together at the moment. That's not her style, Levi."

I pinched the bridge of my nose. "You're right. I know you are, but I don't want her to feel like I think it was dirty. Fuck, I'd happily receive messages like that from her every single god-damned day!"

"But that's not a conversation to have over text. Just keep it friendly, kind, don't focus on her embarrassment. You trying to reassure her over text is only going to make her dwell."

I didn't agree, not entirely. I chewed on the inside of my cheek, tapping out and then immediately deleting a tonne of responses before I finally hit send.

> Levi: Not only did we win our heat, we recorded a personal best time. Nothing you could ever do would put me off my game Honey. Everything is still on track for us to qualify for Paris. I love that you still care

I showed it to Mac, who sighed. "You're so gone for her, Levi." He rolled over and pulled his blankets over his head.

I turned my phone on silent and waited for the three dots to appear. It took forever before they did, and even longer before the message came through.

> Honey: Congratulations! That's wonderful news! Of course I still care. It was never about you

I scrubbed a hand over my stubble, desperately wanting to text her back to tell her that I was so fucking in love with her it hurt. But that wasn't something I could say over text. And it certainly wasn't something I was prepared to say not knowing how she would respond. Or if it was something she even wanted to hear.

So I didn't respond at all. I couldn't trust myself not to blurt out the things I so badly wanted her to know.

———

> Honey: I watched a replay of your heat. You and Mac look like you've been rowing together for years, not months. Good luck in your semi today!

> Honey: How are you feeling about your final?

> Honey: Is everything okay?

> Honey: I hope I'm not bothering you too much, but I'm starting to worry. Did I do something wrong?

> Levi: You've never done anything wrong Honey. But we need to talk when I get home. Face to face. There are things I need to say that I can't do over text from the other side of the world

> Levi: I have to go now. They're calling our race

I shoved my phone deep into my bag and followed Mac down to the marshalling tent. Our final was up next. There were two double sculls teams from Australia who had made it to the final. Us, and the fucking ANU team who had almost taken gold at the ARCs.

Fergus Prince, a complete tosser and one of the ANU team members, smirked at us. "Well, if it isn't Fox, the 'athlete of the year'," he said, eyeing me up and down before turning his smarmy face Mac's way. "I could've kissed Drysdale for injuring himself. Makes our job today so much easier."

I ignored him. Our times in the heat and the semi had both been higher than the ANU team. Prince always talked a big game. It was like he thought he could throw me off by smack talking.

"Or maybe I should just kiss Graham here. But he'd probably enjoy it too much."

I narrowed my eyes at Prince. "Shut your fucking mouth if all that's going to come out of it is shit."

He grinned back. "Jealous? Don't want me kissing your precious Mac?"

I opened my mouth to respond, but Mac put a hand on my shoulder. "Just ignore him," he muttered, his eyes looking everywhere but at me.

"Just ignore him, babe," Prince said, making kissing noises at us. Mac's fingers dug into my bicep.

"Seriously, just don't engage, Levi."

What the fuck was the guy's problem? "How old is he again? He's acting like a fucking child!" I grumbled.

"He's just trying to get in your head. Don't let him."

I knew he was right, but something about the whole conversation left a bad taste in my mouth. I'd already been feeling off kilter about the message I'd sent to Amanda, second guessing every fucking word I sent. I didn't need a stuck-up prick like Prince throwing me even further.

I stared out at the mirror surface of Sava Lake. Two thousand metres of water was all that lay between us and Paris. That was the only thing I needed to be thinking about.

The bang of the starting gun exploded in my ears. My quads strained, my shoulders flexed, and I found myself repeating the same four words I'd often used to concentrate when I first started rowing to drown out the intrusive shit that was bouncing around my brain.

Catch, drive, finish, recover. Catch, drive, finish, recover.

My muscles burned, the sun beat down on me, but all I let myself hear was those four words. I didn't let myself glance around to see where the other teams were, or to check the distance markers, instead focusing on the synchronised pull of Mac's back muscles in front of me. Nothing else mattered but finishing this race.

Even as we crossed the finish line, I felt distant from the cheers coming from the bank, from the announcer over the loudspeaker. It wasn't until Mac's roaring cut through my muffled senses that I blinked, seeing him punch the air.

"We did it, Levi!"

We did?

"Holy shit. We fucking did!"

I laughed through my breathlessness, but my laughter turned to fucking tears without my permission, and I rested my head in my hands, pushing my sunglasses up to press my fingers into my eye sockets, willing the tears to stop.

Elation and relief warred inside me, along with a bittersweet aftertaste that I knew had a whole fuckload to do with Amanda. I needed her like I needed fucking air. Right now, all I wanted was to get out of the shell, swim to the shore if I had to, and call her, just to hear her voice when I told her that we'd won. That she *was* my good luck charm, even if things were completely fucked between us. But I couldn't.

I managed to pull myself together by the time we manoeuvred the boat to the dock and climbed out. Patto was there, a mile-wide grin on his face.

"Have you boys been holding out on me?" he said, smacking us so hard across the backs that my eyes started watering for a totally different reason. "Not only was that a new PB time, but you were bloody milliseconds off of the world record!"

My mouth fell open, my eyes flicking to Mac as he grinned back at me.

"Paris, here we come!" he said with a laugh.

"Holy shit," was all I could manage to get out as I glanced back and forth between my beaming coach, and my beaming teammate.

AMANDA

"Holy shit!" I screeched, almost dropping my laptop onto the loungeroom floor. Alison's eyes were like saucers as I struggled to balance it on my lap, despite my jiggling knees.

"Did I just hear right?" Alison asked faintly. I turned the volume up on the streaming site, where the announcer was repeating that yes, Australia's Sydney Rowing team had won the Double Sculls event, breaking their own personal best time they'd set only days earlier in their heat, but also almost breaking the current world record, too.

"I don't know much about rowing," I said, placing my laptop on the coffee table to prevent another accident, and snatching up my phone with shaking hands. "But this is big … this is big for him … for them, right?"

My fingers fumbled all over the phone screen, opening random apps as I tried to get to messages. My heart was ready to pound out of my chest.

"Uh, yeah, I'd say absolutely smashing their World Rowing Championship final, almost breaking a world record, and securing themselves a spot at the fucking Olympics is a pretty big deal, Manda!" Alison chuckled as she took a sip of her wine. "Now, can we talk about the fact that you called in sick to Frankwright for your shift tonight so that you could watch this live? Because that is not something the Amanda McGregor I know would normally do."

"Huh?" I muttered, finally getting the text thread with Levi open and frantically typing something that I hoped would convey how excited I was for him. How proud I was of him.

How much I missed him …

I couldn't stop thinking about the things that he supposedly needed to say to me face-to-face, and vacillating wildly between heady anticipation of that conversation, and a sickly sense of dread. Because it wasn't just about him and me. It was about him, and me, and his ex-girlfriend, and their baby, and all my issues, and it was all just a huge mess, and one that couldn't be fixed with a simple chat between the two of us.

"Hello? Are you in there?"

I snapped my attention back to Alison, who was waving her hand in front of my face.

"Sorry, I ..."

Alison smirked. "You spaced out because all you can think about is how his arms and thighs bulged as he was rowing?"

I threw her a withering look, trying to ignore the heat rising in my face. Because yes, I had noticed that. I couldn't *not* notice.

"What's stopping you, Manda?"

I looked somewhere above her head. "What do you mean?"

I knew exactly what she meant.

Alison snorted—she saw right through me. "Is it just the garbage-stench ex-girlfriend? Or is the baby an issue too? Look, I wouldn't blame you for not wanting to saddle yourself with a stepchild in your mid-twenties."

"No, it's not that. You know I love babies—for crying out loud, I'm training to be a midwife. If he felt like I was special enough to him to share his child with me ..." I trailed off, my heart thrumming with the sudden image of sharing a life with Levi and his daughter.

Alison grunted. "So, it's just his nasty ex ... you're stronger than that, Manda! Are you really going to let the things she says stop you from being with a man you clearly adore?"

"It's not that simple," I argued weakly. Alison smacked the armrest hard enough to make me jump.

"It is that fucking simple! You and Levi can fix this! He can stand up for you. If he cares, he will stand up for you. And you don't have to let her venom poison you. Not only are you a bloody smoke-show to look at, you aren't just your appearance."

I rolled my watery eyes. "Don't you dare spout out the 'you're beautiful on the inside' line, please. That's almost worse than just telling me I'm fat."

"Own it, Amanda! You're a stunning, sexy fat woman! Stop giving the word so much power! Your size doesn't have any bearing on your beauty. And yes, that scrag might be 'thin'. But she's got nothing else going for her except how she looks. Imagine how fucking empty her life must be, if that's all she has?"

I looked away, wiping at a tear. That was the first time Alison had called me 'fat'. And while it stung, it certainly didn't the way it had in the past, because she wasn't using it to try and hurt me. She was using it to show me that my fatness didn't come with a 'but'. It came with an 'and'. I wasn't attractive, but fat. I was attractive *and* fat. It was just another part of me. One didn't cancel out the other.

"I'm not saying or doing anything until I hear what Levi wants to tell me face-to-face so badly," I mumbled.

Alison laughed. "If you haven't figured out what he wants to tell you already, I've lost all faith in you."

LEVI

"So, apart from consuming too much Rakija, are we going to do anything else to commemorate this momentous occasion?" Mac asked, tipping his shot glass back.

I sipped at my own. I didn't want to get too wasted for what I had planned. The bar we'd found ourselves in was a hole-in-the-wall in downtown Belgrade, with sticky floors and, most importantly, no other rowers frequenting it. After Prince's bullshit earlier, and the murderous looks he'd thrown us as he watched us climb the podium, his team not having placed at all, had been enough for me.

I pulled out my phone, reading again the message I'd found from Amanda when we'd finally collected our gear after all the fucking around that happened post-final.

> Honey: I knew you could do it! I almost broke my laptop I screamed so hard when you crossed the finish line
>
> Honey: I wish I was there, because you really look like you need a hug right now. Tell Mac to give you one for me

I wanted so much more than a hug from this woman. I wanted her riding my fucking lap, crying out my name, arching her back so those tits were right at mouth level.

I wanted her soft, and relaxed, and sleepy in my arms.

I wanted her making sweet remarks as we watched some dorky fucking TV show together.

I wanted her little, secretive smiles as we ate together at home.

I wanted her pregnant with my baby, with a ring on her left hand.

But I'd settle for her on my lap tonight. Just not in the way I really wanted it.

> Levi: I wish you were here too. I suppose I'll have to settle for the next best thing

To reassure her that I didn't mean I was going to go hook up with some random Serbian girl, I slung my arm around Mac's shoulders, pulling him against me. He was drunker than I'd realised —his head lolled against my shoulder as he grinned sleepily for a selfie. I fired it off to Amanda, then pocketed my phone, standing and helping Mac up by the elbow.

"I've got an appointment I need to get to," I said as I led him out of the bar. "You can come with, or I can walk you back to the hotel—you're pretty wasted, mate."

Mac straightened, his eyes sharper than I would have given him credit for. "We're in this together, Levi. I'm in for the whole night."

I shrugged. "Well, it's gonna be an all-nighter. Just be prepared."

The air was cool in the tattoo studio. The artist I'd booked in with had a fantastic reputation online. He was kind of skeezy looking, but the ink on his arms was fascinating—writhing serpents and naked women.

He spoke basically no English, but as Mac browsed through one of the guy's portfolios, he showed me the design that he'd come up with for me when I'd emailed him my idea. And fuck me, it was perfection.

Mac watched avidly as I stripped to my underwear, hopping up onto the chair so the artist could shave and prep my thigh.

"What are you getting?" he asked.

I smirked. "You'll see."

When the design was transferred onto my leg, Mac peered at it, his eyes widening in realisation.

"Is that …?"

I nodded. "Settle in, princess," I said, leaning back in the chair and putting my hands behind my head. "This is gonna be a long night."

Seven hours later, my silent tattooist was partway through colouring. And I was starting to feel the burn. I had a fucking high pain threshold, but seven hours of having a needle dragged over your skin starts to get a bit old.

Mac had been distracting me with stupid songs, or ducking out to an all-night convenience store to grab chips and chocolate bars. But I needed something more.

"If I tell you something that I hate telling people, will you do the same for me?" I asked Mac out of the blue, peering over at him where he sat in the chair, watching the colour filling my tattoo.

"Uh … I …" Mac stammered, then took a deep breath. "Yeah, okay."

I ran a finger across the scar on my eyebrow. "My dad did this to me."

Mac's lips thinned, but he didn't say anything. I was fucking grateful for that. I wasn't sure I wanted to go into chapter and verse about how it had happened. I didn't want to cry in front of the tattooist.

"We had a fight. He grabbed a vase of flowers and threw it at me. It broke against my forehead and a shard sliced right through my eyebrow. Honestly, I was fucking lucky it didn't take my eye out."

The buzz of the tattoo gun filled the silence, until eventually Mac said, "Jesus, Levi."

I huffed out a humourless laugh. "Yep. My dad is a piece of shit. He's never apologised for it either. I don't think he's even once acknowledged that he did it.

"So," I continued, trying to lighten the mood. "I bet you can't top my shitty dad confession."

Mac's eyes slid to the floor. "Don't bet on it." He took a shuddering breath, and suddenly those dark eyes of his locked on mine.

"I'm gay, Levi."

I opened and closed my mouth a couple of times, before realising that I was acting like a complete dick.

"Well, I'm … you've hidden that well, but how is you being gay even close to as bad as my dad throwing a vase at my face?"

Mac sniffed. "My dad's the reason I haven't told you before now. When I was seventeen, I had a boyfriend—a guy from school my mum and dad assumed was my best mate. Things were getting serious between us, but I felt shitty lying to my parents. So … I came out."

I swallowed. "I'm guessing it didn't go well?"

Mac shook his head. "My parents are … they're very conservative. In their minds, if you have those urges you either ignore them, get married to a woman and live like a straight man, or you stay 'celibate'. You don't flaunt your 'lifestyle' to those around you.

"I was banned from seeing my boyfriend. I was told that they didn't recognise my 'choice', and that if I wanted to have a relationship with my family at all, I'd keep it to myself."

Mac's eyes were glistening, and I felt like such a piece of shit for asking him to share something so personal with me. I gripped his shoulder.

"They don't fucking deserve you, Mac," I said quietly. "What about your sister—you said you have a sister with three kids?"

Mac's mouth twitched up in what might have been a smile, but I couldn't be sure.

"She's … more supportive. But she also relies heavily on Mum for childcare, so her support happens in private. Just like my love life happens in private. I hate closeting myself around my friends … but I just don't want to do that with you anymore, Levi. You've been a really good friend to me these last few months."

My throat closed up, and I coughed to try and clear it. "Don't kid yourself, Mac. I've done the bare minimum in this friendship. You've done the heavy lifting. You've been the one to make me open up about my fucking baggage. And when have I ever tried to get you to open up to me? When have I ever showed any interest in helping you with your problems? Fuck, I didn't even realise you had problems you needed to share with someone!"

Mac chuckled, patting me on the hand. "You're an open book when it comes to your feelings, Levi. It's easy to talk to someone about why they feel like crap when it's written all over their face. I've gotten too good over the last decade at hiding my feelings from everyone around me. It's been my survival strategy."

I coughed again. "Well, I don't want you to hide shit from me anymore. We're teammates. Fuck, we're more than that—we're friends." I rubbed a hand over my forehead.

"So, we've both got arsehole parents, but Jesus, yours take the cake. I mean, my dad shits all over my life choices … your parents refuse to even acknowledge the person you are."

I reached for a chocolate bar, unwrapping it and breaking it in half, handing the other part to Mac.

"To shitty parents. May I not become one next month."

Mac tapped his piece to mine. "You won't, Levi. You're going to be a great dad."

"Well, at least now you not being interested in Amanda makes total fucking sense," I said through a mouthful of weird European chocolate. "Because I can't work out how any straight man in their right mind wouldn't want her."

Mac laughed. "I've gotten good at pretending to be interested in women over the years. It's easy to chat to a pretty woman when you aren't trying to get in her pants."

I pinched at my scarred eyebrow. "But you shouldn't have to pretend—especially in front of the rowing guys. Do any of them know, except me?"

"Patto knows. But that man's an iron vault when it comes to personal stuff."

I nodded, thinking about the shit that'd happened with Dad, and how understanding Patto had been. "We really don't give the old fuck enough credit, do we?"

Mac shook his head, as the tattooist gave a final wipe over the finished design.

"You go … mirror," he commanded. I stood, wincing at how tight my body was after over ten hours in the chair, and headed to the mirror.

He'd done a better job than I could ever have imagined. The play of light and shade over her gorgeous body was fucking flawless.

"Well, you have to get her back now, don't you?" Mac said with a grin, standing beside me and perusing the tattoo with his arms folded across his chest. "Otherwise you're a super creep for getting your ex's portrait tattooed on your thigh."

"I think I have a kink for ex-tattoos," I replied, half-joking, gesturing to the Boobzilla on my arm. "But you're right. I need her. I fucking love her. I've just got to figure out a way to make me, and my fucking baggage, a worthwhile risk for her to take."

"She'd be a fool not to take that risk," Mac said, clapping me on the shoulder and heading for the door.

CHAPTER THIRTY-SIX

She's Moved On

AMANDA

"Amanda!"

I turned to see Dr Chris Bentley, technically my boss, seeing as he was the OBGYN I'd been doing my clinical placement with, striding down the hallway towards me in jeans and a button-up shirt with the sleeves rolled to his elbows.

I hadn't had a whole lot to do with Chris during placement, outside of walking patients into his office and occasionally sitting in for an ultrasound. He was a friendly guy, mid-thirties, handsome in the way I had always thought was my type: mildly nerdy, not overly buff, approachable. He had a thick head of light brown hair and warm, brown eyes that crinkled at the corners when he smiled. Which he was doing right at that moment.

Two years ago, I would have swooned over someone like him. Now, all I could think was how his arms were skinny, and too bare of tattoos. And his brown eyes looked dull compared to light-filled hazel ones.

"Dr Bentley, what are you doing over here in public hospital territory?" I asked, trying to mask my exhaustion with a warm grin. I'd just gotten off the last of four night shifts up on the surgical ward, copping the usual abuse from patients in pain, or plain peeved to be in hospital. I just wanted to go home, run a bath and try to forget that I had to do it all again in a few days.

"I work here, too, you know," he reminded me, running a hand through his hair. "I operate on public gyno patients once a week. And please, call me Chris."

I nodded. I hadn't known that. Maybe I should have been paying more attention to the man who had been kind enough to take me on, allowing me to be mentored by Beth, one of the best midwives in the area.

"I was wondering … have you eaten breakfast yet?" Dr Bentley —Chris—asked. I shook my head.

"I normally just grab drive-through on the way home from a graveyard shift."

Chris took me gently by the elbow and steered me back in the opposite direction to my car. I squeaked, not sure what was going on.

"Come and have breakfast at the café with me. I promise their B&E rolls are so much better than Maccas. I have something I'd like to discuss with you."

Feeling like I had no choice, I let him lead me back along the hallway, down three floors in the lift, and into the hospital café. Not the cafeteria where I sometimes grabbed a pre-packaged sandwich on my way into a shift. The actual café, where they made barista coffees, and scones with jam and cream, and apparently really good bacon and egg rolls.

Taking a seat, I grabbed a menu, mostly to put something between me and the set of brown eyes that were peering intently across the table at me. When the waitperson came over to take our orders, I blurted out that I'd have the same as Dr Bentley—forgetting momentarily that he wanted me to call him Chris, and also that I didn't drink coffee. I had to call her back and change my drink order to an Earl Grey tea.

"So," Chris began, and I had no choice but to look at him, because the waitperson had taken away my menu.

"So …" I repeated, hoping he would get to the point sometime soon.

"Beth has nothing but good things to say about you," he continued, fiddling with his watch as his eyes stared me down. "She says you're calm, knowledgeable, you put your patients at ease, you explain things to them in terms they can understand. She told me you've been hands-on and incredibly competent in the birthing suite, working well under pressure. I'm hoping that I'll be able to see this firsthand in the coming weeks—the on-duty obstetrician roster is changing up so I should be on at least one of your nights in the birthing suite in October."

I swallowed at the mention of October. Levi's daughter was due in October.

"Anyway, I'm blathering," Chris said with what almost sounded like a nervous chuckle. "I asked you to sit down with me because I wanted to … I'd like you to come on board as a full-time midwife with me, once you're finished with your graduate diploma."

"Oh!" I said, pressing a hand to my chest. "I …"

"I'm sorry I made it seem like I was working up to something really big. And, I suppose it sort of is. My practice is getting busier, and I need to be able to manage a bigger client roster, which means needing another midwife. You're the obvious choice. You've fit in so well to the practice, Beth thinks you're amazing, Florence says your files are always in perfect order."

My eyes were prickling, and I quickly pressed my fingers to them in the vain hope that I could stem the tears.

"Are … is everything alright?" Chris asked. I managed a watery laugh.

"Yes, everything is definitely alright," I replied, wiping under my eyes at the tears that had managed to leak out. "I feel so humbled that Beth thinks so highly of me. She's been such an amazing mentor; I've been very lucky."

Chris's smile softened. "Don't feel like you need to give me an answer immediately. I just wanted to make the offer, we can discuss this further next time you're in the clinic, if you're interested."

I grinned. "I'd love to accept, right now," I said, and without thinking I reached over and put my hand over his. "Thank you so much Chris."

"I didn't realise the chubby-chaser population in Sydney was so big!"

I stiffened. The voice behind me was deep and vaguely familiar. Chris's eyes flicked above my head, his brow furrowing.

'What did you just say?" he asked of the person behind me. I didn't want to turn, but curiosity got the better of me.

"Theo!" My eyebrows shot up in shock. He smirked down at me, his arm in a sling.

"I'm sorry, you know this man?" Chris asked in confusion behind me. I found I couldn't take my eyes off Theo.

"I … um … yes, this is my …"

"My friend Levi was fucking her for a couple of months," Theo said before I could gather my thoughts enough to work out how on earth I could explain my tenuous relationship with him. "Looks like you've moved on up in the world, though. A fucking doctor! Lofty goal for a timid fat girl!

My mouth went dry, my throat caught.

"I really don't think that you should be speaking to or about her the way you are," Chris said. There was an edge to his voice that hadn't been there a moment ago.

Theo ignored Chris. "So, Levi lost interest in you, did he? I'm not surprised. I mean, you've seen the kind of chick he can pull without even trying. I was shocked you lasted as long as you did—he only chatted you up that night because he thought it would piss Mac off. He hates Mac, so fucking the girl Mac had his eye on was like sweet revenge to him."

What?

I tried to swallow but my throat wasn't working. My hands shook, and I slipped them under the table, weaving my fingers together and holding on so tightly that my knuckles ached.

"You're well out of line right now, mate," Chris warned, standing from his chair and eyeing Theo with intense dislike.

I stood too, the aluminium chair clattering awkwardly to the ground as I struggled to extricate my hips from the armrests. Theo let out a snort of laughter as my face burst into flames.

"I've got to go," I mumbled, pushing past Chris and running in the opposite direction of my car. If either of them said anything more, I didn't hear it.

It wasn't true … it couldn't be true. I thought back to that first night, to everything that had happened between Levi and me from the time we met. Someone who was only interested in what Theo was insinuating wouldn't have acted the way Levi did. Wouldn't have pursued me so vigorously. Wouldn't have wanted to be with me all the time. Would he?

And even if it had become something more to him, if it had started out of some sick need to 'win' me, to stick it to Mac … did that cancel out everything else I thought we might have been building together? Oh God, how could I face him now? How could I listen to whatever he needed to say to me face-to-face?

I managed to make it to an exit, only to realise I now needed to get back to the other side of the hospital where my car was parked. But there was no way I was going back in there. If there was even a slight chance of running into Theo, or Chris, I wasn't taking it.

I powered my way through the gardens that surrounded the hospital campus, barely breathing because I knew if I let a full lungful of air in, it was going to end in me sobbing uncontrollably. I needed to get to my car before I let myself do that.

If only my stupid eyes weren't all stupidly blurry all of a sudden!

"Amanda!"

That voice broke me, and the sob I'd been desperately holding inside burst out. I couldn't see him because of all the tears, but I could feel the heat of him, so close to me. Another sob, and then another. And then his arms were around me, strong, and familiar, and so, so right. Which only made everything so much worse.

"Honey, what's wrong?" he asked, agony filling his voice. He smelled so good, like the ocean, and sun-warmed skin.

"I … I can't," I choked out, wriggling out of his arms, refusing to look up into his face. He took a step back, a distressed sigh puffing out of him.

"Amanda, please," he murmured, but I shook my head, wiping at my streaming eyes.

"No, Levi, not now."

I turned and hurried away, hoping he wouldn't follow me. But kind of wishing that he would.

LEVI

Fucking hell.

Of course, on my first day back in Australia, I'd have to run smack fucking bang into Amanda, completely unprepared. And while I was racing to an obstetrician's appointment with Zilla. An appointment she'd only decided to inform me of via a text message that came through while I was in the air. I'd landed, gotten her message and, jetlagged as fuck, had barely had time to go home and shower before I'd been leaping in my car again and rushing for the hospital. The last thing I needed right now was Zilla deciding I wasn't pulling my weight, and banning me from seeing my daughter.

But all I wanted to think about now was Amanda. All I'd been thinking about since those drunken messages had come through was Amanda. Hell, all I'd thought about since I first saw her in that pool bar was Amanda.

The entire flight home my brain had been on a constant loop of how to tell her, when … where … what the actual fuck to tell her. I'd been jumping wildly between a grand fucking gesture—the kind that she fucking deserved—and just turning up on her doorstep with my hat in my hand. I'd wanted to write a fucking speech before I saw her again, wanted to try and get the mess of raw emotions out of my brain and into something that resembled a coherent argument about why she should give me another chance.

But all the progress I'd made on that front had just flown out of my fucking brain when she'd collided with me. What had happened for her to be that upset? And what the fuck had I been thinking, getting up in her space like that, pulling her into my arms like I still had a right to touch her that way?

But shit, it had felt so good, and so, so fucking right.

I wanted to race after her, to demand she tell me what was wrong. Instead, I stood, watching her run from me, clenching and unclenching my fists and feeling fucking helpless. When she was totally out of sight, I smacked the heel of my palm against my forehead a few times. Would she think that I'd been skulking around her place of work hoping to run into her? Like a complete fucking lunatic?

Fuck, I could stand there and get stuck in my head about the whole encounter, or I could just get the fucking appointment with Zilla and the obstetrician out of the way, even if she was the last bloody person I wanted to see when my head was full of Amanda in distress.

"Your girl is down and engaged," Dr Bentley said, pointing to the monitor showing an ultrasound image of the baby's head, clearly down low in Zilla's pelvic area. "This is great news, considering you're due in three weeks. She's all ready to go, in perfect birthing position!"

I glanced at Zilla, who didn't show any ounce of emotion on her face. I wondered if she'd been having Botox again. I wondered if that was even allowed during pregnancy.

"So, does that mean the birth should be a smooth one?" I asked. Zilla flashed a scowl at me. Okay, so no Botox—her forehead couldn't move like that if she'd had injections.

"There are never any guarantees, Levi," Dr Bentley explained. "The position is good, which is a positive, but there are so many other factors that can impact. But best not to worry about this too much. Your girlfriend is doing great, and less to stress about right now means a more relaxed labour."

"Ex-girlfriend," I reminded him. Zilla shot me a murderous look.

Dr Bentley froze, staring at me like his brain was working overtime.

"Do you have a friend called Theo?" he asked. I went cold, although I had no fucking idea why.

"Uh, yeah. My teammate. He's injured at the moment though. Haven't seen him for a few months."

Dr Bentley nodded, his mouth tight. What the fuck was going on here? Suddenly the weird expression on Dr Bentley's face cleared, and he stood.

"Well, I'll see you two in a week. Unless you go into labour in the meantime. If you do, you can call the clinic, or the birthing suite after hours, and we can work out the best plan of action for you."

With that he basically pushed us out the door. I walked to the counter in a daze, tapping my credit card for the appointment.

"What the hell was that all about?" Zilla demanded as we took the lift down. I shrugged, stuffing my hands in my pockets.

"No fucking idea," I grunted. "Do you want me to come help you assemble the cot and change table that I ordered?"

Zilla sneered. "I already did it. I'm not useless, you know!"

"On your own? Jesus, Emilee, you shouldn't be lifting shit like that at thirty-seven weeks pregnant!"

Zilla rolled her eyes. "Didn't realise you cared about my well-being so much, seeing as I'm just your *ex-girlfriend*," she snarked. "But no, I had some help."

"Who from?" I asked. Zilla's eyes slid away as the lift doors opened.

"Just a friend," she replied. I got the feeling she wanted me to push for more information, so I snapped my mouth shut tight. If she had a new 'friend' it was none of my fucking business.

Just as it should have been none of her fucking business what Amanda and I were to each other.

"If you're seeing someone new, that would be okay with me, you know that, don't you?" I said.

"Seriously Levi?" Zilla snapped. "No, I'm not seeing anyone new. No one wants to date a heavily pregnant woman! No one wants to take on the fucking baggage of someone else's kid!"

Didn't I know it.

"Fucking Sydney Rowing annual dinner," I grunted, adjusting the cuffs on my navy suit. "Why the fuck did they schedule it for immediately after the WRC's?"

"No idea," Mac replied as we entered the ballroom at the Hilton. "But I can tell you I bloody hate wearing a tie." He tugged at his collar.

"Just don't fucking wear one," I suggested, gesturing to my own open collared shirt. "Honestly, who are we even trying to impress anyway, in this getup?"

"Um … sponsors, who pay us … the state premier, who might increase our funding?"

I rolled my eyes. "If our performance in Serbia wasn't enough to do that, I don't see how dressing up and making nice at a bloody dinner is going to help."

Mac fell silent, because he knew I was right. I followed him through the tables, occasionally grunting a hello to people who greeted me, without even really absorbing who I was talking to. My mind was full of Amanda.

I'd sent her a text as soon as I'd seen Zilla drive off after our appointment earlier in the day, asking if everything was okay. She hadn't responded. I was trying not to dwell on that, and failing fucking miserably.

"Uh, Lev," Mac mumbled, jabbing me with an elbow as we approached our table. I glanced up, taking in the other guests already seated. The State Premier and her husband, Patto and his wife, two of the women's Single Sculls rowers—one of them partnered up with a gorgeous looking dark-skinned woman, the other flying solo … and Theo.

"Did you know he was coming?" I asked Mac as we took our seats.

"Nope," Mac muttered under his breath, grabbing the cloth napkin off his plate and putting it on his lap. "He's never responded to any of my texts, never returned any of my calls. I didn't realise his shoulder was so bad it was still in a sling."

Fuck. Neither had I. Was the injury worse than we'd originally thought? Maybe he'd had further surgery. I wouldn't know, because I'd made no fucking effort to reach out to him.

I glanced in his direction, and found him staring right back at me, his eyes narrowed, his mouth pinched. He looked fucking furious. Thankfully the first course was delivered to the table right then, and I could look away.

The Premier was seated to my left. She gushed at me as we ate, going on and on about how my act of sportsmanship at the ARCs had been 'heroic' and 'inspiring', and would I be interested in doing some work with the government to promote their 'sporty kids' initiative, aimed at getting more kids into sport. I grunted and nodded wherever possible. I ended up giving her my email address so she could contact me with details, just to shut her up.

I was so not in the mood for playing nice with people who didn't give a shit about me, only what I could do for them.

I was counting down until dessert hit the table, so I could go home, when the shit well and truly hit the fan.

"So, Levi," Theo said loudly from across the table. It happened during a lull in the conversation, and suddenly every set of eyes at our table looked at me. "Seems you and Mac have gotten over your differences."

I swallowed, chancing a glance at Mac, who gave me a tiny shrug. Great help he was. "Yeah, we've managed to build a strong working relationship together. It served us well in Serbia." There, that was a diplomatic fucking response if ever I'd managed one.

Theo snorted. "I guess desperate times call for desperate measures. I mean, it was only earlier this year that you fucked a fatty just because Mac had the hots for her."

I was on my feet in an instant. Mac stood beside me, one hand on my elbow. The rest of the table was silent, horrified, as Theo got to his feet too.

"What the fuck, Theo?" I asked, my fists clenched by my sides.

Theo smirked. "I just find it hilarious, that you're so desperate for validation that you'd team up with a bloke you hated so much that you cock blocked him just to spite him. You went home with a fucking heifer and kept screwing her for months just to piss Mac off."

"Drysdale, take a bloody seat," Patto warned, getting out of his own chair. Theo ignored him. My breath was sawing in and out of my lungs, my vision tunnelling.

"That's not what fucking happened," I grated.

Theo laughed. "I was there. I saw it all. Poor stupid bitch she was, thought she'd bagged herself an athlete. Lucky for her there's apparently plenty of guys in Sydney who think fat is fuckable—she's moved on to a doctor now."

I hadn't realised I'd moved until I was face-to-face with Theo, gripping him by the jacket lapel. "You are fucking out of line, Drysdale!"

Theo's eyes glinted. "At least I had the fucking decency to set your fatty straight on what you're really like, when I saw her at the hospital earlier today," he muttered, softly enough that only I would hear. "Now she knows that you only fucked her out of your stupid need to beat Mac down."

My ears rang. Amanda, running through the hospital grounds, crying. Pushing me away.

My knuckles burned as they made contact with Theo's face. His head whipped to the side, blood spraying from his nose. He fucking laughed in my face, his breath reeking of alcohol as he lifted his good arm enough to throw a decent punch at my mouth.

I grunted as my head shot backwards, but rage and adrenaline had me pulling my fist back for another shot at the fucker's grinning, bloody face.

I was dragged backwards before I could throw another punch. I turned in fury to find Mac staring me down. For once he wasn't wearing his golden retriever smile. His face was more fucking serious than I'd ever seen it. I was pushed back into a chair.

"Stay put," Mac ordered, gripping my shoulder and holding me down. "You know nothing he's saying is true. You know that better than anyone. Don't make this worse for yourself."

Breathing jagged, I glanced over at where Theo sat, a cloth napkin stained with blood held to his nose. Patto was talking low to him, but Theo was staring right at me, and even though I couldn't see it, I was sure he was grinning like a fucking maniac behind that napkin.

"The cops have been called," Mac muttered. "I don't know what will happen, but at the very least you'll have to go down to the station."

"Fuck," I muttered, dropping my head into my hands. My lip throbbed where Theo had landed his punch, and I could taste blood. My knuckles throbbed from my own punch. I'd just decked my best mate. Ex-best mate.

What the fuck had he said to Amanda?

"Shit, I need to call her," I mumbled, reaching with shaking hands into my pocket for my phone. Mac snatched it from me. I scowled at him, just as four uniform police officers surged through the tables in our direction.

"Now is not the time," Mac hissed, as two cops approached me, the other two weaving in Theo's direction. "I'll keep your phone for you. I'll follow the cops to the station."

With that, he backed away, leaving me to the surly police, who walked me out under the shocked and disbelieving stares of a fucking ballroom full of people.

"Honey, whatever Theo said to you this morning, none of it's true. I promise. Fuck. Please just believe me. I would never ... look, I didn't want to say this over the phone, especially not over a fucking voice message, but ..."

"Levi Fox? Your legal counsel is here," the officer who was supervising my one fucking phone call boomed.

"Fuck! Can I at least finish my call?" I demanded. The officer shrugged, like he didn't care either way. I put the receiver back to my ear.

"If you would like this voice message sent as a text, please press five now."

"Shit!" I grunted, slamming the receiver down and turning back to the officer. "I don't suppose I get a second call if the first one was interrupted?"

"Interview room one," the burly bloke said, gesturing me towards a room. I slouched along the hallway, freezing when I got to the door.

"What the fuck are you doing here?" I demanded. Dad looked up at me, not even a hint of a smile on his face.

"Your brother called me—said you'd gotten yourself into a spot of trouble." Dad's voice was all professionalism. He was in lawyer mode, for now at least. I was sure he'd ream me out about this as soon as he had the privacy to do so.

"I suggest you sit down and tell me what happened," he commanded. I collapsed into the seat, not having a scrap of energy to argue with him.

"Theo provoked me. He got up in front of a table full of people and started spouting shit about … about Amanda. Saying that I only fucked her because Mac wanted her, and I wanted to piss him off."

"Did you?"

I glowered at him. "Did I what?"

Dad sniffed. "Did you sleep with her to annoy Mac?"

I jerked to my feet. "No, I fucking didn't! I saw her across the bar, and I thought she was the prettiest woman I'd ever seen. I couldn't take my fucking eyes off her. Whatever Mac did that night had nothing to do with how I felt. I … I knew that there was something special about her from the first time I saw her. Mac and I've talked about that night since. He had no interest in her."

"Then, if you knew Theo's words were false, why did you let them get to you so much? Why did you lose your cool?"

I gritted my teeth, scrubbing a hand over my face. Dried blood came away on my palm from my split lip. "Because he told her I only fucked her to get back at Mac. Because I love her, and … fuck."

I collapsed back into my chair. "He's probably ruined any chance I had of getting her back. That's why I lost my cool."

I reached up, massaging my scarred eyebrow. It was something I did so often I barely even realised I was doing it, but I noticed the way Dad's eyes were drawn to my hand. To my scar.

"Love makes us irrational," he said quietly. My hand fell away from my face, and I really looked at Dad for the first time in a very long time.

"You're free to go," the burly cop who'd showed me into the room said as he opened the door. "After speaking with witnesses, we've decided not to press charges. The other party has chosen not to press charges either."

Dad cleared his throat and stood. "You've been lucky tonight, Levi," he said sternly, and whatever moment we'd just been having, it disappeared.

Mac was sitting in the waiting area when Dad and I walked out. He stood, holding my phone out to me with a small smile, a ghost of his usual grin.

"You called Xander, didn't you?" I accused.

Mac shrugged. "I wasn't about to leave you in here without any support. And I guessed you'd probably use your one phone call to try and get in touch with …"

I nodded. "Went straight to voicemail. Probably for the best, to be honest. I was in the process of making a fucking fool of myself, but the message timed out before I really dug my own grave."

I looked down at my phone, as Mac ushered me out the door and onto the street, not waiting for Dad who was deep in discussion with the police officer. I could call her again. I could text her, at least that way there was a better chance she would get the message.

It was then that something else Theo said hit home for me. *She's moved on to a doctor now.*

What the fuck? When had that happened? In the week since she'd been sending me texts about fucking herself while thinking about me? Or before that, and she'd just been drunk and messaging me really had been just a stupid mistake?

"Let's go, Levi," Dad said behind me. I flinched when his hand rested on my shoulder, and he snatched it back.

"Mac's gonna drive me home," I muttered, even though we

hadn't discussed that at all. But Mac being Mac, he just smiled and started walking like it was all decided. I turned to follow.

"Levi!" Dad called out, and something in the way he said my name made me stop and turn. He stood, illuminated by the light spilling out through the police station doors, his expression tortured.

"What" I asked.

"You did well—you both did well in Serbia." It was like he had to choke the words out, like offering me praise was that fucking difficult for him. "Your mum would've been so proud."

His voice broke on the final word, and without even pausing, he turned and strode off down the street in the opposite direction. I felt like I'd just been punched in the gut.

"Well, that was … progress," Mac commented quietly by my side. "That *was* progress, wasn't it?"

I shook my head. Not that I disagreed, I just couldn't fucking work out what to make of it.

CHAPTER THIRTY-SEVEN

A Complicated Situation

AMANDA

"How do you hear all this gossip?" I demanded, hoping Brad and Alison wouldn't notice how much I was trembling.

"Have you forgotten what department I work in?" Brad replied. I grimaced sheepishly. I had forgotten that he'd switched from oncology to emergency medicine before he finished his degree. I tried to sip at my tea, but the cup shook too much, so I put it down.

"Did he come into the ED last night?" I breathed. I'd listened to the message he'd left me over and over again. The one from an unknown number where he frantically tried to explain about Theo, then he'd been about to tell me something that sounded … important. And then there was a whole heap of background noise, some swearing, and the message cut off.

"No, but that Theo arsehole did," Brad snarled. Alison rubbed up and down his back comfortingly. "Broken nose. The cops were questioning him. Apparently he made a scene at some fancy rowing event, and Levi got up and decked him."

"With the Premier watching on in horror!" Alison interjected, sounding utterly thrilled. I felt sick.

"What did he do to make Levi so angry?" I wondered, dizziness overcoming me.

Alison quirked a brow in my direction. "Really? You sure you don't already know? My guess is Theo spouted more of the same shit he said to you yesterday morning, and Levi defended your honour!" Alison batted her eyelashes, adding in a dreamy tone, "He's seriously such a unicorn!"

I caught Brad glancing in Alison's direction, something that looked eerily like jealousy flashing across his face. If I wasn't feeling completely twisted up inside about everything Theo had said yesterday, and all this new information, I might have been thinking hard about why that might be.

Alison, who could always read me like an open book, reached over and wound her fingers through mine. "Just call him, Manda. Seriously, just call him and ask him to explain himself. It's not fair for you to take what that arsehole Theo said to you and run with it, without letting Levi have a proper chance to tell his side of the story."

I knew she was right. But I also knew, right into the depths of my heart, that I just wasn't in a place to have that frank conversation with Levi. I needed some space from the hurt of yesterday, from the emotional turmoil. I needed to have some ability to think rationally when I talked it over with him. And that day was not today. I'd had one night off work, but tonight I was back to overnight placement in the birthing suite, and I'd barely slept a wink last night. Not with my head going in circles about Theo, and then replaying Levi's odd message over and over again. I needed to get some serious shut-eye or I would be dangerously exhausted by tonight.

"I can't think about this right now, you two," I said, tipping my now cold tea down the drain and rinsing my cup. "I need to get some sleep. And you probably need some sleep too, Brad," I added. "Sounds like you had far too much excitement in the ED overnight."

Brad chuckled, but Alison smirked. "Oh, he'll be sleeping soon. I just have to help him work out all that adrenaline from running around dealing with emergencies all night long."

I groaned. "I'll be playing white noise through my AirPods, on noise cancelling mode. Just so you know." I left the kitchen, heading for my bed.

Brad mumbled something to Alison, who giggled. My heart ached—for her unrequited love for Brad. For my own messy situation with Levi.

I did something I hadn't done in a long time. I took a sleeping pill. My brain just wasn't going to switch off on its own.

I woke groggily to Alison shaking me.

"Manda! Your phone has rung twice now, and your alarm just went off." She nudged my shoulder again as I blinked, rubbing sleep from my eyes.

"I … gosh, I can't believe it didn't wake me up," I mumbled.

Alison glanced pointedly at the pill bottle beside the bed. "Can't you?"

I ignored her, reaching for my phone. Beth had tried to call me twice. That was unusual, seeing as I was about to head in for a shift with her.

"I'd better call her back," I said, dialling and putting the phone up to my ear as Alison nodded and left the room.

"Amanda, hello," Beth answered on the first ring.

"Hi … is everything okay?"

I heard nothing but her breathing for a moment, and then Beth spoke. "Chris was hoping that you might be able to come in a little early this evening, before your shift starts, so that we can discuss your future."

I sat up straight. "Oh. Um, yes, how much earlier?" I asked.

"Can you be here by seven-thirty?"

I blinked. "Um, yes, if I hurry. I'll have to get off the phone now, though. Shall I come to the birthing suites?"

"No, come to Chris's clinic. You and I can head to the birthing suites after the meeting."

I hung up the phone, dread unfurling in my veins. It had only been yesterday I'd had the conversation with Chris about full-time employment. Why would he suddenly and urgently want to see me about it? I didn't finish my course until November, so it wasn't like getting a contract in place was a priority.

I tried not to read too much into it, jumping in the shower, dressing in record time and snatching a tub of yoghurt and a banana from the kitchen.

"Where's the fire?" Alison asked from the lounge.

"I … uh … forgot there was a meeting planned for seven-thirty. Beth was calling to remind me. Lucky she did, or I would have missed it completely." My voice shook. Alison watched me thoughtfully, but didn't comment.

"Well, have a good shift," she said, but she stood and came over to give me a hug. "I'll see you in the morning."

"Take a seat, Amanda," Chris said, gesturing to the seat next to Beth, opposite him. I sat, clasping my clammy hands in my lap.

"I'm just going to jump right in and get to the point," Chris said, resting his elbows on the desk. "Did you have a sexual relationship with the partner of a patient?"

My stomach rolled over, then dropped to the floor. I glanced to Beth, but she stared impassively back at me.

"I … um …" I stammered, swallowing hard and trying to blink away the sudden stars in my vision. "It's … it's a very complicated situation."

Chris huffed. "Let me make this even clearer. Did you engage in a sexual relationship with Levi Fox?"

"I don't understand," I mumbled, a lump forming in my throat, heat surging to my face. "I … how is this relevant?"

"Amanda, I was about to offer you a full-time role. I need to make it very clear that fraternising with the partners of my patients —even if they are ex-partners—is not behaviour that I condone in my staff."

Tears were falling by this point. "I … we were already together when he found out about Emilee's pregnancy," I fibbed. "They broke up at around the same time she fell pregnant. I promise, he wasn't involved with this clinic at all when our relationship started. I would never …" My words broke off as a sob burst out of my throat.

Beth's warm hand touched me lightly in the middle of my back as I shook. "Why did you not divulge your relationship with Levi when Emilee first came into the clinic, then? Your relationship status with the father of her child might have been a factor for us all deciding if Emilee was the right candidate for you to partner with as a student midwife."

I coughed, and Beth pushed a box of tissues in my direction. I took several, wiping my eyes and blowing my nose.

Pull yourself together Amanda. You haven't done anything wrong.

Well, that was debatable.

"When Emilee first came into the clinic, I wasn't aware that she was Levi's ex-girlfriend. And he also wasn't aware at that point that she was pregnant."

Beth sat back in her chair. "You had a panic attack the first time they came into the clinic together," she muttered. I nodded, sniffing and patting more tears from my eyes.

"I … Levi didn't tell me about it when he found out. We were … our relationship was very new, he didn't want to scare me off with talk of a pregnant ex, until he knew whether things might be …" I trailed off as another sob wracked me.

"You should have told me," Beth said, softly but firmly. I nodded, hiccupping and sniffing.

"I … I didn't want Emilee to know about it. Not after how she …"

"How she what?" Chris asked. My throat closed up, but thankfully Beth took over.

"Emilee was quite rude to Amanda at her first appointment. She made some veiled negative comments about Amanda's size."

My face flamed with shame.

"Are you still in a relationship with Levi?" Chris asked. I shook my head. It was all I was able to do at that point.

"Did you remove yourself from her care team because of your

relationship with Levi?" Beth asked. I shook my head again, trying to swallow back yet more tears to explain.

"Our relationship ended. I removed myself so I wouldn't have to see him." I could have told them the awful things Emilee had said about me, but at that point I was sure it would only make things worse.

"I want you to go home tonight, Amanda. You're too upset to be able to focus appropriately," Beth said. There was kindness in her tone, which only made me feel worse.

"Am I … am I able to continue my placement with you?" I asked. There was an awful silence.

Eventually Chris said, "Yes, you'll be able to complete your placement hours here. As to the offer of full-time work …" I stared down at my shaking hands, waiting for the inevitable.

"As to that, I will need to take some time and put some thought into it. The situation is more complex than I had suspected to begin with. But for now, go home, Amanda, try to relax. It sounds like you've been through a lot the last few months."

I burst into a fresh wave of tears at that. His voice wasn't cruel, nor were his words. But I felt like my whole world was crashing down around me.

"Okay, thank you," I mumbled, and fled the building. Funnily enough, by the time I got to my car, the tears had dried up. I was numb. I turned the car on and drove out of the carpark.

I didn't want to go home. I didn't want to have to tell Alison what had happened to me. I couldn't cope with her fury on my behalf, that they'd blindsided me with their accusations. It would send me into a tailspin.

I did, however, drive back in the direction of Bondi. Just not to my house.

Pulling up, I cut the engine. Before I could talk myself out of what I was doing, I climbed out of the car and went straight to the front door. My hands trembled as I knocked.

"Amanda!" Xander said, surprise on his face as he opened the screen door. "Is everything okay? You look like you've been crying."

I shook my head. If I talked too much, I was going to start crying again.

"Is Levi here?"

Xander shook his head. "Are you on your way to work?"

"No," I said. "Uh, where is he?"

Xander looked awkward. "He left half an hour ago. Emilee's in labour."

CHAPTER THIRTY-EIGHT

Go Time

LEVI

"Fuck, it fucking hurts! Why the fuck does it hurt so much?" Zilla screamed.

"I think it might be time for you to leave," I told the girl who had arrived with Zilla, the one who had been snapping photos and filming random snippets of her labour. But things had gotten to the pointy end really fucking quickly, and her still being there was just creepy.

"But she asked me to document all of it!" the girl protested. I looked over at Zilla, who was panting and gasping and making noises that sounded inhuman.

"She's naked on all fours. It's not like she can post this shit to Instagram," I told the girl. She wasn't even a proper birthing photographer, just some random fledgling 'influencer' that Zilla had taken under her wing.

"But—"

"Get the fuck out, Gabby!" Zilla snarled.

"Whatever," the girl muttered, flouncing towards the door. I plucked Zilla's phone from her hand before she could make off with it, as Zilla started to moan again.

"You're doing just fine, Emilee," Beth reassured her. "You're in transition, that's why it's hurting so much. Just breathe. You don't need to start pushing yet."

I moved up to the head of the bed, standing close, reaching out and patting the back of her hand. She swatted me away. I sighed. I wanted to help her. Something about the way that all of her pretences had been stripped away as her labour progressed—way more fucking rapidly than either of us had expected—made me at least want to try and comfort her. But she wouldn't let me.

"At the moment everything is progressing by the book, Emilee. The baby is fine, you're almost fully dilated. You'll be ready to push very soon."

"I want a fucking epidural!" she screamed. I grabbed a cool, damp cloth from a bowl beside the bed and swiped it quickly over her sweaty forehead before she could push me away again.

"It's too late for an epidural, Emilee," Beth responded calmly. "I can give you some gas, if you'd like."

Zilla groaned again, her body tensing through her contraction. I looked up at Beth over Zilla's naked back. "Gas, please," I whispered. Beth paused, but then nodded, setting up the tube and fiddling with some dials, handing the tube to Zilla, who immediately started sucking on it. As she inhaled, I saw some of the tension leave her body.

Jesus, I needed a shot of that shit. I was tense as fuck, and I wasn't even the one about to push a watermelon out of a tiny hole.

"I feel like I need to push," Zilla said, her voice less harsh, but still strained. Beth looked at me.

"That means you're probably ready to push. Let me check." Beth bustled around the back of Emilee, and I looked elsewhere as she did her checks. She looked up at me and nodded. I chewed on my lips.

"You're ready," Beth confirmed. "When you next feel that sensation, you want to bear down. Try to hold your breath and not make noise—it's easier if you use all your energy for pushing. You might want to hold onto Levi's hand."

I placed my hand in Zilla's, and she gripped me. "It's go-time, Em," I murmured.

"Remember what I said, Emilee," Beth continued. "When we push, we bear down for the count of three, and then we try to relax and breathe through the rest of the contraction. That will minimise the risk of tearing. You can do this!"

"Oh, I need to push," she moaned, crushing my hand. Her face went red, her lips tight as Beth counted her through it.

"Push, two, three … and breathe, Emilee."

Zilla sucked on the gas and pushed when she was told to. I tried my best to just be there for her as she almost broke every bone in my hand, watching all the action going on around me as if from another fucking planet.

My little girl was about to come into the world. A couple of weeks early, and very fucking suddenly. Zilla had barely laboured for three hours at home before things had gotten to a point where she needed to get to hospital fast. She'd already been at eight centimetres when she arrived. She was halfway to the hospital with the rando who had been taking her photos when she called to tell me.

But at least she had told me. I'd been starting to fucking worry over the last couple of weeks about how easy it would be for her to just 'forget' to call me, to keep me out of the room. I had to be grateful that she'd stood by her promise.

When sharp cries began, I thought Zilla had started screaming again. But then Beth was passing a tiny, wrinkly, bloody little body up between Zilla's legs and helping her to turn onto her back, pressing the wailing baby against Zilla's chest and covering them both with a blanket.

A tiny, cone-shaped head, covered in the thickest, blackest hair I'd ever seen.

"Holy shit," I murmured, as Zilla panted, staring down at the bundle in her arms like our little girl was an alien.

"Why is her head such a weird shape?" Zilla asked, a hint of horror in her tone.

"Their heads can be a bit misshapen immediately after birth. They've gone through a big trauma too, coming through the birth canal. It will return to a normal shape within the first couple of weeks," Beth said.

Zilla started to cry. And it was nothing like the crocodile tears she usually put on. Big, gasping, choking sobs, tears streaming down her face.

"Em," I muttered, feeling fucking helpless as she clung to our little girl and sobbed.

"It's normal for emotions to be big right now, Levi," Beth reassured me quietly. She'd been looking at me funny all night, ever since she'd walked into the room about twenty minutes after I'd arrived.

I didn't know what to do, so I grabbed out Zilla's phone, clicked the camera on, and tried to do what Gabby had been doing—capture these first moments.

"Fuck off with that, Levi!" Zilla screeched. She started to push the blanket back, exposing the naked bottom of our baby. "And will someone cut this fucking cord? I want Levi to hold her!"

Waves of emotion ruptured through me as Beth settled Zilla back on the bed, clamped the cord, and held the scissors out to me.

"Do you want to do the honours?" she asked. I glanced at Zilla, not knowing whether she'd be okay with it.

"I don't give a fuck if you do or don't Levi, just someone get this baby off of me!"

I grabbed them and sawed through the thick cord.

"Take your shirt off, Levi, and sit down over there," Beth said quietly to me, collecting the squalling baby off Zilla's heaving chest. I wrenched my shirt off over my head, and seconds later, I was holding my baby girl for the first time.

She was so tiny, and she looked red and swollen, and her eyes were squeezed shut. But she was the most beautiful thing I'd ever fucking seen.

"How can I post photos of her when she's so ugly?" Zilla cried, lying back against the bed and sobbing into her hands.

"She's not ugly," Beth argued gently. "She's just been born. Once she's cleaned up, she'll look much better. In the meantime, let's focus on you. Let's pass the placenta, and I'll get the on-duty OB to come and check to see if you need stitches. You did amazingly, Emilee. Fast labours are very intense, both physically and emotionally."

Zilla continued to weep, and even though I thought she was being fucking ridiculous, calling our beautiful baby ugly, I didn't let it get to me. She'd just birthed a human. She probably deserved a bit of slack.

Bustle continued to happen around the room. Doctors and midwives moved about, Zilla cried or sat in stunned silence. Beth took our baby from me to do some routine tests, swaddling her in a nappy and returning her to me for more skin-to-skin. I marvelled at the tiny thing in my arms, everything else going on fading to a hum in the background.

Zilla got up to shower. I continued to hold our baby. When she returned, she snatched up her phone, pointing it in my direction and then reclining back on the bed. She seemed calmer. Thank fuck.

"Do you want to hold her again?" I asked. Zilla shook her head.

"She's going to need to feed soon, Emilee. Are you sure that you're starting formula immediately?" Beth asked. Zilla nodded.

Beth looked to me. "Well, we have a room ready for you upstairs. We can go up now, and we can get a bottle ready for her."

I stood, cradling the little bundle in my arms. She was starting to snuffle around. I'd read that meant they were looking for food. Beth noticed too.

"Let's have her first bottle down here. It's not busy, we don't need to rush you out of the birthing suite. We don't want a hangry newborn on our hands."

I chuckled as Beth left the room.

"You're a fucking natural, Levi," Zilla said, and for once there wasn't even the smallest hint of bitterness in her tone. I glanced up from our baby to see Zilla staring at her, an odd, tense expression on her face.

"Have you decided on a name?" I asked. "Are we still going with Emvi?"

Zilla collapsed back onto her bed. "I actually don't … I can't believe …" she stopped, meeting my eyes before glancing away guiltily. I wondered what she'd been about to say.

"Lily. You wanted Lily so badly, let's call her that," she mumbled.

I didn't want to cry over the name, but at that moment, I couldn't help myself.

"Hey, Lily," I cooed to our baby girl.

I skipped training to arrive bright and early on the morning Zilla and Lily were due to leave the hospital. Because Lily had been born just shy of thirty-seven weeks, they wanted to keep them both in for a week for monitoring. Zilla had been an emotional wreck for the first five nights, but on my last two visits she'd seemed to be on the up and up. At least I fucking hoped she was—they were about to return to an apartment where it would just be the two of them, and I was fucking terrified that Zilla wouldn't cope.

I'd offered to temporarily move in until she got into a routine, but she'd refused. We still hadn't quite worked out what our custody schedule was going to look like, and I didn't want to push her.

"Can you take her down and wait for me in the foyer?" Zilla asked softly. Lily was sleeping in the little clear plastic crib. "I want to freshen up before I leave."

Thinking it hardly mattered if she was made up with hair done to walk from the hospital to the car, but not wanting to set her off when she seemed to have lost some of her usual vicious streak, I nodded and gently pushed the crib out of the room, along the hallway and down in the lift to the ground floor.

Taking a seat in one of the lounge chairs in the foyer, I gently lifted Lily out of the crib, cradling her in my arms. She didn't even make a peep. She'd taken to feeding like an absolute champ, and was just as happy to take a bottle from me as from her mother. She was already in a great routine of eating and sleeping. I just hoped that the change of environment didn't fuck with that, especially when Zilla wouldn't have nurses and midwives nearby.

I gazed down at Lily, her eyelashes so delicate against her little cheek. Her head was close to a normal shape now, and she looked more beautiful by the day, much to Zilla's relief. I ground my teeth, thinking that her biggest concern about Lily's cone-head had been that she wouldn't be photogenic enough for social media. She might have been less of a bitch to me in the last week, but some things about her hadn't changed.

I wondered, for about the billionth time, whether I should send a photo to Amanda. I hadn't tried to contact her since that fucking horrific voice message from the police station. Which was probably for the best, because my head was a fucking mess.

Was Amanda really with a doctor now? I felt like after our texts while I was overseas, she would at least have had the decency to be straight with me if she'd started seeing someone else. Honesty was her style. Then again, ghosting was also her fucking style.

I looked down at Lily, sleeping in my arms. Maybe I just needed to focus on this little lady and leave my mess of a love life well the fuck alone.

"Levi."

Like it was happening in slow motion, my eyes travelled from my daughter's face, up along the curves of the woman standing in front of me, until I met her eyes.

"Hey, Honey," I murmured, my lips fucking betraying me. I smiled sadly at her. Why hadn't I thought about the possibility that I would run into her here? The entrance to the birthing suites was just to my right.

"She's beautiful," Amanda sighed, reaching towards Lily but stopping, her hand dropping to her side. "What's her name?"

"Lily," I replied, stroking my little sleeping girl's cheek.

"I'm so, so pleased for you, Levi. You look totally in love with her."

I'm totally in love with you, too, I thought, glancing away. I couldn't deny it, no matter what was fucking going on with her … with us.

"How's the new man?" I asked, as if it was totally fine with me that she was seeing someone new. My eyes flicked up to her face, and the utter confusion there stuttered at my heart.

"What…?" She sounded as confused as she looked. My heart kicked up another notch.

"Theo said you were seeing a doctor."

Amanda's eyes darkened. "Theo interrupted me having breakfast with Dr Bentley, who was offering me a full-time position with him once I finish my diploma. I'm definitely not seeing him … or anyone else for that matter."

The weird, tight feeling in my chest that I'd been living with for over a fucking week eased. "There's no one else?"

Amanda shook her head, but she didn't look happy. She looked downright fucking miserable.

"Well, that's good news about having a full-time job to walk straight into," I said, trying to lighten the tense mood. If anything, it got worse. Amanda's eyes glistened.

"I don't know if I have a job, actually. Theo told Dr Bentley that I'd been sleeping with you. Chris wasn't happy that I'd been fraternising with one of his patient's partners."

"Ex-partner," I growled. "And you didn't know … hell, I didn't know … when we first got together."

A tear spilled down Amanda's cheek, and I got to my feet, but she took a step back, brushing the moisture away with a frustrated huff.

"I told them the same thing, but they're still considering my future, because I didn't disclose my relationship with you once I was aware of the situation."

"That's fucking bullshit," I muttered. "I'll tell them that I made you keep it a secret because I didn't want Zi … Emilee to know about us."

Amanda shook her head. "That's a lie, Levi, and I don't want you lying for me. I was the one who wanted to keep it quiet. I was the one who stupidly assumed it would be unprofessional to be open about us in my workplace. Meanwhile it's done more damage coming out the way it has."

Another tear, and she wasn't fast enough this time. Cradling Lily in one arm, I swept in and gently swiped that tear off her cheek with my thumb, letting my hand linger there. Stepping closer again.

"For the record, Honey, I would have shouted it from the rooftops the second you gave me the go ahead. And ... I don't know if you listened to my voicemail ... but the other things Theo said to you, about Mac? Total bullshit. That first night I saw you, it was like a single glimpse of you changed my fucking brain chemistry. Mac might have come over to chat with you first, but I would have been there no matter what."

Her breath hitched, and she flicked her eyes up to meet mine, before glancing away again. "I listened to it. It didn't make much sense, and ... it cut off halfway through you saying something ..." She looked up at me again, her eyes searching.

I couldn't say it. I couldn't tell her I loved her right here and now ... could I?

You might not get another chance, dickhead. Just do it.

"Amanda, I—"

"Levi, you ready to go home?"

Amanda took a big step away from me. I turned to find Zilla standing directly behind me, dressed in pink trackpants and a loose-fitting black t-shirt. Both were brand new and designer. She had a full face of makeup on, her hair was up in a messy bun that looked like it had taken her about half an hour to perfect. There was a small smile on her lips, but her eyes didn't look as malicious as I would've expected.

Fuck. I turned back to Amanda. Scrubs, a low ponytail, her skin completely makeup free. I knew which one made my heart fucking ache to look at.

"Congratulations, Emilee. She's a beautiful little girl," Amanda said faintly, attempting a smile, before turning and walking out the door. I stood frozen until she'd disappeared around the corner of the building.

"She's not over you," Zilla murmured into my ear. I stiffened, turning to her, expecting to see that tell-tale smirk plastered all over her fake face. But she just looked tired.

"I'm not fucking over her either," I replied. Zilla looked away.

"You got the baby capsule fitted in my car?" she asked, changing the subject. I bit my tongue until I tasted blood, nodding and getting ready to take my little girl home.

CHAPTER THIRTY-NINE

I'd Want to Get to Know You

AMANDA

"Please stop me if this question is out of line," Beth began, and my stomach instantly churned. "But … why *did* you and Levi break up?"

I wrapped up the BP monitor for what was probably going to be the last time in this clinic—my placement hours were finished, and Chris hadn't said another word to me about the job offer. I had to assume that he'd decided it wasn't worth it for him.

"I don't think my answer is appropriate. Technically Emilee is still a patient here until she has her six-week follow up," I hedged, walking out of Beth's room and into the staffroom.

"Well, technically you're no longer a student midwife here. So let me ask you this as a friend. I hope you've come to see me as one over the last months?"

I pulled my bag out of my cubby and busied myself rummaging through it. "You intimidate me too much to really feel like a friend," I tried to joke, but it fell flat. I ran my tongue over my teeth, bracing myself to tell the truth.

"Emilee found out. A friend of hers saw Levi and me on a date. She was unhappy, to put it mildly. She said some very hurtful things about me … about my body … about traumatic events from my past, and I just … I realised that I wasn't strong enough, at that time, to stay with him, knowing that meant tying myself to her as well."

Beth was silent for a long time. I couldn't continue to pretend that I was looking for something in my bag, so I zipped it up and slung it over my shoulder, heading down the hall to the door.

"Levi sent me an email last night," Beth called behind me. I froze, but didn't turn as she continued, "He said that when he realised that his ex was pregnant and that you were on her care team, he asked you not to say anything, to keep it quiet. He said that he'd spent three years tolerating verbal and emotional abuse from Emilee, and he was worried that she would be abusive towards you if she found out about your relationship. Is this true?"

I wanted so badly to tell the truth. To say that it was me who had demanded we keep things secret. But I just couldn't. I felt an odd surge of fury mixed with gratitude to Levi for going ahead and doing what I'd told him not to.

"Yes, that's about the gist of it," I muttered. Well, at least he'd been honest about one thing—she had been abusive when she'd found out about us.

"Well, I've really enjoyed working with you, Amanda McGregor," Beth said, and I sighed, because Levi had lied for me, and it wasn't going to make a scrap of difference to my job prospects here.

"I've enjoyed it, too," I mumbled, trying to hold in the tears until I was in the privacy of my car. "I have to go."

With a smile and a wave at Florence the receptionist, I managed to escape the building without any fanfare, and without having to see Chris, who I was sure still found me abhorrent.

"Why is this happening to me?" I muttered crossly to myself, even as my heart fluttered to see him walking towards me. He had his baby —Lily—strapped to his front in one of those baby carriers that were all the rage.

My God, he looked utterly divine. The long sleeves of his t-shirt were pushed up to his elbows, exposing those muscular tattooed forearms. His tanned calves poked out from beneath his khaki shorts. His feet were bare as he strode across the sand in my direction, a tentative smile on his face.

"Amanda," he said, stopping just shy of too close for politeness. Damn my stupid body, I wanted him to step closer. *I* wanted to step closer, to fold myself under his arm and peek at the teeny black head popping out the top of the baby carrier.

"Fatherhood suits you," I said instead, awkwardly rubbing at my arms.

"Lily and I take a walk on the beach every day after I finish training," he explained. "Zi … Emilee gets a break in the afternoons that way, and I get to spend time with my girl."

His eyes didn't leave mine as he spoke, and my heart jolted. I watched his fingers twitching. He wanted to reach out for me. Hell, I wanted to reach out for him. But it felt like too much had happened, like we'd let too much water under the bridge for us to get back to where we were. I almost felt like I was looking at a stranger.

"How is Emilee?" I asked, not missing his tiny wince. I might not have explained myself fully—or at all—to him when I left, but he knew that Emilee had been a big factor in that decision. He was too smart not to realise that.

"She's … different. Less of a bi—less mean." He glanced down at his sleeping baby, and God, I wanted to throw my arms around him and kiss him senseless—him trying to curtail his swearing for a tiny newborn was just about the most adorable thing I could imagine.

But the thought of her changing because of her baby … their baby … sent a pang of fear surging through me.

"Maybe you and she will be able to work things out after all, then." My voice was hoarse. I coughed around the lump in my throat.

Levi looked confused for a second, and then his eyes widened. "No! Uh … I mean, she and I have worked out a way to co-parent without jumping down each other's throats. That's all it'll be between us. I couldn't … she's not …"

He rubbed at the back of his neck. "Walk with me for a bit?"

I found myself nodding, despite my misgivings, and we turned to continue along the Bondi sand.

"Did Dr Bentley come to his senses?" Levi asked. I flashed him a look. It had been a week since I'd walked out of my last placement shift, and I hadn't heard from Chris or Beth.

"Nope. I don't know whether to thank you or shout at you for the email you sent. I think it might have softened Beth towards me a bit, but Dr Bentley still hasn't spoken to me. I didn't want you to have to lie for me."

"Honey, I'd do far more than lie for you," he murmured under his breath.

I hid my shock with a cough. "So … um … how's rowing?" I asked in a sad attempt to change the subject.

"It's … honestly, it's the best it's been in a long time. Mac and I, we're a much better fit than Theo and I ever were. It's fucking— freaking bizarre, but he and I have so much more in common than I would've ever imagined. He worked so damned—darned hard to get us on the podium in Serbia."

Levi ran a hand through his hair. "It's gonna sound selfish as fu —really selfish, but in a way, Theo's injury's turned out to be a posi- tive thing for me."

I couldn't help my smile. "I'm glad. Theo seems like a toxic sort of person, and I think you've had enough of that in your life."

"Theo's got his own issues. If he hadn't done what he did to you, I think I'd be able to forgive him the rest. But fu—far out, I can't forgive him ruining your career. And … I hate him for the hurtful shit he said to you."

Levi grunted. "I don't want to rehash the past, Amanda. We made some mistakes, and I wish I had the chance to start over again with you. Do you think, if we met today, as strangers, with me walking with my baby, would you want to get to know me?"

My breath caught in my throat. "I …" I looked him up and

down. Those eyes, which knew far too much about me, and yet not enough, shone down at me with a light that was all Levi. And I found myself nodding.

"I'd want to get to know you, Levi," I whispered.

CHAPTER FORTY

She Might Be His

LEVI

The tightness in my chest unravelled at her words, and I took a deep lungful of air. Holding out a hand, I said, "Hi, I'm Levi Fox, Olympic Danger Boy and single-dad to this gorgeous little girl."

With my free hand I stroked Lily's silky hair, but my eyes never left Amanda's wide ones. She pressed her fingers to her mouth, then reached out and shook my hand, grey eyes glistening.

"Hi Levi, I'm Amanda McGregor. I'm a … I'm a midwife, and your little girl is so adorable."

I swallowed back my own tears, as Lily stirred in the carrier. "I actually need to feed her, have you got time to sit with me?"

"Yes," she mumbled, and because it felt so fucking natural, I took her hand and led her off the sand, and to a bench in the shade that overlooked the ocean. She followed silently, her hand soft, and warm, but passive in mine. Fuck, I wanted her to wind her fingers through mine, to grip on tight and never fucking let go.

But I had to let go to get Lily's bottle ready. Tipping the formula into the warm bottle, I shook it up, then unclipped the carrier. Her eyes were open, and she started making the little pouty, sucky face she did when she was hungry, and it was bottle time.

"My God, she's divine," Amanda said beside me. She sat close, but not close enough, as I tucked Lily into my arm and offered the bottle to her. She latched on greedily. "She's five weeks old now?"

I nodded. "She's a little champ. She's in the best routine. I was worried that she might make nights difficult for her mother, because I'm not there, but they've been coping really well, from what I can gather."

"How do you … how much time do you get with her?" she asked, and she scooted closer to me, her eyes fixed on Lily. I bit back a grin.

"She's mine from one every afternoon, until about seven-thirty. I mostly take her out somewhere with me for a bit, then we head home for a while, so Uncle Xander can have some time with her too. Molly's obsessed with her."

"Molly? Does Xander have a girlfriend?"

I chuckled. "No, Xander doesn't do girlfriends. He's still hung up on this girl from high school … it was a whole thing … Molly's his Black Labrador. She thinks Lily smells amazing."

"Lily is such a beautiful name," Amanda said, and that tightness started to coil in my chest again. "You've got these lilies on your arm …" Her fingers brushed against my forearm, and fuck me, my dick started to twitch. "Is it meaningful for you?"

I'd kept so much back from this woman. But no more.

"Lily was my little sister. She was stillborn when I was seventeen."

Amanda gasped. "I didn't … oh Levi, I'm so sorry! That must have been so hard for you. Didn't your … didn't you lose your mum at seventeen, too?"

Lily finished her bottle, and I grabbed a burp cloth, resting it and her on my shoulder and giving her a gentle pat. Amanda watched me avidly, her bottom lip caught in her teeth. I couldn't stop staring at her mouth as I talked.

"Mum was diagnosed with stage-three breast cancer when she was pregnant with Lily. The most effective treatments were off the table, because she was pregnant. They did a double mastectomy, but they really needed to do radiation, and hormone therapy, which couldn't be done until Lily was born.

"Mum made the call to hold on as long as possible, and they were able to do some chemo, but it wasn't enough. In the end, the doctors talked her into getting induced early with Lily, at thirty-four weeks, so they could try more therapies. Lily didn't survive."

Amanda's eyes were shiny with tears. Fuck I loved her so much.

"And your mum?" she asked.

I cleared my throat. "Mum hadn't told any of us, not even Dad, that the cancer had spread. She was so much sicker than any of us realised. She died two days after Lily—she never left the hospital. Dad blamed the medical staff for Mum's death.

My Lily burped loudly, and I wiped the spill of milk from her mouth. "Can you hold her for a minute?" I asked Amanda, who brushed a tear from her face, taking my baby in her arms, cradling her and stroking her cheek.

I stood, lifting my shirt off. Amanda looked up with a gasp.

"What are you …?" she asked, shocked, but her eyes roved hungrily over my naked chest. I ached so much. From telling the truth about Mum and Lily, from seeing my girl in the arms of … of my girl.

I turned, pointing to the tattoo on my shoulder. "The clock has four hands. Two for when Lily died … two for Mum."

Amanda raked her gaze over the rest of my arm, at the tangle of roses and lilies. "Your mum's name was Rose, wasn't it?"

I nodded, tugging my shirt back over my head and sitting down beside her. "A week after their funerals, I brought home a bunch of flowers. Roses and lilies. I thought Dad would appreciate the sentiment."

I reached up, rubbing my eyebrow. "I was so fucking wrong. He lost his shit, grabbed the vase and threw it at my face. The vase broke on my forehead and sliced me open. I don't know how I managed to drive to Christa's—my girlfriend at the time—to her house, but her parents took one look at me and took me straight to emergency. Six stitches, and the bruising on my forehead took three weeks to go down. They wouldn't let me go home, wanted to report him for abuse. I managed to convince them that he was just grieving. But even a decade later, I'm still not sure that was really the reason."

"Oh ... Levi ..." The empathy in those two words fucking melted me.

I turned to her. "I feel so much better for having told you all of that, Honey. And fuck, I love seeing you holding her. I've thought about you so much over the last few weeks. Sometimes ... I feel like a piece of shit, but sometimes I think that there's only one thing that could make me love Lily more ... if you were her mother."

Amanda stiffened, and I cursed myself for not filtering my fucking thoughts before I blurted them out. With one last look down at my baby, she handed Lily back to me.

"I have to go. It was ... it was lovely to see you, Levi."

"Don't text her," Mac warned as I pulled the car back out of the parking garage under Zilla's apartment. For the second time this week, some fucker had nicked the second parking space for the apartment, so I had to park on the street.

"I knew that was what you were gonna say," I grunted, pulling up and unbuckling Lily from her car seat, settling her into the carrier as I grabbed the backpack full of her stuff from the seat beside her. Thank fuck for wireless ear buds, my hands were constantly full of baby stuff these days.

"You came on too strong, mate. Texting or calling her now is just gonna freak her out more."

"I hate when you're right," I grumbled, fumbling with the door key and then the lift button, while Lily started to fuss. She was ready for another bottle, which Zilla usually had waiting for her when I dropped her off at seven-thirty. "I promise I'll leave it for tonight. Gotta go, about to walk into the apartment."

I clicked off the call, plugging the code into the lock on the apartment door. As I opened it, strains of voices ... more than one fucking voice ... came from Zilla's bedroom.

"I can't," Zilla sobbed.

"You have to, Em." The other voice was deep, accented and somehow familiar to me. I stopped, waiting to hear what the fuck they were talking about. To try and work out why I recognised his voice.

"It's going to break him. I should never have … I assumed …"

What the fuck? Dropping Lily's bag, I headed for the bedroom door, flinging it open. Zilla was sitting on the edge of the bed, although she jumped up as the door flew inwards. Her face was tear streaked, and she hadn't changed out of the pyjamas she'd been in earlier when I'd come to pick Lily up. Her hair was greasy, hanging around her face. Her dark blonde roots showed in her usually platinum hair.

"What the fuck is going on in here?" I growled, low enough that it wouldn't startle Lily. My heart was racing. Something was very fucking wrong. I turned and saw the owner of the deep voice, and recognition trickled through my blood.

"You're the … the chef from the restaurant that night—*Comida Orgasmo*!" I accused. The dude returned my stare, a mix of defiance and sympathy on his face, which only made the hollow feeling in my gut worse. "What the fuck are you …"

I turned to glared at Zilla. "He's the 'friend'? The one who sent you the picture of me with Amanda?" Zilla stared down at her hands. Fuck. I'd felt like he was paying a creepy amount of attention to me that night.

"Mateo," he said. "And … yes … I sent the photo, I'm sorry. Em and I …" He glanced towards Zilla, who stood there, shaking and teary. She turned to me.

"Levi, give Lily to Mat, he'll give her a bottle. We need to talk."

I took a step backwards. "You want me to give our baby to some fucking rando?"

The Mateo prick stepped closer. "I've been here every night since they came home from the hospital. I've fed Lily most nights."

"What the fuck, Emilee?" I demanded, as Lily started to pick up on my stress, fussing with more fervour. I unbuckled her from the carrier and lifted her to my shoulder, patting and rocking, as much to calm me as her.

Zilla wouldn't meet my eyes. "Just … please Levi. I don't want you holding her when I …" Her voice shook, and she looked so fucking broken and miserable that shock thrummed through me. Wordlessly I handed Lily over to the fucking Mateo guy, who popped her on his shoulder and left the room, closing the door quietly behind him.

"Seriously, Emilee, I'm freaking the fuck out right about now," I muttered. She still wouldn't look at me.

"Sit down, Levi," she mumbled.

I shook my head. "I think I'll stay right here, thanks."

Emilee shrugged, her bottom lip trembling, and nothing like the way it did when she was faking her tears.

Holy fuck.

"Mat's my … my boyfriend," Emilee said in barely more than a whisper. I gritted my teeth, but managed a shrug.

"So fucking what? I said it would be fine if there was someone else. You deserve to move on as much as I do."

"We've … I was seeing him before you and I broke up."

I sat down hard on the end of the bed. My mouth moved, but no words came out. My throat was dry, like it would crack if I tried to force sound out.

"Say something, Levi," Zilla begged.

I coughed. "You were cheating on me." It wasn't even a question. I thought about Lily's black hair. And Mat's black hair …

"She's not mine, is she?"

Footsteps faded, then came closer. I managed to look up. Zilla was holding a box out for me.

"I honestly don't know, Levi. I … Mat and I used condoms, just like you and I did."

I snatched the box with hands that shook, reading the words but not making any sense of them.

DNA Laboratories At-Home Paternity Test.

"What's this?" I asked, turning the box over and over in my hands.

"I … I made Mat promise that he wouldn't do one until you did, since … since you've thought she was yours from the start. I'm … I'm so sorry, Levi," she whimpered, and I looked at her properly for the first time in weeks. She was definitely not the same person she'd been before she gave birth. That woman wouldn't have been broken up inside at the thought of lying to me. Hell, she *had* fucking lied to me, for nine months. She'd known Lily might not be mine, but she'd let me think it, all that time.

I wanted to feel angry. I wanted the fury to scream and rage at her. But all I felt was fucking numbness creeping through my limbs.

"She might not be mine."

"Please, just open the test. I'll go get you a swab from Lily, and you can take it all home with you now."

I stood, although how my legs held me up, I had no fucking clue. "I'll get her sample. How can I trust that you won't fuck that up and lie to me about that, too?" My voice was monotone, which only made my words sound even harsher to my ears. Zilla let out a sob.

"Okay, Levi," was all she said, as I stalked out, tearing the box open on the kitchen bench, refusing to look to the lounge where fucking Mateo was cradling my baby girl like she was his.

Fuck. She might be his.

CHAPTER FORTY-ONE

Tropical Holiday

AMANDA

"Do you really think this is a good idea?" Alison asked as I shoved a bunch of t-shirts into my suitcase.

"It's been more than two years since I've seen them," I replied, as if the length of time since I'd last visited my parents was the real reason I was frantically packing a bag for my last-minute flight to Cairns. "Timing works well—placement is over, I took time off from Frankwright to study for exams, I only have a week of classes left and I can attend them online. That gives me a fortnight with Mum and Dad."

"And a bit of space from a certain tattooed Danger Boy?" Alison prodded. I glared at her.

"It's hardly getting distance from someone who I never see anyway. I could stay in Bondi and have the same amount of distance."

"Bullshit," Alison scoffed. "You said you ran into him at the beach yesterday. Whatever he said to you has got you running interstate."

I sat on the edge of the bed, tugging my hair out of its ponytail and plaiting it instead, keeping my hands busy.

'Honey, I'd do far more than lie for you.'

'Sometimes I think that there's only one thing that could make me love Lily more … if you were her mother.'

"Does it really matter what the reason is?" I demanded, hoping anger would get her off my back. I should have known better.

"Is running the right thing to do here, Manda?" Alison asked, her voice quiet and reasonable. "Either pull yourself together, tell him what you need from him to make things work between you, or give the poor guy some closure."

I knew what she was saying was rational, and fair, and the right thing to do. But my head was a whirlwind, and I couldn't work out the first thing about what I wanted with Levi, let alone how we could make it work.

I was scared. I was terrified to fall back into the place we were in before, where we were falling for each other without making our life together work for us. Even now I was struggling against the need to head straight down to the beach, knowing he took Lily there every day around this time.

"Everything you're saying is right," I agreed, grabbing a pile of undies out of my cupboard and tossing them into the suitcase. "But why can't I take a couple of weeks to really think about this before I go making a huge decision?"

Alison stood, coming over and wrapping her arms around my waist. "You can. I won't stop you, my darling. Just … please don't overthink this and talk yourself out of taking a risk. I think Levi is it for you. I just don't want you to lose your chance because you're afraid."

"If I lose my chance in a fortnight, then things weren't meant to be between us anyway," I mumbled, bowing my head so that Alison wouldn't see the tears welling. "I'm nearly finished packing. Can you book me an Uber?"

"Sweetie, I'll drive you to the airport," Alison said, planting a kiss on my shoulder before walking out of the room.

LEVI

I let out a long breath, glancing up and down the busy street. People bustled past me on their way to or from their lunch breaks, typing on their phones.

None of them had any fucking idea just how momentous what I'd just done was. My sample and Lily's sample were right now inside the building behind me, being taken to a lab to be analysed. I'd paid the extra fee to have the test expedited, but that still meant I needed to wait two to three days for the results.

How the fuck was I going to function?

I headed for my car, climbing in and staring out the windscreen. I hadn't told anyone what was going on. Not Xander, not Mac. But the tightness in my lungs was fucking impossible to ignore. I needed to get it off my chest to someone.

I drove.

I breathed a sigh of relief when I saw her car parked out the front of her house. Climbing the steps, I banged on the front door. And waited. And banged again.

Nothing. No one was home. Or she knew it was me and was hiding.

Fuck.

I collapsed into the chair on the front porch and let my head fall into my hands. I hadn't slept last night. What if Lily wasn't mine? I couldn't even think about it, it made me feel so fucking sick.

I loved that tiny little girl. Fuck, I loved her so much it hurt. But if she wasn't mine, I had no right, no need to be in her life. Clearly Mateo had been sleeping over every night, doing all the night-time daddy duties. He was already a part of her life. And she was so little, me disappearing from her world would mean nothing to her.

But fuck, it would break me.

I'd lost track of how long I'd been sitting there when footsteps roused me from my misery.

I looked up, my frown deepening when I saw that it was Alison and not Amanda.

"Jesus, Levi, you look like shit!" she said, and she actually sounded concerned. "What's wrong?"

"I need to see her. I need to speak to her ... to tell her ..." I choked up, tears welling in my eyes. Alison sat down on the porch beside me.

"Sorry, Levi, I just dropped her at the airport. She's heading to Cairns for a fortnight to visit her parents."

I stood, pacing the creaky old timbers of the porch. "Fuck. I wanted to talk to her face-to-face, but this can't ... she's in the air now?" I turned to Alison, who checked her watch, shaking her head.

"Not for another forty-five minutes."

I snatched my phone out of my pocket, dialling her number. It rang, and rang ... and went to voicemail.

"Amanda, please, just ... call me back when you get this. I really fucking need to hear your voice right now. I'm not ... Things are shit. I just need to talk to you, okay?"

I hung up. Alison stared at me, worry written all over her face.

"This isn't just about wanting her back, is it?" she asked softly.

I shook my head. "Something really fucking awful happened last night, and ... stupidly, probably ... she's the first ... the only person I want to talk to about it."

Alison unlocked the door, holding it open and gesturing me inside. I hesitated, until she grabbed me by the arm and practically dragged me in.

"Is Lily okay? Is that what the problem is?" Alison asked as she bustled into the kitchen, flicking the switch on the kettle and grabbing cups and teabags.

"She's fine," I grunted, "I don't want to talk about it."

"Not to me, anyway," she replied, arching an eyebrow. "You know, when things are shit in your life, and there's one person, and only one person, who you want to talk to about it, that's generally because you love them."

"I do love her," I said. "I fucking adore everything about her. I just ... I want to tell her, but every time I get close to saying the words, she disappears on me."

"So don't let her disappear on you. Find a way to corner her, and lay all your cards on the table. And there better be a big fat card about how you plan to rein in Boobzilla."

I looked up at her in shock. "How did you know I called her that?" I asked.

Alison laughed. "Best friends tell each other everything. I know more about you than you'd like me to admit." She pointedly glanced down at my crotch. "She says it's magic."

I shook my head and stood, not in the mood for her games. "Zilla won't be a problem," I muttered. After the shit she was putting me through with Lily and fucking Mateo, she knew she had no right to even whisper something nasty about Amanda again.

If Lily wasn't mine, I could cut Zilla from my life for good. That thought left a bitter taste in the back of my throat.

"I've gotta go." I headed for the door.

"I'll text you her address in Cairns," Alison called out behind me. I stopped halfway down the hall.

"Why?"

"Oh, just in case … you never know when the mood might take you, and you suddenly feel the urge for a tropical holiday."

Fat fucking chance of that happening. Until I knew what was going on with Lily, I couldn't go anywhere. Or talk to anyone.

"Jesus, Levi. Have you even showered in the last two days?" Xander called out through my bedroom door. I rolled over in bed, brushing crumbs off my sheets.

I'd lied to fucking everyone around me. Xander, Mac and Patto, Zilla. They all thought I had the flu. It had been the best excuse to steer clear of training, to keep Xan off my back … and Zilla wouldn't want me infecting Lily. I'd holed myself up in my bedroom, sneaking out only to eat and use the toilet, when Xander was at work.

I ached to see Lily's tiny face, to hold her little body in my arms, but I knew I was in no fucking state to be trying to care for her. And if the results came in showing I wasn't her father … well, at least I wouldn't have to say goodbye.

I'd tried to find positives in case I was right, and she wasn't mine. I tried to tell myself that meant I could cut all ties with Zilla. It meant that things might be easier with Amanda, if … when we finally talked things through.

But in the end, I'd rather have a harder fight to get Amanda back, and keep Lily. Only problem was, I didn't get to make that choice. A tiny saliva sample from each of us would decide our fates.

"You feeling any better?" Xander continued, knocking lightly on the door. "You even awake?"

"I'm awake," I groaned. Barely. I'd been so fucking miserable that sleep was the only thing that I wanted to do. If there was a pill that could have knocked me out until the exact moment the test results arrived, I would've signed up for that shit like lightning.

"Does it stink in there the way I'm imagining it would?" Xander asked.

I sniffed, wincing at my own stench. "Probably worse."

Xander grumbled something incomprehensible under his breath. "Do you want your mail? There's an Express Post envelope here for you."

I fell out of bed. It had barely been forty-eight hours. Could the results really be here so fucking fast?

Standing up, I wrenched the door open, snatched the envelope out of Xander's hands, and slammed the door in his face.

"What the hell is going on, Levi? You don't have the flu! Why are you getting urgent mail from DNA Laboratories?"

I ignored him. Hands shaking, I turned the envelope over, sticking my finger under the tab and tearing it open. But I couldn't bring myself to pull out the papers inside and look at them.

"Will you just bloody talk to me?" Xander demanded. I stood, reaching over and opening the door for him before sitting on the bed again.

"Christ, you weren't wrong when you said it smelled worse in here than I was thinking," Xander said, but even with his nose wrinkled, he still sat beside me. "Will you tell me now what the hell has had you holed up in here for two days pretending to be sick?"

I handed him the envelope. "I need you to read this to me," I said. When he didn't take it, I shoved it into his chest. "Please, Xan."

He took the envelope, giving me a bewildered stare. I dropped my head into my hands, clawing my fingers into my hair.

"What's this about?" he asked.

"Just read it. It'll be pretty fucking obvious once you do."

The rustling of paper sent my heart hammering against my ribs. I was going to be sick.

Just fucking breathe, Levi. You can't change what's in there, but you need to know.

Xander didn't say anything for a very long time.

"This is … Lev, this is a paternity test …"

"What the fuck does it say?" I asked.

"Uh …" More rustling. "The alleged father cannot be excluded as the biological father of the tested child. Based on the analysis listed above, the probability of paternity is 99.9999999999%."

Fuck.

Wait.

"Read that again?" I breathed. Xander repeated himself. Was I hearing right?

"Does that mean …?" I muttered, still confused.

"Lev, if there was any doubt that Lily was your baby, it's just been refuted. She's your kid. Now will you tell me what the hell is going on here?"

I jumped to my feet. "It doesn't fucking matter. She's mine!"

I ran for the bathroom, showered in record time, and raced back to my bedroom, where Xander still sat on my bed, staring at the papers, eyebrows furrowed.

"Why did you get tested?" he asked. I scrambled into a pair of boxer briefs, snatching the papers from him. He glanced up at me, eyes widening when he saw the tattoo on my leg.

"When did you get that?" he demanded.

"Serbia," I replied, dragging on some running shorts and a t-shirt.

"Does Amanda know?"

I shook my head. "But she will. She fucking will."

I laid the document out on the kitchen bench for Zilla to see, then headed straight for the bouncer, scooping Lily out of it.

"Hey my girl," I crooned. "I'm sorry I ghosted for a couple of days. I'm back now, and I'm not going anywhere." She gurgled at me.

"You're happy about this?" Zilla asked, shocked. I turned to her. She was pale, her cheeks sunken. Her clothes were stained and she looked like she'd lost weight the way they hung off her.

"Are you fucking—freaking serious?" I asked her, swaying side to side with my girl resting against my shoulder. "I'm over the goddamned moon, Emilee."

Tears pooled in her eyes. "I … I just thought you'd be off the hook if she wasn't yours. Nothing would tie us together anymore."

I huffed. "Em, we're over. You clearly know that. You've moved on—you moved on while you still had me on the hook. Am I bitter about you cheating on me? Yeah, a little. Am I angry that you lied to me about the chances Lily was mine? Absolutely. But I was in love with this little girl before I even met her. Shit—sugar, I've been a total mess these last few days thinking I might never get to be with her again."

Emilee hiccupped out a sob. "I … I don't know what to say, Levi. I was scared at the beginning. I hadn't announced our breakup on socials, and I … I didn't want to do that and then immediately turn up pregnant—that's never a good look. It was easier to keep the breakup on the DL and … well I knew you would do the right thing by her … by us. Things with Mat were so new, and, I'm not gonna lie, I thought posts of you and me with a baby would boost my following."

She sat down on a kitchen stool, leaning her elbows on the

bench. "Mat wanted me to come clean. But I was too caught up in the lie by then. I … Levi, I'm not doing well. This is so hard. Even with Mat here helping of a night … it's been so much harder than I ever thought.

"My body …" She stopped talking to gasp through a sob, "I hate the way I look. My stomach is a fucking wobbly mess." To emphasise, she dragged the loose t-shirt up enough that I could see the loose skin there, criss-crossed with red stretch marks.

"It just looks like you had a baby six weeks ago, Emilee. Cut yourself some fuck—freaking slack! You don't have to be picture perfect every second of the day!"

"I've made a living out of being fucking perfect, Levi. But I can't do that and be a mother. It's too much. Mat's been my rock these last few weeks, and you … you've been so great too, taking her every day. You're a really good dad, Levi."

She pinched the bridge of her nose, but tears slipped out anyway. Real fucking tears, nothing like the crocodile variety I'd gotten so used to. "I'm … I'm not well. In my head."

I sighed. "Em, you haven't been yourself. It's been obvious. You hardly leave the house. And I know that's got a lot to do with not wanting people to see you looking anything but Insta-ready. Being a new parent is fu—bloody rough. I'm glad you've had Mat here to support you, and you know I'm always here to help out with Lily. But maybe you need to get some professional help?"

Zilla nodded, wiping away more tears. "Mat wants me to take a break from Instagram. He says I just need to focus on how I feel about myself, and not what everyone else is thinking about me."

As much as I hated to admit it, Mateo sounded like a switched-on kind of guy. I probably wouldn't have felt so charitable towards him if the paternity results had gone the other way.

"I think he's right." A sudden, fucking insane thought popped into my head.

"What if I took Lily for a few days? To give you a chance to rest, to talk to someone about your mental health, get some sleep, whatever you need."

Zilla's eyes narrowed slightly. "Why? Why would you offer to do that, Levi?"

"Because she's my baby too, and ..." Anything I tried to come up with at that point would sound ridiculous, so I blurted out the truth.

"I need to go to Cairns, but I ... I don't want to miss my time with her."

"Why do you need to go to Cairns?" Zilla asked.

"Amanda's up there." I waited for her to screw up her nose, to make some bitchy remark. But her eyes filled up again. That was when I was sure that she was struggling.

"Mat sent me that photo of you with her because he was trying to convince me that I could move on, go public with him. He told me that you two looked so in love, that *you'd* moved on, so why shouldn't *I* move on, too?"

"But instead you came to my house and abused me," I muttered. "Screamed some really fucking awful shit about her. And she was in the bedroom, heard everything you said. She left that night without saying goodbye."

Zilla dropped her head into her hands. "I thought ... I didn't want you, but I didn't want anyone else to have you, either. And I was shocked—she clearly had something that I didn't, something that made you look at her the way you did. Plus, I was panicking. In my head I had this picture where, online at least, you and I could be a little family with Lily. Where I could post pictures of you with her and pretend like we were together and happy and ... perfect. And I couldn't easily fake that if you were out in public with another woman, looking like you'd hang the moon for her. I was fucking stupid."

"You were more than stupid," I said. "But you *have* moved on now. You have Mateo. I want ... I need Amanda. And you don't get to try to drive a wedge between us if she'll have me back. I think you owe me at least that much after everything."

Zilla ... Emilee ... stared at me for a long time, wiping her tears away as they rolled down her cheeks. Lily started to fuss, so I took her into her room and changed her wet nappy.

Emilee came in as I was dressing her again, carrying a bottle. She handed it to me, gesturing for me to sit in the rocking chair. I sat, Lily latching on hungrily as I watched Emilee grab a big bag from the wardrobe and sit it open on the change table. She started packing clothes, nappies, burp cloths, blankets. When she left the room, returning with a bunch of clean bottles, a bottle brush, sterilising equipment and formula, my heart started racing.

"What are you doing?" I asked. She gave me a tight smile.

"If you're taking our daughter on a tropical holiday, I'm making sure she has everything she needs. You'd better book yourself a flight."

CHAPTER FORTY-TWO

Two Little Games

AMANDA

"Tell me about how you're feeling about your body," Gillian asked me over the phone.

"Well, I think you'll be proud of me," I replied with a little smile. "I'm currently lying poolside wearing a two-piece, and no board shorts, and I don't feel self-conscious."

I didn't add that I was lying poolside in an over fifty-five's retirement village, and the only other person at the pool was in her late sixties and napping on a sun lounger.

"And how do you feel about wearing these swimmers in public?"

I looked down at my body. The tankini was white with a black palm frond pattern. "I feel … cute," I replied, a little shocked to realise that I meant it. "I think I'd feel okay about wearing this out and about back home with my friends, actually."

"That's some very positive progress, Amanda. Now, are you ready to talk about him?"

My brain groaned, but I managed not to do it out loud.

"It's a little bit funny, don't you think, that I was finally ready to talk about one man I had issues with, only to replace him immediately with another?" I knew I was deflecting, and I knew that Gillian would see right through me, even from over two-thousand kilometres away.

"I think this one actually means more to you than the other. And that makes him even more difficult to talk about. Perhaps a similar exercise to your letter to Thomas might be helpful in sorting out your feelings?"

"I … I really don't think that will help," I argued weakly.

"Well, it's something to—" I tuned out as a shadow fell over me. I glanced up to find Mum. Even with her big, Audrey Hepburnesque sunglasses on, her face looked agitated.

"Sorry Gillian, my mother needs to speak to me urgently." I muted the phone before Gillian could respond.

"Is something wrong, Mum?" I asked in a hushed voice. I didn't want the other lady to overhear, even if she appeared to be napping. According to Mum, gossip spread like wildfire through Cassowary Quay Lifestyle Village.

"Oh, I was hoping you might be able to answer that for me, Miss," Mum replied, and she lifted her glasses so she could pierce me with her accusing eyes. She hadn't called me Miss since I was about fifteen. "Do you think you could enlighten me as to why our doorbell just rang, and when your father answered it, there was a very large, very attractive tattooed man on the other side, holding a baby and asking if he could see you?"

I gaped at her, lifting my phone and unmuting it just long enough to say, "I've got to go, Gillian."

"No, Mum!" I hissed, tugging my arm from her grip and heading through the back door of the villa, which allowed me to sneak to the spare bedroom, avoiding the living areas. "Let me at least put some shorts on!"

Mum glared at me. "I just want to get to the bottom of this, immediately! Who is this 'Levi' fellow, and how does he know where we live? And why have you never mentioned him to me? Good Lord, Amanda, he's delicious!"

"Be quiet!" My face was flaming, and I realised with a horrified jolt that the only pair of shorts I could find in my messy luggage were the denim ones I'd worn *that* night. But there was nothing for it —if I didn't sort myself out and go into the living room, I was worried Mum would invite Levi into my bedroom to chat.

What on earth was he doing here? And he'd brought Lily with him? Did that mean Emilee was somewhere nearby? How had he known their address?

"Alison," I muttered darkly, buttoning the shorts and storming out to the living room before Mum physically dragged me out there.

And then he came into view, and I froze. A light scruff covered his jaw, and he was wearing a very fitted black t-shirt and grey running shorts, which left nothing to the imagination.

God, no wonder my mother was a thirsty old thing, calling him delicious. I wanted to peel him out of those clothes and run my lips and tongue over every inch of him. I was suddenly hot and achy in places that I did not want to feel hot and achy when standing in a room with Mum and Dad.

"Levi," I breathed, all thoughts fleeing my mind. And then I looked down, to see Lily lying on a little quilted mat, kicking her legs and peering around with interest. "Oh, she looks so much bigger than a week ago!"

Levi's eyes didn't leave mine once. "She's had a growth spurt. Hey, Honey." He took a step towards me, then seemed to come to his senses, realising that my parents were watching our interaction like it was bingeworthy TV.

"Can we … talk outside?" I suggested. Levi's eyes roved over my body, lingering on the substantial amount of boob on display in the tankini top.

"Yeah, okay," he murmured, turning and bending towards Lily. Oh God, his backside in those shorts was almost better to look at than the front. Almost.

"Oh, leave Lily with us, Levi!" Mum practically gushed, hurrying over and taking a seat near where Lily lay, squeezing Levi's forearm as she did. "It'll be good grandma practice!"

Okay, so Mum knew Lily's name. How long had they interrogated him before she came to get me?

Why on earth was he here?

I headed straight through the screen door and out onto the front lawn, staring down the driveway until I felt him, warm and solid, standing behind me.

"Why are you here?" I asked breathlessly. The curtains twitched across the drive. Levi showing up unannounced with a baby in tow to visit the McGregors' single daughter was going to be the biggest gossip of the year.

"You didn't call me back," he murmured. Holy Hell, his mouth was right next to my ear. I shivered despite the sweltering heat.

"I came up here to get some … some clarity," I mumbled pathetically. His hands were on my arms, and I should have been shaking him off. I should have been putting some space between us. But it felt so good. Too good.

"Well, I already have fucking clarity when it comes to you, Honey. That's why I'm here."

My breath hitched. "What … what do you mean?"

His fingers dug into my arms. Not enough to hurt, but enough to feel … claiming.

"I mean I love you, Amanda. I fucking love you. And I'm not letting you ghost me again."

My entire body felt simultaneously doused in icy water and set on fire. I wrenched my arms out of his grip so I could turn to face him. But then I spotted my parents, openly watching us through the front window. Oh my God, Dad had actually gone and gotten a bag of popcorn.

"This is not the place, Levi," I hissed, my heart thrumming in my chest. With a glare at my parents, I grabbed his hand and pulled. "Come on. We do need to talk … somewhere other than here."

LEVI

Amanda tugged me down the drive, past the identical single level villas with their identical gardens out front. I didn't know what to think. I'd just blurted out that I loved her. Where was my well-rehearsed fucking speech now?

I glanced back, seeing her parents waving at me through their suddenly open front blinds. Maybe she really had meant we needed more privacy. But did we need privacy because she was going to reject me, and I was going to be a total pathetic mess …

… or because she was going to say exactly what I wanted to hear, and we definitely wouldn't want her parents to witness what I planned to do to her if that happened?

Fuck. I'd never been this nervous in my life. I tried to focus on the warmth of her hand in mine, but all that did was make me realise just how clammy my palms were.

"Come in here, there should be somewhere private for us to talk," Amanda muttered, dragging me through a glass door with a plaque that read, 'Recreation Centre'. Several people looked up at us as we blasted hot air into the air-conditioned space, and more than one of them raised their eyebrows as Amanda hauled me past their tables.

Amanda muttered something about gossip as she headed for a door at the far end of the space. She opened it and led me into a dimly lit room, letting go of my hand as she turned to close the door behind us.

When I saw what was in the room, I couldn't hide my grin.

"Coming full circle, are we?" I asked with a low chuckle. Even in the mood-lighting of the pool room, I could see her blush. The air conditioning was cold and I couldn't help but notice Amanda's nipples puckering against the thin fabric of her swimmers.

"Explain yourself," Amanda demanded, crossing her arms over her chest. I opened my mouth to speak, but she cut me off. "Did you actually come all the way up here—with a six-week-old baby in tow —to tell me that you love me?"

I leaned back against the pool table. "Yep," I replied, smirking at her. I sure as shit wasn't feeling as cocky as I was acting, but it seemed to throw her off balance, so I figured I should roll with it.

"Oh," she said, and the pink in her cheeks spread to her chest, her cleavage. Fuck me, I was not wearing the right shorts to conceal my rapidly swelling dick. I noticed her glance down, then blink and turn her face away. "I … Levi, you shouldn't have blindsided me with this."

"I disagree." I stood, heading over to the wall where the cues hung, grabbing two and a chalk cube. "I think when you're blind-sided is when I'm likely to get the most honesty out of you."

"I've never been anything but honest with you!" she said, her hand automatically reaching out to take the cue from me. I stepped closer, right into her personal space.

"You omit a lot, though, don't you Honey?" I murmured. I was flying completely by the seat of my pants, but hell, I was going to roll with the crazy idea that had just popped into my head. "But we're going to fucking fix that right here and now." I started pulling the balls out of the pocket nets and racking them up. "I know you like to play games with me. So, here's our game. For every ball you sink, you get to tell me one thing that's worrying you about the idea of us. And for every ball I sink, I'm going to tell you something too."

Amanda's breath hitched, and just like that first night, I couldn't take my eyes off her tits as they rose and fell in time to her shallow breaths. Fuck, she was the sexiest woman I'd ever laid eyes on.

"What kind of thing?" she whispered.

I winked. "You'll have to play to find out."

You'd better fucking hope this crazy idea of yours works.

"Uh … I … Okay, but I get to break," she said. I chuckled, anticipating what was about to happen.

"Be my guest, Honey." I stepped back. "I promise I won't play dirty."

Her eyes flashed, and for a split second, I was sure she was disappointed by that. But she lined up her shot, and just like I'd expected, two solids dropped into pockets. She glanced at me, then away, licking those pink lips.

"Okay, well … are you here alone? Or did Emilee come up with you?"

I cleared my throat. She was pulling out the big gun first. "Emilee's in Sydney. She's got a boyfriend. She knows how I feel about you. When I told her I wanted to come up here to talk to you, she was the one who packed a bag for Lily and told me to book a flight."

Amanda's mouth dropped open. "She … she was?"

I nodded. Amanda seemed to compose herself, although the confused set of her eyebrows was so fucking endearing—I wanted to kiss that little line between them so badly.

"And she was okay with you taking Lily interstate?"

I nodded again. "She's been struggling with her state of mind. She was able to keep the worst of it from me because she's had her boyfriend staying over and helping her at night-time. But I think she was happy to have a bit of space to try and get some support for herself."

"Oh … okay then," she mumbled, looking perplexed as she turned back to the table to take another shot. I reached out and gripped her waist. The little breathy sound she made when my hands touched her had me biting back a groan.

"You sunk two balls, Honey," I reminded her. "You have to tell me something else that's worrying you."

I stepped back, giving her space. She turned, eyes glassy, the tops of her breasts flushed.

"I'm … I've done some stupid things when it comes to men in the past. Trusting a man is … it's hard for me," she mumbled, staring firmly down at the floor. I strode closer again, pinching her chin and lifting it until she had to look at me.

"If you're talking about that arsehole Thomas Blackthorn, I know all about him. And I can't believe you could even for a second think that anything Emilee, or anyone else, said about you and him was true. He was a total fucking psychopath, what he did to you … and to Mel, and everyone else he hurt … none of that is on you!"

I dropped back, letting her go. "I … I hope you don't think I would do anything like that to you, Amanda."

"I … of course I don't, Levi!" she said with conviction. "I just … I've always had a fear in the back of my mind, that if … when people find out about what he did, and my involvement with him, they'll … they won't want anything to do with me."

I threw my arms out wide. "Well, I know what he did. And I know that you're his victim as much as anyone else. And I'm right here, with all that knowledge, and I'm telling you right now, I don't give a flying fuck about any of it."

Amanda flinched. Shit, I had sounded too angry. But I was angry. I was fucking furious—that psycho had done such a number on her.

"Well, I guess … well," she stammered. Without another word she turned back to the table. The pool shark in her returned, and with steady hands she took her next shot—an easy one for the bottom pocket. She missed by too much for it to be anything but intentional.

"I guess you're up," she said, innocence dripping from her voice like honey. I was being played. She'd decided she wanted to avoid having to talk to me about her worries. Well, either way, this worked for me. She didn't realise that I had a whole catalogue of things she needed to hear lined up in my brain. And I only needed eight.

Her deliberate miss had set me up a perfect shot to the centre pocket. I took it, and before the ball even sunk, I turned to her, fixing her with my gaze.

"Honey, I love sitting and drinking tea together, and I fucking love how you dunk your Tim Tams into your tea until the chocolate is all melted, and you have to lick it off your fingers. But I love it even better when you let me lick it off." My voice had turned deep and hoarse, and fuck, I was getting hard. She glanced down at my dick, and then away again, her perfect tits heaving as she sucked in air.

I adjusted my dick, taking a breath to try and get it to deflate a bit, before I stepped back to the table. I lined up and sank another ball.

This time I walked around the table to where she was standing, trailing a finger down her arm before resting my palm over her fingers. Her body shook, her breaths sharp and shallow.

"I love how caring you are. How you make an effort to remember little things that mean a lot to me. But I sometimes worry that you put other people's feelings ahead of your own." With my free hand I stroked her jaw. "You shouldn't, by the way. Your feelings are very fucking important to me. I want them to be important to you, too."

"I …" Amanda started, but I pushed a finger against her lips, silencing her.

"I'm not done," I said, meeting her wide grey gaze, my expression serious. "One thing this whole experience has taught me is that opening up to each other is … it's really fucking important, Honey."

I cleared my throat. "I'm sorry if you ever felt like I kept things back from you. I'm … it's fucking difficult for me to talk about how I feel, I've spent so many years believing that my feelings aren't important."

"Oh, Levi—"

"Please, just let me say what I need to say, or I'm not going to get it all out," I muttered, eyes downcast, my voice hoarse from trying to hold my emotions at bay. "I don't ever want you to think that I wasn't as open with you as I should have been because I didn't think you deserved those parts of me."

"I never—"

I pressed my finger tighter against her lips, stroking my thumb along her jaw. She huffed out a tiny, frustrated breath that almost made me laugh.

"I didn't think I deserved you. I didn't want to burden you with why I'm a total fucked up mess. I didn't think you'd want to stay with me … with all my baggage. I figured you'd have your fun with me, and run before … before Lily arrived. I couldn't let myself let you in … because I knew that if I made myself vulnerable, if I told you how I really felt, and you left, that would have broken me."

I felt her hand on my shoulder, and I swallowed down as much of my emotions as I could. I needed my wits about me, not to turn into a blubbering mess. "Fuck, it did break me. Just because I didn't tell you back then, doesn't mean I wasn't feeling it."

Her fingers squeezed my shoulder, and I dropped my hand from her face, letting myself look at her again. Her eyes were glistening with unshed tears, the way I was sure mine were.

"Levi, I … I know what it's like to have things from your past that still impact you, every day, that are just too difficult to talk about. I mean, Hell, I couldn't bring myself to tell you about … about Thomas. So, please, don't ever think that you weren't enough, or that your life was too messy for me. I know all about messy lives."

I blinked, too fucking raw from her words to continue to meet her gaze. Clearing my throat, I forced my attention back to our game. I eyed two potential shots off down the cue before making my decision and taking the shot. The nine-ball rebounded off the side, but came through for me, sinking into the top pocket.

I looked up at Amanda, who had followed me around the table, eyes wide. She was close. Close enough to drag into my arms, to lift up onto the table and kiss senseless. But I couldn't. Not yet.

"I love that you hate folding your washing," I said, trying to lighten the mood again after dragging it down so much. Amanda's eyes widened and a little, disbelieving giggle fell from those perfect pink lips.

"That's … strange," she said. I couldn't help myself. I reached over and ran a finger along the hem of her shorts. The ones that had fucking tormented me from the first moment I met her.

"Is it? I love it, because I want to be the one who helps you fold it. Honey, I want all your little, insignificant moments." I stopped just short of slipping my hand underneath the hem and running it up that creamy thigh. I removed my hand, watching her squirm for a second before turning back to the table.

I lined up my shot but missed.

"Bugger," she muttered under her breath, which forced a chuckle out of me.

Barely glancing at the table—she'd given up all pretence of actually trying to sink a ball—she took a shot. It ricocheted off the bottom of the table, but somehow managed to sink in the centre pocket.

"Damn it," she growled, turning to me, eyes blazing.

"I'm a fat girl."

I took a step back at the aggression in her tone. "So fucking what? You think that's something that will keep us apart?" I asked, shocked.

"You're not going to deny that I'm fat?" She folded her arms across her chest, which just squeezed her tits together, until all I could see was the dark crevice between those two creamy mounds.

"Fuck that noise," I growled. The disbelief in her eyes almost undid me. "I'm changing the fucking rules," I announced, tossing my cue aside and striding up to the table, taking the eleven-ball in my hand and dropping it into the nearest pocket. I reached out to her, dragging her arms away from her chest, resting my palms on her waist, rubbing my thumbs up and down from the bottoms of her tits to her lush hips.

"I love your curves. I love every luscious fucking inch of your body. Your tits feature in every one of my dreams. Just thinking about your perfect arse gets me hard." I stepped closer so she could feel the length of my dick, straining against my shorts, as I pressed my lips to her ear to murmur, "I want to worship every single part of you with my mouth, my tongue. Every. Single. Part."

She was panting. I didn't give her a second to think. I grabbed another one of the striped balls, dropping it into a pocket. My fingers dug into her waist.

"I love that you look just as beautiful in a faded old t-shirt and yoga pants as you do in a slinky dress, or expensive lingerie. But I love that you look the most beautiful when you're naked and moaning underneath me."

"Levi," she murmured. I pressed a single finger to her lips, silencing her. I had to move away from her to collect the next ball, practically throwing it into the pocket before leaning my hands on the table and staring her down across the felt.

"At the beach last week, I fell in love with the way my baby looks in your arms. And I love imagining us one day giving Lily a little brother or sister. The thought of your belly all round with our baby…fuck, Honey, I fantasise about it."

"Levi, stop," she begged, her eyes wide, her cheeks flushed. I shook my head, smiling determinedly at her as I tossed the second-to-last of my balls into a pocket.

"When something momentous happens in my life—good or fucking bad—the first person I want to talk to is you. When we won gold in Serbia, all I could think about was calling you to celebrate, and I hated that we weren't in a place where I felt okay doing that. And … last week something happened that nearly broke me … and the only person I wanted to talk it through with was you. You're my person, Honey."

"What happened?" she whispered. I shook my head.

"Later. I still have an eight-ball to sink." I picked it up and walked around the table with it, until I had her wedged between my body and the table. Slipping it into the pocket behind her, I brushed my lips against her cheekbone, her jaw, bringing them so close to her mouth that her breath was mine.

"I just fucking love you, Amanda. And I hope that you feel the same way. I know I come with a shitload of baggage, but I'm not going down without a fight here. Things are better when I'm with you. It's as simple as that."

She leaned away, putting space between our mouths. I barely dared to breathe. Had I done it again? Come on too strong? Had I read this whole fucking situation wrong?

"Do you remember that other game we liked to play?" Amanda asked. My brain was so full of the smell of her, of the feel of her heat against me, that I had no fucking idea what she was talking about.

"The 'I want' game," she reminded me.

I sucked in a breath. "I remember." Was she about to tell me she wanted me to stop? Her eyes flicked to the ceiling, as if she were searching for the right words.

Fuck.

I relaxed my grip on her body, putting space between us. Her eyes flashed to mine, and she reached out, gripping my waist and pulling me back against her.

"I want you," she whispered.

At first, I was sure I'd misheard her.

"You want …"

She hiccupped out a little laugh. "I want to try this with you … really try it. I … I want this with you … and Lily. I want your messy life, and all your baggage. I want it so badly, Levi."

My groan was swallowed up as our mouths collided.

CHAPTER FORTY-THREE

Welcome Home

AMANDA

"So, tonight's *the* night, isn't it?" Alison asked, leaning against my doorway. I scowled, adjusting the hem of the new boho dress I'd bought. It was white with flutter sleeves and a deep V neckline showing plenty of cleavage.

"You look hot. But honestly, after you've made him wait two weeks to get back into your pants, you could show up in a sack and his magic penis would be poking a hole in his jeans."

"Don't try to flatter me," I grumbled. "I still haven't forgiven you for not giving me a heads-up that you'd sent him to my parents' house!"

Alison chuckled. "Well, it worked out for the best in the end, didn't it? You two are as loved up as ever … or at least you will be when you get his dick back inside you tonight."

I sighed, plonking myself on my bed and pressing my hands between my trembling thighs. I'd built the night up, in my own mind at least, to the point where I'd worked myself up into such a state of nerves, I was worried I'd take one look at him naked and pass out.

"Why did I decide we needed to take things slow?" I whimpered. "And why did I decide that we needed a hotel room to … reconnect?"

"Because you're a romantic at heart, and you wanted to do things the right way this time around," Alison explained. "And because you know that you're both going to be screaming the whole place down tonight, and at least at a hotel you don't have to continue to live with the people who will have the pleasure of over-hearing you."

It had been three weeks since Levi had melted me with his declaration of love in the pool room at the rec centre. Thinking of it still made my chest go squish. And the kiss we'd shared … I'd felt that in every single cell of my body.

But after several minutes of kissing, and maybe a little grinding, We'd broken it off. What could so easily have happened between us wasn't appropriate in a public room at a retirement village. And it certainly wasn't appropriate knowing that my parents were waiting back at their villa to find out what the hell was going on with us … while also caring for his infant daughter.

So, we'd agreed—no sex until we got back to Sydney. He had a hotel for three nights in Cairns, and we spent that time doing something we'd never done. We dated. Well, we dated as much as a single parent of a newborn dates.

We visited Cairns Aquarium, where every woman of child-bearing age practically lost their panties at the sight of Levi wearing Lily in her carrier. She slept through almost all of it, while Levi and I wandered and talked. He joked about pranks he'd played on his brother as a kid, and told me how he got into rowing—his mother had been an Australian champion in her teens and early twenties, and she'd been the one to encourage him to persist with it. She'd even coached him and Theo when they first started the sport. The love he still felt for his mum shone in the unshed tears in his eyes when he spoke about her. I'd squeezed his hand extra tight for a good half hour afterwards.

When we'd taken a break to feed Lily, I'd confessed that I hated being an only child, but had never breathed a word of it to anyone before. I'd shyly said that I definitely wanted to have children of my own one day—more than one.

When he'd whispered, "you've already got one," and handed the milk-drunk little bundle over to me to cuddle, I'd almost burst into tears.

He'd shared the story of Lily's birth with me, how Emilee's labour had been fast and intense, and how holding Lily for the first time, all naked, and bloody, and wrinkled, had felt like it had changed his biology. He'd told me about discovering Emilee had been cheating on him, and the awful days while he waited for paternity test results, and his utter relief that Lily was one hundred percent his. That had earned him a lingering kiss from me, with Lily nestled between us, fast asleep.

To try and lighten the mood, I'd told him about the masturbating mother who had been my first official childbirth experience as a midwife. He'd been equal parts amused and insatiably curious about it, and it rapidly morphed into a discussion on orgasmic births, and orgasms in general, until I'd blushed furiously as he chuckled and ran a thumb over my heated cheek.

We'd eaten fish and chips on Cairns Esplanade in the early evening, before Lily got fussy and needed to be back at the hotel for bedtime. The next night we'd ordered takeaway Chinese food and eaten it at a table by the pool at Cassowary Quay with Mum and Dad, who had fussed over Lily like she actually was their grandchild. Mum hadn't missed a single chance to comment on Levi's muscles, or his 'unique' eyes, or his very handsome smile, all while throwing the most wicked side-eye in my direction.

One night, once Lily was down, we'd cuddled on the lounge in his hotel room and watched something quietly on the TV. Well, we had the TV on quietly while we made out on the lounge like teenagers. But clothes stayed firmly on, and I didn't sleep over. I couldn't trust myself not to give in to the ever-growing need for him, but I was determined that if we were going to do this properly, we had to do things the right way around this time—not just fall into bed together.

Back in Sydney, things had gotten a little more serious. Once the buffer of my final uni exams was over, there was the Emilee issue to contend with. Levi had said we needed to get it all put to bed as quickly as possible, and while the thought of coming face-to-face with her had terrified me, I'd known it was the only way. Like ripping off a Band-Aid.

"I promise she'll be on her best behaviour, Honey," Levi had reassured me. "Look, I doubt you'll get an apology out of her—that's not her style. But … she's changed, Amanda. I can't fucking explain it, but something about becoming a mother has changed her."

I still hadn't been able to fully contain my trepidation when I went with him that evening to drop Lily back to her mum's house. Emilee had walked out from the bedroom, and while her footsteps had stuttered when she saw me, awkwardly standing just inside the door, she'd forced a tight-lipped smile onto her face.

"Nice to see you," she'd muttered.

"You too, Emilee," I managed. "You look really well."

She did. She had that new-mum, perpetually tired look, and she wasn't as perfectly presented as I remembered her from the few appointments we'd had together. But it actually made her look more … human.

She huffed. "I look like shit, but thanks for lying to me. You …" she'd taken in my cut-off jeans, white t-shirt and cardigan, and I braced myself for the inevitable put-down.

"You look … nice—that's a cute outfit." While it was obvious the words had cost her, it hadn't felt like she was lying.

"That went so much better than I expected," I'd said to Levi as the lift took us back down to the carpark.

Levi had raised a brow. "*So* much better? What the fuck were you expecting?"

I'd shrugged. "She didn't call me a whale or accuse me of being dirty and desperate. That's progress."

I'd been aiming for light-hearted and humorous. What I'd gotten in return was his huge, hard body pinning me to the wall, his knee pushing between my legs, big hands tangling in my hair, tugging my head to the side, and a hickey sucked into my neck while I moaned and ground myself against his muscular thigh.

"I'm feeling fucking dirty and desperate right now," he'd grumbled. "Fuck, Honey, this no fucking rule better be over soon."

"Tomorrow night," I'd breathed into his ear as he continued to nibble and suck at my collarbone. "I've got to work until five, so pick me up at eight, once you've dropped Lily home for the night."

And here I was … 'tomorrow night' was no longer in the future. Gazing at my reflection in my bedroom mirror, I fingered the mottled blue mark on my neck, where he'd branded me in that lift.

"Do you think that maybe the particulars of my plans for this evening might be a bit much to ask of him? I'm scared he might …"

"Might what?" Alison demanded, "Ravish you? Screw you nineways from Sunday? Turn vampire and bite your neck again? Isn't that what you want him to do?"

I rolled my eyes. "You know what I'm talking about."

Alison came up beside me, wrapping an arm around my waist. "Levi would never do anything that you weren't totally into, you know that. So just be honest with him, and everything will work out." She stood, heading for the door. "I have to get ready now too. Brad's taking me out for Italian tonight."

My eyebrows shot up. "He's taking you on a date?"

Alison smirked. "If I'm talking to him about it, I call it 'pre-fuck-fest-carb-loading', but between you and me, yeah, I'm claiming it. Date night with Dr Jacobs!"

I grinned at her retreating back.

"I want all the goss on everything that *goes down* tonight, Amanda McGregor!" she called from her bedroom door.

And just like that, the nerves flooded back in full force.

LEVI

"Goodnight, angel," I murmured to Lily. She was having a bottle with Mateo, who I had to admit was a fucking decent guy, really. He had one night a week where he didn't work at his restaurant, and he spent it taking on the lion's share of the evening baby duties so Emilee could get some rest. I was also pretty sure he was the reason Emilee wasn't acting like Zilla these days. Between him and Lily, it seemed that she'd actually found things that mattered more to her than her Instagram account.

With a nod to Mateo, I quietly left the apartment, waiting until I was in the lift before I made the call.

"G'day," Mac said.

"How's it all going?" I asked, not beating around in the bush. "I'm just leaving Emilee's now. I was gonna go straight to Amanda's to pick her up, but I can let her know I'm running late if you need me back there to finish up."

"Nah, we've got it under control. Just about to lock up and get out of here. There is no way I want to be within a ten-k radius of this place, knowing the christening you and Amanda will be giving it tonight."

I chuckled. "Thanks mate. I owe you one. Well, I probably owe you a shitload more than one, really."

"I'm not keeping count," Mac assured me. "Anyway, gotta go, I too have a date to get ready for."

My eyebrows shot up. "Why have I heard nothing about this?" I demanded. "Where did you meet him?"

Mac cleared his throat. "Not Grindr, if that's what you're wondering. I … my sister actually set us up. He's the biological father of a girl one of my nieces goes to preschool with. He co-parents with her two mums."

I grinned. "He sounds great. Well, fucking enjoy yourself tonight, Mac."

"Thanks, I will, Levi. You too."

"Oh, I plan to," I said, ending the call and climbing into my car.

Halfway to Amanda's my phone pinged with a text. When I pulled up at the next set of lights, I surreptitiously checked the screen.

> Alison: I cancelled the hotel room like you asked, free of charge (you're welcome). I gave them a very convincing sob story and they were super sympathetic. You owe me, Danger Boy. You better give my girl a night she'll never forget!

I sent back a thumbs up as the light turned green. When I pulled up outside Amanda's house, Alison was walking down the path. She saw me, waiting by the letterbox for me to get out of the car.

"She's very nervous, Danger Boy," she murmured. "Be gentle with her tonight, okay?"

"Well, there goes my plan for surprise anal," I joked. Alison guffawed, but quickly fixed me with a beady stare.

"I'm not even slightly joking, Levi. Tonight might be an even bigger deal for her than handing over her V card to you."

With that she flounced off down the street, leaving me to watch her, feeling perplexed as fuck. What did Amanda have to feel nervous about?

A tiny inkling of a reason started to whisper in the back of my mind, but I pushed it aside, because if I let that thought take root, I was going to be hard as steel before I got to the front door. Not to mention if I was wrong, I'd be so fucking disappointed.

"What was Alison talking to you about?"

My head snapped up, and my jaw dropped.

"You're a fucking angel," I murmured. She stood in the open doorway, light spilling from behind her like a halo. Her white dress skimmed those beautiful thighs. I didn't even need the hot fantasy that had been taking root in my mind a moment ago. Just the sight of her and my dick was about to rip out of my trousers.

"Hi, Levi," she replied, her voice breathy and low, which was doing nothing to alleviate the steel rod in my pants. "How are you?"

I strode up to the door, wrapping an arm around her waist and pulling her close. "So much better now I'm with you," I said honestly, dragging her against me, snaking a hand around her neck and tilting her jaw up with my thumb, nipping her bottom lip before soothing it with my tongue. She gasped, and as much as I wanted to deepen the kiss, I sighed and stepped back.

"If I keep that up, we won't make it out tonight. I'll be pushing you up against the door frame and ripping your panties off."

Her blush was the most adorable thing I'd ever seen.

"Let me just get my bag, hold on." She disappeared back down the hallway, returning a moment later with a large leather bag, a nervous smile plastered on her face. I took the bag from her, cupping her cheek.

"You good?" I asked quietly. She nodded, biting her lip. I thumbed it gently until it popped out from between her teeth.

"Mine," I reminded her darkly, taking her hand and leading her to the car, handing her into the passenger seat.

"So, where are we going?" I asked, as if I hadn't completely screwed with her not-so-secret plans. I had what I hoped was a much better surprise in store for her.

"I … uh … there's a nice restaurant in the city, just near the Park Hyatt. So maybe just park somewhere near there?"

I tried to hide my smirk as I pulled onto the street. Once we were out of Bondi and on the road, I reached over, putting my hand on her thigh, just below the hem of her dress. She shivered, and my grin widened.

Making her come tonight was going to be so much fun. And I'd had plenty of time to fantasise new ways to do it. Fuck, I'd been jacking off multiple times a day just thinking about how things would go when we finally fell back into bed together.

"Um, this isn't the way into the city," Amanda said in confusion.

Laughter burst out of my chest. "There's been a change of plans tonight, Honey. Sorry to spring it on you, but there's somewhere else we really need to be tonight."

"Oh. That's a …"

"If you're worrying about your room reservation, don't. Alison sorted that for me."

"She what?" Amanda's voice was shrill. "You weren't … it was supposed to be a surprise!"

"She cancelled it. No charge. And it was a surprise when she told me. A really fucking nice one." I slid my hand just slightly under the hem of her dress, and she gasped.

"Well, where are we going, then?" she asked, her voice shaking slightly as I kneaded the flesh of her inner thigh. Any higher than this and she was going to push me away. She didn't like me to touch her too high on her legs.

"You'll see," I replied, taking a left and continuing further away from the city. Amanda's leg started to jiggle under my palm.

"Don't be nervous," I murmured. It's a good surprise." I fucking hoped she would think it was a good surprise.

"I'm fine," she insisted, but the jiggling didn't stop.

By the time we pulled up outside our destination, Amanda's breaths were shallow, and she was chewing almost viciously on her bottom lip. I decided not to play games with her and make her stop —fuck, my heart was starting to hammer, and my palms were sweating.

What if she thought I was coming on too strong?

Well, she should be used to it by now, shouldn't she, dickhead?

"Where are we?" Amanda asked worriedly as I helped her out of the car. She glanced up at the building in front of us, then back at me, a little line forming between her eyebrows. I reached out and smoothed it away with my thumb, before reaching into the car and grabbing her overnight bag. The one she'd packed thinking we'd be staying in a five-star hotel tonight.

Fuck, I hoped she liked the new arrangement instead.

"Come inside," I whispered, taking her hand and turning towards the apartment building. It was an Art Deco, three storey place, painted cream. I fumbled with my keys until I found the right one, unlocking the glass door into the lobby.

"We're going up," I said, heading towards the wide staircase,

Amanda following timidly along behind me. At the top of the stairs were four doors—two on each side of a wide hallway. I took her to the furthest on the right, pulling out another key.

The door swung open and I stepped inside, turning back towards Amanda.

"Welcome home, Honey."

CHAPTER FORTY-FOUR
Inked Into My Heart

AMANDA

"Oh my God," I breathed, stepping into the apartment on shaking legs. Battery operated candles adorned an ornamental fireplace, a rug and a two-seater lounge in front of it. More candles covered the kitchen bench to the right, and a circular dining table.

"Do you like it?" Levi asked, and I realised he looked as nervous as I felt.

"What … what do you mean, home?"

He rubbed guiltily at the back of his neck. "Well, it doesn't have to be … home, that is … for you. But I figured I needed to get out of Xander's, get myself somewhere that Lily could have her own room, so I can take her overnight sometimes. And Mateo took over the lease on Coogee with Emilee, so I can finally afford my own place again. Mac and some of the rowing boys helped me set up the furniture today."

He reached out and took my hand again, drawing me into the apartment. "But I'd fucking love to think that you'd live here with me … maybe not straight away, if you're not … if that's too soon. But I want you to feel like this is your home, too. Even just on the nights you stay over."

"Levi, I ..." I broke off, overwhelmed with the aching rush of love I felt for him. His brows furrowed.

"You don't have to answer me right now. In fact, fuck it, forget I said anything about it. You hungry? I have some takeaway menus here." He let go of my hand and strode over to the kitchen bench, fumbling with a bunch of brochures, his eyes looking everywhere but me. I giggled. I rarely saw him so flustered.

He glanced up at me, eyes wary. I followed him into the kitchen, putting my hands on his hips and resting my forehead against his warm, solid chest.

"I love you," I murmured, tilting my head up and pressing my lips to his. He stood frozen for a split second, before his arms curled around me, dragging me closer until all of me was pressed against his impressive body. He deepened the kiss, licking and nibbling at my lip until I opened for him, then plundering my mouth in that hot, possessive way that made me ache between my legs.

"I fucking love you, too, Honey," he growled against my mouth, before moving to kiss my jaw, nibble at my earlobe.

"Can we eat ... after?" I whispered. Levi stilled, his breath hot and tickly against my neck.

"After what?" he asked.

I laughed breathily. "After you take me to see our new bedroom."

With an incoherent groan, Levi's big palms stroked down my back until he gripped my butt, lifting me. I squeaked, but wrapped my legs around his waist as he carried me through a doorway to a small hall.

"Lily's room's that way, bathroom straight ahead," he said in a rush, turning and striding the other way. "And this," he said proudly, laying me down on a bed and climbing on top of me, "is our bedroom. Brand new bed. Very sturdy. Will withstand the kind of hard fucking you love."

The bed was massive, with a slatted timber bedhead. More candles decorated both bedsides. He'd really gone all out with the ambiance tonight. I wanted to test the limits of this bed with an intensity that took my breath away, but I had something else I wanted to try first … if I could work up the courage to ask for it.

Levi manoeuvred me up the bed until my head hit the pillows, nudging my thighs apart until he was nestled between them, the hard ridge of his penis pressing right where I needed it. I couldn't help myself—I rocked my hips against him. His light-filled eyes rolled back in his head as he let out a little puff of air.

"Need this dress off you," he muttered, kneeling and reaching between us to drag the hem up my legs. I lifted my butt so he could pull it free and sat up so he could slip it off over my head.

I bit my lip, glancing up at him as he took in my underwear. His eyes darkened and he scrubbed a hand over his mouth.

"Is this …?" he asked hoarsely. I nodded, knowing exactly what he meant. It was the white lingerie set I'd been wearing in the photo I'd texted to him.

"Fuck me, I want to take this off you with my teeth," he growled. I sat up, scooting back a bit to put some space between us.

"Levi, I … I think we should play the 'I want' game again," I said, my words coming out in a rush before I lost my nerve.

Levi's eyes never left my breasts as he replied, "What do you want, Honey?"

I swallowed. My nipples were hard and aching beneath the lace of my bra, just from the way he was staring at me. "I …" I stopped to take a few quick, shallow breaths. Levi watched, jaw clenching and unclenching like he was only just hanging onto his control by the thinnest thread. I was about to lose my nerve.

"I want you to tie me to the bed and …" another quick breath, "and make me come with your mouth."

Those light-filled eyes flooded with black as his pupils overtook is irises. "Are you … don't fuck with me about this, Honey," he murmured.

"I've never been more serious in my life."

His body collided with mine, knocking me back onto the pillows, his mouth taking mine, rough and desperate, and so delicious that I clenched around nothing, wetness rushing to soak my panties. His tongue branded my mouth, hot and demanding, and I returned his need, tangling our tongues together, biting and sucking on his mouth, clawing my hands into his hair. His body nestled between my legs once more, his penis hard and needy, the seam of his pants rubbing right against my already swollen clitoris.

His mouth broke away from mine as his hand made its way down my body. "Once I tie you up, Honey, this," he cupped my hot, wet core in his palm, "is mine. You want me to stop, you need to say the words. But otherwise, you let me do this my way, okay?"

I nodded, swallowing down my fear, my worries.

"Fuck," Levi muttered, his head dropping until his forehead rested against my shoulder. "I don't think I've got anything to tie you up with."

I managed a very nervous giggle. "I have two silk scarves in my bag out by the door."

He glanced up at me, smirking. "You came prepared tonight." Planting a kiss to the swell of each of my breasts, he jumped off the bed and practically sprinted out of the room, returning in record time with the scarves. He stood in the doorway, just taking in the sight of me in my bra and panties. He palmed his erection through his trousers, eyeing me hungrily.

He stalked forwards, crawling up the bed until he loomed over me. Reaching behind me, he unclipped my bra, drawing it slowly down my arms. I shivered as the cool air hit my bare nipples.

"I'm going to take my time on these tonight," he said, his fingers trailing up my arms and down across the curves of my breasts, cupping them and running his calloused thumbs over my nipples. A little moan burst out of my throat, and I squirmed.

"But first I need to stop you wriggling so much." He gripped my wrists, drawing them above my head and securing them together with one of the scarves. My breaths became even shallower as his chest brushed my bare nipples. He fiddled at the bedhead with the other scarf, as I tried to crane my neck to see what he was doing.

Gripping my jaw in one strong hand, he caught my mouth roughly with his, sucking my bottom lip into his mouth and biting down just hard enough to have me gasping and throbbing. And then

I felt the soft, cool silk of the other scarf pass between my tied wrists, and the tug of him tying it tight.

He leaned back, gripping my hips and dragging me down the bed until my arms were fully extended. His cheeks were flushed, his eyes glittering as he took me in.

"Fuck, Honey, your tits look so amazing like that," he growled, bending to suck a nipple into his mouth. I cried out, arching my back to his mouth as he tugged on it with his teeth, before soothing with his tongue, and moving to the other one to repeat the torment of pain and pleasure. On and on for what felt like forever he teased my breasts with nothing more than his mouth, until I was panting, and begging, and my panties were completely soaked.

But then his mouth trailed down my body, and all the nerves I thought I had under control started to flood straight back.

LEVI

Amanda's nipples were rosy red and glistening as I kissed my way down her body. Fuck, the skin on her stomach was so warm and soft. I nibbled at the giving flesh, my dick so hard in my pants it was fucking painful.

Her body stilled beneath my mouth, the needy wriggling she'd been doing turning tense. I glanced up her body. Her eyes were fixed on the ceiling, her jaw tight. I sat up.

"You never have to do anything you don't like, Honey," I reminded her, even as I pushed against this barrier she was erecting between us, stroking my fingertips up and down from the undersides of those round tits to the waistband of her panties. "Are you not enjoying this?"

Her eyes darted to me, and away again. "It feels good," she said, her voice as tense as her body. I had to do something about that. I reached down and cupped her pussy through her underwear. Fuck, she was soaked.

"I'm sensing a 'but'." I slid one finger along the seam of her pussy through the fabric, until some of the tension relaxed, and she was panting and bright-eyed.

"Are you going to tell me what the 'but' is?" I asked, finding her clit and circling it.

She shook her head, rolling her hips to my finger. "It doesn't matter … just do what you need to."

I took my finger away, and she grunted, finally looking at me. "Don't stop," she whined.

"Oh, I'm not going to stop," I warned her. "Whatever is freaking you out, you better start talking, or I'll have to spank this pretty pussy instead of eating it."

To show her I wasn't joking, I palmed her roughly between her legs, then gave a light slap right on her pussy lips. Her body jerked, her arms straining against the ties. Her eyes went glassy. She'd fucking enjoyed it.

"Something about my mouth on your pussy terrifies you, doesn't it?" I asked. She didn't answer.

Another slap on the wet fabric that separated me from her beautiful pussy. She moaned this time, writhing.

"I think you enjoy having your pussy spanked a bit too much. Maybe I should threaten not to slap you, that might convince you to talk," I muttered. She whimpered.

"I … I want to try it so bad," she gasped. She wouldn't meet my eyes.

"But …" I prompted, feathering my hands up and down her belly once more.

"But I'm worried you won't like it."

I couldn't help the bark of shocked laughter that burst out of me. "Fuck, Honey. I've been dying to devour your pussy since the first time I laid eyes on you. The thought of your legs wrapped around my head, my lips and tongue lapping up all of your delicious wetness …"

I couldn't help but run the heel of my palm along my rock-hard dick. "I'm scared that it'll be so good I'll blow in my pants."

"I'm worried that I'll … that my legs are too big and …"

"And what?" I asked quietly, leaning down and pressing a kiss to her bellybutton.

"And I'll suffocate you."

Fuck. Was that the only thing that had stopped her? With a growl, I dragged her panties off her legs. Her beautiful, shapely legs. I pressed her knees until her legs were wide, her pink, swollen pussy glistening in the candlelight. I gave it another light slap, watching as she squeaked and writhed, as her clit swelled.

"That was for being a good girl and telling me the truth," I muttered, before climbing up her body and cupping her cheeks in my palms, forcing her to look at me.

"And this is because you're fucking beautiful, and perfect, here," I kissed her forehead. I slowly kissed down her face, throat, chest and breasts. "And here. This skin here is so fucking lovely," I whispered against her belly, continuing to kiss down, nipping at her hips, then sitting up and stroking down the length of both her legs, "All the way down to here." I lifted one of her feet, pressing a kiss to the top, kneading the arch of her foot until she moaned.

"And I don't know what ... or who ... put that stupid fucking idea into your head," I muttered, putting her foot back on the bed and settling between her legs, kissing up the inside of one thigh, then the other. "But even if it were possible for these gorgeous thighs to suffocate me while I'm eating you out ... which, by the way, it's fucking not," I kissed them again, glancing up to see her watching me, eyes bright, some of the wariness melting into need, "then I'd die the happiest fucking man on the planet."

I spread her thighs wider, thumbing her swollen pussy lips and parting them. Fuck, my dick was aching worse than it ever had before.

Get yourself under control, Levi! Make this unforgettable for her.

"I'm going to eat you now, Honey. Because I can't think of anything that will make me feel happier right now than to feel you come on my tongue."

I dipped my mouth to her dripping pussy.

AMANDA

My brain was still scrambled from the electric shocks of pleasure that had zinged through my body when he'd slapped me between my legs the way he had. I vaguely realised I'd just told him the truth. And he didn't care.

And then his tongue licked me from my entrance all the way up to my clitoris, and the moan that forced its way out of my throat at the sensation was guttural, and wanting, and it matched the one that burst from him. The one that vibrated against my clit.

"Fuck, you taste like heaven," he growled against my hot, aching flesh, his thumbs spreading me wider, his tongue lapping at my entrance, thrusting inside, until I was writhing under him, panting and sweating and shaking with need. His tongue felt so different to his fingers, to his penis.

When he suddenly sucked my clitoris between his lips, the tip of his tongue flicking at it as it swelled and pulsed, I practically levitated off the bed. With two strong, warm hands, Levi pressed my hips back to the bed, holding me still as he sucked and licked and nibbled and drove me higher, and higher, and higher. My head thrashed against the pillow, my arms struggled against the silk scarves, and every panting breath was a tiny scream as he pressed his face deeper into me.

"I'm going to … oh, God, Levi!" I cried out as the pleasure overwhelmed me and I exploded against his mouth, pulsing wave after pulsing wave of my orgasm pounding against his still lapping tongue. Even once I came down from that high, and my sensitised flesh started to feel overstimulated, he continued to kiss, and lap and press the flat of his tongue against my clitoris.

"Levi, you need to stop … oh God," I moaned, "it's too much!"

He lifted his face to grin at me. My arousal glistened on his nose, cheeks and chin, and I swallowed back a moan at how hot that view made me.

"Remember how I said we were doing this my way, Honey?" he said darkly, and I gasped as one finger slid inside me. "You are going to come again on my tongue, right now, and once you've done what you're told, you can have my dick inside you. Deal?"

I rocked against the slow torture of his finger moving in and out of me. "Uh … okay," I managed.

"Good girl," he murmured, pressing a sweet kiss to each hip before his mouth descended once more. I was still insanely sensitive, but that brief reprieve while he bossed me … and the teasing of his finger inside me … had tilted the sensations just to the pleasurable side of painful.

He was ravenous, sucking on my clit so hard I practically screamed, before changing to teasing, tickling, featherlight flicks with his tongue. His one finger inside me continued its slow, rhythmic breach and retreat, his free hand pressing down on my abdomen, which somehow made everything intensify to the point where it was all too much.

"I can't, Levi, it feels … oh!" I gasped as he added another finger, picking up the pace of his thrusts as he flattened his tongue against my clit, rubbing it and the super sensitive skin around it until I was in a frenzy of lust. And then he curled his fingers inside me and sucked hard on my clit, and I was done, detonating against his mouth.

He let me slowly come down from that one, kissing me gently, his fingers still inside me as my muscles pulsed around him. When he finally lifted his head and removed his fingers he gazed down at my flushed, sweaty body, licking the arousal off his fingers, as if he hadn't almost drowned in it moments ago, before wiping some of the wetness from his cheeks and chin, and climbing over me. He was still fully clothed, but his penis was the hardest I'd ever felt it as it rested against my very well-loved flesh.

"Honey, I will be doing that to you at least once a day for the rest of my fucking life, I don't care if I have to keep you tied to my bed for all fucking eternity. That was … fuck … that was better than sex."

I giggled, feeling slightly drunk, trying to reach up to bring his face to mine, only to realise that I was still tied to the bed. He fumbled with the knots, releasing my hands, taking them in his and massaging my palms and wrists.

"I think you might've forgotten what sex feels like," I murmured, gripping his head and pulling him down for a kiss. "Although, yes, that was … I wish I'd let you do that sooner."

Levi eyed me with those light-filled amber eyes. "It takes a lot of trust to let a man give you an orgasm that way, honey. I'm … I fucking love that you trusted me enough to let me do it."

"I love you, Levi Fox," I whispered against his cheek, reaching for the bottom of his shirt and pulling it over his head. "Now, let me remind you how good sex is."

"How good *our* sex is," Levi corrected me, scooting to the edge of the bed to drag off his trousers and boxer briefs. My eyes widened, my mouth popping open as his bare thighs came into view.

"What is … that's …" I stuttered, staring in shock. Levi glanced down at his leg, then back at me, a sheepish grin on his face.

"Oh, yeah, that. I forgot you hadn't seen it yet."

I sat up taking a closer look at the new tattoo. "Is that me, in …" I reached out to touch the skin there, only to be distracted by his penis bobbing against his belly, twitching as I touched his skin.

"It's you. It's a fifties pin-up style version of the photo you sent me when I was in Serbia. I found an artist in Belgrade who barely spoke English, and he did it for me after we won the final."

"Why?" I asked, even as the thick, throbbing length of his penis took all my attention. I slid my palm from the tattoo, along his groin, to cup his testicles. He groaned.

"Because you sending that photo was my good luck charm. I wanted to wear it always." He chuckled, pushing me back onto the bed before rolling on a condom and climbing on top of me. "Plus, I love that every time I look down, there you are, riding my thigh."

"Well, you … you really are intense, you know," I mumbled. "You had me permanently inked into your skin." He brushed a strand of hair from my face, stroking his thumbs over my cheekbones.

"You're permanently inked into my heart, Honey. What's a little tattoo compared to that?"

I swallowed back the sudden lump in my throat, reaching up to pull his mouth down to mine. He kissed me, tenderly, lovingly, as he slid into me. I had to break away from his mouth to let out a huff of pleasure at the familiar feel of him inside me.

"Well, since it seems I'm on a roll with trusting you with things that I've always felt uncomfortable about, perhaps … maybe … I could try riding you for real," I murmured against his shoulder as he slid in and out with agonising slowness.

Levi stilled inside me, lifting up to stare into my eyes. "Fuck me, Honey, you can't say things like that when I'm trying not to come the second I'm inside you." He stopped pressing his lips together and closing his eyes. His head moved just slightly, but rhythmically.

'What are you doing?" I asked.

"Counting by sevens to get myself back from the edge," he replied, his eyes still closed. "I have to do it every time I'm inside you, because you feel like …"

He let out a long breath through his nose, resting his forehead against mine and moving his hips slowly. "You feel like home, Amanda."

It was me who gripped his chin this time, lifting his head so I could press my lips to his, before cupping his face in my hands. "Another time then. I think the first time we christen our new home we should be making love when we do it."

Levi nuzzled his nose against the side of my face. "Honey, every single time we've been together, I've been making love to you."

Then he wrapped his arms around me, and I wrapped my legs around him, and we made love until both of us were crying out and the world was just Levi and me.

TWO EMAILS

LEVI

"No … this can't be right …" Amanda muttered, staring at her phone as we sipped tea at our new kitchen bench.

"What can't be right?" I asked, coming up behind her and wrapping my arms around her.

"This," she said shortly, holding the phone up to me. "You can read it out loud to me, that might help me make sense of it."

I peered at the screen. "Dear Amanda. On behalf of Dr Chris Bentley, I am emailing you with a formal letter of offer for a position as full-time junior midwife …" I stopped, taking the tea out of her hand and putting it down on the counter before spinning her around and whisking her into my arms.

"You got the job after all!" I said, pressing a kiss to her mouth. She kissed me back, but it felt like her mind was somewhere else. I broke away. "Isn't this what you wanted?"

Amanda's face was so adorably confused that I had to fucking laugh.

"Well, yes, but …" she said, and sucked her bottom lip between her teeth. I dragged it back out with my thumb.

"Do I need to remind you again who that lip belongs to?" I

asked darkly, watching her face flush. "Now, stop worrying, and talk to me!"

"I was sure that he was never going to offer me a job. I've been applying for other positions. I have an interview lined up next week."

I shrugged. "Maybe he heard that you were about to get poached out from under his nose, and he finally came to his fucking senses," I suggested. Amanda didn't look convinced, but she took her phone from me and put it down.

"Maybe. I … I don't know if I want to work for him now, though. Not after the grilling he and Beth gave me about you."

I pulled her into a hug. "Well, you're fucking amazing at what you do, you've passed your exams with flying colours, and if he thinks enough of you to offer you a job, I'm sure he'll give you a glowing reference. You have options, Honey. You have the power here."

Amanda tilted her head up and kissed me on the chin. "You're right. And you're wonderful. And we need to get moving."

We'd spent the entire night making love. At first it had been slow sex, but the next time she'd needed me hard and fast, the way she loved it. She'd given me a blow job that had me seeing stars, and as the sun rose, she'd let me lick another orgasm out of her.

But now, she had to go back to her place, probably both to shout at, and hug, her best friend for double crossing her to help me with my plans. And then she planned to go shopping for a bunch of stuff to keep here at my place. She wasn't quite ready to 'officially' move in with me, but she said she wanted it to feel like home to her, and I was okay with that. Sure, when she finally said fuck it and decided to move in properly, I'd be over the moon, but I knew she wasn't going anywhere. She was mine. My person.

Meanwhile I was spending the morning grabbing as much of my stuff from Xander's as I could, before I had to pick Lily up for our afternoon together.

"I'll text you when I'm done with my shopping, I'd love to spend some time with you and Lily today," Amanda said as she climbed out of my car at her house. I got out too, coming around to walk her to the door.

"I've been thinking," I began, wrapping an arm around her waist and pulling her against me. "We should talk about what to call you when Lily is around. So that she starts to learn her name for you early on."

Amanda pressed a kiss to my cheek. "You are adorable, Levi Fox. I'll have a think about it, but off the top of my head, what do you think of Mandy? It's what I used to get in high school a lot, and I think it has a nice ring to it."

I cupped her jaw and kissed her deeply, pulling away just before it got to the point where my dick would start to respond. "I like it. Sounds close to 'Mummy', without stepping on Emilee's toes."

"We can talk more tonight, once Lily goes home," Amanda whispered. I gripped her hips and pressed her against the door, covering her mouth with mine.

"We can talk more tonight, after I've made you come at least three times," I murmured into her ear, nipping the lobe and chuckling when she shivered. I stepped back, adjusting myself. I always went too far with her. It was fucking impossible not to.

"I'll see you after lunch, Honey. I love you."

"Love you too, Levi."

Xander was out when I got to his place. Since he didn't work on a Sunday, I assumed he'd taken Molly out for a walk. Since he'd gotten Molly, he'd stopped screwing his way through the single women of Sydney every Saturday night. Or maybe it had been since he'd signed the contract for this TV show he was going to be starring in soon. I laughed to myself. He was probably trying to clean up his act so he didn't look like a total fucking sleaze once he was famous.

I texted Mac to thank him again for all his help yesterday, but I didn't get a response, which was unusual. Mac was normally an early riser. I chuckled. Maybe he'd gotten lucky with the guy he'd gone out with, and they were still sleeping it off. I fucking hoped that was the case, for Mac's sake. He deserved a bit of good luck in the romance department.

I set the kettle to boil for another cuppa, and while I waited, I went into my bedroom, bundling my wardrobe into a bunch of bags and my suitcase, and taking that out to the car. I stacked a few boxes of things I hadn't bothered to unpack in the whole time I'd lived with Xander into the back seat. Now I had my own place again, I could finally settle in properly.

I sat down at the kitchen bench to drink my tea when the door opened and Xander walked in, unclipping the lead from Molly's collar. She galloped up to me, practically climbing my leg, woofing loudly and demanding that I pick her up.

I reached down and scratched her head. "Sorry, Mol, you're getting too damned big to be a lap dog!"

"Jesus, don't burst her bubble! She still climbs up into my lap every time I sit down on the lounge," Xander said, dragging his shirt off over his head and wiping sweat from his forehead with it. I noticed that his chest and abs were looking cut.

"You been working out more, Xan?" I asked with a smirk. "Don't want all your soon-to-be-fans to think you've got a dad-bod?"

Xander sneered, heading for the kitchen and grabbing a bottle of water from the fridge, slugging half of it down in one gulp.

"It's in the bloody contract," he muttered. "I have to maintain a 'certain body type'."

I guffawed. "Yep, they want to turn you into a thirst trap."

Xander leaned his elbows on the bench opposite me, taking his phone out of his pocket and playing with it. "Look, it's probably good for me to keep in shape. I'm thirty next year. I should be taking my health and fitness more ..."

His words trailed off as his jaw slackened, the phone dropping onto the bench.

"What the hell is wrong with you?" I demanded. "You're not having a fucking stroke or something, are you, old man?"

"Fuck," Xander muttered, reaching into a cupboard and dragging down a bottle of Scotch. "Fuck." He didn't even bother with a glass, just slugged straight from the bottle.

"Are you gonna tell me what the fuck this is about?" I asked, snatching the bottle from his hands and screwing the cap back on. "You can drink away whatever is eating you once I know what the fuck it is."

Xander ran a hand through his hair, then sighed, his eyes coming up to meet mine. Fuck, he looked pale under his tan.

"Did you get a bad text message or something?" I asked. "Fuck, you haven't tried to copy your brother and gotten someone pregnant have you?"

"Worse," Xander muttered hoarsely. "I just got an email confirming the crew for the show. It starts shooting on the first of December."

"So fucking what?" I grunted. "You knew it was going to be soon, you said they wanted to start in summer."

Xander made a weird half cough, half choking sound. "It's not the timeline that's the problem. It's the showrunner."

"The what?" I asked. "I don't know all the fucking fancy TV lingo, Xan, you'll have to be a bit more specific."

"The producer in charge of the day-to-day-running of the show," he mumbled.

"Is it someone you don't like?" I pressed. Xander shook his head, massaging his temples.

"It's worse than that. It's her."

For a second, I had no fucking idea what he was talking about. "It's who? Fucking say something that makes sense, please!"

But then my brain caught up, and my mouth fell open just as Xander said exactly what I should have guessed he was trying to say all along.

"It's Georgie."

Acknowledgments

My husband, you're always there to come up with weird names for people, places and things when my brain just won't do it for me. You've encouraged this little authoring folly of mine.

Lani Belle, critique partner, beta reader, all round cheerleader, you often have more faith in my characters than I do. This book is out in the world now because of your enthusiasm.

Elena, as always, your feedback and editing have improved this book out of sight. If Mac gets his own book, it will be because of you!

Leisha, you absolutely nailed the cover … again!

About the Author

Layla has been writing stories ever since she could pick up a pencil and shape words. The most memorable works of her tween and teen years included a rap version of 'Little Red Riding Hood' and an embarrassingly pornographic high school camp/murder mystery (which was possibly a sign of things to come).

Layla studied Communications at Newcastle University in NSW, Australia, and worked as a buyer and marketing coordinator in the education sector, before joining her husband in the family retail business. That's still her day job (she's very lucky her boss is pretty lenient, or she'd never get any writing done).

Layla lives on an acreage in regional NSW with her husband, two rambunctious children, four mostly feral cats, and an ancient German Shepherd who still thinks he's a puppy. Oh, and some angry Plovers that swoop her every spring without fail.